THE

AEON

CHRONICLES

BOOK 2

April M Woodard

DISTANT WORLD PRESS

THE AEON CHRONICLES

For information, contact:
P.O. Box 2020
Villa Rica, Georgia 30180
http://www.aprilmwoodard.com

Cover design by SHANNANTHOMPSON ART
Edited by Tiffany White www.writersuntapped.com
Proofread by LTT Editorial Services https://ltteditorial.com

ISBN: 978-1-7322490-4-2

First Edition: February 2019

Distant World
PRESS

"TUT, TUT, CHILD!"
SAID THE DUCHESS.
"EVERYTHING'S GOT
A MORAL, IF ONLY
YOU CAN FIND IT."

— CHAPTER 9, THE MOCK
TURTLE'S STORY

Alice's Adventures in Wonderland
-Lewis Carroll

The gold-engraved pin barred a perplexing emblem. At first glance, it looked like an owl. The wings' tips were down, and the crown was pointed, hovering over the 'A.' Sophie tilted her head, realizing it was her king's emblem, upside down. This was a symbol of the rebellion, a symbol of treachery.

Aalok's signet.

The Aeon Chronicles
Book I

CARPENTER

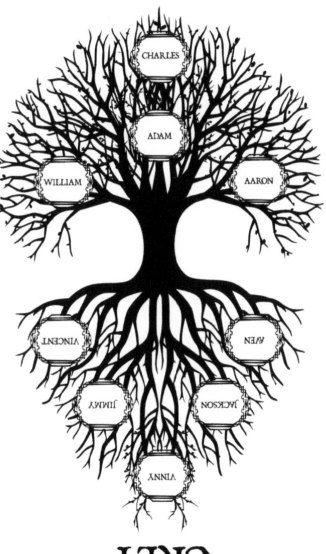

CHARLES

ADAM

WILLIAM

AARON

VINCENT

AVEN

JIMMY

JACKSON

VINNY

CREY

ANGEL EYES

DEATH. It's something you can't outrun, but Claire sure as hell tried to. She focused on the remnants of the crumbled lighthouse ahead, the pounding of her feet on the wet sand, and her heavy breaths. A morning run on the beach was her reality. Not the dream from last night, not the images swirling around in her brain. No matter if she thought she had died, thought somehow she had been evaporated to dust by a bright light; she was alive.

Her racing heart and the sweat beading down her back proved her existence. Still, she couldn't ignore how vivid and real the end of the dream had felt. Even when her eyes had flung open to the sound of her phone's alarm, the frightening images still lingered.

"Claire!" her best friend's voice called behind her—another confirmation she wasn't dreaming.

Taking in labored breaths of the thick salty air, Claire slowed her stride. She glanced over her shoulder, one hand on her hip, another on her chest and spotted Laura.

Laura cursed faintly, flinging her flip-flops off her feet. She jogged toward Claire, dressed in her usual skintight yoga pants and an off the shoulder cropped sweatshirt.

"Hey," Claire said.

"Don't hey me," Laura snapped. "What the hell are you doing?"

"Running."

"Running?"

"Walking swiftly?"

"You were in a full-blown sprint," Laura fussed, wiping the sweat from her brow. "I beeped the horn, but you just kept going."

"Where's your car?" Claire glanced over Laura's shoulder, finding her freshly waxed cherry-red sedan. It was the latest model, equipped with the convenience of a self-driving option, which Laura often used to sleep on the way to work.

"The street, dummy, and I'm illegally parked. If some stupid kid scratches the door with their hover scooter again, I'm gonna have a bitch fit."

"Oh yeah. Filling your lungs with toxic chemicals will totally calm you down," Claire chided, watching Laura smack a pack on her palm. "Eighty percent of smokers die from—"

"Gosh, mom," Laura mocked, putting a cigarette between her lips. "I didn't know it was Lecture Laura Thursday." She wrinkled her nose at the incoming tide. "At least the strawberry scent will cover up the smell of fish piss."

"Why do you live by the beach again?"

"To annoy you," Laura mumbled through the cigarette in her mouth. She lit it, taking a long drag as if it was her last before an execution. "And I'm not ready for Daddy to cut the cord, so a salty toilet at a distance is manageable."

"You know it does this after a storm. The smell will roll away in a few days." Claire reached down to catch the plastic wrapper that Laura had carelessly let dance away in the wind. "And it wouldn't be so dirty if people would stop throwing trash in it."

"Don't start with that hippie crap. You sound like those damn protestors. 'Stop global warming! Save our oceans!'" Laura said, pounding the sky with her fist. "It's so annoying. I mean, not that I agree with the government taking away the right of people to swim in shit."

Claire glanced up at the sky to the hum of a drone flying above. "It's getting pretty bad." She ignored the fact that her face was on a screen in real time at a government facility. "Think the state will issue a curfew like last time?"

"Pfft. If they do, they'll have to lock me up in the patty wagon with the tree huggers. I have plans tonight."

"With?"

"Depends on who's at the bar." Laura grinned, taking another drag.

Claire shook her head at her friend's promiscuity. "Do you have to work today?"

"Duh."

"So why are you here so early?" Claire glanced at the digital screen on her sports watch.

Seven a.m.

3

"You always sleep in until nine," Claire noted.

"We need to talk about the flight," Laura said. "I know I said we were going with Clint in the private jet, but he's gotten super clingy. I need my space. Joey said he would and since I haven't banged him yet, he offered to fly the Cessna. I know what you're going to say, but there's no reason to . . ."

Laura's words became distant until Claire could hear nothing but the lapping waves and a muffled voice echoing in her mind.

In the dream, the ocean reflected a crimson moon, making the sea appear as if filled with blood. The noise of the tidal wave was steady, like the static hum from the inside of an aircraft. It tried to drown out the words from her angel's lips, but she heard them, held onto the hope in his words.

For I am yours . . . he had said, squeezing her arm gently.

Claire lips trembled as she squeezed the angel's arm back, gazing into his bright blue eyes. They were a sea of turquoise, a sea of calm.

And you are mine, her dream-self answered.

"Claire!" Laura snapped her fingers, her irritated face coming into focus. "Earth to Claire. Hello?"

Claire sucked in a sharp breath. "Yeah, right. Next Friday. I wrote it on the calendar."

Laura put her hands on her hips. "Why the hell are you so spacey?"

Claire hesitated to answer, digging her toes in the sand. "Just a bad dream last night."

Laura's voice softened. "About your father?"

"No. It was about the wave and that angel guy."

4

Laura cocked a brow. "Oh, the angel guy."

"Don't start."

"The handsome hooded blonde again." Laura bit her lip, grinning.

"Don't look at me like that."

Laura threw up her hands. "Hey girl, it's you who's dreaming him. Although, if he showed up in my dream, I would have made sure it had a happy ending."

"That's because your mind is perverted."

"Says the nun who hasn't dated anyone in three years."

Claire shrugged. "I'm looking for something serious."

"And how do you expect to find Mr. Right if you don't date? I mean you won't even give anyone a chance to get to know you."

"Anytime I let someone close they only disappoint me."

"You mean when you tell them you see stuff."

"I don't see stuff." Claire lowered her voice and glanced over her shoulder. She was thankful the beach was vacant but took notice of the red blinking light on the surveillance cameras posted along the street. She knew they could hear her, that the all-seeing eyes watched her every move.

Claire hated hiding the truth, especially from her best friend, but she didn't want to be flagged again. Seeing stuff. Imagining things that weren't there. That kind of talk put you on a list that required you to get help or be sent to a therapy facility. She couldn't go back on the drugs; she couldn't go through any more sessions, dredging up painful memories of her past. She would keep up the lie. She would pretend, like always, that everything was okay.

"I just have no interest in dating," Claire said casually. "It's overrated."

"Claire, if you're still upset about, well you know, what happened that night, you can talk to me."

"I don't need your 'first time' talk again," Claire grumbled. "Or any mention of my birthday."

"I'm just saying I'm totally on your side. Taylor was a prick. I mean, I would know. I slept with the guy."

"You slept with him?"

"Yeah, a week after you did."

Claire crossed her arms. "While I was in physical therapy?"

"What? I was curious after you told me he had a big—"

"Don't say it."

"You totally exaggerated by the way. But you haven't seen enough weenies to know the difference, so I forgive you. Let's see. Who is someone I *haven't* slept with? Oh! Mark."

"Mark. The guy who works at the convenience store and gives you free cigarettes and booze if you flash him?"

"Yeah, he's kinda cute and obviously generous."

"I'm starting to question your morals—and taste in men."

"Everyone has faults, Claire. We can't all be perfect little angels like you."

"At least I'm not a matchmaker from hell."

"This is about you Claire, not me. Look, I get it. Really, I do."

"Get what? That I don't want to date someone that's shallow?"

"No." Laura took Claire by the face and smushed her cheeks as if she was the cutest baby in the world. "That no one can compare to your cutie, pootie, mubby, wubby."

"Stop." Claire giggled, swatting Laura away. "It was nothing like that."

"Sure it wasn't." Laura grinned before bending down to tighten her shoelaces. She made a face as if disgusted that the bubbling surf dared touch them.

"It was like—like he understood me," Claire continued. "Like a soulmate. I can't explain it."

"Oh. So you were dreaming of your soulmate. The perfect guy saving you as the world comes to an end!" Laura threw out her hands as if she was in a dramatic play, shouting to the sky. "One last kiss so intense that now you must find your eternal love before it's too late!" She laughed and turned back to Claire. "Sounds to me like the perfect end to an erotica novel."

"How would you know? You don't even read."

"Claire you can't ignore the reaction your body makes when you think of this hooded dream guy."

"What reaction?"

"You're blushing."

Claire shrugged. "My face is hot."

"Are other places?" Laura shot a glance to Claire's groin.

"You and your one-track mind." Claire sighed as an alarm buzzed against her wrist. She tapped the screen on her watch and swiped to the calendar app. "I have to get going. What time are we leaving next week? There are a few things I need to do for Mom before Vegas."

"You didn't hear me, did you? We leave tomorrow."

Claire's gaze snapped to Laura's. "Wait—what?"

"I'm sorry, okay? I had to change the date because next week I have tickets to that concert and . . ."

Claire narrowed her eyes, daring Laura to finish her sentence. She was always changing plans, always making up excuses.

"And next week was full."

"Oh my gosh, Laura. You told me you had this booked six months ago."

"Something else you and I are opposites about. You, Claire, are organized. I, on the other hand, am a procrastinating hot mess. I told you I planned to book it. I never said I did."

"How many miles away are we from the city?"

"Well, because of my last-minute lateness, I got us an upgrade on the strip," Laura chirped. "A hotel called and left a voicemail, so I called back."

"A hotel called you? Like real person? Not a bot?"

"Yep."

"Great, so you've been scammed." Claire let out a frustrated breath. "When we get there we won't even have a place to stay. Laura, *you* are the maid of honor and *you* were supposed to plan the bachelorette weekend. Not me. And yet here I am making sure that everything is ready for Jenna when we're not really friends. She's never liked me. She just needs an extra body in a dress for pictures because Wayne has five groomsmen."

"Would you stop bitching and listen? So this guy I spoke to on the phone, Mal, holy hell, Claire. His voice was"–Laura grunted and bit her lip–"so sexy. I'm gonna ask for him when we get there. I think I can get us some VIP passes to Chippendales."

"Which hotel?"

"It's a surprise." Laura widened her eyes, flailing her fingers as if something magical was about to happen.

"I hate surprises," Claire grumbled.

"I know." Laura wiggled her brows and turned around. "I'll see you in the morning. I don't have to say what time because you're always like an hour early or something."

"What's wrong with being punctual?"

"What the heck does–you know what? Never mind. Joey said we're taking off at seven."

"Is your dad okay with your flyboy taking the Gulfstream?"

Laura shrugged her shoulders. "Dad won't know."

"Laura–"

"Chill out. He's going out of town. We'll be back before he will."

"I really wish you wouldn't do things behind his back like that."

"Gosh, mom. I guess it really is Lecture Laura Thursday." Laura rolled her eyes, combing her fingers through the bleached highlights in her hair. "Meet me for lunch. I'm craving nachos. No wait, a hot dog with chili and onions, oh and some cheese fries."

"I'm surprised that's the only weeny on your mind."

"Claire." Laura laid a hand to her chest, pretending to be in shock. "Did you just make a crude joke?"

"Don't get used to it." Claire smirked. She bent over, stretching, readying herself for another sprint.

"'Bout time I started rubbing off on you." Laura shoved Claire's shoulder playfully as she straightened.

"You're not. And about lunch, Mom wants you to come over and try her new crab cake recipe. She wants to get it right before the guests arrive."

"You didn't tell her?"

"It was only a notice email. Two months behind doesn't mean foreclosure."

"I told you Daddy would help. Let me ask him."

Claire shook her head. "I can't. And I can't take any more of your allowance. I'm going to talk to the bank, see if I can work something out. Get a second job if I have to."

"Yeah, as if you need another excuse to give me when I ask you to go out."

"So, yes to lunch?" Claire asked.

"I do love some crab cakes. Real crab?"

"Yes"—Claire laughed—"real crab. Although, I don't get how you hate the smell of the ocean but love seafood."

"Crab smells like crab, not fish piss. I'll be there. Although a hot dog did sound good."

"Hot dogs are so bad. You do know what they're made of don't you?"

"But they taste so good." Laura licked her lips, acting as if talking about them was turning her on.

"See ya later, deviant." Claire laughed, hugging Laura's neck. She turned and jogged toward the lighthouse.

"Like I know what that means, but I'll take it as a compliment," Laura called. "Just remember, weenies are good too! Weenies are good!"

Claire couldn't help but smile at Laura's crudeness, but she didn't look back. She increased her stride, thinking of the angel with the turquoise eyes that she couldn't shake from her mind.

KITTEN CALL

AVEN Crey lazily opened his eyes, hissing at the metal cuff biting into his sore wrist. He cursed under his breath, vaguely remembering the night before. Falling asleep after the act was never good. There would be no way to make a clean break now.

He glanced around his sleek and shiny modern bedroom, looking for his clothes. His pants were inside out on the hickory hardwood floor, his button-down shirt tossed over his black leather chaise lounge.

Shifting his naked body, he sat up, attempting to squeeze his hand free from the vice, but the cuff was locked tight. Hearing the whoosh of the toilet flush from his bathroom, his eyes widened. Snapping his head toward his nightstand, he set his gaze on his cell phone, laying under a pair of bright pink lacy underwear. He reached, sliding his fingers across the four empty liquor bottles and cringed as one of them slid to the edge.

Twisting under and around his hanging arm, Aven carefully picked up his phone and texted "911." The water from the faucet was running, so he still had a few seconds. He slid his phone under the sheets and pretended to be groggy as a naked woman stood at the threshold of the bathroom door.

"I wanted to let you to get some rest so you could play," she said, tracing her body with slender fingers.

Aven shook his wrist, jingling the cuff against his poster bed. "Good cop, bad cop?"

"Uh huh."

"I'm guessing I'm the bad cop?"

"Oh yes. Very, very bad." The redhead sauntered to the end of the poster bed and slid her hand down the metal brace.

"Then maybe you should punish me." Aven motioned her to come to him with his finger. He had no intention of sleeping her again, but for his plan to work, he would have to play her game.

The redhead crawled onto the bed and sat, legs straddling him. As she leaned down, her fiery curls tickled his face. Ignoring the pain in his left wrist, he wrapped his right hand around the back of her thigh and squeezed, letting out a throaty growl.

The redhead moaned but flinched as the bedroom door flung open and slammed against the wall.

"What the hell?" a girl with blonde hair and fiery blue eyes screeched.

"Katharine!" Aven shoved the redhead off of him. "It's not what you think!"

"Who the hell are you?" The redhead glared.

"Who the hell am I?" The blonde's face twisted as she took a step forward. "I'm his wife, you stupid bit–"

"Whoa, whoa, whoa! Honey, just—just calm down." Aven's free hand was up in the air as if in surrender to her rage.

"Calm down? Calm down? Screw you and your whore!" The blonde stomped forward and seized a red stiletto on the floor. She reared back, flinging it over her head. Aven dodged the flailing object, and it smacked the black leather headboard an inch from his face.

"You're married?" The redhead twisted to him. "When did that happen?"

"Secretly. Can't have in the tabloids." Aven laughed nervously. "But we separated."

"Separated? You lying scum!" The blonde picked up the other high heel and chucked it at Aven but missed him, knocking over the lamp on the nightstand.

Snatching up her skimpy grey leopard dress from the floor, the redhead slipped it on. She headed for the door as the blonde continued to scream, throwing Aven's clothes.

"A year of counseling! Just wait until he hears about this! You dirt bag! You low life piece of—" She growled like a wild animal. "What about the kids?"

The redhead whipped around again. "You have kids?"

Aven simply shrugged his shoulders. "Still waiting for the DNA test to get back."

The blonde lifted Aven's dress shoe in the air, aiming for the redhead who held up her hands. "Ma'am calm down. I'm not his mistress."

The blonde walked right up to the girl, white knuckling the shoe, coming inches from her face. She smiled as if daring the redhead to blink. "I think you should go unless you want me to shove this where the sun don't shine."

The redhead slipped out the door, and the blonde ranted on until the front door to Aven's mansion slammed shut. As if a director had said cut, she tossed Aven's shoe to the side and smoothed back her hair.

"Geez, Kitten. Where did that come from?"

Kitten combed through her ash blonde hair, twisting the wavy long strands up into a messy bun. "You know, Aven, I think after all these years I'm finally realizing I'm too good at acting to be some playboy's assistant."

"Is that what you tell your friends? You're a playboy's slave?"

"Slave?" Kitten let out a laugh. "Don't flatter yourself."

"I didn't, you did."

"Why didn't you take her to a hotel?"

"I thought she was a prostitute."

"You went looking for someone on the Vegas strip? That's stupid. You could catch something."

"Haven't yet. Courtesy of our brilliant scientists at InfiniCorp."

"Solace is still going through clinical trials. They can't be sure their miracle drug keeps you immune to diseases. When they say 99-percent chance that leaves a 1-percent chance." Kitten huffed. "What were you thinking?"

"I was thinking of a good night's rest, and it's the one thing I haven't tried."

"So what? You cruised the strip and just picked the one that looked the least strung out?"

"I planned to eeny, meeny, miney, mo, but when I pulled up they were fighting like rats as if I was the last stale Cheeto on Earth. I think I'll go there more often. It was way too easy."

"Aven."

"The redhead, Officer Reed, pulled out her badge halfway down the strip. I pulled over, turned on the lights. It didn't take long for her to recognize me."

"And you brought here because . . ."

"She wanted to see my *massive* mansion."

"Why didn't you tell her no?"

"Because she-devil in the backseat insisted with icy fingers wrapped around my throat." Aven winced at the sting of his wrist and cursed under his breath. "Help me out of these cuffs will ya?"

"Just because your demon expects you to sleep with a new girl every night doesn't mean you have to."

Aven watched as Kitten shuffled to the nightstand and situated her tattered college sweatshirt hanging off her shoulder. It was from her own one-night stand years ago, one she had confessed to Aven. But unlike Aven's nightly rendezvous with strangers, Kitten's sexual encounters were few and far between.

"Says someone who's had ten hours of beauty rest without a single nightmare," Aven remarked.

"Thanks to you it was only eight hours," Kitten grumbled. She bent over and picked up the lamp, sitting it back in place. Curling a lip, she slid the lacy underwear away with an empty liquor bottle. She looked around the nightstand and behind it, shoving the empty bottles left to right before kneeling on the floor, searching around the bed. When she rose from her scavenger hunt, she wasn't holding a shiny key like Aven hoped.

"This is the only part I like about acting like your crazy ex-wife." Kitten sighed, smiling at the cherry-red stilettos.

"Ah, yes. As if you don't have enough shoes in your closet from my little escapades." Aven grinned. He thought about all the times Kitten had come to his rescue. Five years they had been doing this. He would sleep with a stranger and message her if he had fallen asleep. This accidental doze off had been the fourth time now.

"Just my size," Kitten cooed, smoothing her hand over them as if they were her precious pet.

"Key, Kitten," Aven urged, jingling the chain.

Kitten put the shoes down. "What would you ever do without me?"

Aven followed her gaze as it traveled to the sheet partially covering his bare hips and moved his hand out of reach. Kitten huffed, gripped his hand, and jerked it toward her. The lock clicked, setting him free from his steel bond.

Rubbing his raw wrist, Aven glanced up with a grin. "The better question is, what would you ever do without me?"

"Get dressed. You're late and Vincent's already asking me where you are. Should I tell him it's because of your drunken night with the newbie cop or because you had to get fitted for a new suit for the charity ball?" She asked, holding up her phone.

He wasn't listening. He sang to himself, shutting the shower door.

"You're such an ass," she said to no one.

Typical Aven. Always shrugging off responsibilities.

She thought about walking right in and telling him she quit, but she knew if she did that it wouldn't go well. She would stutter over her words, seeing the steam rising over his toned body. She shook her head.

Suffer through it, Katharine. Suck it up.

Holding up the red stilettos, she smiled. "Hello, my beautiful darlings." She glanced back at the bathroom door, biting her lip. No. She would leave him to shower alone; although, the thought of strutting in wearing only high heels had crossed her mind. She braced herself on the dresser.

"Don't be stupid," her reflection ordered, glaring back at her. She squeezed her eyes shut, drew in a deep breath, and put on the stolen stilettos. She entered the personal elevator in the hall with her head held high and glared at the mirrored reflections of herself in the steel doors.

"You're a lioness, not a kitten," she coached. She would not let Aven get to her. Not today. She pressed the ground floor button and exited Aven's home, crossing the manicured lawn like a model on the runway to her canary-yellow Porsche. She slid her sunglasses on her face, traced her mouth with blood red lipstick, and emailed Mr. Delgato that Aven Crey would be thirty minutes late.

DYING WISH

"WHAT are you reading, Will?" the hospice nurse asked, setting her knitting bag on the rocking chair beside him.

"Briar Rose," he replied softly. He forced a smile, glancing at his bedridden mother. She was sleeping peacefully.

For now.

When she woke the pain would be back, along with no memory that he was her son.

"Sleeping Beauty. No religious undertone in that one," the nurse, Olivia, pointed out. She grabbed a pair of rubber gloves from a box. "I sure do miss real books. I used to love going to the library as a kid. Times have changed."

Will's brows furrowed at the empty bookcase built into the wall of his mother's room. It had once been filled with her favorite stories. Now there were only dusty hand-crafted knickknacks, sentiments she had kept since his childhood. He wondered what he would do with all her things when the time came, if he would put the house up for sale and disappear from town again. Without her, there was no reason to stay.

"Keep reading," Olivia urged. "She can hear you."

Will wet his lips, tapped the screen of his tablet, and continued reading as Olivia changed a bag of fluids. He paused to the sound of the squeaky wheels of the IV pole, hoping it didn't wake her, but it didn't. Nothing could wake her but the pain.

"Don't mind me," Olivia said, wrapping the blood pressure cuff around her patient's arm. She didn't flinch as it inflated and squeezed her bicep. She was still and quiet, her chest rising and falling with each steady breath, accompanied by a slight wheeze. Will took in a deep breath, wishing he could give her his healthy lungs. As a hush filled the room, he found the place he left off.

"However, she was not dead, but had only fallen into a deep sleep." Will paused, staring at the word "dead" as his dream from the night before trickled back into his mind.

There was destruction and a tidal wave. He strained, trying to recall the glowing girl, the angel he was holding before the light in the sky blinded him. His mind repeated the words he had said, what he had vowed. He had leaned down to kiss the angel.

The loud slap of a rubber glove pierced his ears.

Will blinked free of the image of the angel's lips.

"How is she?" he asked Olivia in a hushed tone.

"The same." Olivia informed.

"They said she wouldn't . . ." Will propped his elbow and rubbed his brow with calloused fingertips. "They said six months."

"Doctors think they know everything, but they forget the Creator has his own timing." Olivia sat next to Will and took out some tangled yarn from her bag. She untangled it with her light brown fingers, wrapping it into a ball.

"I know you're probably wondering why he would keep letting her hold on like this," she said, "suffering day in and day out, drugged up, hardly able to speak, but he knows when the time is right."

The Creator.

There had once been books about him, but Will had never had the chance to read them. He had only seen versions of them behind glass in museums. Religious text had once been available in libraries and stores but had been banned the year he was born. It was a result of riots and book burnings as war broke out, but the countries came together to make peace. They agreed to ban all religious text, monuments, and anything that offended people.

Citizens were now monitored on the internet, scanned, fined, and incarcerated if caught with religious text out in the open or if caught posting it online. It kept the peace between the nations, or so the news told. Will knew better. He knew war never truly ended.

"Adam . . ." his mother croaked.

Will jumped out of the rocking chair and ran to his mother's side. "Mom?"

"Adam wait," his mother cried, gripping the sheets.

"Mom, it's me. It's Will."

Her eyes fluttered open, looking at Will as if he was a stranger.

After pressing the button for morphine, Olivia took out a pen from her scrubs and quickly scribbled on her clipboard.

Holding the creased and cracked paper between his fingers, Will gazed at the glossy image of his mother in her younger years. But when his eyes met the baby in her lap, he inhaled sharply, folding the letter back over the picture.

"Mom, I already took care of your will. You have nothing to worry about."

"No, Will. There is still one more thing left. Please . . . look at the picture."

Will licked his dry lips and did as she asked. "I don't remember your hair being this long when Aaron was born."

"That's because this picture was taken when I was twenty-three."

"Twenty-three?"

"Look closer."

Will's stomach knotted, picking apart the details of the photo. His mother's hair was long, jet black, cascading down her shoulders to her elbows. She was smiling and so was the baby with bright blue eyes and matching hair color.

"Look at the date on the back."

Will flipped the picture over. The date written in cursive was a year and a few months before he was born; next to the date was a name he was unfamiliar with.

"Who's Aven?"

"Your brother. He's your brother, Will."

Will tried to swallow the knot in his throat as realization hit him. "Older brother."

"Yes."

Putting the letter and the picture down on the bed, Will ran his fingers through his dirty blonde hair. He paced the room, trying to ignore the tingle of his crawling skin, but it was no use. He might as well have been standing in a plane, contemplating a jump. His stomach flipped like it had in military training. Only now, fear laced his insides, and there was no parachute to ease the fall.

"Did Dad know?"

"Yes, and it's the reason he's dead."

Will's stopped pacing and put his hands on his hips. He stared at the floor, trying to sort through his thoughts.

Dad's death? Had he not been killed in the line of duty?

He rubbed his eyes, hoping he had fallen asleep in the chair, but when he opened them again he was still standing with shaky breaths. His gaze traveled to his mother's quivering lips, to the IV taped to the back of her hand that clutched the sheets.

"I need you to find him Will," Kate rasped. "There's something important I have to tell him."

Will didn't respond. He was still trying to wrap his head around everything his mother had confessed. He had a brother he never knew existed, a past his mother had never told him about.

"Will, please. He needs his mother."

Will glanced up, his gut twisting. "Why didn't you tell me?"

"You were so young and when you got older . . . I didn't know how to tell you. I thought you would never forgive me, I thought . . ."

Will uncrossed his arms, came to his mother's side, and sat down on the bed. Gently, he took his mother's hand in his and slid his thumb across her thin skin. "I forgive you. I just don't understand."

Kate squeezed Will's hand but was too weak to keep a grasp. "Your daddy came to visit me today. He said he's taking me home soon. There's—there's something he wants you to have. In his bedside table is a box."

Will went around the bed and pulled open the nightstand drawer. He shuffled around a few wrinkled papers, a small screwdriver, and an old rusty army knife until he found the box.

"Your grandfather told him to make sure you have it."

"Grandpa? How did he—"

"We are all reunited Beyond the Veil." Kate smiled and glanced at the box. "The code is 755."

Flipping the combination to the numbers, the box clicked open. "What's this for?" Will asked, holding up a brassy skeleton key.

"It will unlock the truth," Kate rasped.

Shoving the key in his pocket, Will came to her side and offered a glass of water, but she pushed it away.

"Give me your word, Will," Kate croaked. "Promise you'll find Aven."

"I promise."

THE MAN

RAIN dripped down Will's face as he surrendered to the guns pointing at him from over his head. He blinked a droplet from his long lashes and called out over the thunder.

"Come on, Jer. Is this really necessary?"

"Password," a crackling voice ordered over the speakers from the secluded ranch.

"You know it's me."

"The way people get their faces rearranged these days, one can't be too sure."

Will sighed. "You're the man."

"Didn't catch that."

"You. Are. The. Man."

"Damn right I am."

The yard went black as the floodlights died, and Will lowered his hands. He watched as the guns folded in and retracted into the ground, covered by artificial brush.

At a creak from the front door, Will lifted his gaze to his friend, finding a smug smile plastered across his tan face.

"Think you have enough artillery in the yard?" he called over the pouring rain.

"Will, you know I don't do that anymore," Jeremiah whispered.

"Still like it black, right Will?" Julie poked her head around the corner from the kitchen.

"Yes, ma'am," Will called.

"Jeremy just got us this new coffee maker. It takes two seconds to brew," Julie said. "Can you believe it?"

"Oh?" Will answered, keeping his gaze on Jeremiah. "Technology these days. To think I'm still brewing it the old-fashioned way." Will leaned closer to the Jeremiah. "Please. It's her dying wish," he whispered.

"Okay," Julie said, coming in with two steaming mugs. "Black for Will, café latte for my man."

"Thanks, Jules," Will said.

Julie smiled and handed her husband his mug.

"Hey baby. Why don't you go get the sonograms?" Jeremiah said. "I want to show Will how big—"

"His feet are?" Julie lifted her brows.

Jeremiah held a space from his hands. "Enorme."

"The doctor keeps telling him it's the umbilical cord"—Julie rolled her eyes—"but he won't listen. I'll get you a towel, Will. I can't believe Jeremy didn't offer you any dry clothes."

Jeremiah's mouth dropped open as if to protest.

"Thank you, Jules." Will grinned wide.

When Julie's footsteps creaked from above, Will pulled his chair closer to Jeremiah, keeping his voice low.

"I think for Julie's safety you should keep this between you and me."

"Will, if this is another—"

"Just hear me out. In this letter, Mom said she used to be a scientist. She worked for a medical corporation. They had a secret military project called Genesis. The serum they tested made the soldiers stronger, faster, heal quicker."

Jeremiah narrowed his eyes. "I'm listening."

"The guy in charge of the whole operation, Jackson Crey, and her ended up having a relationship. She got pregnant. Had a son."

"Your half brother."

"When Jackson's father, Vinny, found out, he was furious. Mom wrote that Vinny kept calling the baby a mutt. That he wasn't a pure blood."

"Pure blood?"

"Yeah, I don't know what that's all about. All I know is Vinny swore he was going to kill him, and a week later, Vinny came up dead. Ruled a suicide. Mom wrote that she suspected Jackson and his brother, Jimmy, murdered him. Her suspicions were confirmed when my dad approached her while he was with the CIA, said he knew she had discovered the serum was a cure. Dad told her he would get her out, but she had to stay in and get proof on the murder. She wrote that there was never any proof, but those last few months she was in, she caught onto something big with the serum."

Jeremiah lifted a brow. "That it gave the soldiers super powers?"

"Not just that. She wrote that she woke up one night, listening to Jackson on a COM, whispering. She watched the feed the next day, listening to it over and over again. She said the soldier kept yelling at no one as he put the gun to his head–as if he was being told to do it–that he couldn't stop himself from pulling the trigger." Will sat back and crossed his arms. "Sound familiar?"

"Too familiar."

"She was in for two more months before she and Dad fell in love. When she found out she was pregnant with me, Dad planned to get her out of there, but Mom refused to leave."

"Because of her other son."

Will gave a slow nod. "So Dad came up with a plan B. But Jackson found out. She wrote about the night they had planned to escape. Jackson and she were fighting. Dad came in to get her. They fought. It ended when Dad shot Jackson. His brother Jimmy walked in and saw his dead brother bleeding out on the floor. My mom stepped in front of Dad as Jimmy pointed a gun at him. She said Jimmy let them go but wouldn't give up his nephew. Mom wrote about how Dad faked their deaths with a car accident, moved them out here, how they kept their heads down. The rest of the two pages are just– they're really sad."

"So, your dad made her leave her kid?"

"I think the guilt got to him. My mom wrote that when my brother was ten, Dad had got called to go back in and get the formula that Jimmy had in a safe at his home. But my dad diverted from the plan, tried to get my brother to come with him; Jimmy caught my dad, and they struggled. My mom said that Dad's partner, Caleb, came back the next morning, told her everything that had happened–at least everything he had heard over the COM."

"That's how your dad died."

Will rubbed his scruffy face. "Yeah. Quite a different story from what I was told as a kid."

"Damn."

"I think it's all connected, Jer."

"Will." Jeremiah sighed. "You following the white rabbit will only get us one place. And that's falling down a hole, six feet under. Or worse. Floating in an ocean in the Pacific off the coast of Mexico as shark food."

"Baby," Julie called down the steps. "I couldn't find the first sonogram, but I did find a few photos from all of us at prom."

Will put the picture in the envelope, stuffed it back in his rain jacket, and took a sip, acting as if he hadn't been talking about his father's death.

"What I wouldn't give to go back in time." Julie grinned, handing the pictures to Will. She sat on Jeremiah's lap and kissed him. "Remember how we danced all night?"

"I remember telling the limo driver to pull over so I wouldn't have to pay for detailing." Jeremiah poked at her.

"At least Will held my hair back while you hit on Hannah."

Will gazed at the picture of him in his teens, then the girl next to him. Hannah. His ex-fiancé.

"Will? Are you okay?" Julie asked, sitting up.

"Yeah." Will cleared his throat and looked to his watch. "Hey, uh . . . I should get going."

"Tell your mom I'm praying for her," Julie said, hugging his neck.

"Bye Jules," Will said, forcing a smile and walking out the door. He waited for Jeremiah to shut it before he spoke.

"She still thinks I broke up with Hannah before I left, doesn't she?"

"I never told her any different." Jeremiah sighed, leaning against the porch post. "For all Jules knows you were missing in action, and by some miracle you were found alive."

"She can never know the truth. It could put her and the baby's life in danger."

"That's why I hope this isn't some wild goose chase again."

"Think you can find my brother?"

Jeremiah raised a brow. "Will. You're talking to the man."

MNEMONIC

A feather quill paused over a papyrus because of a knock on the door. Claire replaced the quill in the inkwell and rose from her chair. When she opened the door, a young man with onyx hair and stone-gray eyes stood on her doorstep. He smiled and bowed.

"Milady."

"Hello again." Claire curtsied, lifting her lilac chiffon dress. "May I help you?"

"Yes, I believe you can. I have come to ask permission."

"Permission?"

"To take you for an afternoon stroll—if I may."

"It would be my pleasure to take a walk with you."

"I assure you the pleasure is mine," the young man said, offering his arm.

The two walked in the dales chatting about their meeting in the library. They climbed the hills, to a meadow of barley, lavender, and wildflowers. When a pink cherry tree and a picnic laid out beneath it came into view, the young man offered Claire a small bouquet of lavender flowers. Claire sniffed the flowers and sat with him on the blanket as he offered her a package wrapped with cotton twine. The scent of coco filled her nose as she took out a chocolate and placed it in her mouth. Salted caramel tantalized her taste buds as she glanced around the landscape. This place was too vivid, too otherworldly, to be real.

She and the handsome young man talked for hours about music and dancing before he leaned forward, taking a wisp of Claire's hair blowing across her cheek in the lavender breeze. His fingers traced her high cheekbone, paused, and lingered at her chin.

"Do I have your permission to kiss you?"

Claire leaned back, surprised at such a request, but as the young suitor took her gently by the neck, she lazily closed her eyes and leaned toward his lips.

FRIDAY, 12:09 P.M., LAS VEGAS

"Claire! Wake up already!"

Claire's nostrils flared to a smack on her arm. She squinted her eyes, wiping the drool from her chin as the scent of chocolate and lavender faded.

"You really need to get that drooling thing under control," Laura teased.

"Are we here?"

Claire sat up and glanced out the small window of the plane, finding the wing and the landing pad.

"Of course we're here. Everyone's getting their stuff from cargo." Laura rolled her eyes. "So the drooling, is it only when you're in a deep sleep? What do they call that . . . remy or something?"

"REM sleep." Claire groaned as she stood and stretched her stiff back. "You should Google stuff sometime."

"Hurry up, woman. Check-in is in twenty minutes," Laura said, patting Claire's butt.

Swatting Laura's hand away, Claire grabbed her backpack and stuffed the wrapper from her granola bar inside. She glanced out the window again, finding her friends parking their luggage and taking pictures of one another. "How long was I asleep?"

"I don't know. The whole trip?" Laura gulped down her glass of champagne before slamming the window shade shut. "You dreamed about him again, didn't you?"

"Who?" Claire asked, pinching the bridge of her nose from the headache coming on.

"The blonde mystery dream boat."

No. She hadn't, but she didn't want to tell Laura she had dreamed of a new angel. An angel with a charming smile, shiny onyx hair, and stormy blue eyes. Stretching her neck without an answer, Claire followed Laura to the plane exit.

Laura placed a hand on her hip and threw her other one in the air as if she was a supermodel, posing for a magazine. "Viva Las Vegas, ladies!"

The three girls standing next to their suitcases cheered with spirit fingers.

Claire let out a low moan at the noise.

Cheerleaders. Always so loud.

Claire had never been a cheerleader. Only a dancer. A quiet, elegant dancer. She rubbed her temples before shuffling through her purse, searching for her phone. Jet lag or the sleeping pills must have caused the headache. She didn't know which.

"Holy shit!" Laura shrieked.

"What?" Claire asked, slightly annoyed at Laura's tug on her blouse. She exhaled in relief, finding her phone and drew it from her purse.

"Is that him?" Laura squealed, pointing to a man in his late twenties, walking around his plane.

Claire tried to glance out the plane, but as Laura shoved her forward, her phone fell to the floor with a thud.

"Dang it, Laura!"

Cursing under her breath, Claire bent down to retrieve her phone under her seat. As she straightened, she pressed the service icon, letting out a sigh of relief when she saw the green light. But then she groaned as the screen on her phone went dark.

Great.

Claire fumbled to get Laura's grabby hands off of her. "Why are you freaking out?"

"Oh, my God! Just look already!" Laura shouted, twisting Claire around by her shoulders.

FRIDAY, 12:15 P.M., LAS VEGAS

Will's stomach growled as he exited his private plane. He knew he should have grabbed something but had felt rushed watching the minutes of his mother's life ticking away on his watch. Locking the door of his plane, Will rubbed his thumb over the skeleton key on his keychain. He had wondered what it unlocked the whole flight there, but he knew finding out that secret would have to wait.

Bending over to retrieve his luggage from the cargo, Will grumbled to himself. When he had left South Carolina, it had been brisk. He had been slightly chilled from the rain after his visit with Jeremiah, who said he would find Aven's address, but there was still no word. An hour into his flight, Will had thrown on the white hoodie he had brought. It was his little brother Aaron's lucky hoodie. Will knew he would need all the luck he could get to find Aven in a city like Las Vegas.

Throwing his duffle bag over his shoulder, Will glanced around the orange dusty landscape. A desert. There was no place he hated more. Knowing stories of Vegas, how there was no AI watching the city, he reminded himself to make it a quick trip. A big city, any city, was not the kind of place he wanted to be in long, anyway. It was too loud, too busy for his liking. He missed the quiet and stillness of the countryside, the spring rain, and the fresh air.

Sweat beaded his forehead as he cleared a tickle in his throat. Each breath of air he inhaled burned his sinuses as he made his way toward the steps to the pilot lounge. Two steps

"That's true," Laura said, smiling. "But what if your Prince Charming is right here in Vegas, and you'll meet him because it's like destiny or something?"

"Destiny?" Claire raised a brow. "Since when do you believe in that?"

"I don't know. Now. I mean maybe that fairy tale crap people used to read before the book burnings had some truth to it. Maybe there is something serendipcious going on."

"Serendipitous."

"Whatever, just remember, I'm your maid of honor, and if you do find him here and plan to get hitched by Elvis, I get to pick out the dress."

Claire groaned. "Why did Jenna let you plan the bachelorette party again?"

"Because I'm fun, and I have great taste."

"You got lucky we're not staying at one of those crappy motels a mile away from the strip."

"If I hadn't shrugged off booking, we wouldn't be staying at the Luxor, now would we?"

"Like I said, you got lucky," Claire said, watching Jenna, Brittney, and Khloe take selfies, no doubt posting them on social media. Social media. More like kiss your privacy goodbye. All it took was for someone to look up your name on Google. All your information was there. Every picture you took, your location, anything you had ever posted. If you were logged in, anyone could read your life story.

"Just you wait. This is going to be a night you'll never forget." Laura winked. "Unless you do forget because you wake up with a hangover like I had last Saturday. I really wish I could remember whose house I left my earrings at, but I don't want to call Josh, or Blake . . . or his brother to find out. That would be awkward."

"Don't expect me to take care of you again. I liked those slippers, and how the heck you crawled into my window is beyond me," Claire said as they made their way to the exit.

"I keep telling you, Claire, it's the yoga. Ladies! Everyone together for a picture."

While Laura handed her phone to a stranger passing by, Claire tied her sweatshirt around her waist. The girls huddled together for a pose, making kissy faces. When Claire looked up to smile, the room spun and as her eyes met a pair of brown work boots. Her fuzzy gaze traveled to a white hoodie with a gold emblem lying over a navy duffle bag, hanging on the shoulder of a guy with blonde hair.

The golden emblem seemed familiar to her, but she couldn't make it out. As her vision zoomed in, the gold embossing appeared as a crown and wings over an "A." Flashes zipped through her mind: a crystal castle, a white horse on a beach, laying in an ocean, and a gauntlet and soldier standing before her.

Time sped up, and Claire found herself staring at the sliding doors of the airport exit. She stood in a daze, straining to bring something to her memory, but her attention snapped to Laura who stood beside a man in a suit and hat, holding a sign.

"Ladies, our chariot awaits!"

THE LITTLE

BLACK DRESS

FRIDAY, 7:25 P.M., LAS VEGAS

"HEY, Mom. I made it. Sorry I didn't call sooner, my phone died." Claire pulled back the curtains, looking out the small slanted window of the hotel room. She didn't look down. She knew if she did she would get dizzy. Her fear of heights had always been an inconvenience, but more so now as she tried to take a picture from the 7th floor.

"It's okay, sweetheart," her mother said from the speakerphone. "How was the trip?"

"Good," Claire answered, gazing at the landscape through the palm trees at the brightly lit city. Las Vegas was bustling with cars and people, making her wish she were back home. She missed the sound of lapping waves from her quiet bedroom.

"You used the sleeping pills again, didn't you?" her mother's faint voice asked.

"Hold on," Claire said and went to shut the door of her room. It hardly muffled her friend's laughing or the music from their portable speakers. "What were you saying?"

"What hotel are you girls staying at?"

"The Luxor. Laura got us a last-minute upgrade. We're sharing a room, but the beds are so big we could have fit at least two other people in here. The wall is even slanted like a pyramid. The bathroom is as big as one of our guest rooms at the Inn," Claire explained as she leaned toward the mirror and wiped the smudged mascara from her lower eyelids. She made a face at herself, drawing back the bags under her eyes.

"Any plans tonight?"

"Dinner, and then after we're going to this nightclub in the hotel called LAX."

"LAX. I remember going there."

"You went to Vegas?"

"Long before I met your dad. I remember making out with this really handsome guy and—"

"Mom."

"Didn't it close?"

"It was recently renovated a few years ago. From what I searched online the nightclub is a room of red velvet and gold. Here, I'll send you a screen shot. Laura reserved the VIP section. They're already talking about how drunk they're going to get, but I don't—"

"Claire," her mother chided. "You're twenty-two, you're not married, and you don't have kids. You won't be young forever. It's okay to have fun. You're supposed to."

"Yeah, but—"

"One day you'll realize that once you settle down. You can't reverse time, Claire, and when you get my age, it flies by."

Claire situated the wrapped towel on her head and tucked the loose one around her chest between her breasts. "How are you holding up, you know, with unpacking and things?"

"By things, you mean how am I handling the anniversary alone?"

"Yeah." Claire bit her lip, regretting bringing it up.

"Honey, we've talked about this. Remember what your therapist said? You're only hurting yourself when you keep dwelling on the past. I know you don't want to go back on the medication but...it's been a year. If you're still having a hard time maybe—"

"No. I'm fine I just...I really miss him," Claire said, tearing up. "Don't you?"

"Of course I do. It took me a long time to make peace with it. I know one day you'll make peace with it too. He wouldn't want you to be sad."

"Yeah, I know."

There was a space of silence until her mother cursed.

"Mom?"

A horn blared from Claire's phone speakers.

"Mom! Are you okay?"

"Sorry. These stupid self-driving cars think they can just pull into a lane without putting on a blinker. I hate them being on the road. This jackass in the rear seat is completely oblivious that his AI almost killed me and him."

"Wait. You're not at the house?"

"Don't worry. I locked the door this time. Took me three times to get that new thumbprint password to work, but it did. Do you want me to text you a screenshot of the app saying it's secure? I'll have to wait until I get to the airport but—"

"I thought you had someone booked this week?"

"Just my luck, they canceled."

"Canceled . . ." Claire rubbed her forehead. They needed that booking to make the electric bill payment this month. "Okay, um, hey, uh don't forget to scan your digital receipts when you get gas, go easy on the credit card, don't spend over—wait. Did you say airport?"

"I was wondering when you would take a breath." Her mom laughed. "Your brother called. He said Beth is going to have the baby tomorrow night, so I booked a flight to New York."

"She's going into labor? I thought she still had a few more weeks left?"

"You know how doctors do things these days. OB decided he needed a vacation to the Bahamas, so he moved the C-section up."

"I don't see how that's healthy for the baby."

"Me either. When you were born I had you all natural. I still remember the sound of your raspy little cries. The nurse kept talking about how green your eyes were. Your father was concerned about that birthmark on your wrist. I think he thought maybe the umbilical cord had hurt you."

Claire glanced at the brown line on her arm. Her birthmark. As a child she thought it was ugly, but now it looked more like a thin bracelet. She traced a finger over it with furrowed brows, thinking of her father. He had wanted to make sure she was okay. He had always been protective of her, had always kept her safe. Guilt crept up Claire's spine as her eyes welled with tears. She clutched her necklace. "How long will you be gone?"

"Oh, only few days. I'll be back before you and the girls get home from your trip."

"I'm sorry I can't go with you."

"I bet. You have been talking about going to New York for years."

"I have to admit, I'm a bit jealous."

"You've wanted to travel the world since you were a little girl. Maybe you should go back to school, become a flight attendant."

"A plane that goes hundreds of feet in the air? Mom, I had to drug myself just to get here."

"Maybe one day you won't be afraid of heights anymore. They have that new drug out, what's it called? Solace? I saw the commercial the other day. Doesn't have many side effects. I could make an appointment with Dr. Seresh when I get back."

"That's okay. I'll pass."

"All right. Hey, I'll bring you back a souvenir."

"And I'll bring you back a one of those gaudy Vegas t-shirts from the gift shop."

"Deal. I love you, honey. I'll see you next week."

"Hey, be careful okay? I hear New York's crime is higher than ever this year."

"I'll be fine. They have those surveillance cameras on every corner now. They even have those new police AI. They're creepy to say the least, but I'll be safe. Don't you worry."

"Tell Ryan I miss him. Make sure you take lots of pictures and videos. I want to see my little nephew. Even if it's the middle of the night."

"Okay, honey—Hey, Claire?"

"Yeah, Mom?"

"Have a drink for me. Get one of those red fruity ones with an umbrella."

"Mom." Claire groaned.

"Just one. It will help you loosen up."

"One."

"I love you, baby girl."

"I love you too."

Claire pressed end on her phone, but as she did something yanked her towel, jerking her head back.

"I heard that."

"Heard what?" Claire unwrapped her towel and combed her wavy hair with her fingers.

"Receipts? Really Claire."

"I want to make sure Mom does it right this time. Last year she had over two thousand dollars we could have deducted."

"Your job is so boring. Why did you go to school for bookkeeping again?"

"You mean accounting?"

"Whatever, yeah, that."

"Because Mom had just bought the Bed and Breakfast and she needed someone to help her. She's good at cooking and I'm good at numbers, so I figured why not?"

"No, you're a saint. You sacrificed your life dreams of becoming a dancer or pianist for that lame job so your mother wouldn't have to pay someone."

"You know I couldn't keep dancing after my ankle surgeries."

"You used that as a crutch after you got off the actual crutch. Your ankle is fine."

"Fine. It's called growing up." Claire threw her damp towel over her arm and shoved Laura. "Something you should do, unless you plan on being a yoga instructor all your life."

"Guys like it when I tell them my profession. Oh wait." Laura snapped her fingers and shook a finger. "I just figured out why no one wants to date you."

"It's not my job. It's because I don't want to waste my time dating."

"No, you're picky and you keep expecting something magical to occur when you meet someone. You should be looking for a guy who is single, hot, and rich—not a soulmate."

You mean shallow.

Claire went to the bathroom for her makeup bag. There were only a few items in there. Mascara, cream eye shadow, and light-tinted lip gloss.

"Let me do your makeup and hair." Laura jumped up from the bed and snatched Claire's makeup bag from her hand.

"No way. You'll paint my face like I'm some circus clown. I'll look like a total sleaze." Claire snatched back her makeup bag back and held it up in the air out of Laura's reach.

Sticking out her tongue, Laura went straight to the closet and pulled out a navy dress with a white floral print. "Did your grandma pack your suitcase for you?" She went to the dresser and pulled out Claire's drawer, lifting out a pair of folded white bikini underwear. "And these. Is she hiding in your suitcase? Because you brought things like you were going to a family reunion or something."

"Briefs are comfortable."

"Comfortable." Laura tossed the briefs in the drawer and shoved it closed. "Okay, wow, you're in desperate need of a makeover, honey." Laura curled her lip and went back to the closet, taking out the navy dress. "Please tell me you're not wearing this tonight."

"What? You said bring a dress."

"A black dress." Laura sighed, pulling up the event she had sent Claire on her phone. "Didn't you see the word black in black bold letters?"

"I guess I read over that."

"Apparently you did. On purpose. You hate black, but that's no excuse. I do something organized for a change, and you just completely ignore my effort."

"Laura you know I haven't worn a black dress since . . ." Claire's voice trailed off. She couldn't say the words.

"Sweetie, I hate to be a bitch, but tonight isn't about you. We're taking pictures, like a ton of them. You don't want to look like some random chick that photo bombed, do you?" Laura went to her suitcase and took out a Victoria's Secret bag.

"No, but I didn't bring a black dress," Claire said, brushing her hair. "I don't even own one."

"You don't?" Laura asked with a mischievous grin, reaching into the bag. "Well, that is strange. I could have sworn I saw something—oh wait, ta da!"

Laura held up a slim and very short spaghetti-strap dress with tags on it and waved her hand over it like it had just magically appeared.

"Why does that look familiar?"

"Because it's yours, dopey. You gave it to me when you cleaned out your closet a few summers ago. Anything remotely dark went into a box. Now you have nothing but ugly floral prints and solids that make it look like you go golfing on the weekends or something."

"I like simple."

"A color-coded closet is simple?"

"It looks nice. Like a rainbow."

"No, you obsess over things and take time keeping everything perfect to keep your mind off whatever's bothering you. It's like your OCE keeps you halfway sane or something."

Claire bit the inside of her cheek. Laura was right. Except for calling OCD, OCE. "You know if I don't keep myself occupied, all I'll think about is how Dad isn't making French toast, or how he used to sit in his La-Z-Boy on Sunday drinking a beer before a cookout, or how I would get onto him about his scruffy face when I would kiss him goodnight. Distractions are all I know."

"I'll make sure you are completely distracted tonight. I'll even request the DJ to play our song so we can dance," Laura said, taking out a pair of black lacy underwear and bra from the Victoria's Secret bag.

"You wouldn't."

"Oh, I would. Remember the routine?" Laura pressed a button on her phone, playing a song Claire knew all too well.

Laura mimicked the moves to their routine, adding in some other provocative moves.

"No. I can't." Claire laughed, covering her eyes.

"Girls! Claire is dancing tonight!" Laura jumped on the bed, bouncing Claire up and down. She swung the black bra around in the air like a lasso, swinging her hips. As she yelled over the music, Jenna, Brittney, and Khloe all piled in the room on the bed to join her. "What happens in Vegas . . ."

"Stays in Vegas!" the girls said in unison.

Jumping off the bed, Laura snagged her makeup bag from her luggage. She glanced over her shoulder at Claire with puckered lips and said, in a dramatic voice, "Come, come darling, let me make you beautiful."

WHITE MAGIC

Friday, 5:22 p.m., Las Vegas

"WHAT took you so long?" Aven asked.

Kitten huffed at him, throwing a white garment bag over her arm. "You're welcome."

"But I didn't say thank you."

Kitten kicked the front door shut with her heel and shoved the garment bag into Aven's chest. "I'm late because I got held up at practice. If you looked at my schedule on your phone for once, you would know that."

With her nude heels clacking on the onyx floors, Kitten followed Aven up the glass stairs of his mansion and into his room. As his bare chest brushed past her, she tried to ignore the skipping beat of her heart and the sweet scent of his cologne. She averted her gaze from the reflection of his defined abs in the mirror and typed a search for local gyms. She quickly erased it, knowing she wouldn't follow through with the membership.

Although Kitten had a slim figure, full perky breasts, and plump round behind, she was self-conscious of her body. Not to mention tight jeans and crop tops didn't grab Aven's attention; he had seen it all. Curvy, thin, dark skin or light; he had entertained every type, and Kitten could tell he was getting bored of it.

After three years, Aven had racked up quite a "body count" as they used to call it. A joke that had clearly been forgotten by Aven after body number two hundred, but Kitten hadn't lost track. The redhead was number three hundred and eighty-six.

Aven hung the garment bag in his massive walk-in closet, filled with suits, slacks, and dress shirts. Everything he owned was black. Well, everything except the white-collared shirts, most of which he would discard because of makeup stains from his escapades.

Aven smiled at himself in the oblong mirror, flipping down his collar over a bright red tie. Red. It was the color of desire, of passion, and his favorite color, but only because it was guaranteed to pull focus. He glanced at Kitten in the reflection, finding the room unusually quiet with her in it. She gazed at his bookshelf, looking for illegal literature as always.

She had given him a lecture on the ones with religious undertones just a few weeks ago, but Aven didn't care and neither did the local police. That point had been made by his last encounter. No one could touch him in this city. Money was power, and he had plenty of both.

"Learn anything new, or are they teaching you old tricks?" Aven asked, snapping his cufflinks.

"That's funny coming from someone that knows a few."

"They're teaching you simple science, Kitten. Not magic."

"And Rose?" Kitten asked. "What do you call what she can do?"

"What Rose can do is a gift. Not to mention her lineage. At the rate you're going, you won't understand the basics of vibrational healing until you're eighty."

"Oh, I will, and one day when you need me, I won't come running to save you."

"You can't help but come to my rescue." Aven smirked. "Wife."

Kitten warned him with her eyes before turning her gaze to the shelf filled with tattered and worn hardbacks. She put a finger to a few of them before tilting her head to read a title.

"Poe? Really Aven. That guy was demented." Kitten plucked Shakespeare's *The Merchants of Venice* from its nook and flipped through it.

"Or tormented." Aven cocked a brow, straightening his collar.

"Your pet crow still tapping on your window?"

"He's not a pet, he's a pest, but yes."

"I told you I'd call someone."

"Don't bother," Aven said, clipping on his cufflinks. "If it's Nehia's doing, it will only come back."

"How do you get away with keeping such depressing, illegal, what did they call it? Literature?"

"The feds could care less about my choices in, yes, literature."

"You have *Macbeth* and *A Midsummer Night's Dream* and . . ." Kitten squinted her eyes. "I can't even read these other titles they are so faded. Is this one new?" She held up a worn copy of *Dante's Inferno*. "*La Divina Commedia* . . . Comedia? Since when do you read comedies?"

"Durante degli Alighieri."

"Speak English. I didn't go abroad like you did."

"*The Divine Comedy* is not a comedy. There were only two styles of classical literature in the Middle Ages: tragedy and comedy. Tragedy meaning a tragic ending. Comedy, a happy one."

"Happy?" Kitten flipped through the book. "Is this the one about the nine circles of hell?"

"Mm hm."

"You read all of this"—Kitten looked up from the book—"in Italian?"

"Several times."

"And you like reading about hell because . . ."

Aven lifted a brow in the mirror.

"You bought this around the time she-devil began haunting, didn't you? I'm sorry. I couldn't find Bree. Hell doesn't have a P.O. Box. If you want, I can start searching for her again."

"No. I'll find a way to rid myself of Nehia without Bree."

Uncomfortable silence filled the room, and Kitten bit her lip. The only reason she had started taking classes to learn magic was to help Aven keep the demon away. But she never told him that, and she was far from knowing how to do any protection spells.

Kitten put the book back in its nook. Clasping her hands together, she rocked on her toes. "So."

"So . . ." Aven leaned toward the mirror and glared at a lipstick stain on his collar.

Kitten added a note in her phone to change dry cleaners and shivered as Aven rolled his shoulders out of his shirt. Finding herself staring at him in the mirror, she shifted her gaze to the floor as he walked past her and back into his closet.

"Today was elementals."

"So you played with gemstones, did you?" Aven called from out of his closet. When he returned, his freshly pressed white-collar shirt was buttoned. He wrapped the red tied around his neck and headed back to the mirror to tie it again.

"Do you want to see what I learned or not?" Kitten asked as she came to help him.

Aven sighed. "If I must."

"Don't seem so thrilled," Kitten grumbled, shoving the knot of the necktie to his throat.

Aven grunted. "I'm starting to wonder if you do that on purpose."

Ignoring his remark, Kitten went to his dresser, dumping his keys and wallet out of a decorative bowl. She sat on the bed, took a bottle of water from his dresser, and placed it in her lap. Setting the bowl in front of her, she took off the top and began to meditate.

Aven loosened the knot of his tie, making sure to not make a sound. He turned smoothly on his heels to face Kitten. Her eyes were closed, and she took in deep steady breaths, just as he knew she had been taught. He crossed his arms, rolling his eyes. The meditation part always took the longest, and he was bored already.

Magic. To Aven the word was a joke. People could imitate supernatural abilities but never fully understand a true gift if they didn't have it. And Aven didn't think Kitten had any, unless the school had proclaimed a look to kill as one.

After a long moment, Kitten raised her hand above the water bottle and said, "Water, my friend, my partner, my world, the only thing I ask of you is for a little control."

Aven scoffed.

"Shut it, Crey," Kitten threatened, cracking open an eye. She closed it again and continued to concentrate as Aven watched unamused. To his surprise the water rose up from the bottle, following her hand. She moved the stream up into the air, forming it into a bobbing sphere, hovering it a moment before she glided her hand toward the bowl. Aven was impressed at first, but he knew a true gift couldn't be disrupted. He couldn't help himself.

Clearing his throat, Aven smiled, because just as he expected, her hand trembled at the sound. Seeing Kitten struggle to keep her concentration amused him more than her newfound Ability. He curled his lips as the water orb followed her hand again before he faked a sneeze. The bubble burst and fell into Katharine's lap, and onto bed.

"Aven!" Kitten slapped her hands against the wet duvet. "Do you have to be such a—"

"Ah, ah, ah," Aven said, waving his finger in the air. "Manners, Kitten. You know the rules. If you ever want to be a proper witch, you'll have to watch that pretty little mouth of yours."

"Don't do that."

"Do what?" Aven asked as a playful smile tugged on his lips.

"Try to smooth things over with your charm."

The smile deepened as he tilted his head. "I thought you were immune to my charm?"

"Does it look like I'm falling all over myself after a compliment like every other girl you come in contact with?"

"Ouch. Someone's in a mood today."

"Maybe I'm just tired of making up excuses for you after your dirty deeds," Kitten snapped.

As Aven slid his hands in his pockets and dropped his gaze to the floor, Kitten immediately regretted her words. His encounters. A slap in the face would have hurt less. It was never a choice. He had to entertain, had to feed the demon's desires. That was his price to pay for making a deal with a devil. She shouldn't have gone there, but the truth was it killed her to see him with anyone.

Nothing but torture.

She imagined what it would feel like if he kissed her the way he did his encounters—caressed her neck, whispered in her ear with that sultry husky voice that made her knees weak. She loved him and hated him with a passion he would never know, a desire she could never expose.

"Katharine—you know you're beautiful. I don't have to tell you."

Kitten stared at the wet duvet and folded her legs under her. "All girls like compliments. It would just be nice to hear you give me one for once."

Listening to his quiet footsteps, Kitten watched Aven walk to his bed as if afraid she would extend her claws again. He rested his hands on the edge of the black leather footboard and leaned forward, fixing his gaze.

"You have men chasing you all over town," he said in his hushed tone. "Why does it matter what I think?"

Kitten forced her shoulders to shrug. "Because."

"Because I'm your boss?"

Kitten clenched her teeth, trying to ignore the thumping of her heart. Afraid he could hear it, she leaned back, pressing her teeth against her lips. She concentrated on the sharp stab of them but held his gaze. He was daring her to blink, daring her to look away.

A staring contest.

She wouldn't let him see how much he affected her, like he did all women. She had known him all his life, knew his charm, his tricks, but few people could get close enough to know his shortcomings like she did. Kitten was the only one who knew about the demon, how the succubus was once satisfied by Aven's music, but now, was only pleasured by the deep groans and moaning in the middle of the night.

The longer Kitten stared into Aven's stormy grey eyes, the more thoughts entered her mind of her and him together. She quickly reminded herself that it didn't mean anything. He had made a statement and that was it. A simple truth. Katharine Reece was beautiful.

She held back a frown, knowing that Aven Crey would never see her as more than just that. His pretty, sweet, and understanding childhood friend. Nothing more than just the pet name that she was. Nothing more than Kitten.

With a flutter of Kitten's lashes, the game was over.

"You blinked." Aven grinned, tapping her nose playfully.

"Stupid boy." She punched his arm—always her reaction to his arrogance.

"Sore loser." Aven gently shoved her on the shoulder as he stood. "May I remind you that witches are to be humble. You may want to take that sass down a notch if you want to achieve a title. If you like, I could ask Rose to give you a private lesson."

Aven smoothed his hands over his jet-black hair and glanced at Kitten in the mirror. He just had to poke at the tiger, couldn't refrain from one more playful remark. Rose. She knew that was just an excuse to entertain one of the most beautiful witches in the Circle. He had been trying to sleep with her for years and not just because she was beautiful, but because she always brought friends. Nothing pleased the demon more than two or more encounters at a time.

Kitten snatched up the plastic water bottle, and it crunched in her fist as a noise rose from her throat like a rabid dog.

"Clean this up, will you?" Aven said, casually taking his wallet and keys from the dresser. "I can't have my bed looking like I've already had company."

Rearing back, Kitten chucked the bottle toward Aven's head, but before it made contact with his face, he laughed—"See you tonight Kitten"—and shut the door.

SHE-DEVIL

Friday, 7:02 p.m., Las Vegas

AVEN killed the ignition to his blacked-out motorcycle and tapped the chip behind his ear that was connected to his phone. A hologram popped up from his watch, displaying the name Vincent Picture. Aven rolled his eyes but answered with another tap to the skin chip.

"I know what you're going to say," Aven said. "Look, don't worry about Delgado."

"We need him to sign off on the paperwork," Vincent said sternly. "If you want Partner, I suggest you be on time for once."

"I was only twenty minutes late." Aven smoothed down his hair in the side mirror and took off his riding glasses.

"Forty. Forty minutes and twenty-three seconds late. Have you no sense of time? I don't think you're ready to go to Singapore."

"I'm so ready for Singapore."

"No. I should go. This deal is too important."

"So what? I learned Mandarin for nothing. Well, not for nothing, but . . ." Aven said, taking off his leather gloves with his teeth. He thought about the girl he had hired—hadn't taken too long before she made it on the body count list.

"I suggest you go alone or only take Katharine. If you're serious about the company, then you won't be playing. You'll be working."

"I'm good at both." Aven laid his gloves under his helmet on the seat. "What's business without a little pleasure?"

The trip had been on his mind for months. He wondered if he should take Kat. She always kept him in line, was always there if he woke up in a cold sweat from his night terrors, and she kept the clingy females at a distance when he was out for a drink. There were nights he was too tired to entertain, his body too worn from pleasing the opposite sex. With Katharine around, there was a chance at a quiet night of reading before the nightmares came.

"We're about to save millions of lives," Vincent said.

"And make millions in the process."

"You know it's not about the money, but it's billions, Aven. Billions. Remember that next time you're late."

"How can I forget? Hey, I'm heading to the club to check on things. Can we talk about this when I come up?"

"Make sure you're here by eleven. We have a guest who arrived this afternoon."

"Newly initiated?"

"No. An old friend. You'll remember once you see her."

"Keep me in suspense, then. I do love surprises. I'll be up shortly."

Aven ended the call and entered the Luxor hotel, heading for the elevator. Whistling a tune, he pressed the button for the rooftop and the party, but as the door closed, a chill ran down his spine.

"Sinner," a sultry voice whispered, tickling his earlobe with invisible icy lips.

Aven shrugged off a shiver down his spine as the elevator dinged and opened to the casino. Beautiful young women waiting to enter his elevator gave him a quick once-over and rushed to get inside. Aven nodded politely and excused himself, slipping through them to the elevator opening across the hall. Pressing the button for the lobby, he glared past his reflection in the steel doors to the unseen presence behind him.

"A little early for you to be showing up," he said to no one.

"Billions and billions," the voice hissed.

"And so the devil appears."

"What is money the root of?"

The haunting always started with a rhetorical question. Tonight, just like every night, she was giving him a choice to choose right or wrong. Aven never understood why the demon gave him a warning. Maybe it was to break down his confidence for control. He wasn't sure. Either way, he knew what she wanted. He always knew, no matter the question, the choice was the same. Take the high road and be tormented in his dreams or add another name he would soon forget to the body count. But he hadn't planned on giving in. Not tonight. A week of entertaining had been enough. His body and his mind needed a break.

"The path to paradise begins in hell," the demon quoted. Aven slit his eyes at his disfigured reflection, watching the smoky shadow dance like a slithery snake down his cheek. He alone could see it. He alone knew why the lights flickered. Claws formed from the smoke, wrapping around his neck and squeezed until the elevator dinged.

The doors opened to the floor of the nightclub and Aven's shoulders fell as he sighed,

"And to a place I come, where nothing shines."

EARTH ANGEL

THE music of LAX silenced the demon's whispers as Aven entered the night club. He sucked in a deep breath of cigarette smoke, fighting the urge to head for the vending machine in the back to grab a pack.

Forcing a confident smile, he made his way to the bar, passing women, young and old, swiveling in their chairs to get a good look at him. His lips drew up, overhearing their giggling as he leaned against the bar. He nodded to the bartender, José, who was flipping bottles in the air with ease.

"Hey boss," José said, pouring a steady stream of blue liquid into a shot glass. "The usual?"

"Surprise me." Aven shrugged, his playful countenance returning. He gazed around the room. It was packed and he was glad. More people, more noise, more candidates to pick from. His gaze wandered back to the bar and to a woman in her early forties putting a cigarette between her lips.

"Allow me," Aven offered, reaching into his inner pocket. He took out his silver butane lighter, held it out, and thumbed the starter.

A possible taker.

He hadn't planned to satisfy the demon tonight, but the woman was beautiful, and by the looks she was giving him, he doubted she would care if he left after the deed was done. He waited for the demon to approve, but there was no sign, no icy draft on the back nudging him forward.

The woman smiled seductively, took a puff and opened her mouth to speak, but Aven's attention was brought to a noise up in the VIP section as a group of girls screamed with excitement. They held up their shot glasses, clinking them and tilting back their heads—all of them except a petite brunette who sat in a booth glaring at her phone.

"That's like the third or fourth bachelorette party this week," Aven said, still trying to catch a glimpse of the brunette.

"Oh yeah, but this group is bangin' and I mean bangin'," José said, placing a napkin and Aven's usual glass of bourbon in front of him.

Aven raised his brows. "I said surprise me."

José was grinning but not at Aven. His attention was on the VIP section.

"Have we been enjoying the view, José?"

"You know me, Mr. Crey. Always the looker never the hooker. I have yet to master the magic and charm you so easily possess."

"True, José. So very true."

"Hey," José said in a hushed tone, leaning over to Aven, "here comes one of them now. How about you give me a lesson?"

Out of the corner of his eye, Aven watched the short brunette come down the stairs, holding a glass of ice. She was the same girl that had been on her phone, the same girl he had tried to get a better glance at. He couldn't see her face past the brown barrel of curls, only her lips in a tight thin line. She was irritated about something, and he was curious as to what.

"I'm sensing this one is not open to conversation," Aven said, taking a sip of his bourbon.

"Oh come on." José rested both hands on the bar. "I thought you liked a good challenge?"

"Oh, I do. Just not tonight." Aven glanced in the other direction to some young women sitting at a table, eyeing him. He gave his bedroom stare and mentally picked which of them he would be taking back to his room, but the demon didn't give him a hint. She was silent, but he could feel her legion of demon dogs lingering nearby, watching and waiting.

An icy finger pressed against Aven's chin. Finally, she had chosen. But the demon didn't direct his head to any of the girls he had been looking at. Instead, she twisted his face to turn his attention back to the petite brunette coming his way. This was the one the demon had chosen. This was the one who she desired him to ravish tonight.

"Come on, show me how it's done," José begged.

How it was done.

It was always easy for Aven. A little flirting, a few sleight-of-hand magic tricks, but not every possible taker was the one the demon wanted. The first few weeks were easy. Aven had his pick, but now, she would play with him, point out girls that ended up having boyfriends or were too drunk to walk. No matter if the demon had chosen a girl that was too incoherent to speak, he would look for another or go home alone. He never stooped so low as to take advantage of someone. He made sure they were making the choice.

He wondered if the demon was playing with him now. He would take the chance. Even if this wasn't the girl the demon wanted, he could at least show José how easy it was to lighten someone's mood.

"Watch and learn, José. Watch and learn." Aven flicked his jacket and rolled his shoulders, conjuring his ego and confident mask. He leaned on the bar and pretended to check his watch, but as he lifted his gaze, he was met with green eyes and an indescribable wave of familiarity.

Light, like a star, a blinding sunburst, filled his vision as a flash of recognition struck Aven. The music muffled as the commotion of the crowd became distant and far away. The milky halo around the girl blurred as the motion of the room came to a standstill around her. Bodies froze in place, but the girl was in slow motion, still coming toward him, her gaze holding his. Her eyes were so bright, so very green with hints of gold. Somehow, he knew those eyes, knew this stranger's face. He struggled, straining his mind, trying to remember not where, but when he had met her before.

There was a consuming peace as she neared, a sense of euphoria. His chest warmed as if her brightening halo were rays of the sun, as if she was the sun herself. A scent of coconut filled his nose and a soft breeze flowed over him. The room faded to black, and in the blink of an eye, Aven was in a meadow, standing on top of a hill. He held a white rose as an angel walked toward him through the poppy flowers. She smiled brightly, seemingly overjoyed by his appearance, but the vision melted away before he could take her in his arms.

Aven blinked, finding himself no longer in the meadow, but standing on the sticky carpet of the nightclub. The bodies of the room had taken motion again and music filled his ears.

The girl reached for the bar with a trembling hand and gripped it tight, waiting for José. Aven took mental notes of her face. Her lips were a faded coral, no doubt from the lipstick wiped off at dinner and never reapplied. Her lashes were long and thick but caked with mascara. Her eyelids were a smoky charcoal, blended into a thick black cat eye. It was all wrong.

In his mind, Aven didn't remember her with makeup but a natural beauty with pink cheeks, sun-kissed skin, and eyes that sparkled like jade stones. She was the angel from the vision, standing in a place of sanctuary.

He studied the girl further as she straightened the pink tiara on her head, seemingly annoyed it had been poking in her scalp all night. When José came toward her, Aven caught a wince through her forced smile.

"Yes, ma'am?" José asked with a wide grin. He shot a quick glance at Aven and brought his gaze back to the girl, giving her his full attention.

"Yes, hi, another on my tab please?" The girl's fingers still trembled as she slid her glass, half filled with melted ice, on the bar.

"Coming right up, miss." José took the dirty glass, tossed the ice and sat it beside the other line of dirty glasses on the large metal sink. While the girl watched the bartender fill her cup, her gaze darted to Aven, who averted his, acting as if he was watching the people over her shoulder. It was clear she wasn't convinced and Aven knew he had to play it off.

Casually leaning against the bar, Aven finished off his whiskey and tapped the rim of his glass, avoiding the brunette's sideway glance.

"Coming right up, boss," José said with a wink.

While Aven waited for his drink, he fought the need to meet those green eyes again. Like a magnet he felt the pull, a tug as if someone was pushing him toward her. It wasn't the demon. No. This force was soothing, but urgent. Losing his senses, Aven's gaze shifted to her hand resting on the bar with a sudden desire to touch it.

Before Aven realized it, he was staring again at the girl again, tapping his fingers anxiously against the bar. The girl lifted her gaze from her phone to his drumming fingers, then back to her phone. Aven stilled his fingers, reminding himself he was supposed to be showing José how to pick up even the most uninterested of women. Smoothing down his tie, he brought back his mask of confidence. He stared with intention until the girl met his gaze.

"Hi," Aven said smoothly.

"Hi," the girl said flatly, averting her gaze back to her phone.

Aven gave a quick glance at José. He was attending to customers but watching closely.

This is not how it's done.

"Having a good time?" Aven asked.

"Not really." The girl sighed, not bothering to look up.

Fail.

With a raised brow, José placed another drink on the bar. Aven hadn't realized he had drunk the last one so quickly. Nodding a thank you, Aven tapped his phone.

A ding rang out on the register and José tapped the screen. "Very generous of you, Sir. Thank you."

Aven shrugged with a small smile.

The girl scoffed.

Not impressed by charm or money. Noted.

"Anything else?" José asked, his head forward but his eyes on the brunette.

"How about the drink special for this lovely princess?"

"You got it." José snapped his finger and pointed with nod.

The brunette glanced at José, then at Aven, and scoffed.

Aven tilted his head. "What?"

"Princess?" she asked with a disapproving look.

"Sorry." He flashed his white teeth before taking a drink. "Mistook you for royalty."

The girl reached for the cheap plastic tiara and blushed.

Step one. Find a way to make conversation. Done.

"Oh, right. The crown," the girl said, situating the tiara straight.

"It's rather convincing."

"It's rather dumb." The girl scrunched her nose and glanced over her shoulder to the VIP section. "The bride insisted."

Aven shook his head as if he understood the bridesmaid's predicament. "Brides."

"Your order, miss, and the Craven Casino Cocktail," José said, setting the drinks in front of the girl.

She glanced at Aven with furrowed brows.

"It's on the house," Aven assured her, hoping she would feel obligated to stay.

The girl met José's gaze. "Put it on mine, please."

"Yes, ma'am." José nodded and tapped the screen on his register.

"Thank you," the girl said. She glanced up at Aven and held his gaze.

Say something to her.

Aven was speechless, too captivated by the way her emerald eyes sparkled. Before he could part his mouth, the opportunity to make conversation fled as she turned away, heading for the stairs.

"Have fun!" he blurted over the crowd.

The girl turned, looking at him as if he had stupid scribbled across his forehead.

"You too," she answered back and quickly made her way to the stairs, trying not to spill the drinks.

Heat spread through Aven's neck as he brought his gaze to the bar, his face twisting in disgust. "Have fun?" he asked under his breath. He rubbed the back of his neck to ease the pin pricks and looked up at the girl moving around people to get to her party. When she finally got to her private VIP room, a blonde her age smacked her on the arm and threw her hands in the air.

Had the girl done something wrong? Was her friend jealous? Maybe the blonde was her girlfriend?

"Hey boss, don't sweat it," José said, wiping down the bar with a dry rag. "She's been drinking virgins all night. She's probably just uptight, ya know?"

"Virgins?"

"Yeah. She's had like three glasses of cranberry juice tonight. She comes and gets it herself."

"Huh."

"Maybe she's hungover from the last night or something."

"She's definitely something." Aven took a sip of his bourbon, unable to take his eyes off the brunette. "How long have they been here?"

José swiveled, snatching the tablet from the register. "About two drinks each, two round of shots, and one order of cheese fries, extra crispy. I'd say about an hour, hour and a half."

"How old is the brunette?"

José slid his finger across the screen. "She's of age. Twenty-three tomorrow according to her ID."

"What twenty-two-year-old doesn't drink? She a guest?"

"Floor seven."

"Explains why they were here so early," Aven said, watching the brunette twirl her straw with her fingers. He was good at figuring out body language. She was fidgeting, and he was curious as to why.

As José attended to another customer, Aven drank his bourbon, fighting back and forth with himself. He thought about going up the stairs and talking to her. He could properly introduce himself, but that would be out of character for his alter ego. He silently quoted his own rulebook in his head.

RULE 24: NEVER MAKE YOURSELF LOOK DESPERATE.

The longer Aven gazed up at the girl, the more his need to be near her again plagued him. He strained his mind to conjure another vision. Nothing came, at least, not until the girl did something that struck him, something he felt he had seen her do before.

Aven's vision zeroed in, and he watched as the girl tucked a loose curl behind her ear. The room fell dark and another flash came.

A meadow of wildflowers appeared at Aven's feet. He watched them sway, taking in a deep breath of their sweet scent, mixed with a salty breeze. The wind ruffled his hair as he listened to crashing waves somewhere in the distance.

Wishing to stay in that moment, Aven waited to lift his head. He would do anything to keep the sense of bliss consuming him. There were no words to describe the serenity, no poetry to compare its peace.

The moment Aven looked up, he found the angel. She stood on the edge of a cliff, looking out to sea. Sunrays glittered her white gown that waved in the wind, and a white halo of light encompassed her, expanding. Somehow she knew he would come. She knew he would be there, looking for her, and she for him.

Tucking stray hairs behind her ear, she glanced over her shoulder, but the instant Aven took a step to go to her, he fell into darkness.

When light filled his vision again, Aven found the angel, lying in his lap under a blossomed Japanese cherry blossom. She smiled up at him, hugged him, and her brightness expanded again. As Aven held her closer, he took comfort in the warmth of her halo, somehow knowing that he was the reason she glowed.

Petals of pink fell around them like slow drifting snow, landing in her hair, on her cheek. Aven gently brushed away the flowers as she laughed.

Her smile. His gaze was fixed upon it, desire drawing him down to kiss her soft lips. The angel glowed, leaning up to meet him. At the light brush of her lips, her brightness blinded him, and she was gone.

Sucking in a sharp breath, Aven blinked back to reality. There was no longer an ocean breeze or scent of lavender—just the odor of burning tobacco and cheap perfume that filled his nostrils.

Aven rubbed his eyes as a disco ball danced across his face. He shifted his weight and felt something cold and wet stuck to his leg. He cursed under his breath, seeing the ice from his glass on the carpet and the last sip of bourbon on his dress shoe. Kicking the ice to the side, he shook off the drops of whiskey from his shoe and smoothed back his hair. He smiled to people passing by, acting as if nothing was wrong. But something was wrong.

Strange visions were not new to Aven, but having them this clear was. They had never been anything wonderful either. Not of a place that felt heavenly, never of a beautiful angel in his arms. Glancing back up at the brunette, Aven was certain that the girl with green eyes was his way back to that safe haven of light.

At a sharp whistle from Aven's lips, José came over. "Yeah boss?"

"Send the next round on me. Put a note that says, 'Congrats to the beautiful bride.'"

"You sure you wouldn't rather me put 'Enjoy your last night of freedom?'" José asked.

"Let's not be so honest, shall we?" Aven smirked. "She might get cold feet, and I can't deal with that kind of guilt."

10

SUIT GUY

"WHY are you ignoring the hottie in the suit?" Laura screeched. She reached for Claire's phone but missed.

"Uh, probably, because he's trying to get in my pants?" Claire answered, wrinkling her forehead. "Don't you watch movies? That guy is acting like one of those suave stalkers that get all buddy, buddy with the bartender by paying them to slip a roofie."

"What horror movies do you watch? This is more like a chick flick, and you're acting like the weirdo whose too goody-goody to let the hot piece of ass hit on her. And then the dumb dude still falls for her, and when they screw, it's like a damn miracle the chick's an amazing lay. It's complete bullshit." Laura scooped up the "on the house" drink from the table before Claire could stop her and gulped it down.

"Laura!"

"What? I'm checking to see if it's drugged." Laura licked her lips.

"That was so stupid," Claire chided. She stared at Laura, gripping her phone tight as Laura leaned back against the booth cushions. "Well, was it?"

Laura sat up as if she was a rag doll, wobbling her head. "Oh yeah," she slurred. "I feel good." She rubbed Claire's arm and then patted her face. "Claire you're sa' pretty. Rook at dat cute button nose." Laura tapped Claire with her finger and laughed.

Claire stood and took Laura by the arm, trying to bring her dead weight to her feet. "Come on. We need to get you to the hospital."

Hitting her elbow on the wooden booth on the way down, Claire yelped as she fell at a tug on her wrist.

"I'm kidding!" Laura giggled, wrapping an arm around her neck. "Geez!"

Claire shoved Laura away and pulled down her dress. "You're such a jerk."

"And you're so gullible. It's clean. God, Claire, you freaked over nothing. He was just being nice."

"Nice or not. Men still have one thing on their mind."

"Women are no different, honey. You just don't know what you're missing"

"Missing? Laura. Look at him." Claire gestured. "What guy wears a suit to a club? And the staring thing is just—he's probably a serial killer."

"I told you to stop watching those shows. Your innocent little mind can't handle it."

"Documentaries."

"Boring."

"He fits the profile. He's a compensating creep."

"I wish that constipating creep would stare at me."

Claire gave a sideways glance. "One. I'm buying you a dictionary app for Christmas. Two, your taste is men is seriously disturbing. Thirty percent of crime in the U.S. is committed by a narcissist."

"Narca-what?"

"I'll Google the definition for you."

"Okay, sweetie," Laura said in a motherly tone, gesturing for Claire's phone. "I think you've had enough screen time for today."

"In a sec. Mom just sent me a message. Colt was just born. It's taking forever for the pictures and video to load. Are you sure this place has Wi-Fi?"

"Message Mom a picture of that tall drink of water. I'm sure she can appreciate it."

Claire's face twisted in disgust. "Gross."

"What?"

"It's my mom, and I'm getting a visual I know I won't get out."

"Your mom was young once."

"Yeah, but she would never dream of doing something like that."

"Oh, trust me. Mama would totally hit that handsome devil."

"I think I need to go to the bathroom and throw up now."

"It's not like you'll see him after tonight. For chrissakes, go talk to the guy, Claire."

"I did talk to him. I was even polite after his lame attempt to hit on me."

Laura snatched Claire's phone.

"Hey!" Claire shot to her feet, reaching for it. "What's your problem?"

"I'm not the one with the problem. You've been acting weird all day. When we walked into the hotel you were staring at that Luxor sign like it was a bad omen or something."

Claire crossed her arms and shrugged. "I was taking a mental snapshot."

"No, you were staring off again, being all weird like after—"

"Don't go there." Claire glared, prying her phone from Laura's grasp. She fell back into the booth and texted her mom.

Staring at the images of her nephew, Colt, an ache swelled in her chest. She wished she were in New York. She had always been very close with her brother until he moved. The night before he left, he told Claire the pay raise was something he couldn't refuse. She knew it was a lie, knew it wasn't because of his job opportunity. It was because every time he came to the house it reminded him of their dad, how he was gone. Claire could only assume it was her own guilt that brought on the hallucinations, because not long after Ryan left, Claire was sent to the Psychiatric Center.

Her therapist had said the recurring dream of the tsunami wave was merely a metaphor for the storm inside of her, that if Claire wouldn't let go, her depression and anxiety would keep getting the best of her, swallow her up, drown her. The angel was a symbol hope, an example of the strength inside of her.

"If you go talk to him I'll leave you alone," Laura said as if offering a truce.

Claire let out a long breath. Laura's nagging was getting to her, but she couldn't talk to the guy at the bar, not after what she experienced. The flashes always happened the same way—always a warning she was going to hallucinate—but this time it had been different.

She had stood in place as the room blurred and noise fell silent. The stranger at the bar came into focus as everything and everyone came to a stop. The bartender's bottle was frozen in the air; the people at the bar posed as if they were wax figures set up in a museum. Looking past the stillness of the room, Claire brought her focus to the man in the suit staring at her.

His hair was thick and black as midnight. It was combed back neatly but fell over his well-manicured furrowed brows and into his grey eyes. His eyes. Claire remembered the overwhelming familiarity of their softness, tinged with a hint of pain. At first they were like a dark storm, but they lightened, flecking with shards of icy blue.

A sharp stab spread across Claire's chest. She didn't know why, but it was as if something very sad, something heartbreaking had occurred between them. In that frozen moment of time, her heart whispered. It told her to go to him, told her that this man, this stranger had been torn away from her some distant time ago and fate had brought them together again.

"Claire." Laura snapped her fingers in front of her face.

Claire blinked and shook her head. "I'm not doing it, so you can just stop asking."

"When was the last time you even—"

"Laura, I mean it."

"Well you should at least—"

"No. And your relentless attempts at bullying will not persuade me otherwise."

"Why do you always use those big smart words that make you sound so dumb?" Laura asked, flopping down beside her.

"I prefer simple English to Yappanese. Look. We have this argument every time we go out, and every time the answer is the same. You're just mad because I'm the only person in existence who ever tells you no."

"If you won't talk to tall, dark, and handsome, *I* will." Laura shoved Claire and stood.

"Be my guest." Claire gestured with her hand but kept her eyes on her phone.

"If I'm lucky, I'll be his."

TEQUILA

"YOU know what?" Laura asked.

Claire lifted her gaze as Laura swiveled on her heels at the top of the steps.

"What?"

"You're lame." Laura jabbed, snatching up Claire's phone again. "And because I'm your best friend, I'm going to make damn sure your birthday doesn't suck this year."

Tugged by her wrist as if she was a pouting toddler, Claire was dragged to the dance floor. Not once did Laura loosen her grip. Even as she stood at the DJ booth, she held Claire firmly.

Oh no. The routine—my punishment for sulking.

The moment Laura let go, Claire spun on her toes to make a break for the exit, but three grinning faces blocked her way.

The bridesmaids held their stance, arms crossed, chins lifted. They reminded Claire of the National Guard. She had seen them on the news last summer during a riot after another government shutdown.

Claire sighed. "She's asking him to play that song, isn't she?"

"Laura? No." Jenna laughed.

"She wouldn't dare," Khloe teased.

"Here." Brittney offered Claire a shot. "You might need this."

Claire stared at the yellow liquid in the tiny glass as Laura came up behind her. Her friends circled, licking their chops like hungry lions; laughed like drunken hyenas.

This place isn't a club. It's a jungle.

"Come on, Claire." Laura shifted her shoulders as she danced. "You know this routine like the back of your hand."

Claire's heart thumped in her chest as her blood ran cold. There were too many people, too many eyes looking at the bride-to-be and her crew. Yes. She did know the routine, but she wasn't about to do it in front of all of these strangers.

As a song ended, the loud commotion of voices in the room died down as the DJ spoke into his microphone. "Before she says 'I do,' Jenna and her crew are going to give us a little show."

Claire clutched the shot glass, staring at the room of strangers with wide eyes before she met Laura's gaze.

"I'm not doing that dance." Claire's voice quivered, as did her hand as she handed off the shot to Laura. "And I'm not drinking this."

"Best Bitches. Remember?" Laura argued. She glanced at Khloe and Jenna. "Grab her."

Four hands held Claire firmly in place as she struggled to break free, but there was no escape.

"Liquid courage, honey," Laura said, pressing the shot glass to Claire's lips. "Bottoms up."

The stout stench of tequila burned in Claire's nostrils as it dribbled down her chin and neck, but she opened her mouth and swallowed the putrid liquid, forcing herself to swallow. Her stomach churned, twisting in knots as she coughed. She swiveled around, lurching for the table behind her and snatched a drink, not caring whose it was. The gulps of orange juice eased the burning in her throat, but it met her gut like a bag of rocks.

"Atta girl!" Brittney said, patting her back.

When Claire straightened, she forced her screwed up face to smooth as Brittney offered something small that looked like candy. "What's that?"

"If you don't want to throw up, you'll take it," Brittney said, closing in the space as she looked around the room.

Claire hesitated. Drugs. She had never taken them and didn't want to start now.

"Come on, Claire," Brittney urged. "I know it's hard. I know today is—I miss hanging out with you. We were all best friends, well, except Jenna. But don't you remember what it was like? All the sleepovers, all the time we spent together on the bus for competitions? You and I were close, and then you just . . . you left us. It's never been the same."

Claire stared at the pill a long moment. She knew she had secluded herself, made up excuses not to see her friends, and busied herself with work at the Bed and Breakfast.

Brittney put the pill in her hand. "It will help you forget."

Claire clenched her teeth, ignoring the little voice in her head telling her to stop, to walk away. But the urge to vomit was too strong. Tossing the red pill to the back of her throat, Claire swallowed it, gulping down an offered drink from Brittney's other hand.

Morals. Claire had them, but tonight, she would ignore her conscience. Just for one night she had to prove she wasn't strange, that she didn't constantly feel like running away.

"Let's see what you got ladies!" announced the DJ as the song for the routine boomed with bass.

Claire chugged the rest of Brittney's drink and wiped her mouth with the back of her hand. It only took seconds before her head was swimming. Her body went lax and a tickle danced in her stomach. The pill. It was taking effect, and quick.

Finding her balance again, Claire took in a deep breath and smoothed back her hair as the liquor buzzed in her veins. A giggle rose, but she stifled it, clearing her throat. She was going to show them. She was going to show them all.

Strutting to the dance floor, Claire broke out in the choreographed dance to the chorus line. She slid left to right with her friends, just like they had during the year they won nationals in tenth grade. The onlookers of the club made a circle around them and cheered. When a spotlight landed on Claire for her solo moves, the crowd grew louder. A wide smile spread across her face. This was the person she used to be; this was the Claire who never thought twice about having fun.

When the song ended, the crowd clapped and hooted for the girls as they joined hands with a bow, ending their routine.

Claire laughed as her friends tugged her back to their table where a few guys approached, handing them some shots.

"Fun size is back!" Laura announced holding up her glass.

Claire lifted her chin with pride, ready to tilt back the shot, but the little voice inside her came calling again.

The memory of her sixteenth birthday came to her with images of shots of tequila, dancing with Tyler, making out with him, losing herself in the moment.

My fault. I'm the reason he's gone.

Bracing a hand on the table, Claire held her balance, but she couldn't ignore the ache swelling in her chest, couldn't ignore the memory of the flames licking the ceiling.

Steadying her shaking hand, Claire glanced over her shoulder, finding a beer bottle on a vacant table. Relief spread through her as she picked it up, finding it light. Flipping it upside down, she emptied the remaining backwash at the back of her heels and held up her shot glass.

"Drink up bitches!" Laura shouted, holding up her shot.

The girls screamed, clinked their glasses, and drank in unison. Claire followed suit, but unlike her friends, she didn't swallow. Instead, she placed the beer bottle to her lips and spat the tequila inside. Letting out a hoot, she slammed the shot glass down on the table.

As a waitress came around to gather the empty glasses, Claire put the beer bottle on her tray and sat down, asking her politely for a bottle of water. She thought she had done it, that she was in the clear, but to her dismay another tray full of drinks was placed in front of her.

"Courtesy of the manager." Another waitress smiled, handing Jenna a note.

While Jenna read the note out loud, Claire looked over her shoulder to the bar. Suit Guy smiled, lifting his drink as if to say, "you're welcome."

Rolling her eyes, Claire swiveled back around in her seat, watching as the girls huddled around Jenna, reading the note. Jenna blew a kiss to the manager and the waitress handed out the red drinks. All of them were decorated with white paper umbrellas, all of them but hers.

Glaring, Claire looked back at the bar to the manager who held up his glass again. Her friends followed suit, holding up theirs and accepted his offer. Her friends sucked down their drinks, but Claire didn't drink hers. Instead, she slid a cherry from the plastic sword and popped it in her mouth. She didn't taste any alcohol but just to be sure, she took a small sip. Cranberry juice. Now knowing the drink held no liquor, Claire tilted back, hoping it hadn't been drugged.

"Oh, look at who got something special." Laura wiggled her brows, taking the red the paper umbrella from Claire's glass. She twirled it in her fingers, spinning it left to right. "Red must mean he's in love," she teased

"Come over here!" Jenna slurred as she called to Suit Guy. She waved her hands in the air as if she was about to drown and he was manning a lifeboat.

Claire giggled at the bride-to-be and her desperate attempt. The pill. There was no ignoring how it made her feel, and she wondered if she would have a headache in the morning. Regaining her composure, Claire watched as the rest of her friends motioned for the manager to join them.

When the manager didn't come, Jenna climbed over Brittney and Khloe, stumbling toward him to thank him in person. Wrapping her arms around his neck, she made a sloppy attempt to kiss him on the cheek. The manager must have complimented her bridal crown because Jenna touched it and laughed while she composed herself.

Was he going to use that line on all of her friends?

Averting her gaze, Claire looked over Brittney's shoulder to the phone in her hand. The Vegas hashtag popped up with pictures and a video of their dance routine. The numbers under the video were gaining, two hundred likes and counting.

Just great.

With a huff, Claire dared to shift her gaze back to Suit Guy, and just as she has suspected, he was staring at her again.

"He can't keep his eyes off of you, Claire," Laura said, elbowing her. "Go talk to him, for chrissakes!"

"Have I ever told you how much it bothers me that you say chrissakes?"

"Like I listen." Laura rolled her eyes. "Oh look, here he comes! I call dibs, ladies!"

As her friends jumped up and circled around Suit Guy like a bunch of young teenagers meeting their favorite rock star for the first time, Claire stood calmly. Taking her time, she took steps toward him, coaching herself to be polite but froze in place to a stranger's voice behind her.

"Hello, beautiful."

12

TONY

CLAIRE'S body tensed as she slowly turned, wrinkling her nose at the stench of cheap cologne. Face to face with another guy in a suit, she glanced at his greasy combed back brown hair and his cracked dry lips as he flicked his tongue.

"Can I help you?" Claire asked, glancing at his suit. She halfway thought she was hallucinating him, that the pill made her imagine a slightly less attractive form of Suit Guy. But as her gaze shifted to the other women gawking at him, she knew he was real.

"Want to dance?" the new suit asked.

"No thanks, I'm good," Claire answered as the tips of her ears burned. An alarm. This was the reaction her body made when she was near someone that was trouble. This guy hadn't been in the club long. She would have noticed another suit in the room by now. Still, she wondered if the manager knew him or if they were friends.

"Come on. It's just a dance. I saw you out there. I'd like you to show me how to dance like that," he said.

"I'm not a dancing instructor, but if you want lessons, I'm sure you can look up a studio nearby," Claire quipped, halfway surprised at her cocky response.

She glanced back at her friends and the sexy Suit Guy, who glared.

"Don't be such a snob. I saw you looking at me when you came in."

Claire spun on her toes and glowered. "Excuse me?" she asked, balling up her fists as heat flushed her body. She was ready to lay the guy out on the floor, take him down a notch. If her dad had taught her anything as a child, it was to stand up for herself, especially to guys like this.

"Come on sweet cheeks." He reached for her hand, but Claire took a step back, bumping into someone behind her. A rumble from his chest vibrated against her back, his tone stern.

"Tony."

Claire swung around to find Suit Guy, his eyes narrow with irritation at the man behind her.

"Crey," Tony said, lifting his chin. "Looks like you have your hands full. How about you let me have this one tonight?"

Suit Guy gave a slight smile. "I don't think she's interested."

"Why don't you let pretty little green eyes tell me that," Tony challenged.

Claire opened her mouth to defend herself, but Suit Guy spoke.

"Shouldn't you be at the party?"

"I was, but Vincent is looking for you. He says you're ignoring his calls. Again." Tony brought his gaze back to Claire and smiled. Her stomach twisted in knots. There was no way to make a clean break between them.

"Ah, well you should run along and tell him I'll be there shortly."

"I thought I'd have some fun first." Tony slid his tongue along his lower lip and wiggled his brows.

Claire's stomach rolled.

"Well, I think you should have fun elsewhere," Suit Guy said. "These girls are having a bachelorette party. And as you know, I can't have the future husband come back here for a fight, now can I? Besides, you know what happened last week."

"An honest mistake, but I don't see a ring on this one's finger," Tony said smugly, looking at Claire's hand. He took a step back and gestured for it. "You don't need the owner's permission to talk to me. Let me buy you a drink, maybe then you'll change your mind about dancing."

Claire's eyes darted to the table and her chair. "No, thank you. I have one," she said, brushing past Tony. She snatched up Brittney's drink, taking a few sips from the straw, and sat, acting as if she wasn't listening in on the two suits' conversation.

"Don't make yourself look so desperate." Aven gave a cocky grin, blocking Tony's way to the brunette.

"You've got some nerve, Crey."

"Lots of nerves." Aven took his associate by the shoulder and squeezed. "And if you keep getting on them, my mouth may slip about your mess up a few months ago."

Tony's eyes went wide.

"Why don't you go to the casino," Aven said, keeping his eyes locked, pressing his thumb into the pressure point of Tony's trap. At the widening of Tony's pupils, the light fading, Aven glanced back at the brunette, releasing his hand. "High stakes tonight."

"Stakes?" Tony mumbled with a blank stare.

"Make some money. I'll meet you up at the party for a game of poker later," Aven said, casually, looking at his watch. "Tell Vincent to give me twenty minutes."

"Money," Tony said.

Aven took a betting chip from his pocket, flipped it in the air, and snapped his fingers before he caught it. "You like money."

Tony blinked at Aven, then he looked around the room.

Aven placed the betting chip in Tony's hand.

Tony looked at it and at Aven. Confusion was plastered on his face. He looked over his shoulder, doing a double take at the brunette.

Aven turned him quickly, pressing the soft spot of Tony's collarbone again. This time Aven meditated, making sure he had Tony's full attention.

You don't want her. She's nothing to you. Most likely a lousy lay. What you want is to take all of my money. Money. You want money.

Over and over in his mind Aven repeated the words, squeezing Tony's shoulder tight.

Finding only a brown rim around Tony's wide pupils, Aven snapped his fingers in Tony's ears.

"We'll play a private game after the party. Just you and me," Aven offered, patting Tony's arm. "Tell Vincent I'll be up soon."

"After the party . . ." Tony said, glancing at Aven's expensive watch. "Vincent . . ."

"Twenty minutes, tops."

Tony met Aven's stare. "Twenty minutes." He blinked. Came to. "I'll tell Vincent."

"Good man." Aven grinned. "I'll see you shortly."

Watching Tony go in the direction of the exit, Aven glanced back at the brunette he had saved. She was taking a phone, an old model, and putting it to her ear. He stared, wondering who she was speaking to. "I love you too," was all he could gather as he read her lips. A tinge of jealousy spread through him as he wondered who Ryan was.

Disappointment came quickly to Aven, realizing the demon had been toying with him. She didn't want this girl, she merely wanted to remind him of the type of woman he could never have. He was cursed because no one, especially this angel, would ever want to be with someone who dealt with devils.

Although the brunette never made eye contact, he nodded to her as if to say goodbye, and turned. His eyes reflected the pink neon light of the cigarette machine as he made a straight line for it. The rules of his elite club were strictly against smoking, but Aven didn't care. Patting the lighter in his jacket pocket, he headed toward the neon light, ready for a release.

DEVIL IN DISGUISE

PERSUASION. It always made Aven edgy. He needed the nicotine to calm him down, a buzz to ease his tense shoulders. Halfway to the cigarette machine, he paused in his steps as a voice called over the music.

"Sir!"

Aven turned in surprise as his gaze met the brunette walking briskly to stand in front of him.

"Yes, miss?"

"Thank you," she yelled over the music.

Aven shook his head and cupped his ear. He knew what she had said, but he wanted to hear it again.

"I said," the brunette began, but the music stopped as she yelled again, "thank you!"

Aven held back a smile as her cheeks flushed, and she gazed around the room as people stared.

Aven slid his hands in his pockets and shrugged. "Just saving a damsel in distress."

The girl tucked her hair behind her ear.

There it was again: the tug, the magnetic pull. Remembering the vision, warmth spread through Aven's being.

The girl's forehead wrinkled, and Aven realized he had been staring at her again.

"Okay," she said with a nod. "Again. Thanks." She turned and took a few steps back to her table.

A cool draft came as the brunette walked away, taking her light and warmth with her. Even if she wasn't what the demon wanted, he still had time. He could still spend a few moments longer in the sunlight, perhaps be taken to the safe haven once more. The demon could wait to be entertained. By midnight she would get what she wanted. She always did.

"If you really want to thank me, you can dance with me," Aven called out without a second thought.

The girl whipped around. "Excuse me?"

Aven paused for a moment. He hadn't meant to say that.

Now who's acting desperate, Crey?

He gave his charming smile, the same one he had practiced for years, and came to stand in front of her. "If you want to thank me properly, you'll dance with me."

"I can't dance to this music," she said, shaking her head.

"I mean real dancing."

"Real dancing?"

Before she could say another word, Aven took her hand and led her to the DJ Booth. Fire blazed through every fiber of his being at their touch, but he ignored it and shouted up to the DJ. "Hey Jordan!"

The DJ slid his sunglasses down his nose as Aven mouthed the song. Jordan smiled, slid his sunglasses back over his eyes, and tapped the glowing screen in front of him.

As the girl followed him to an empty table, Aven unbuttoned his jacket, laid it neatly on a chair, and took her hand again. This time the fire was comforting. It spilled over him as if a pitcher of warm water had been emptied from above.

This feeling was familiar, one he had never forgotten, one he had longed for. He flashed back to his childhood, to a memory of his mother. It was the time she had wrapped him in a blanket and kissed his hair. The day she had died. He wondered if his mother sent him this girl, this angel, because in that very moment of their touch, Aven believed she was the only way to escape his never-ending darkness.

Putting the thoughts in the back of his mind, Aven glanced up at the DJ who asked the crowd to make way for another performance.

"You're serious?" the girl asked, standing wide eyed as "Devil in Disguise" began to play.

Aven brought her to the center of the dance floor and grinned wide. He rolled up his sleeves neatly and took her hand, placing his other hand on her hip. "You're not the only one who can jive, Princess."

As Aven spun the girl out and pulled her into his arms at the chorus, the crowd cheered. Dancing with this girl had been one of the most natural things he had ever done. He was surprised, and yet, he wasn't, by how their movements flowed together. Every step was in sync as if reading one another's mind.

Aven's heart raced. Butterflies filled his stomach. It was the way the girl smiled at him, the way his chest swelled, ready to burst from joy every time they laughed.

There was no amount of money, no luxury that could replace this feeling. Happiness, true happiness, was right there with him, twirling in his arms. And for the first time in his life, Aven realized it couldn't be bought.

As the song ended, Aven pulled the girl to his chest and dipped her. He paused for a few pounding heartbeats and smiled brilliantly, never breaking his gaze. Her eyes. He now knew he had seen them before the visions. Maybe he had dreamt of her before his hauntings and somehow had forgotten her beautiful face. He vowed in his heart, he would never forget again.

With his gaze darting to the girl's lips, Aven fought against the urge to kiss her. He almost had in the vision. Focusing on her ribs expanding and contracting, the crowd's applause that grew louder, Aven pulled the girl to her feet and gestured for her to take a bow.

"Are we even now?" the brunette asked, lifting her head from her curtsy.

Aven grinned with a nod. "Yes, we're even."

"Good."

The girl's mouth parted as if she wanted to say something, but she turned away. Her warmth went with her again, but Aven couldn't be left in the cold. Not after what he felt during their dance. Money couldn't buy happiness, but it could be a bridge to it.

"Hey, Princess."

The girl turned, but not slow enough. Aven caught a hint of the smile she was trying to hide. He didn't hide his, pleased by the nickname he had chosen for her. "You look thirsty. Can I buy you a drink?"

"Sure," she answered with a shrug.

Aven slipped on his jacket and lead the way to the bar where José stood with a goofy grin, shaking a mixer in his hands.

As Aven pulled a stool out for the brunette, she glanced at him, seemingly surprised by the gentlemanly gesture, and sat down. Taking a paper napkin, she dabbed her forehead and chest and Aven sat across from her.

"Where did you learn do that?" she asked.

"What?" Aven cocked a brow. "Dancing?"

"I've never met a guy that would jitter in public unless a trophy was involved. You don't seem like a dance competition kind of guy."

Aven feigned offense. "That's judgmental."

"I've taken dance all my life and none of the guys that competed were–"

"Wearing suits?"

"No."

"Handsome?"

The girl pressed her lips, shaking her head as if to hold back a laugh. "You own this club, don't you?"

"And the hotel."

"Well, businessmen such as yourself," she said, eyeing his suit, "don't usually take jitterbug lessons in their leisure time."

"Who says?"

"So you take classes?"

The DJ announced another song for the bachelorette party, and a short moment of only chattering voices filling the room gave Aven the chance to lean forward and whisper,

"Can you keep a secret?"

"Depends on the secret."

"You seem fairly trustworthy."

"Do I?"

Again there was a moment between them, an intimate one. But it was soon interrupted as José served the Craven Casino Cocktail to the girl and a glass of Aven's usual.

Aven took a step back and straightened. "You may want to go easy. That'll sneak up on you."

"I don't think you have to worry about me." She took a sip. "Thank you, by the way. It's very good."

"My own concoction."

"So what's your secret?"

"For the drink?"

"No, how did you learn to dance like that?"

Aven tilted his head and leaned against the bar. "You really want to know?

The girl nodded once.

"Alright. I'll give you a little background history," Aven said. "Very personal, but, like I said, you seem trustworthy. You wouldn't try to blackmail me or anything, would you?"

"Depends on if you start acting like that jerk who approached me earlier."

Aven let out a light laugh. "I like your honesty."

The girl smiled and nursed her drink.

"When I was nine," Aven began. "I learned to waltz. The young girl I was partnered with hated the waltz, and our teacher, Miss Salizzoni, was very strict. Lucky for us, she took breaks after about an hour into our lessons. She'd say"—he faked an Italian woman's voice—"stay here, and I'll be back in an hour. Practice your steps, and when I return I expect you to know them."

The brunette laughed at his attempt to mock his former teacher. "Did she really sound like that?"

"You don't like my accent?"

The girl covered her mouth and shook her head as if she was a bit embarrassed for him, but Aven didn't care if anyone was looking. He wanted to make her laugh. Every time she did, her eyes brightened with her smile and her warmth soothed him.

"Hm. Thought I was always good at impressions, anyway, we knew where she was *really* going."

"Oh yeah? Where was she *really* going?"

"The pool house to get close with the gardener Philippe."

"Oh."

"Something about gardeners." Aven shrugged and took a sip of his drink. "So for an hour the girl and I would be alone to do whatever we wanted. One day we were playing hide and seek. I was in the closet hiding and started snooping around, looking at some old DVDs in a box."

"DVDs? Those disk things people used to watch movies on?"

"Ancient, right? I was naturally curious and pulled them out, dusted off the TV, and plugged it in. It took me a while to figure out where to put the shiny round object, but when the movie played, my partner shouted at me to leave it in, that she wanted to dance to the fun dancing lesson."

"I'm guessing that fun dancing lesson was jitterbug?"

"1950s. The Great Charleston. I grumbled a bit, but after she punched me in the arm I followed the moves. A few steps later I was having a good time. It was far better than the waltz."

"What happened when your teacher came back from her break?" the brunette asked, putting break in air quotes.

"We would scramble to put the stuff back in the box, shut the closet, and resume our positions. We learned the waltz eventually, but nothing could match our jitterbug skills, or tango for that matter."

The girl's phone vibrated on the bar. She picked it up and pressed the screen, scrunching up her face. She looked over her shoulder at her blonde friend who was still typing.

"Tell your friend you're in good hands. No more creeps will bother you."

"She's not worried about that."

"No?"

Clearing her throat, the brunette turned back around. "She's thrilled I'm talking to you."

"Is she now?"

At his words, the brunette gave Aven a strange look. He wondered if he had done something wrong. She fluttered her lashes as if trying to shrug off whatever it was that bothered her and turned her phone around for Aven to see. He nodded at her friend's text, filled with exaggerated emojis. When the phone vibrated again, the girl turned her phone and stared at the screen with narrow eyes.

"In fact," she said, "she wants to know if I'm bringing you back to the room and if I am"—she read the text out loud—"to program the lock to say, 'do not disturb.'"

With a huff the brunette swiveled in the bar stool, shaking her head no, but the blonde only grinned, making an obscene, even proactive, hand gesture.

"She's—" Aven began.

"Nosy?" the girl snapped, swinging herself around.

"No."

"Annoying?"

"I was going to say persistent."

"Yes, she is. Persistent. About everything," she said, circling the ice in her glass with her straw.

"You're not big on drinking, are you?"

The brunette parted her mouth, tilting her head slightly.

"The ol' bottle trick gave it away."

"You saw that?"

Aven shrugged his shoulders. "Maybe."

"I never drink. I haven't since I was sixteen. Laura, my crazy best friend"—she head-gestured—"practically dragged me here kicking and screaming. She's been insisting I find someone to . . ."

"To . . ." Aven knew, but he wanted the girl to admit that she truly was as decent and honest as he assumed.

Pink spread through the brunette's cheeks past her sparkling blush as she gazed at a couple making out.

"Someone to what?" he asked, trying to bring her focus back on him.

The girl gave a lengthy sigh. "Someone to hook up with. She's been trying to get me to drink so I'll have a good time."

"She doesn't know about the virgin Cape Cods?"

"Thank you, for earlier," the girl said, fidgeting with her straw. "It was thoughtful of you."

"You're welcome."

The brunette took a small sip before looking over her shoulder at the blonde taking pictures with the bridal party.

Aven was cautious with his next words. "Would you mind me asking why you don't drink?"

"Let's just say one really bad hangover ruined me for life."

"Well"—Aven smiled—"I feel honored you're having one with me." He held out his glass and the girl tapped hers against his with a clink.

"I'm being polite," she said. "You saved me from having to knee that Tony guy in the crotch."

"I don't take kindly to men forcing themselves on women. I'll be sure no one else does while you're in the hotel."

The words tumbled out of Aven's mouth. He knew he had crossed the line, telling the girl he would see to it she wouldn't be bothered. He quickly tried to think up something to recover with, but the girl spoke.

"That's a bit much," she said, raising a brow.

"Just making sure to keep good reviews. People Google that stuff before they book, you know."

"As a matter of fact, I do know." The girl covered her mouth, but her shouldered bounced. "My mother and I own a Bed and Breakfast in Georgia."

"I'm not the only entrepreneur then."

The girl giggled but tried to compose herself. Aven waited patiently, knowing she had taken the little red pill. It wasn't one from his company; it was one from the black market. Uncontrollable giggling was a side effect. He mouthed to José to bring a glass of agua.

The girl cleared her throat and sat up straight. "So what? You'll have spies watching my every move to make sure people treat me with respect?" She took a few more draws from the straw, and Aven thought to take the drink from her. He gave José a look, telling him to hurry up with a pointed stare.

"Got to keep the ratings up," Aven replied, trying to act as if what he said was a joke.

"Well then"—she gave a faint laugh—"I'll have to be sure to give you five stars in my review."

"I look forward to reading it." Aven flashed a genuine smile.

When warmth came from the girl again, he realized that's all she wanted. Honesty.

The longer Aven looked into her eyes, the more he craved the feeling from the vision. He knew he had to find a way to spend more time with her, to keep that feeling a little longer. Glancing at his watch, he noted the hour.

Time for a little magic.

TRICKSTER

CLAIRE was grateful Suit Guy broke his gaze to glance at his watch. She had been lost in his grey eyes, lost in the power of them, the confidence. He was right. She should have gone easy on the drink.

Lacing her fingers, Claire observed the polish she had picked off her nails. She needed something in her hands, something to fidget with until she could find a way to politely leave the bar. Taking a cherry from the plastic sword on the rim of her glass, she lifted her chin. "I don't think I have ever been to a hotel that has gone so above and beyond for their guests."

"We do what we can to have repeat visits." The manager winked.

"Right," Claire said, scrunching her nose. "Well, I appreciate your chivalry, but I assure you I can slay my own dragons." She pointed the plastic sword at the handsome stranger.

"Can you now?"

Another rush of heat swept through Claire as the manager stared. She caught herself from leaning forward and pushed back her shoulders.

Get it together, Claire.

"This princess is quite capable of taking care of herself," she informed him. "I don't need a knight in shining armor to come to my rescue."

"Oh, but Princess, surely you know you cannot slay dragons without magic."

Claire gave a light laugh. She was grateful it wasn't a giggle. Her previous giggle fit earlier had been hard to control. "You know magic?"

The manager reached into his jacket and withdrew a deck of cards, shuffling them. "As a matter of fact, I do." He spread the cards out on the bar. "Pick a card."

"Any card?"

"Any card."

Claire looked over the deck and picked a card in the middle and looked at it.

"Now don't show me. Remember it well, pick up the cards, and put yours back in the deck."

Claire memorized the card and slid hers back into the deck.

"Alright now shuffle them," he instructed.

Claire shuffled the deck and offered it back.

"You hold onto them," he said, his expression suddenly serious. "Now look in my eyes and try not to blink."

A long moment of silence passed as they stared at one another.

"Am I making you uncomfortable?" the manager asked with a slight smirk.

Claire thought about his question for a moment. She couldn't figure out if she was uncomfortable or not. She liked the attention Suit Guy gave her, but then again, she felt uneasy, as if this whole time he had been undressing her with his eyes. She ignored her instincts and kept her focus.

"Got it."

Claire blinked, wetting her dry eyes.

"Got what?"

"Your card."

Claire tried to hand the deck back, but the manager shook his head.

"We don't need them. You can lay the stack on the bar."

"Don't you need to find my card?" she asked, putting the cards to the side.

"Nope," he said, taking a napkin from a holder. He unfolded it, smoothed it out, and took out a silver lighter from his other inner pocket. "If you will be so kind as to assist me, milady."

Claire stared at Suit Guy for a long moment. The word "milady" struck her with a wave of familiarity. She shifted her gaze to his silver lighter, seeing the engraved symbol. She swore she had seen the signet before. It looked like the one she had envisioned in the airport, however this one was upside down.

Blinking, Claire glanced up at the manager. "You want me to light it on fire?" she asked, taking the lighter. She grazed her thumb over the etching, trying to understand why it seemed as if she knew it. Her stomach tightened as a flash came to her mind, and the etching took the form of a lapel attached to a red suit, worn by the dark-haired angel she had dreamed of on the plane.

"Please," the manager said. He had been waiting patiently and Claire realized she had better come back to reality.

"Okay." Claire thumbed the starter, setting the napkin up in flames, but before it reached Suit Guy's fingers, he flicked his wrist.

Before her very eyes, a card appeared out of thin air.

"Tada," the manager said, holding out the card for Claire to look at it. "Is this your card?"

Claire batted her eyes, completely astonished. "How did you know I drew the five of spades?"

Suit Guy appeared confused and twisted the card to look at it. "The five of spades?"

"That's right."

The manager laid the card down, taking the deck and sorted through the cards. "That can't be your card," he said, slipping his hand pockets as if he lost something.

Claire laughed at his confusion. "It is." She took the card from the bar, looking it over front to back, still wondering how he did the trick.

"If I remember right, it wasn't a spade."

"And what makes you think that?" Claire asked, handing the card over to him.

"Because," he said, leaning toward her, "this is your card." When he flicked the five of spades, the queen of hearts appeared before Claire could blink.

"How did you do that?" she asked.

"A magician never reveals his secrets." He grinned, placing the deck in his pocket.

Claire's laugh was faint at first until a giggle turned into a fit of laughter. There was no controlling it this time.

The manager gave a laugh that sounded a bit nervous. "Is that funny?"

"Oh, you're good." Claire pressed her lips hard, holding off the tickle in her stomach as she brushed the ash off her phone with a napkin.

"Comes with practice." Suit Guy shrugged and took a sip from his glass.

Claire couldn't help but laugh again. She stood and wiped the running mascara under her lower eyelids. The pill Brittney gave her was hitting her hard. "Now I've seen everything. Magic tricks and pick up lines." She straightened her tiara and took a few steps away from the bar. "I forgot I'm in Vegas."

"Would you like to see another trick?"

"No, I need to get back to my friends." Claire turned, but as she caught the twinge of panic in his eyes, her laughter halted. His expression was part fear, part desperation, hidden behind a smile.

No matter the guilt Claire suddenly felt, she knew the longer she stood there, the harder it would be for her to leave. Forcing a sweet smile, she held out her hand. "It was very nice meeting you Mr., uh . . ."

"Crey, Aven Crey," Suit Guy said, shaking her hand gently but longer than expected.

"Claire Grace. A pleasure to meet you, Mr. Crey. You have a lovely hotel," she informed him, drawing back. "I'll be sure to add in my review that the entertainment was above all of my expectations."

Waiting for Aven to speak, Claire caught him staring at something past her. No. He was staring at her cheek.

She brushed her cheekbone, finding the loose curl beneath her ear. It was the same loose curl that always went rogue. She remembered cutting it as a child, how her mother had fussed when she saw the trimmings in the sink.

"It is. I should be thanking you," he said, taking her hand again. "For you have exceeded all of mine, Your Grace."

As Aven kissed her knuckles, a fire blazed through every inch of her skin. The same had been felt when their hands had touched before their dance, only this time, a vivid vision came to her mind.

Claire's breath hitched and she froze when Aven's attire changed right before her eyes. Instead of a black suit, he wore a white uniform, slightly wrinkled and smudged with something like soot. They were standing at a golden gate as people in gowns and some kind of otherworldly attire passed through it. A pain deep within her chest ached as she met Aven's eyes. It was the same she had felt when she had first seen him. Only this time, guilt consumed her.

As the vision faded, Aven's white attire seeped into black as if ink drenched his uniform. The vision was blotted out, and only a man with raven hair and matching suit remained.

"Have a good night," Claire mumbled all too quickly and turned, walking away toward the steps. Whatever that vision was, the man in the black suit was connected. This was not the same blonde angel she had seen from her dream of chaos. This was a dark and mysterious stranger taking his place.

SHOOK UP

WITH a trembling hand, Claire pressed her palm to her chest, trying to control her sharp breaths. Whatever that flash was, it felt real, too real. She was going to lose it. She was going to have a panic attack. The heat that had flushed her veins at the touch of Mr. Crey's lips turned to ice as she topped the steps and met Laura's eager stare.

"I saw him kiss your hand!" Laura squealed, gripping her by the arm. "What did he say?"

"Nothing much. Showed me a magic trick."

"Details woman!" Laura shouted, shaking her.

Laughing, Claire gently pushed Laura back. The giggly feeling tickled her stomach as her head swam.

Stupid pill.

"Well." Claire sighed, shuffling through the mound of purses on the red pleather bench. "He's handsome, charming, and completely full of himself."

"Mm. I love a confident man." Laura licked her lips.

"I'll be back." Claire grabbed the black sequin clutch Laura had loaned her and went to the steps.

"Where the hell are you going–don't say the bathroom again."

"The room."

"Oh, are you going back to his place or ours?"

"Neither. I'm going to ours. Alone."

"You're turning in? What the hell, Claire?"

"I'll just go up for a bit. I feel dizzy." Claire wasn't lying. She did feel dizzy. Between the wave of familiarity, the drinks, and the pill, her head felt like a merry-go-round.

"I need to lay down. I'll come back in an hour."

"Liar. You'll fall asleep watching some sappy movie on TV."

"I won't watch sad movies. And I'm too buzzed to fall asleep. I'll go drink some water, rest, and be back soon."

"We have water here."

"Laura, please. I danced, we had fun, and we'll be here all weekend. Just let me go up for like thirty minutes, and I promise I'll dance with you guys when I get back."

"Fine." Laura huffed, giving her quick hug. "Thirty minutes. If you don't come back missy, I will drag your pretty little ass right back down here and make you dance to something you absolutely hate."

"Deal." Claire smiled, but then she frowned as Laura glanced to the manager at the bar.

"Just know that you gave up dibs on sexy pants. What's his name?"

Claire didn't know why she hesitated to tell Laura, but she did. "Aven. Aven Crey. You were right. He is nice and very . . . eloquent."

Laura snapped her gaze back to Claire. "Speak English, woman."

"He's very well spoken. Sophisticated. Not like the guys you're used to. Actually, you know what? Never mind. You won't be able to keep up."

"Oh, I can keep up," Laura said, putting her hand on her hip. She tipped her nose in the air. "But can he?"

"Have fun." Claire smiled, but it was forced. She was secretly hoping Laura wouldn't go talk to him. For some reason she was suddenly jealous, regretting her words as she watched Laura eye Aven.

"I'll be back in a bit." Claire steadied herself with a hand on the railing and walked down the steps.

"I mean it, Claire," Laura called down to her. "Thirty minutes or else."

Claire waved her other hand in the air, not looking back. She kept her head down, quickening her stride past the bar. She didn't glance up at Aven, didn't follow the compulsion to say goodbye. With furrowed brows she climbed the stairs, feeling as if Aven was burning a hole in her back with his eyes. It wasn't the sudden heat that made her pause. It was the tug, the voice in her heart that whispered for her to stay.

16

CASINO STALKER

ALTHOUGH Aven made small talk with the woman he had lit the cigarette for, he watched Claire out of the corner of his eye. She paused on the steps as if she might turn to look at him, but she hastened her stride.

His shoulders slumped in disappointment. Sipping his bourbon, he kept his focus on her over the rim but clenched the glass tight as he watched Tony ascend the steps after her.

"Shit," Aven said under his breath.

Am I losing my touch or is the demon messing with me?

"José," Aven called to the other end of the bar.

"Yeah boss?"

"Get Jestine here another. I'll be back in a few."

"Yes, sir."

"Excuse me." Aven gave a quick smile at Jestine and swiftly made his way up the stairs.

Darting into the casino, he furiously texted his cousin.

A: Tighten your leash. Your boy is at
it again.

Pressing send, he kept his distance, but his gaze was on the brunette as she made a straight line for the elevators. With no text back from Vincent, Aven clenched his teeth and caught up to Tony, slamming him against a slot machine with one swift swoop.

"What the hell, Crey?" Tony gritted out, shoving him back.

"You know all I have to do is say one word to Vincent and you're out. Stalking is very much against the code."

Tony spat. "I'm not stalking anyone."

"No? Not even that feisty brunette you tried to dance with earlier?"

Feisty. The perfect word to describe her.

Even if he hadn't come to Claire's rescue, Aven knew that she could have handled herself. But he hadn't wanted to give her the chance to slay her own dragons. He wanted to be her knight.

"Why is it any of your business? You've slept with every girl in the Circle, and what? I can't entertain an out-of-towner? You can't claim everything you set your eyes on, Crey. So stop being such a selfish di–"

"Ah, ah, ah. Manners."

"Screw you."

The doors to the elevator closed as Aven caught a glimpse of Claire in it with a group of people. As his shoulders relaxed, he brought his gaze back to Tony with a smirk. "I don't swing that way, but if you want to dance, I'll dance."

"So proud of being a man-whore, aren't we?"

Nodding as if he was admitting his status, Aven pursed his lips. "Man-whore."

His least favorite nickname.

"That's right," Tony taunted. "So fuck off."

As Tony walked away again, Aven took him by the shoulder and squeezed. Even if he wasn't going to persuade him, he could intimidate him.

"You see, Tony. The difference between my man-whoring and yours is that no one makes complaints, now do they? Maybe if you were gentle with the delicate flowers instead of stomping on them, they wouldn't have to go to Vincent to file complaints and you wouldn't be on parole."

"I'm on parole because you make what I do your business. Your pillow talk cost me two grand in fines."

"Then if I were you, I'd stop following that girl, go back up to the party, and start doing what you do best. And I don't mean getting so drunk off the open bar that you have to be carried back to your room. I mean kissing the rings."

"One day you're gonna get yours, Crey." Tony bit his lips, shaking a finger. He turned to go to the elevators but paused and looked over his shoulder with a grin. "You know what? You can have the snobby bitch, she's probably a terrible lay anyway."

It took everything Aven had not grab a fist full of Tony's hair and smash his smug smile into a slot machine. The need to protect Claire's honor was instinctive. He hardly knew her and yet, his hands were clenched tight in his pockets.

Aven kept his cool facade and smiled. "Be a good boy and tell Vincent I'm on my way."

As Tony got in an empty elevator, Aven blew out a long breath. He texted Kitten a warning, apologizing in advance that Tony was in a mood.

New or not, Tony was crossing lines. He wasn't just disrespectful to women, but short-tempered and abusive.

RULE 1: NEVER, EVER, DISRESPECT A LADY.

Aven's phone vibrated in his hand.

```
V: I'll talk to Tony. Come up to the
party. Your surprise is waiting.
```

Another message, but this time from Kat. She had sent a puking emoji next to Tony's name then,

```
K: Hurry up!
A: Be up soon. Handling some business.
K: What? A quickie?
A: Ever known me to rush?
```

Walking into the elevator, Aven grinned at his witty reply to Kat, pressing floor seven.

HEAVEN'S DOOR

WATCHING Claire lift a shaky hand to the lock scanner, Aven approached slowly. He had to let her know he wasn't trying to be a creep.

Was he a creep? He did follow her to her room. It wasn't purely infatuation. Or was it?

Aven cleared his throat making his presence known.

Claire flinched and swung around, pressing her back against her door.

"A gorgeous girl like you really should be escorted to her room."

The words. They had tumbled out of his mouth. He told his alter ego to take a hike. He didn't need him. Yet.

"Gorgeous?" Claire scoffed. "Wow. Okay, first of all, gorgeous is a bit much, and second, why are you stalking me?"

Aven caught the flicker of her gaze from his eyes to his lips but pretended to ignore her wandering eyes. He tilted his head, surprised by her answer. "That's a first."

"What is?"

"I suppose I was wrong to assume beautiful women appreciate compliments. I apologize if I have made you uncomfortable. That was not my intention."

"Then what are your intentions, Mr. Crey?" she asked point blank, crossing her arms.

Aven was again captivated by how her eyes brightened at her righteous indignation.

Feisty indeed.

His fingers twitched in his pocket, holding back the urge to reach out to graze her high cheekbone, to trace a finger down the light freckles on her slender nose. He wanted to hold her again, feel her warmth, but Claire wasn't expelling waves of sunshine like she had been before. The space between them was cold.

"Tony was following you," Aven admitted. "I didn't want to take a chance he'd detour from the party upstairs, which might I add, is where I'm supposed to be. Instead, I'm making sure one of my guests is safe and sound in her room."

Claire relaxed her posture. "Is he that bad of a guy?"

"When Tony drinks he doesn't think clearly, or at all really."

"You were worried about me?"

There was a pause before Aven spoke. Was it truly for her safety or his own self-gratification?

"Yes."

When Claire's arms fell to her side, Aven relaxed, relieved that his answer had been accepted as the truth, but he tensed again as his phone buzzed in his pocket. He let out a sigh of relief, reading Kitten's message. Tony was at the party but making his way around the room to talk to every girl in the Circle.

"I must be going," he said, placing his phone in his jacket pocket. "I promised someone a dance."

When Claire's forehead wrinkled, Aven's lips turned up. In a way, he hoped he had made her jealous, made her wonder just as he had, who was on the other end of the phone.

"I hope my attempts to be chivalrous haven't affected your review."

"No." Claire blinked. "And, uh, thank you again."

"My pleasure, milady." Aven gestured for Claire's hand, but she didn't budge.

Aven hid his disappointment with a slight smile, slipping his hands into his pockets. "Have a pleasant night, Ms. Grace."

"You too."

As the door to room 755 clicked shut, Aven forced his heavy feet to go toward the elevator. It was as if the hallway was knee deep with rushing waters, as if an unseen force was pushing him back. He glanced over his shoulder. Something was telling him to stay, telling him that he could have all of life's questions answered if only he would talk to Claire a little longer.

The vision from the nightclub flashed in his mind again.

Heaven.

That was the only way to describe that place: pure, unimaginable contentment.

Fighting against the invisible current, Aven continued toward the elevator where he knew the demon would be waiting. He anticipated the icy draft of the demon's breath, the unrelenting taunting, her hellhounds gnashing their teeth when he woke at midnight. This was his curse, the consequence of the choice he made years ago.

Waiting on the elevator to arrive, Aven drew back his sleeve and glanced at his watch.

Nine p.m.

Only hours before the demon would appear. If he didn't find someone to entertain soon, the ghosts of his past would return.

He had to take the edge off. Had to get another stiff drink. He would go to the party, socialize, and although he was tired of the same women of the Circle, he would take one back to his room.

When the elevator dinged, and the doors slid open, a chill slithered down Aven's spine. It was the welcome of hell's pleasure and pain, the welcome of another night of dancing with the devil.

Claire shut the hotel door and took in a deep breath of fresh linens. The scent of them lured her to the turned-down bed, where white fluffy robes were folded neatly. She traced her fingers along the plush cotton, ready for a long hot bath.

Then she saw it: the golden wrapper of tiny chocolates. They called to Claire as if saying it was almost time, as if telling her to not waste another minute and taste their sweetness. Glancing at the clock, Claire frowned.

Nine p.m.

With a sigh, she sat on the bed, pressing the soft terry cloth robe to her cheek. It wouldn't be long before she would have to go back to the club. Although she desperately wanted a hot bath, Claire placed the robe to the side, kicked her heels from her feet, and set her phone's alarm for ten minutes. She clutched the tiny chocolate in her hand, closed her eyes, and leaned back on the bed.

Taking in steady, even breaths, Claire entered the place between awake and asleep, finding herself in a dream she had never had before.

A bright yellow sun was above. Its rays warmed her, making rainbow prisms sparkle from her beaded gown. Chocolates wrapped in a paper package and cotton twine were on a blanket. When she glanced up, the man above her smiled, and she reached for him, smoothing away his soft raven hair to see his grey eyes and glowing face. Darkness soon seeped in like ink, blotting out his face, and he was gone.

Claire found herself standing in another place. It was cold, dim. She was looking for a white horse; there was a bonfire, people gathered by it, clothed in black smudged robes. They were whispering, staring at her. She wasn't supposed to be there; she wasn't one of them. Smoke filled her nostrils, burning her eyes. The urgency to leave clutched her chest. She needed to go back. She needed to return, or he would be upset with her.

He who?

Lifting her gaze from her ashy feet she saw another him. It was the angel from the meadow, the one with dark hair and grey eyes that peered up. His face was torn, full of pain.

The guilt returned. Somehow, Claire knew she had broken his heart.

The dream seeped into black again.

Claire found herself in someone's arms. She was with the dark-haired angel in a tent. They were dancing to music. Someone entered, startling her.

It was him. The blonde angel from her recurring dream. He was angry, standing by a white horse. The horse was sad, and suddenly, so was she.

She was leaving with the angel, the warrior. Someone called out to her. She tugged on the horse's mane. The dark-haired angel came to her, took her hand, kissed her knuckles, and whispered.

The beauty of free will is that you have a choice . . .

Aven couldn't hear the ding of the elevator as the doors opened and closed on the parking deck floor. He had been too deep in thought to notice the button he had pressed. The only thing on his mind was the vision.

Remembering that peaceful place, the warmth, his chest ached. The tug deepened as he stared at number seven of the screen. He crossed his arms—holding back the urge to press it—and glanced up at his disfigured reflection in the metal doors.

Finding the lack of confidence plastered on his face, Aven uncrossed his arms and rubbed his neck. He rolled his shoulders as if he could roll off his mixed emotions. Whatever this tether was, it begged him to press Claire's floor. The more he tried to ignore the urge, the further the compulsion deepened.

Letting out a heavy sigh, Aven took out his phone and messaged Kitten that he was on his way up and to save him a dance. As he lifted his thumb to hit send, he paused as an icy draft grazed his cheek.

"Time to play," the familiar voice whispered.

Aven swallowed hard. The despicable demon had returned, just as he presumed it would. If it was a game she wanted, he would play, but this time, he would let fate decide.

PINKY SWEAR

PUTTING a hand to her throbbing head, Claire sat up slowly. She wondered how she got on the floor. She never felt the fall from the bed.

Was I sleep walking again? Did Aven slip something in my drink after all?

No, it was something else, something that had been going on with her for a long time. Dreams. Visions. She had been dealing with them ever since she was a child. This time it was different. This time, the vision felt more like reality, and her reality now felt like the dream.

She couldn't tell her mother about this. If she did, another visit to the therapist would be scheduled. By law it was required to report anyone's unusual behavior, even your own family. Claire couldn't see her therapist again. She had vowed to herself not to take anymore drugs or go to anymore counseling sessions. She would face this head on.

With the room still spinning, Claire put a hand to the wall, bracing herself, but slipped. The scent of cocoa filled her nose as she brought her hand to her face. The tiny chocolate bar she had been holding was smeared all over the palm of her hand, and now the wall.

A knock at the door made her jump.

With a groan, Claire steadied her wobbly legs. She braced her shoulder against the wall and swung open the door.

Not Laura.

"Mr. Crey."

"Miss Grace. I'm sorry to bother you again."

"No, it's alright. I'm glad you're here."

"You are?"

"Yes. I, um, I wanted to ask you a question."

"Of course. By all means."

Claire wanted to ask him if they had somehow met before tonight, but now that he was standing there before her, she didn't have the guts.

Say something not psychotic.

"Is room service open? I figured I should eat something, soak up the alcohol. I tried to lay down, but I'm still a bit dizzy."

Aven gave a faint laugh. "Twenty-four hours a day."

Good save. Wait...why is he here?

"I scanned my finger for permission to charge my card," Claire tried to explain with furrowing brows. "Laura's waiting for me downstairs, I was just about to go back down and–"

"Do you want to go to that party with me?"

Claire's lashes fluttered. "I'm sorry? I thought you asked me to a party."

"I did. Do you know how to waltz?"

"Do I know how to—yes, I do but I—why do you want me to go to a party with you?"

"Because I would hate for you to spend a night in your room alone,"—he glanced down at Claire's balled up fist— "eating cheap chocolates when there are plenty of gourmet desserts upstairs."

Claire's face went red with embarrassment as she hid her hand behind her back.

"You'll be back by twelve. I promise."

"You're joking?"

"Not at all."

"Why would you want to take me? If you can't tell by now I'm not exactly a party girl."

Aven gave a sideways grin. "Is 'I thoroughly enjoy your company' a good enough answer?"

Claire could see Aven meant what he had said. There was no alter ego standing before her. There was only a man in a suit with soft, hopeful eyes. "You enjoy my company?"

"You're very-honest. It's refreshing, really. I think we would have a good time."

"But I don't drink and—"

"You don't have to drink. I'll have the bartender make you virgin Cape Cods all night."

Claire eyed Aven with suspicion. "I hardly know you, Mr. Crey."

"You will. Hopefully, well enough to call me by my first name."

"I can't."

Aven's smile fell.

"I'm supposed to be going back down to Laura and the girls."

"We can swing by the club on the way back."

"Well, it *would* shut Laura up for the rest of the trip. She's been like a crazed monkey on my back."

Aven offered his hand. "Then let's go drive her bananas."

Claire glanced at his hand but didn't budge. "Why are you so adamant about me having a good time?"

"Because, Ms. Grace," Aven closed in the space between them and set his gaze, "the stakes in life are too high for you to dwell on what might have been. And I don't want you to look back ten or twenty years from now and say to yourself 'I should have gone with that dapper young man in the suit.'"

A laugh rose from Claire's throat. "Dapper?"

"It would be a good distraction from whatever you have been frowning about all night." Aven lifted his gaze above her forehead. "And I'll bring you back before your carriage turns into a pumpkin."

"Ah, I see." Claire smirked, taking off the lopsided tiara. "The whole princess thing again." She crossed her arms, making sure to hide the chocolate, although it was obvious he knew. "So if I'm Cinderella, then who are you?"

"Prince Charming, of course."

"So Charming, say we go to the ball and dance all night, then what?

"The magic will end, and you can go back to shoveling cinders and mopping floors."

"You'll bring me back to my room, expecting nothing in return, just because you enjoy my company?"

"Yes. I will be a complete and utter gentleman," Aven said, putting his hand to his chest with a slight bow.

Eyes. They never lied. Not to Claire. Every word out of his mouth had been the truth. Still, she wanted his word. Claire cocked a brow and held out her chocolate-free hand, pinky lifted. "Swear it."

"What are we, like five?"

"If you intended to keep your promise, you will swear by the pinky, good sir."

"Is my word not my bond, fair maiden?"

Claire ignored the skip of her heart and raised her hand higher, wiggling her pinky.

Aven grinned and shook his head. "You're full of surprises, Ms. Grace."

"I'm not big on surprises."

"I quite enjoy them."

"Swear it."

Clearing his throat dramatically, Aven lifted his head high as if it was an honor to stand in Claire's presence. "I, sir Aven Crey of Las Vegas, Nevada, swear by the royal pinky that I will be a complete gentleman from this moment forward, concerning, Her Majesty, Claire Grace of . . ."

"Tybee Island, Georgia," Claire informed him.

"Of Tybee Island Georgia. To thee, I do swear."

Aven locked his pinky with Claire's and they shook.

"And," Aven said, typing on his phone. He then tapped Claire's phone to his. "I'll do you one better."

A ding rang out, and Claire looked at her messages, finding a digital copy of Aven's license.

"If I cross any lines tonight you can have the knights hunt me down and throw me in the dungeon."

"If you insist," Claire said, saving the photo to her camera roll. "But if you do disrespect my nobility, I won't have you put in chains."

"No? Then what will you have?"

"Your head, of course."

"Fear not, Your Majesty." Aven opened his palm with a flourish, revealing the five of spades wrapped like a rose. "I wouldn't dare disrespect the queen of hearts."

GOING UP

AVEN stood patiently in the hallway, waiting to accompany Claire to the elevator. She had asked for ten minutes, no doubt to wash the chocolate from her hand. He had been curious why she had it smeared between her fingers but didn't ask as she appeared and they entered the elevator.

Pressing the button to the top floor, Aven exhaled in relief. There was no cold draft, no demon's icy fingertips on the back of his neck—only pure warmth and sunshine beside him. To Aven, Claire was like the first day of spring after a long cold winter, but as her warmth faded like fall, he frowned.

"What's wrong?" he asked her reflection in the steel doors.

"I can't go to this party."

"Why not?"

Aven watched Claire glance down at her black cocktail dress and then at his suit. "Well, look at me and look at you. This dress was thirty bucks. Your suit looks like it cost five hundred dollars or something.

"Two."

"That suit was only two hundred dollars?"

Aven grinned. "Two thousand."

"See what I mean!" Claire threw out her hands. "Your friends are going to be dressed up, and I'll be walking in like something you found on the corner. Especially with this face job Laura did on me."

Aven had to agree. The makeup had struck him as too much when he had first seen Claire in the club. Underneath it all, he knew she was naturally beautiful, but it was covered up by thick mascara and black sparkly eye shadow. Still. That didn't hide her confidence or grace.

"By the way you carry yourself they'll know right away I'm not paying you by the hour. If you don't want to go I can take you back to your room," Aven offered.

"No. It's better I'm not there when she comes to look for me. Hopefully, she'll think I changed my mind and went to your room."

Aven's lips twitched, and he gave a sideway glance at Claire as her cheeks flushed.

"But I don't want to go to your room. I mean"—she let out a frustrated breath—"at LAX, she insisted I take you back to our room, or go to yours. I want her to think that's what's happening because, she's always like, 'Claire you've only slept with three guys' and, 'stop being such a boring nun.' But I don't see the point in casually sleeping around. I mean, all my friends make it seem like it's some grand accomplishment or like it's so amazing. Clearly, I'm doing something wrong. I mean, the movies make it seem like it's so much fun, but it's not. It's awkward and uncomfortable. I've been called a prude since I was fifteen, but it's not like I haven't tried to have a relationship. I've had three semi-serious boyfriends who all turned out to be jerks, and having sex with them was just not what I thought it would be and—"

Aven smirked as Claire tried to catch her breath. Rambling. No one in the Circle thought rambling was attractive, but not everyone was him.

With flaming cheeks, Claire glanced at Aven's grinning face in the steel doors. She was mortified, having blurted out the reason for her relationship status, which to her, was none of this guy's business.

"And I've said too much," she admitted, drawing out the words.

Aven held a confident smile and leaned over slightly. "Most men don't know how to please a woman properly."

Claire shivered slightly at his husky voice.

"Love making is not a sport, it's an art."

Blood thrummed in Claire's veins, throbbing in her heart, and as Laura had said, in "other places."

"Prude, huh?" Aven asked, breaking the uncomfortable silence. "Laura's nickname for you?"

"She also calls me an old maid, goody two-shoes, Ms. Perfect. I'm boring and predictable. I wasn't always this way, but when—" Claire caught herself. The reason she stopped having fun, the reason she felt guilty for being normal was related to the shame of her chocolate-smeared hand. There was too much to explain, and she wasn't ready to be that honest with someone she hardly knew.

"When I was staying up late studying for finals, she was skinny dipping at pool parties. Saturdays I was at the dance studio, practicing choreography for competitions. I played piano on Sunday morning at my mom's worship center while she was nursing a hangover from the night before. And when I wasn't competing or playing piano, I was helping my mom or volunteering. According to my best friend, I don't dress slutty enough, I don't express myself with a foul mouth as I should, and I'm way too picky when it comes to dating."

Claire waited for Aven to say something, but he didn't. He stood, still grinning wide, staring at their reflections.

Claire's nose crinkled. "And now I'm basically ranting."

"Please, by all means, continue. It's rather adorable."

"Adorable?" Claire asked flatly.

"Yes, very."

"Great. So now I'm an adorable prude," Claire grumbled.

To Claire's surprise, Aven came to stand in front of her. He tilted his head and leaned down as if to make sure Claire listened to him closely. "Despite what your friend thinks, there are men that find morality attractive."

Claire stared at Aven, trying to ignore the pounding of her heart at her breastbone.

He raised a brow. "You don't believe me?"

"Well, I haven't met any."

Aven narrowed his eyes before leaning back, pressing a button on the screen behind him. Claire's heart skipped as the elevator stopped with a slight jolt. While the bell rang out in an annoying tone, Aven tapped the screen again, ceasing the ear-piercing sound. He turned back to Claire and set his gaze.

"Good morals are nothing to be ashamed of, Ms. Grace."

"I'm not ashamed," Claire lied, fidgeting with her fingers. "It's just, the way I was raised, no one seems to be looking for–"

"Demure?"

Claire averted her gaze to the ground, but Aven lifted her chin gently.

"You should be proud of who you are." He tucked the hair in her face behind her ear. "If others can't see what's behind those gorgeous green eyes, well, it's their loss."

Claire shivered as Aven's gaze shifted to her lips. Catching herself from leaning forward, she blinked.

"Wow." She laughed nervously, crossing her arms. "Did you learn lines like that from a movie or something?"

Aven stood upright, but a mischievous smile still played on his lips. "Or something." He pressed the call button on the screen of the elevator.

"Yes, Mr. Crey," a male's voice answered.

"Riley, I need you to meet me at the craps table in fifteen minutes. I'm sending you a list."

Claire gave Aven a sideways glance, watching him type something in his phone. "What are we doing?" she whispered.

"I have your list, Mr. Crey. I'll go get everything immediately."

"Thank you, Riley," Aven said and pressed the button again, ending the call. "Change of plans, Princess," Aven said, pressing Claire's floor.

"You're not going to your party?"

"Eventually. For now, the soiree can wait."

Claire scrunched her brows, thinking of the someone he had promised to dance with. "Won't your friend be disappointed?"

"Most likely."

Aven didn't say another word until the elevator doors opened to her floor.

"Change into something comfortable," he requested, gesturing for her to exit. "I'll meet you at the casino bar in thirty minutes."

Claire exited, but before she could open her mouth to ask any more questions, Aven winked as the elevator doors closed shut, leaving her guessing what the handsome stranger had in store.

VIVA LAS VEGAS

"SEVEN!" the stickman announced.

The players at the craps table whistled and clapped.

"We won again?" Claire asked Aven in disbelief.

"Yes, milady. We are triumphant," Aven said. He gathered his purple chips and placed them in the slot in front of him before leaning to Claire's ear.

"Last roll, Princess. Everyone's betting on you."

Claire surveyed the players giving her eager stares. There were young and old men nodding, clapping, and rooting for her. She glanced back at Aven. "What if you lose?"

"How can I lose with my lucky charm standing beside me?" Aven held out the die.

Claire took in a deep breath and blew on them slow. As a sly smile tugged at Aven's lips, he tossed them. There was a hush at the table as Claire covered her eyes—listening to the clatter of the die against the table—but as a roar exploded from the men, she peeked.

"Seven!" the stickman shouted.

The players clapped for Claire, and she curtsied with a slight smile.

While the gamblers gathered their chips, a player approached. He appeared to be in his sixties, wearing a tan cowboy hat. Claire thought of the colonel for Kentucky Fried Chicken, looking at his pointed white beard and curled up mustache.

"Little lady," he said in a strong southern twang, "you have made me a very rich man tonight." His gaze went to Aven as his eyes twinkled. "She's a keeper. I'd lasso that gal if I was you, son."

Aven nodded, offering his arm to Claire, who blushed. "An angel from Heaven. If I'm lucky she won't fly away."

"Then grab her by the wings and never let go." The cowboy cackled and tipped his hat. "Ya'll have a good evening."

Claire took mental pictures of the cowboy's tan fringed suit and brown snakeskin boots. It was against the rules to take pictures in the casino, but she would tell her mother about him and her winning streak playing craps.

"What are you going to do with your winnings?" Claire asked as Aven escorted her to the bar. He pulled out a stool for her and ordered a virgin strawberry daiquiri and a glass of bourbon.

"Something fun," he replied, bringing his attention back to her.

"You're all about fun, aren't you?"

"Yes," he said, wiggling his brows, "as you'll be before the night's through."

Claire thanked the bartender for her drink and then glanced back at Aven. He was quiet, taking sips of his bourbon and staring at her.

Again? What is his deal?

She hated that he was always staring. No. That was a lie. She was elated his eyes were always on her, that she had his full attention. She kept telling herself she shouldn't like it, reminding herself he had to have an ulterior motive. All men did.

"So what is this fun you speak of?" Claire asked, stirring the red slush in her glass.

Aven leaned on the bar and folded his hands. "I made you a bucket list."

"A bucket list?" Claire laughed. "I'm not some terminal patient, you know."

"No, but you act like one." He took her hands in his; one on top of the other. Claire tried to ignore the skipping of her heart as he gave a gentle twist of her wrist.

Still not used to things appearing out of nowhere, Claire tried guessing what it could be poking her palm. When she lifted her hand, she frowned at the present.

"What's this?" she asked, suddenly uncomfortable. She couldn't meet Aven's eyes, and the longer she stared at the tiny red box topped with a gold bow, the deeper her heart sank.

"Open it."

Claire swallowed, wetting her dry throat before she opened the box. Inside on a red velvet pad, lay a beautiful silver charm, stamped with a well-known and very expensive brand.

The tiny dotted gems on the cubes sparkled in the soft lamplight as Claire held up the sterling silver pair of die.

Aven reached into his inner suit pocket, revealing a silver charm bracelet and snapped it around her wrist.

Riley. He was the man speaking on the other side of the screen in the elevator. This must have been on Aven's list.

The gesture was thoughtful, but Claire didn't want to accept Aven's gift. She didn't want a present.

Not today. Any day but this day.

Glancing up, she found Aven mirroring her expression. It was the first time she had ever seen him frown.

"You don't like it?" he asked.

"No, it's beautiful," Claire admitted. "I just—I don't understand why you're doing this."

"I'm not sure I follow."

"I made it perfectly clear I'm not sleeping with you. You do know that, right?"

"I have no intentions of trying to take you back to my room, Ms. Grace."

Claire searched his eyes for a long moment; as if he knew she was asking for the truth, he held her stare.

A few thudding heartbeats later, Claire's shoulders fell with relief. Regardless of his genuine gesture, she needed more of an explanation. "Then why do it?"

Aven bit his bottom lip but couldn't seem to hold back a brilliant smile. "Because of your adorable rant."

That stupid rant.

Claire regretted it. She had always let her mouth get away with her. Maybe one day she would learn to keep it shut. "No, really. I mean this is a bit much for someone you just met."

Aven's brows furrowed slightly as if it were painful for him to form the words he was about to say. "It's very rare to meet someone with, shall we say, decency?"

"I can't possibly be the only decent person you've ever met."

"You'd be surprised. Just about everyone I know pretends to be someone they're not. This is the first time I've ever met someone with such pure, brutal honesty. Someone who called me out on my, as you put it, lines?"

Who is this guy and where did he come from?

Claire watched Aven press his thumb to his phone, giving the bartender what she assumed was a hefty tip. He took out his wallet, slipping out something she had only seen behind glass.

The crisp, green paper was smooth, bearing the image of Benjamin Franklin's face. It seemed to smile at her as Aven dangled the hundred-dollar bill from his fingertips. With his other hand, he withdrew the lighter Claire had lit the napkin with at the bar and thumbed the starter.

"You know what that's worth, don't you?" she asked with wide eyes.

Aven grinned and set the corner of the money on fire. As it singed the face of Benjamin Franklin's chin, Aven closed his fist around the flaming paper in a dramatic way. Tiny plumes of smoke escaped his grasp. He opened his hand again, waving his fingers in the air and letting the ashes drift to the ground.

Seeing the smudges on his hands, Claire's mind flashed to the dream she'd had earlier in her room. Sooty robes and dancing bodies around a bonfire were clear, but this time she was standing afar from them, watching as if in another body. She was hidden in a thicket, observing the party until a sooty hand gripped her arm tight. Her shoulders tensed as if she could feel the slurring man tugging on her, digging his grimy nails into her skin.

Claire squeezed her eyes shut, clutching the edge of the bar. There was no slowing her racing heart, no way to untangle the knots in her stomach.

No. Not now.

Trying to avoid an anxiety attack, Claire opened her eyes and focused on Aven's hands as he wiped his fingers with a napkin. The soot was gone and so was the grip of the sooty hand that had flashed in her mind.

"Claire, I have money to burn. Sometimes I do it, literally, just to get a rise out of people," Aven informed her. "It would be much more satisfying to spend it on someone other than myself for a change."

"Does this bucket list involve anything else foolish and impulsive I should know about?"

Aven pulled back his sleeve looking at his watch. "Come on. If we are going to time this right, we'll have to hurry."

"Do you like bikes?" Aven asked, escorting Claire out of the Luxor hotel.

"We're riding around Vegas on bicycles?"

Aven chuckled. "Not exactly. I'm glad you braided your hair. Wouldn't want it to get tangled."

The braid. It had given Aven another wave of déjà vu when the elevator doors opened and Claire stepped out to the casino floor to meet him. His heart had fluttered as she came toward him. He had bitten his lip, watching the sway of her white pleated skirt. He envisioned his fingers gazing her thighs at the hem but caught himself. Reminding himself again of the mental note he had made, he kept his gaze above her shoulders, above her nose, because even her lips were too tempting to look upon.

That had been proven in the elevator.

Claire raised her brows. "Tangled?"

Aven took his wallet from the back of his jeans and approached his blacked-out motorcycle.

"I thought we were riding a bike."

"This is a bike."

Claire's eyes grew wide. "I've never ridden one of these before."

"Good," Aven said, placing his wallet inside the small leather bag. "This will get you ready for what else I have in store."

"What did you put on that list?"

"Only one way to find out." He handed her a helmet and sat on his bike. It started with a smooth putter and then roared as he twisted the handlebar.

149

"Don't you need one?" Claire asked, pointing to the helmet. "I mean, won't you get pulled over if you're not wearing it?"

"Let's just say the rules don't apply to me."

"But what if we get in an accident?"

"You worry too much," Aven said. He got off his bike and helped Claire tighten the strap on the helmet.

"Like I haven't heard that before," she huffed. "Am I going be safe with you?"

Aven paused from the straps and met her gaze. "Yes."

"Promise?"

"I promise," he vowed, lifting his chin. He wrapped his pinky around hers, gently turned her hand, and lightly kissed her knuckles. He hadn't intended to linger so long, to breath deep the scent of her skin, but he did. As the smell of coconut lotion made its way into his senses, Aven pictured Claire and him on a beach, basking in the sun. He forced himself to let go of the fantasy and slipped away from her grasp.

Claire's heart thundered against her chest at the hot touch of Aven's lips. She wondered what his mouth would feel like on hers as he withdrew his fixed gaze.

He mounted his bike and revved it. "Tick, tock, Princess,"

Steadying herself with Aven's shoulders, she lifted her leg, and tucked her skirt snuggly beneath her, hoping it would stay put.

"Those pipes get hot so keep your feet on the pegs," Aven shouted over his shoulder.

Claire tugged at the strap beneath her chin, before she steadied her white Converses on the foot pegs.

Lifting the kickstand, Aven balanced the bike with his black riding boots. One hand rested on his leg, the other turned the throttle as he backed out of the parking spot.

Claire looked around for something to hold onto, but there was nothing but the man in front of her.

Earlier, she had imagined what kind of body was under Aven's suit, but as she clasped her hands in front of him, she didn't have to imagine anymore.

"Comfortable?" Aven yelled over the engine.

"Yeah," she yelled back. A lie. Yes, the seat was cushiony, but her insides were a balled-up mess. She coached herself to stay calm, to remember why she was doing this. She couldn't back out. Not now. Because after tonight, she could rub it all in Laura's face that she rode around Vegas with sexy Suit Guy.

Fun size was back with a vengeance.

As Aven approached the street, Claire caught him smiling at her in the side mirror. "Hold on," he shouted over the thundering pipes.

Claire squealed as Aven pulled onto the strip. She tensed her legs around him, and pressed her cheek to his back.

"Open your eyes, Claire."

"If I do I'll throw up!"

"You're not going to throw up. Just open your eyes."

Claire peeked through one eye and lifted her head, finding Aven grinning ear to ear in the side mirror. Behind him was a girl she hardly recognized. This was the Claire she knew before the tragedy, the same Claire who didn't let fear hold her back.

"A full moon," Aven said, glancing up. "I think you should howl, let out your inner animal."

"What?" Claire yelled in his ear.

"Howl."

"Now?"

"Howl," he said, drawing out the word.

"No! Everyone will think I'm crazy!"

"They won't, watch."

Aven beeped the horn and wailed like a wolf as a self-driving cherry-red mustang with the top down zoomed by. The women inside sat up and crowed as Aven revved the engine and took off down the strip.

"See," Aven shouted. "Now you do it."

"I can't! I'll fall off!"

"May I?" Aven asked, reaching back.

Claire didn't give permission, not exactly, but she also didn't say no. She watched as Aven's fingers inched her skirt from her knee and wrapped around the thick of her thigh. When he followed suit with his other hand, her body locked up.

Aven stroked his thumbs across her skin, no doubt to ease her grip around his hips, but it only made her tense. She flushed with heat and her breaths grew heavy as a sudden urge consumed her.

This must have been what Laura had been talking about. This was what she had been missing out on all those years: the yearning, the tension-building. She struggled to ignore the oscillations of the seat beneath her, the throbbing between the space of her skirt. But when Aven tugged her gently against his back, she let out a soft whimper at the dizzying pleasure that suddenly came.

"I've got you," he assured.

Claire nodded and released her grip, but when the bike leaned, her gaze darted to the handlebars with panic.

"Put your hands back on the wheel! I mean, the thing you steer with!"

"Not until you let it out."

"No! I can't!"

"Cruise control," Aven ordered the bike.

"Cruise control on," a smooth female voice announced from the blue screen. Aven leaned back against Claire, weaving in and out of the lanes. A car horn beeped behind them, but he didn't replace his hands on the handlebars.

"I can do this all night, Princess."

Claire hated peer pressure but complied with a tiny yelp.

"Louder. Vegas can't hear you."

At Aven's light squeeze on her thighs, she let out a feral cry.

"Fun, isn't it?" Aven called out before placing his hands back on the handlebars.

"You're crazy!" Claire laughed. She curled her fingers through Aven's belt loops and sat up tall.

"Vegas playlist," Aven ordered the bike. "Song five."

While Elvis's "Viva Las Vegas" played from the motorcycle's speakers, Claire gazed around at the flashing city sights. She watched the jugglers on the sidewalk, the partygoers trolling the streets. When a holographic projector in the sky exploded in fireworks, she glanced up. The trails of sparkles rained down, flashing images, ads of all the latest attractions in town.

SEE THE FOUNTAIN LIGHTS OF THE BELLAGIO.
TAKE A RIDE ON THE GONDOLA AT THE
VENETIAN.
COME TO PARIS. SEE THE EIFFEL TOWER.

Claire's heart leapt at the image of Lady Liberty, and she thought of what her mother had said.

Be young. Have fun.

In was in that moment that Claire realized she had to live. That was, until Aven spoke.

"How are you with heights?" he called over his shoulder.

"How high?"

"Oh, only five-hundred-and-fifty-feet-in-the-air high."

"I think you should take me back to the hotel."

"Why?"

"Because I'm terrified of heights."

"You're what?" Aven shouted.

"I'm. Afraid. Of. Heights," Claire yelled over the noise of the traffic speeding by.

Aven's lips twisted into a roguish grin in the side mirror. "Well, I guess I'll just have to cure you of that."

SECRET SCIENCE

THE black and red charms on Claire's new bracelet clinked together as she scooped up another bite of chocolate cheesecake. She slid the silky cream across her tongue and relished the aftertaste of the tart raspberry sauce. Unlike her previous birthday cakes, this one was eaten without an ounce of guilt.

"You act like this is some kind of treat." Aven noted.

"It is a treat, I mean, I've never been to this place before."

Aven narrowed his eyes, and Claire knew he was on to her. That was twice she had caught herself from blurting out the truth about her secret.

She averted her gaze to his gift. In addition to the pair of die from the Luxor hotel, there was a charm of the Sphinx of Giza, the Eiffel Tower, and the iconic Vegas sign. Aven had taken her around the world in only a few hours, snapping pictures of them at every major attraction. She had never once mentioned it was her birthday, never once told him why she was grateful he had been a distraction.

Twirling the Statue of Liberty charm with her fingers, she murmured a vague explanation. "I don't eat chocolate."

"You don't eat chocolate?" Aven leaned forward, tilting his head. "You just ate half that cheesecake, so I know it's not an allergy."

"No. Nothing like that."

"Care to tell me?"

"It's um . . ." Claire stopped herself and looked down at crumbs left over from their dessert then back up to Aven. "It's kind of a personal secret."

"How intriguing." Aven leaned in closer, resting his elbows on the table. "A dark, chocolaty secret. You may not know this about me, but I'm very good at keeping secrets."

"You don't want to know. Believe me. It will ruin the night."

Aven tilted his head and stared at Claire a long moment. When she didn't fess up, he shrugged his shoulders and stood, pushing his chair under the table. "Then I guess I can assume you're ready to go see what's next on your bucket list? I'll go pay." He turned to go to the register.

"Wait," Claire said, almost desperately.

Aven sat back down, looking at Claire intently.

"I'll tell you part of the secret."

"I don't want to make you do anything you don't want to."

"No, I want to," Claire said a bit too eagerly.

Aven had mentioned a little bit about curing her of her fear of heights when they had sat down in the bakery, but when the cheesecake came, there was no more talk of it. He had been quiet, watching her as usual, seemingly pleased by her reaction to his choice of dessert.

Claire glanced around the room at the people eating scones, éclairs, and cakes. They weren't giving her a second glance, but she felt like they were secretly listening, spying. Her gaze darted to the upper corners of the bakery, but there were no cameras, no one watching or listening to what she was about to confess. Nevada was the one and only place people could go and not be watched.

"I only eat chocolate once a year," Claire admitted.

"Once a year? Not on Easter or Valentine's Day?"

"I stopped getting Easter baskets when I was ten and I don't get chocolates on Valentine's Day."

"Just today?"

"Just today, or tonight, actually. Right around midnight."

"Hm," was all Aven said.

Claire pushed their plate to the side. She wanted to tell him more, tell him the true reason she fasted chocolate only to binge on it one night out of the year, but she wasn't ready, not yet. "So um—you said you could cure me?"

Aven leaned back in his chair, crossing his arms. "You have your secrets, and I have mine."

"You're not going to tell me?" A smile tugged at Claire's lips. She was getting used to the trickster, the flirt.

Maybe his alter ego isn't so bad.

Aven lifted his chin slightly with a smirk. "Perhaps part of it."

There was a long pause of silence as she held his gaze, but then her eyes fluttered. Whatever this little staring competition had been, she lost.

"You blinked." Aven grinned.

"Are we going to keep playing games or are you going to tell me?"

"It's better if I show you." Aven stood up and dragged his chair closer to Claire's. As the pegs of the chair squeaked across the floor, Claire looked around the bakery at the few people eating. No one was paying him any mind. She felt they should. He was the most handsome guy in the room, could have easily been have been mistaken for a young Elvis Presley, not an impersonator but the real deal. But no one looked. Even as they walked past him, sporting their tourist attire of Vegas t-shirts and khaki shorts. Claire reminded herself she would have to get her mom a t-shirt at the gift shop.

"I've made you a promise," Aven said as he sat. "Now it's you who must promise me."

"Promise what?"

"What I reveal to you now cannot be told to anyone."

"More magic tricks?"

"Magic, yes. Tricks, no."

"So this magic—it's real?"

"It's more like ancient science. The brain is a very interesting part of the body. A muscle. You can train it to do powerful things. Thought is the key. Our thoughts dictate our choices and our choices dictate our life. Fear is linked to something in the subconscious. Most people overcome those subconscious fears in various ways. Some use subliminal tapes, meditation. Others use prayer."

Aven took Claire's hands and put them together as if forming her hands to do just that. "The way I do it has been passed down for centuries, but few know of it."

"How does it work?"

"There's a signal in our brain. It's like a light switch. You can turn the light on"—he spread his fingers over her palm, tickling it—"or off." He closed her palm and held her hand in his. "Your brain vibrates off a specific frequency. When you are tuned to the right frequency you can train your mind to do things most people can't do."

"Is this some kind of advanced science or something?"

Aven grinned but didn't answer her question. "For this to work you have to be completely open-minded. And I can't do it without your permission."

"Permission for what?"

"To use a key phrase."

"Key phrase for what?"

"It's how I'll flip the switch to wake you. You won't know what the phrase is, but it's something with meaning, something we have both said before."

"Is this some kind of hypnosis?"

"It doesn't matter what you call it, what matters is the intention." Aven gave Claire's hands light squeeze. "Do I have your permission, Ms. Grace?"

Claire hesitated a moment, looking at their hands. When she brought her gaze back to Aven's, she gave her answer. "Yes."

As if it was another trick, Aven's hands suddenly warmed, and he rubbed his thumb along the back of her knuckles.

"Look in my eyes, try not to blink. You failed last time."

"That was a test?"

"You need to hold my stare as long as you can. You'll want to close your eyes, but don't. Just focus on me, on my touch."

Claire held her gaze as long as she could, but when Aven's touch grew hotter, her lashes fluttered as did her heart. "I don't think a staring contest is going to cure me."

Aven's glare intensified. "Shh. No talking. Focus. Take in a slow, deep breath and a long, slow exhale, but keep your eyes on my pupils."

Claire did as Aven instructed and took in a deep breath while holding his gaze.

"You're very comfortable, very warm," Aven said in a whisper. "You're safe."

Aven's hands grew hot as they slid up her arms. Claire's body relaxed, and the heat comforted her. He drew her closer by her shoulders until there were only inches between them and gently pressed the muscle above her collarbone.

In the black circles of Aven's grey eyes, Claire found a flicker like a flame. It grew brighter as his pupils expanded. Her body felt light, weightless, and just as Aven had said, she felt the sudden urge to close her eyes. As they fell shut, it wasn't darkness that welcomed Claire as she expected, but a blinding white light that consumed her.

THE WHITE ROOM

CLAIRE'S eyes fluttered open to the sight of a small room. It was white. All white. There was no furniture, no windows. Nothing. She walked to one of the four walls to touch it, but with each step she took, the wall moved further away. She glanced around, looking for something, anything other than the nothingness.

"You're safe," the voice echoed.

"Aven?" Claire turned in a circle, finding Aven behind her, dressed in an all-black suit.

"Stay calm," he said softly. "Slow deep breaths."

Claire did as he asked, taking in deep breaths through her nostrils, concentrating on the rise and fall of her chest.

Aven held out his hand, as if asking Claire to trust him. "Ready?"

At Claire's nod, Aven took her hand and then her other.

"Think of a place," he said. "The most beautiful place possible and only that place."

Clearing her mind, Claire thought of a place she remembered from her dreams. A place of peace, of beauty. As images of that place filled her mind, the walls of the white room became soft as if they were clouds surrounding her.

Something warm and wet appeared beneath her. Shifting her weight, Claire glanced down as the fog cleared, finding rocky ground. Warmth met Claire's back and she turned, letting go of Aven's hands. The clouds parted, revealing the place she had pictured, the paradise of her dreams. The landscape of the sea sparkled in the sunlight. The lapping waves kissed the sand that glittered on the shore. Tropical trees swayed in a light salty breeze, and colorful birds flew across the sky.

Claire's ears filled with the sound of rushing water, and as she looked below her feet, she could see rushing water cascading over the edge of the cliff.

"Do you see this too?" she asked Aven, keeping her gaze on the tropical landscape. "This place?"

"No. This is in your own mind. I'm just the comfort to guide you through."

"I feel like I know this place. Like—like I've been here before. But not in a dream."

"This place was a time before your fear, a time where you had no care to jump, but you can't stay here, Claire."

"Someone else was here with me . . ." Claire said, turning to Aven behind her. "Can we wait just a little longer?"

Aven took a step forward, offering his hand. "It's time to face your fear."

When Claire turned back around for one last glimpse, she squinted at a glowing figure that appeared before her.

Turquoise eyes glinted as a familiar face smiled. It was him. It was the angel from her dream.

"See you at the bottom," was all he said before he leapt backward.

Claire reached her hand toward the mist, but it soon turned to white smoke that burned her eyes.

The stench of burning wood filled Claire's nose, and she coughed as the white smoke turned into black clouds. Choking on it, she glanced around the bedroom, knowing where she was. This was the place of her accident; this was the moment that had haunted her for the past seven years.

Finding the window beside her just as she remembered, Claire rushed to it and struggled to get it open. Knowing it wouldn't open, she turned to the bed. Tyler's bed.

She paused, looking at the wrinkled sheet before she grabbed it. Ignoring the guilt of what had occurred before this moment, she wrapped her hand, and punched the glass. Relief came as it shattered. Unable to control her coughs, she quickly unwrapped her hand, tossing the sheet aside. Grabbing hold of the window frame, she hissed.

How could I have forgotten?

Blood trickled down her palm, and she could again feel the burn as she plucked the shard of glass out. She snatched up a pillow from the bed and ripped a shred of its case in a rush. Tying it around her hand, she reminded herself that this wasn't real, that it was only a memory.

Careful not to cut her hand again, Claire gripped the window frame and climbed onto the scratchy roof. She glanced down over the edge and saw a dark lawn filled with faces—all horrified. Among the faces of her friends was someone who hadn't been there before. He stood, gazing up at her calmly with his hands in the pockets of his black suit.

"This is where it happened," Aven called up to her. "But you already knew that. That's why you're here."

"Wake me up!" Claire cried, gripping the window.

"You have to overcome your fear, Claire. Where are you? What happens before your fall—or did you jump?"

Claire shifted her gaze from Aven to Laura and then her other friends from school, pointing. Then she looked behind them to the firemen, getting a ladder ready. "Where is he?"

"What happens next, Claire?" Aven shouted.

Claire squeezed her eyes shut and swallowed. "I was on the roof, I was scared. It was so high, and I took a step to climb down but—" Claire heard a sound, a sound she had never forgotten. It was the same low moan as trailing thunder, a haunting echo that again made her quiver.

The hair on Claire's neck stood up as she turned back toward the window. She was ready to let go and climb down, but she knew what happened next. Flames crawled up the frame and bit her fingertips as smoke poured out of the house. Jerking back with a scream, Claire flung her hand away and fell, sliding down the slanted shingles. Scrapes and cuts from the scratchy surface burned her legs, her arms. Tears rolled down her face as she wept, but she dared to look to the window. She was never able to look away in her dreams. It was no different now.

With wide eyes, Claire cringed. The smoke demon appeared. Its red eyes glared as it bared its jagged teeth. It roared out of the window, clutching her arms with blazing claws. Claire cried out, gripping the gutter with her other hand, but her raw blistered fingertips begged for her to let go as she looked at the fall beneath her.

"Claire," Aven called out to her. "What happens next?"

"Wake me up!"

"Let go, Claire."

"I can't!"

"Yes, you can. I'll catch you."

"Tell my dad to get out of the house!" Claire wept. "Please! He's going to die! He's going to die because of me!"

Claire's gaze darted to the window as the smoke monster drew back into the house and then exploded with a fiery rage.

"Claire, I'm going to say the phrase."

"Tell them to help him! It's eating him alive!"

"Claire," Aven called out, "I promise—"

With a creak of metal, the screws popped from the gutter and Claire's grip faltered. She reached for the house, watching everything slow around her and then come to a stop. Her body had been rendered weightless, suspended, frozen in midair. She focused on the fire, but no longer saw a monster. The flames were beautiful, soft, like tattered ribbons, dancing in a summertime breeze. And then, before Claire could blink back her tears, her stomach dropped, and she slammed into a wall of utter darkness.

Jolting awake with wide eyes, Claire gasped. She loosened her grip, finding her clammy fingers wrapped around a neck. A steady pulse came through it as the familiar scent of sweet cologne filled her nose.

Peeling her damp forehead away from Aven's cheek, Claire leaned back and met his eyes. Before the white room they had been light blue lakes with icy shards peeking through, but now they were dual storms of grey clouds, sparking with lightning.

"You didn't jump," Aven whispered, smoothing her damp hair from her eyes, "you fell."

"You were there. How—how did you catch me?"

"You saw me?"

"You said—you said I promise, and then I woke up."

At the clinking of silverware and people in conversation, Claire glanced around the bakery. No one looked in her direction, no one seemed to care that Aven was holding her in his lap.

"Three minutes," Aven said checking his watch. "That's the longest anyone's been under."

Claire shivered at the tickling of a tear on her cheek, but she didn't wipe it away. She was too weak, too rattled to move. She didn't realize how badly her hands were shaking until Aven squeezed one gently. He gazed at her for a long moment, his stare sympathetic as if somehow he felt her pain and sorrow.

"Did you see what happened?" she asked, although he had told her on the cliff that he couldn't.

Aven cupped her face and caressed her tears away. "Time to go, Princess."

As Aven parked his motorcycle, Claire gazed up at the High Roller Ferris wheel. It was much bigger than the ads she had seen around town. Round white pods hung on the end of the tall circle instead of the rickety carts she had seen in school textbooks. Vivid hues of pink, purple, green, and blue lit it like a round rainbow. This was no Ferris wheel; it was a spaceship, ready to take off.

Sucking in a sharp breath, Claire took off her helmet as Aven leaned the bike and kicked the stand forward.

"You ready for this?" he asked, taking her hand.

Claire nodded, trying to calm her trembling fingers. She was still shaken up from the memory of the fire but was soon soothed by Aven's gentle touch.

"I won't know unless I try, right?" she said.

"I've called ahead to make sure we can be alone. I don't want you to be uncomfortable around a bunch of people in such a tiny space."

Feeling more at ease, Claire followed Aven's lead to the entrance. He asked her politely to wait inside the pod and after a few minutes, he was back, holding two drinks in his hands.

"I told the bartender to make it just like the one at LAX."

"Thank you," Claire said, grateful for something to take the edge off her shattered nerves.

A crackle of the speaker above announced the song choice "Courtesy of Aven Crey" and the pod released and rose.

Claire gulped down the drink and scrunched her face. Her stomach bubbled at thought of how high they were about to go. "Can you tell them to bring it back down if I get too scared?"

"Yes," Aven assured her, "but I would hate for you to miss the view." He took her drink and put it on the table nearby and held out his hand. "May I have this dance?"

"Is dancing supposed to keep my mind off the fact we are about to be five hundred feet in the air?"

"The drink won't begin to calm your nerves for at least another"—he looked at his watch—"oh, thirty seconds?"

Aven quietly counted down from thirty, and Claire couldn't help but crack a smile as he swept her around the small room.

"So I was right." Aven grinned, leaning them side-to-side.

"About what?"

"That dancing with me makes you smile."

"Maybe it's dancing in general."

"No." Aven dipped Claire as the song ended and gave his charming smile. "It's definitely me." He kept his eyes locked with hers, setting her back on both feet gracefully. Keeping his hands on her waist, he brushed his cheek to hers and whispered, "Close your eyes."

Claire closed her eyes, hoping Aven was about to kiss her. Instead, he smoothed his hands down her waist to her hips and turned her.

"Now open them."

Opening her eyes, Claire gazed past her and Aven's reflection, focusing on the fuchsia and gold neon lights of the Las Vegas skyline. Drawn to the sight, she pressed her hands against the glass, losing her breath as she glanced past her feet. For the first time in her life, Claire wasn't trembling with terror at being at such a high height, but with joy.

Aven stood beside her. It was quiet for a few steady heartbeats until a jingle came from Claire's bracelet. She looked at it and smiled, finding a sparkling charm of a Ferris wheel that hadn't been there before.

THE CHOICE

"DO you have enough pictures to get the monkey off your back?" Aven asked, taking Claire's helmet. He placed it on the bike before offering his arm.

Claire laughed. "Oh, she's definitely going to go bananas. Claire Grace, touring a hot Vegas night with sexy Suit Guy.

"Suit Guy, huh?"

"I have to admit," Claire said, entering the elevator, "you do look rather dashing in it."

"I'll take that over compensating creep,"

Claire's smile fell. "How did you know I—"

"I can read lips." Aven shrugged. "Comes in handy with my work overseas. I've had a lot of practice, but your friend's exaggerated facial expressions made it easy to find out what you two were talking about."

"You have real estate in different countries?"

"Yes, but owning property is something I do for fun in my spare time. My medical company is how I make my living."

"Which medical company?"

"You've probably heard of it." Aven glanced up at the ad scrolling across the holographic banner above them.

Claire's mouth fell open. "You own InfiniCorp?"

"Half. My cousin owns the other. It was passed down in my uncle's will."

"So are you COO?"

"No. We have technology for that. I'm more of a brand ambassador. I go to other countries, explain what InfiniCorp has to offer, and hand out samples. But regardless of what the media says, there are still many countries that don't care for Americans." Aven slid a finger across his throat. "Reading lips has kept me alive."

"How many languages can you speak?"

"Twelve."

"Twelve. Wow. I failed French in high school. I couldn't imagine having to learn so many."

"Oh, Je suis désolé. Treize. J'ai oublié le Mandarin."

"Treize," Claire said, after counting on her fingers. "That's thirteen, right?"

"See, you weren't such a bad student."

At the ding of the elevator, Claire stepped out, allowing Aven to escort her to her door.

"Thank you for keeping your word."

"Of course, milady." Aven bowed. "I am, after all, a gentleman."

"And for the bracelet."

Aven held a cleaver grin, clasping his hands behind his back. "You're supposed to get presents on your birthday."

"How did you know it was my–" Realization hit her. "Right. Lip reading."

"Happy Birthday."

Claire's brows knitted together as she averted her gaze to the ground. Happy. Her birthdays were never that.

"What you faced in bakery. It was on your birthday. I'm sorry, I–"

"No," Claire said all too quickly. "Don't apologize. I'm the one that should be sorry."

"For?"

"Falling in your lap like that."

"It's quite all right, I assure you."

"No. What you did for me–there's nothing I can do to repay you."

This man has everything. Except . . .

"All I can offer is the rest of my secret. I'll tell you, but not here. Somewhere quiet. In case I spaz out again."

Aven's face twisted as if he was in pain. "It's getting late."

"Right. Of course." Claire shook her head. "The party. I'm sure your friend is wondering where you are."

Aven stared for a long moment before he finally spoke.

"There is one place," he said in a grave voice. "But if I took you there, I would be breaking my word."

Claire held her breath. She knew he was talking about his room. She held his gaze, ready to offer her hand and part ways, but something tugged at her heart, something faint whispered,

Say yes. Say you'll stay.

"It's your choice," Aven said, never breaking his gaze.

The word choice, the way Aven was looking at her with his tortured expression, made Claire flashback to the vision of the campsite. She again saw the sad, dark eyes that watched her leave, but this time, the vision moved forward, showing her something she hadn't seen before.

She was in a throne room made of gold under an arbor of roses, and before her was the dark-haired angel, waiting in anticipation for an answer.

I hope that choice is me.

Claire's lashes fluttered, bringing her back to reality.

Aven was still there, still waiting for her answer. His gaze was fixed, and Claire wondered if he would ever blink.

Say yes. Say you'll stay.

The whisper repeated; compulsion washed over her, and Claire's words were uttered much too quickly to revoke. "Bring me back in thirty minutes?"

"As you wish, Princess."

PENTHOUSE

AVEN watched Claire glance around his Penthouse suite. It was roomy with a large leather sofa, a stocked bar, and a baby grand piano. She lingered at the piano but passed it, going to the window wall to view the Vegas landscape.

Guilt crept up his spine. He had used his gift, persuaded her to come here. He had broken her trust without her even knowing. Worse, he had lured her into the den of the demon.

Say yes. Say you'll stay.

The words he had repeated over and over echoed in his mind. Selfish. That's what he was. He hated himself in that moment, hated how relieved he had been at her answer. But if a part of her hadn't wanted to come, she wouldn't have. She could have told him no, could have walked into her room without a second thought. That was the trick to his gift, that's why it always worked with his encounters. Yes, she had chosen to come with him, but with influence.

Aven ordered two coffees and messaged Kat. He asked her to come to his room, to barge in like she had so many times before, but his thumb paused at the send button as Claire spoke.

"The light is so beautiful."

Aven lifted his gaze, narrowing his eyes. He wondered if he was in another vision, if this night had all been a dream, because as he looked upon Claire's petite silhouette, he found it encompassed in a halo of white. It was a revelation, the pluck of the perfect cord ringing in his mind, telling him that Claire had been the reason the demon had stayed away.

Light overcomes the darkness.

It was one of Paula's quotes. It had been passed down from her mother, and her mother's mother. Ancient Truth, she once had told him.

Words of Old.

Drawn to her glow, Aven came to Claire's side to soak up her warmth. He gazed into the black void of space through the window, searching for a star to wish upon. Finding none through the parted clouds, he pleaded with the Heavens instead, praying to be with the angel a little longer.

"Do you ever wish you could go back in time?" Claire murmured.

Aven gave a sideways glance, but she didn't look at him. Instead, she lifted a thin gold chain from her neck, revealing a skeleton key pendent that had been hiding beneath her top.

As she looked at the necklace with sentiment, Aven remembered his childhood. His mind pictured the glass cases, the skeleton keys of all sizes displayed along the walls of his uncle's study.

"A birthday gift?"

"From my dad," Claire answered with tears pooling in her eyes. "I'll never forget how quiet that morning was, how I fussed at him to shave his beard when he kissed my forehead.

He had pointed to the fridge, told me not to open my birthday present until he got home for breakfast the next day."

"What was in the fridge?"

Claire's smile replaced a grimace. "Chocolate cake."

"Cake for breakfast? I think I would have liked your dad."

"A tradition since I was five." Claire paused for a moment and looked back out to the city, her face sullen again. "The night of my sixteenth birthday, I was about to fall asleep when Laura slipped through my window. She convinced me to sneak out after my mom went to bed, to a party a few blocks away. The only reason I went was because Tyler, the guy I had a crush on, was there. I was anxious to talk to him, trembling like always. So I drank too much, way too fast. When Tyler finally came to talk to me, I didn't think twice about going upstairs with him when he asked me to."

"Everything seemed perfect." Claire sighed. "Candles had been lit, music was playing. He had made it special for my—" Claire's voice cracked. "Um, I had never—" She scrunched her face, and Aven knew she didn't want to explain her first time. Countless encounters had told him how uncomfortable it was.

"It's okay, Princess. You can skip that part."

Claire appeared relieved and continued. "After it was over, someone banged on the door, and Tyler left to go break up a fight downstairs. I went to the bathroom and got dressed. It didn't take long before I smelled the smoke, and when I opened the door, the fire was crawling up the walls. I ran to the window, but it was stuck. I did as my dad had taught me and wrapped a blanket around my fist and broke the glass, but I still cut my hand trying to get out."

Claire grazed her fingers over the scar along her open palm. "When I stood on the roof I saw the fire truck coming in. I knew it was my dad's by the number. I kept asking everyone below where he was, kept looking for him. They kept saying everything would be okay as the ladder rose, but . . ."

Aven could tell by the tremble in Claire's voice that what she was about to say next was harder than admitting her first time was unpleasant.

"I had just started a new medication for my anxiety."

"Explains the trembling," Aven noted, glancing at her hands. "What did they give you?"

"Seritol." Claire swallowed and picked her nails. "They handed me a sample packet before I left my session that day. I guess I should have paid attention to the side effects on the label."

"Quetiapine. Convulsions, upset stomach, difficulty breathing, drowsiness, and hallucinations."

Claire's gaze darted to his at the word "hallucinations."

"What did you see?" Aven asked, taking her shaky hands to comfort her.

"There was a backdraft, but in my eyes, it was a monster, a demon made of flames. It roared from the bedroom, burned my hand. I let go and slid down the roof. I tried to hold onto the gutter as long as I could, but–"

Claire winced.

Aven squeezed her hands gently as a long pause fell between them. "You fell," he murmured.

"I heard the crack when my ankle broke, but after that everything went black. I was in the hospital for about a day. When I was released, I couldn't even stand at my dad's funeral. When I got home, I wheeled myself to the fridge, finding the box with my cake and a card with my necklace inside. I put it on, ate my piece of cake alone while my mother cried in her room. I covered the other piece my dad would have eaten and put it back in the fridge. My mom let it stay in there for two months. I don't think she had the heart to throw it out. In a way I think we both thought if we left it there, we would wake up one morning to my dad at the kitchen table, eating it."

"That's your secret."

"I have issues. And because of them, I almost didn't come to Vegas."

"But then, you wouldn't have met me." Aven gave his charming smile.

Claire wiped her tears and gave a light laugh. "I guess it's true what they say."

"What do they say?"

"That everything happens for a reason?"

Aven held Claire's tearful gaze. He wanted to kiss her lashes, kiss away her heartache. He leaned forward, ready to comfort her, but a knock came from the door.

Claire exhaled in relief seeing the bellboy in the hallway. She still worried that Aven would at some point make fun of her, tell her what she saw was crazy, but he hadn't. Not yet.

While Aven tipped the bellboy, Claire went to the piano. She traced her fingers along the glossy ebony surface but refrained from tapping the ivory keys. Pain ached in her chest as she remembered the last time she had played. The notes rang in her mind. She again saw the memory of a glossy casket sitting in the Worship Center, how her mother had wailed over it.

"You're not a flowers kind of girl, are you?" Aven asked, handing her a cup of coffee.

Claire's shoulders relaxed as the warmth from the cup soothed her stiff, frigid fingers.

"I love flowers," she answered, glancing at the vase full of red roses on the piano top, "but I prefer them in pots so I can plant them outside. One day I want to plant a garden, have a bench to sit on, a place to talk to the flowers."

"Ah, a Lewis Carroll fan, I see."

"When you grin, it reminds me of the Cheshire cat."

"Do I look that mischievous?"

"At times." Claire smiled as her gaze went back to the piano.

"Do you play?"

"I used to teach after I graduated high school to pay my college tuition."

"Sit and play something."

"No, I can't. I'm rusty."

"I'll play one with you." Aven put his cup to the side and sat down on the bench, patting the spot next to him.

"No really. I—"

"All right teacher"—Aven grinned, playing a playful tune—"I'll play. You grade."

Claire sat her cup next to Aven's and pressed her lips together as she sat on the bench. Her eyes darted left to right, watching Aven's fingers trail up and down to the upbeat score of Nikolai Rimsky's *Flight of the Bumblebee*. There was no need to give him pointers. His form was perfect.

As Aven played, Claire's mind took her back to her first piano recital. She recalled the itchy pink tulle dress she had to wear, how the hairpins had poked her scalp from her tight bun. But all of that didn't matter when she played, because that had been the first time her father had seen her perform. When she stood to curtsy, he had run down the aisle to the stage. Beaming with pride, he offered a bouquet of a dozen red stem roses.

That's my Claire Bear.

"If you play with me," Aven said, slowing his pace with another tune. "I'll tell you another one of my secrets."

Claire snapped back to the present as Aven tapped the keys to the tune of *Chopsticks*. She shook her head no, but as Aven reached to her side of the piano, she relented and joined in. She giggled as her heart raced. They played faster, and faster, and then, the duet was over too soon.

"I forgot how much fun that was." Claire laughed. She lifted her gaze to Aven's, finding him staring again.

"Another contest?"

"No."

"Then what?"

"Happiness looks good on you."

Claire blushed, tucking her hair behind her ear. "How long have you been playing?"

"Since I was two," Aven answered, playing a melancholy solo. "Most of my early memories were of her and I at a piano. She taught me how to play. She had brightness about her. A lot like you."

"Had?"

"She passed away a few months after my second birthday, car accident."

"I'm sorry."

Aven finished his song and gazed at Claire a long moment. "Play something from the heart."

"From the heart?"

"Yes. Bare your soul."

"Bare my soul . . ." Claire put her hands on the keys, then took them off again, shaking her head. "I can't."

"Just think of everything you've ever held inside and let it out through your fingertips."

Aven watched Claire take a deep breath and exhale through pursed lips. With eyes closed, she played a song so deep, so meaningful that Aven believed he had glimpsed at one of the deepest parts of her soul. The song was like an angelic hymn but dark and sorrowful. And then, the sentimental score was over too soon. Claire sniffed and slipped her fingers from the ivory keys.

"An angel of music." Aven didn't hold back this time and wiped a tear from her cheek. "You're even more beautiful when you cry."

Claire wiped her eye and cleared her throat. "Your turn to be vulnerable."

"Vulnerable?"

"Yes. Bare your soul."

Vulnerable. It was a foreign word to Aven. He had never let his guard down with anyone. Kitten was the only person he had ever let in, ever let see this side of him. He had never told his encounters about his past, never let them see him for who he was.

A sad, broken little boy.

But Claire wasn't an encounter, and he vowed in his heart that she would never be.

The score he played was about her. In the notes was every emotion, every sigh, and every word he hadn't said out loud. She sat, watching him, looking as if she could hear the lyrics he was singing in his head.

A buzz came from Claire's pocket.

"Laura must be looking for me," Claire informed him, silencing her phone.

Aven stood with Claire and forced a smile as he walked her to the door. "Thank you for letting me keep my head, Your Majesty." He bowed, taking her hand, and kissed it. "But before you go . . ."

Aven gave her wrist a gentle tilt and let go, letting Claire reveal the glinting crown charm in her palm.

"For my nickname at the bar."

"No," Aven corrected gently. He snapped the charm on her bracelet. "To remember to hold your head high." He lifted her chin. "Never look down or the crown slips. You have a beautiful soul, Claire. Never be ashamed of who you are."

At a ring from her phone, Claire tapped the screen to silent it and scrunched her face. "She's probably wondering what's taking so long."

A weight, as if the demon was sitting on his chest, made it hard for Aven to breathe. He knew as soon as he departed from door 755, the demon would return and order him to find someone to seduce. He would do as she requested; he always did.

With one last gift to give, Aven held out his clenched fists to Claire. "Pick one."

"Always a game with you," Claire pointed out, tapping his left hand.

Aven revealed an empty upturned palm with a sly grin. Claire picked his right hand and he opened his left, revealing a white paper napkin, wrapped like a rose.

"Until you get that garden."

Claire took it and twirled it in her fingers. "A thousand times, thank you."

"It is I who should thank you, milady."

"Thank me for what?"

"For being you."

When Claire smiled, her halo of white returned. Aven couldn't help but want to be encompassed in it. His fingers curled into his palm, holding back the urge to touch her, to kiss her gently on the cheek, to say goodbye. But he reminded himself of the promise not to cross that line.

But Claire did.

Her kiss was feather light, innocent even, but it made every fiber of Aven's being want to sweep her up in his arms and hold her tight. He knew if he did, he would never let go.

His face hardened as he bit his lower lip, trying to gain back control.

"I'm sorry." Claire frowned, putting a hand to her forehead. "It's—It's probably the alcohol. I should go."

"I've always been a man of my word, Claire, but with you—I find myself to be nothing but a liar."

In each step Claire took back, Aven took one forward, until her back was against the wall. His eyes wandered from her lips to the dip in her collarbone, to the smooth line of her neck, and then to her silky brown hair.

Brushing back her curls, he took her by the nape of her neck, painfully slow, and leaned down, satisfying his hunger with the taste of her lips.

Claire yielded, going limp in his arms and stifling a soft moan. The sound of her light whimper only made him thirst for more, and he pressed her harder against the wall. He let his hands explore the hills of her figure, let them venture over the glorious and soft terrain under her shirt. But as his fingers dared to roam the blooming valley beneath her skirt, Aven drew back with a throaty growl.

"If you don't leave now"—he exhaled against her mouth—"there will be nothing left of my chivalry."

Claire met his gaze, searching his eyes, searching for truth. There was no mask that Aven could bring forth to convince her, no alter ego to take his place, no tricks, no spells of persuasion. It would be him and only him that took her to his bed, but only if she chose to.

"Par tes lèvres, mon péché est purgé," Aven whispered.

He kissed her again; this time slow, gently, asking permission with soft sweeps of his tongue. Claire's answer, the reply to his unspoken request, came with only a soft sigh against his lips.

"Par tes lèvres, mon péché est purgé,"
"By thine lips, my sin is purged."

MORNING

SATURDAY, 4:02 A.M., LAS VEGAS

AVEN woke from a dream of him standing on the shore in a tropical paradise to the light scent of coconut. Lapping waves quieted as his lazy gaze met the nape of Claire's neck. He smiled to himself, finding the small hickey he had left in the crease of her shoulder. He kissed the splotch with sentiment and pulled her in close. He was ready for sleep to find him again, ready for another dream of standing in the sun. But there was only a cold draft that came the moment he shut his eyes.

"I thought that I was in Heaven," a slithery singsong voice echoed.

No.

Cracking open an eye, Aven found his demon, hovering above the bed. Her shadow moved across the wall as she sang Elvis's "Devil In Disguise," taunting him with every line.

Not Now.

Grabbing his phone from the nightstand, he let out a heavy sigh. It would be hours before dawn. He couldn't stay. No matter how much he wanted to get more sleep, to hold the angel, he couldn't risk the demon getting in Claire's head. He would leave. He wouldn't ruin how perfect the night had been.

After dressing, Aven conjured a sheet of notepaper from a small desk. He formed it into a rose, and made it appear on the nightstand next to Claire's phone. He requested the words from his mind to ink themselves inside the folds. It wasn't an apology for leaving but a thank you for the most wonderful night of his existence.

He stood above Claire, stuffing his hands in his pockets, and gazed at her for a long moment. He thought to kiss her goodbye, to whisper three little words he had never said with intention. He knew it to be true, had known it the moment he had laid eyes on her. He felt he had always known, that he had said it long before they had even met.

Leaning down, Aven wet his lips. He was ready to say the words, ready to admit that Claire had his heart. But before he could mutter them, the icy fingers of his demon wrapped around his throat and squeezed.

SATURDAY, 5:10 A.M., LAS VEGAS

Claire fluttered her lashes, drawing in a breath. The sweet scent of roses made her heart skip a beat, remembering how Aven had caressed her body with the silky petals. Drawing the sheets over her naked body, she sat up, finding the other side of the bed empty.

With a soft sigh, she reached for her phone and rubbed her sleepy eyes. Finding only a black screen and her reflection looking back at her, Claire let out a groan.

Dead battery. Great.

"It's called a charger."

Claire froze to a female's voice coming from the other side of the bedroom door. She wondered if she was imagining it, if she was still dreaming.

"I've called six times. You're phone better be dead, or you'll be when I find you," the sassy voice snapped.

No. The voice was real.

With her heart pounding in her throat, Claire reached for her clothes, and fell into the floor with thud.

Crap.

Hearing no footsteps coming her way, Claire quietly wrapped the sheet around her chest and crawled to the door. Peeking her head out, she found figure to the voice. The girl's back was turned, her nails tapping against the piano that she and Aven had been playing only hours earlier.

"Just wait until I get a hold of you, Aven Crey," the girl said, slamming shut the piano.

Walking quietly on the pads of her feet, Claire made her way to the Penthouse entry as the girl cursed at her phone. She turned the knob, wincing as it clicked open, but slipped out, never looking back as it shut. She ran down the hall, tripping on the sheet, and darted into the ice machine room. Pressing her back against the wall, she prayed no one had seen her dramatic exit.

Stupid. Stupid. Stupid.

Claire rubbed her face. It was hot to the touch, burning with embarrassment. She assumed the girl was Aven's girlfriend, if not someone he knew well enough to know where he had been staying.

After Claire dressed in a hurry, she tossed the sheet to the side, finding an ice bucket on the floor.

Good excuse.

She filled the bucket to the top with ice and peeked around the corner. The girl had exited Aven's room and was coming in her direction. Claire hated lying, but she hated confrontation even more. She had to pretend. She had to act like she wasn't in the Penthouse suite last night.

Whistling a pleasant tune from her lips, Claire stepped out of the ice room and walked down the hall.

"Excuse me?" the girl's voice called.

Claire paused in step and glanced around the empty hall for a moment as if confused. When she finally turned, her mouth parted slightly, taken back by the beautiful face of the girl she had evaded. She was around Claire's age and height. Her blonde hair was long, bleached out to an ashy white. The tips of it were pastel pink, which faded into her matching pink blouse. Claire guessed she was a model with her long legs and slender figure; if not that, maybe a Las Vegas show girl.

"I'm sorry. Are you talking to me?" Claire asked, pointing to her chest.

"You didn't happen to see someone coming out of the penthouse suite, did you?"

The heat from Claire's cheeks spread down her neck, prickling it like a desert cactus.

Keep calm.

The blonde's Barbie doll face pinched slightly, and she tilted her head with narrow eyes. "Well?"

"Um, no. I've just been getting ice." Claire smiled, taking her gaze from the girl's banana yellow heels to glance at the bucket.

"Gets pretty hot in Vegas, doesn't it?"

"Yeah." Claire laughed nervously.

"Well, I won't keep you."

Claire nodded and headed down the hall, but the blonde spoke to her again.

"Oh, by the way."

Claire paused and cautiously turned.

"You have a rose petal in your hair." The girl smiled. "Just thought you should know."

COMFORT FOOD

SATURDAY, 5:17 A.M., LAS VEGAS

"HONEY, what in the world are you doin' here at this hour?"

Aven glanced up at his godmother, Paula, who stood above him with a hand on her hip.

"I just had a craving for some chocolate chip pancakes."

"Mm hm." Paula's brown eyes gave a pointed stare. "You never come this early unless somethin's up."

Aven rose to his feet and slid his hands in his pockets. He glanced over Paula's shoulder, watching his demon stand in the street. Her hellhounds appeared out of thin air beside her. They gnashed their teeth, growling. As they came toward him, Aven brought his gaze back to Paula. "Maybe I just missed you."

Paula squinted, puckering her brown lips like fish. "Hmph." She turned to the empty street, puffing out her chest. "All ya'll! Get on outta here!" she shouted, waving a hand in the air. "Shoo devils! Go back to where you came from, spirit of Samria!" She turned back to Aven. "I done told you, baby, you don't have to deal with all that mess."

Aven shrugged. "Do I ever listen?"

"Stubborn as a mule." Paula sighed, unlocking the door. "Come on, baby. They ain't gonna bother you in here."

Aven smirked at his demon that glared at him from an abandoned hover car with a busted window.

"Stay." He pointed at her and the hellhounds before walking into the eatery.

The bell of the door resounded through the little establishment as Aven sat in his usual booth by the window. He watched his demon and her legion of hounds as they strolled down the pavement. He hoped they were stalking someone, anyone else, to torment. It was a selfish thought, but insomnia did that to a person. A sigh of relief escaped Aven's lips as the devils disappeared into smoke.

Soothed by Paula's singing and the clatter of plates, Aven withdrew his phone from his jeans. He thumbed through the missed calls from Kitten and her very rude but amusing messages.

K: I met your encounter. She's cute. Next time let me know, would ya? Oh, btw. Housekeeping didn't appreciate the bed of roses.

Aven wiped the corners of his mouth and swiped his phone to the photo app, ignoring the voicemail alerts popping up from Vincent.

"I done told you baby, you ain't gotta put up with that nonsense," Paula said behind him. "I'm guessin' you didn't entertain any young ladies last night?" she asked, placing a glass of cold milk down in front of him.

"No, I did." Aven sighed, pausing at the picture of him and Claire at the Vegas sign. "But it was different this time."

"I don't want to hear details, sugar." Paula held up her hands and shook her head. "And I ain't gonna judge you, but you need to be changin' your ways. That's no life for you. You need a wife and a family, maybe even some pretty babies."

Aven let out a throaty laugh. "I'm not exactly a family man."

"You never know until you try. You have enough money to live comfortably the rest of your life. Ain't that enough?"

"It's never enough."

"Hmph. Money is the root of all evil."

Aven grinned. Paula was using one of her many quotes again, and as always, he countered it. "Money makes the world go 'round."

"Go after selfish ambition and evil shall follow." Paula shook her finger and made her way back to the stove as it dinged.

Aven had no witty reply to that one, only the harsh truth. "The Old Ways don't apply to the world today."

"That's man's words," Paula said. She favored her hip as she shuffled her feet the table. She laid Aven's breakfast in front of him and pointed to the ceiling. "The words of the Creator are forever, baby. Never changin' always applicable,"

Paula said, placing a hand on Aven's shoulder. "Let us give thanks."

Aven closed his eyes at her touch. He always did out of respect when she prayed over his meal.

"Oh, mighty Creator, Father of all. Watch over my godson. Keep him safe, keep temptation from him, and guide him to your wisdom. And if it be your will, send an angel to watch over him."

Aven batted his eyes at the word angel and glanced to the photo of Claire, thinking of her halo.

"For even when the adversary is pulling us down into the deep," Paula continued, "we shall climb above, toward you, on that mountain of truth. Praise be to you, oh mighty King. Forever."

When Paula squeezed Aven's shoulder, ending her prayer, Aven smiled at her. "Thank you, Mama."

"I want you to eat everything. Ya gettin' skinny boy." Paula fell into the chair next to him with a grunt. She glanced at his phone, and Aven wished he had locked it to the home screen.

"My, my," Paula said, "look at that sweet face. What's her name?"

"Claire." Aven's forehead wrinkled as a dull pain spread across his chest. "Claire Grace."

Paula picked up Aven's phone and slipped on her glasses. "She looks shy. I'm guessing she's not from 'round here?"

"No, she's a guest at the hotel."

"Look at those bright eyes. You should date her honey."

"I sorta did. Last night."

"And?" Paula asked, scrolling through the photos.

"And she lives too far away. Tybee Island."

"Georgia? So you found yaself a real southern peach. Be like that *Gone with the Wind* movie and go sweep her off her feet."

Aven chuckled. "That may have worked centuries ago, but courting is no longer considered a romantic notion. It's stalking."

Paula razzed her lips, handed back Aven's phone, and stood. "This world is nonsense. My grandmamma and granddaddy courted. You don't see love like that anymore. Fifty years. Now that's true love. Marriages lasted back in those days you call old."

Aven sighed, thumbing through the photos again.

"Wait! Go back a few."

Aven swiped his fingers across the screen. "This one?"

"What's that surrounding her? Looks like she's glowin' or somethin'."

Aven had always told Paula about everything going on in his life, but he didn't know how to explain his gifts. He had kept that bit of information to himself. "It's the lights reflecting in the lens from the sign," he lied, wondering how his phone could have captured her aura.

Paula raised her brows. "Or maybe your mama sent you an angel. I tell ya, baby, the Creator knows our prayers before we even say them out loud."

Aven thought about the visions, thought about how the succubus had left him alone, let him sleep for two hours peacefully without any tormenting dreams. He was curious, however, why she had returned. Had it been because Claire fell asleep?

"It was the first night in a year I'd had a good dream," Aven admitted.

"Baby, I done told you what to do 'bout them spooks and them nightmares. You know they mess with you because of that witchy woman. She was filled with her own legion. She'd walk in here, and I could just feel her evil. Her eyes were always glazed over, like she was hungry for souls or something. I swear she done made a deal with Samria himself."

Bree Delaroche. A mistake I can never take back.

Aven ate his pancakes slowly as Paula busied herself in the kitchen. Now and then he would glance out the window, looking for his demon and her hellhounds. They hadn't reappeared. Yet.

Perhaps they really are torturing another sorry soul.

When Aven was finished with his meal, he gulped down his milk and tapped a pay icon on his phone. Sending Paula much more than the meal was worth, he pressed another icon, requesting a driverless cab.

A ding rang out.

Paula pulled her phone from her apron and shook her head. "I made that meal for you cuz I love you, not so you can send me money to pay the power bill," she fussed, coming to his side.

"Last time I was here you were behind," Aven said, standing.

Another ding came from Paula's phone. She gave Aven a disapproving look. "Sugar, them pancakes ain't worth no two hundred dollars.

"Kindness is priceless."

Another ding rang out and Aven's grin widened.

Paula put a hand on her hip, looking at the notification. "Now you're just being cute. I already paid the rent."

"Save it for next month. I'll be out of town."

"So you didn't get partner?"

"Not yet," Aven informed her, ordering a bottle of liquor. The app replied with the place and time of delivery out loud.

"Boy, it is too early for you to be drinkin'," Paula fussed as she picked up his empty plate and glass.

"You know I can't sleep without it."

"This life you live is only gonna kill ya, honey."

Aven forced a smile and kissed Paula on the cheek. "Thank you for breakfast, Mama."

"You're welcome, baby." Paula gave Aven a light pat on the back. "You come back soon, now. Don't wait another month again."

"I'll come back tomorrow. How's that?"

"Knowing how you keep your word, I'll hold you to it." She winked at Aven and he winked back.

"Bye, baby. Be good now."

"Yes ma'am." Aven pushed open the door open, only to be greeted by fangs on the sidewalk. The demon dog growled, and another appeared from smoke, foaming at the mouth.

Paying no mind to the hellhounds, Aven entered the driverless cab and tapped the wireless connection on his phone. The speakers of the car announced his address as the hologram lit up, showing the route that would take him home. Laying his head back on the seat, Aven wet his lips, thirsting for the bottle of bourbon that would be waiting on his doorstep.

SAVIOR

SATURDAY, 5:32 A.M. LAS VEGAS

CLAIRE shrugged off a cold chill that ran through her and yawned. She squeezed her crossed arms tighter across her chest, wishing she had a light jacket. According to the front desk clerk, the girls never had a reservation for their room.

Stupid scammers.

The gift shop clerk had informed her the nearest convenience store was only a few blocks away and apologized for not having her charger in stock. Claire wasn't too thrilled with the idea of walking alone on the Vegas strip, but she had to call Laura.

Claire assumed Laura had used her father's credit card to book another hotel for the weekend stay. Until she could find out which one, she was on her own, trudging down the sidewalk of Sin City.

There were no drones to watch for crime, no cameras to scan the faces of possible drug traffickers, only flashing ads and holograms of showgirls at every turn, announcing,

WELCOME TO LAS VEGAS, A CITY OF FANTASIES, A CITY WITHOUT CONSEQUENCE. WHAT IS YOUR PLEASURE?

Quickening her stride past the hologram showgirls to her left and right, Claire fixed her gaze on the sign of the convenience store across the street.

"Pretty lady!" a man in a top hat called out. "Free tickets!"

Claire held up her hand. "No thank you."

"Come on, they're free," the man insisted, catching up to her. "You'll love the show. Magic, illusion." He waved his hands as if he could make something appear.

Claire took the card, reading,

BE DAZZLED AND AMAZED

Her gaze darted to the stranger's face, seeing him focused on Aven's gift. Her ears burned and a prickle of anxiety poked her neck as she fought the urge to run. She thanked the man and averted her gaze to the crosswalk and a group of huddled teens going across the street. She took a step to follow them, but a jerk on her arm and something hard pressing into her back made her freeze in place.

"Don't even think about screaming," a gruff voice said in her ear.

The tips of Claire's ears burned as she took two steps back. Bile rose in her throat when an arm snaked around her waist, forcing her under the MGM hotel sign.

Her abductor shoved her against the supporting column, invading her personal space. "If you scream"—he glared, revealing the gun in his hand—"you're dead."

"What we got here?"

Claire's eyes darted to her left, finding the figure of a deeper voice coming out of the shadows.

"From the looks of it a silver bracelet." Claire's abductor grinned. Claire swallowed the acid lining her throat as her abductor's rancid breath met her cheek.

"Silver sure is high this year," the man from the shadows noted. He snatched up Claire's wrist and pressed her pointer finger to his phone.

Licking his chipped front tooth, the man from the shadows smiled as the blip of the money transfer rang out. "What else you got, sweetie?"

"Lookey, lookey," her abductor said, fishing out her necklace between her breasts.

"Please"—Claire fumbled to take off Aven's gift—"my dad gave me that before he died. Take the bracelet but not that."

"Daddy's girl," the man from the shadows teased.

With one swift tug, Claire's necklace snapped from her neck. Her whole body shook with fear and anger, and although she had at times doubted an all-powerful Creator existed, she prayed to him.

Finding a newfound strength, Claire dug her nails into her palm. She laid her thumb tight over her knuckle just as her dad had taught as a child.

You're a strong, independent young woman, Claire, her father's voice echoed in her mind. Be brave.

Drawing back her elbow, Claire focused on her abductors nose, but before she could extend her fist, something white whipped past her vision with a smack.

Claire jumped back as a stranger in a white-hooded sweatshirt and jeans elbowed her abductor in the face. As her abductor stumbled back, cupping his cheeks, the man from the shadows flipped out a knife.

Her savior dodged the rusty blade as the man from the shadows cut through the air, aiming for his chest.

Her gaze darted back to her abductor as he wiped the blood from his lip and reached around his back.

"Watch out!" Claire warned.

As if he was from a spy movie, the hooded stranger lunged and twisted her abductor's wrist back. The crack of his fingers and the wail from his lips made her stomach churn.

Her abductor cursed and held his limp hand while the hooded stranger dismantled his gun like a plastic toy and tossed it into the bushes.

As if on cue, sirens wailed down the street, and the criminals scampered down the sidewalk. They turned the corner and were gone.

The hooded savior picked up Claire's necklace and grabbed her hand. It was all too fast, too sudden for Claire to react as a flood of images filled her mind at their touch. The wave of familiarity left her breathless, much like the first time she had seen Aven. Only these visions, she knew she had seen before.

Claire didn't object as the hooded man opened the passenger side door to his car; she sat, watching the police cars wail down the street until their red and blue lights disappeared.

"Are you hurt?" he asked, shutting his door.

Claire fixed her gaze on the driver side. There was her hero, his face hidden beneath a white hood. But as he slid it back to his shoulders, revealing himself, Claire's heart stopped.

With the speed of a hovering rail train, images zoomed in Claire's mind. It was her recurring dream. Once it had been blurry, but now, it seemed to weave itself together, stitching moment after moment into her mind. Every instant from start to finish was coming in clear. The wave was coming again, but she heard her angel's words and felt his touch—clearly this time.

"Sophie, look into my eyes. What color are they?"

"Blue..."

"Remember the blue of the ocean that day we met, remember Bevol and days spent in paradise? You will see it again. All perish now, but one day we will live again, with

Aramis, with our friends. It will all be just as it was before, and we'll be together again."

My warrior. My protector.

Your Guardian, her mind whispered back.

"Miss?"

Claire blinked out of her daze. "What did you say?"

"Are you hurt?" he asked again.

Claire shook her head. "N-no. No, I'm fine. You're . . ."

"You're trembling." Her savior peeled off his hoodie and offered it to her.

Claire took it with gratitude and put it on. She rubbed her hands together in the sweatshirt's oversized sleeves, exhaled in them, and then inhaled. The scent of fresh-cut grass and Old Spice filled her nose. It was the same scent her father carried on warm summer days, a comforting smell she remembered from her childhood.

Did Dad send him? Did the Creator hear my prayer?

"What hotel are you staying at? I'll give you a ride back."

Claire stared at the stranger, still trying to be sure she wasn't dreaming. Surly everything that had just happened couldn't be real.

He furrowed his brows. "I'm not going to hurt you."

"No, it's—I know you won't, not after saving me, I just—" Her words trailed off as she gazed into his sea blue eyes.

"I'm Will. Will Stryde."

Claire looked down at his offered hand, and then to his wrist. Air rushed from her lungs, seeing a birthmark. She shook his hand, looking at her own birthmark in disbelief.

They're identical. This can't be real. Wake up, Claire!

"Claire Grace." She said, finally.

Lifting her gaze, she found Will's eyes soft but searching. *Did he see the birthmark too?*

"Where are you staying?" he repeated, slipping his hand away. He started the car, putting it in gear.

"I don't have a hotel."

Out of the corner of her eye, Claire watched Will tilt his head and then look her up and down.

"I'm not a hooker," she blurted, whipping around. "I mean, my friends—" She exhaled a frustrated breath. "It's a long story."

The stranger glanced at her trembling fingers. "You can tell me about it after we get you something warm to drink."

TEA

CLAIRE sat in the red booth across from Will and watched as the menus popped up on the table screen. The twenty-four-hour diner welcomed its new customers with bright graphics and music. Claire reached out to put her finger on the scanner, but Will beat her too it.

"Thank you," Claire said, drawing back her hand into the oversized sleeve. Although she hated not being able to pay her way, she knew she didn't have a single bitcoin to her name. She couldn't afford the overdraft fees, not when the mortgage was so behind.

When a list of Will's food and drink preferences appeared as dancing icons on the screen, he frowned.

Claire could tell by his furrowing brows he didn't like his privacy invaded. She had never cared for it either, but it was the way the world was. Catching a quick glance, she looked at his information. His birthday, his license number, even his state of residence, was out for anyone to see.

Tapping yes on the coffee icon, Will lifted his gaze. "Cream and sugar?"

"Just a water please." Claire smiled politely.

Will gave her a look and then scrolled through the menu, finding a tea icon and added it to his order.

The word chamomile sparked a memory in Claire's mind: of her father, of a bad dream that had woken her one night, the warm mug he had brought her, and the prayer he had said with her before putting her back to bed.

"Will you excuse me?" Claire said, heading to the bathroom. She didn't want this guy to see her cry, didn't want him to ask if she was okay again. She wasn't.

Will rubbed his five o'clock shadow and stared out the window. He thought about the touch of Claire's hand, how it had brought back the memory of last night's dream.

He was standing on the beach, peering down at the girl with the long brown braid. She was terrified, weeping.

Emotions flooded him, now seeing Claire as the sorrowful angel. In the dream he had kept his gaze, ignoring the raging wave, and comforted the girl with a tearful kiss goodbye.

"Here you go, honey," a waitress said, sitting down two steaming mugs.

Will blinked from the memory of the dream. "Thank you."

"Is your girlfriend okay?"

"We're not—"

"Oh, I'm sorry I assumed you two were together. You make a cute couple."

Will gave a sheepish grin.

"Let me know if you need anything else."

"Yes, ma'am."

Girlfriend.

Claire wasn't that, but in Will's heart he felt she belonged with him. He rubbed his brows, telling himself it was stupid. Déjà vu was brought on by stress. Nothing more. She couldn't be the same girl he had sketched and painted these past seven years. It was only a coincidence. But as Will stared into the black abyss of his mug, his soul whispered a contradiction.

Claire blinked back the burning in her eyes, grumbling over the black tint shedding off her long lashes. She scrubbed her eyelids hard with the wet, scratchy paper towel. She didn't care if it felt like sandpaper. She was tired of looking like a hooker.

After combing through her frazzled hair, she braced herself on the sink, staring at her reflection.

"Get it together, Claire," she said to herself in the mirror. "It's a coincidence. Nothing more." Her gaze darted to the gold-embroidered emblem on Will's sweatshirt: Navy Seal.

It was the same emblem her father had on one of his hats she wore as a child. The vision from the airport trickled back into her mind, and the room blurred. Her only focus was on the symbol as it changed.

The embroidery seemed to weave itself again, re-threading the wings of the eagle, lifting them. The titian peak centered in the form of an A, and an infinity symbol laced across it.

Claire pupils widened, but then shrunk as the flash of the new emblem left her vision just as quickly as it had come.

Stop it, Claire. Stop acting crazy.

Combing back her hair one last time, Claire built up the courage to leave the restroom. She meekly sat in the booth with a polite smile and wrapped her fingers around the hot mug in front of her.

"Thank you."

Will gave a quick glance from his mug. "Don't worry about it."

"No—I mean for taking on those thugs. If anything had happened, I don't know what my mom would do."

"The world's pretty crazy, huh?"

"Yeah."

She took a small sip of the tea, soothed by the hot liquid gliding down her throat. Cupping the mug, she stared at the sediment in the bottom.

A vision came of a delicate teacup, a bright light beside her, an omniscient presence.

"Better?" Will asked, interrupting her thoughts.

"Yes," Claire answered with a sweet smile. She glanced at Will's information on the screen again. "So are you here for business or pleasure?"

"Neither. I'm looking for my brother."

"He lives here in Vegas?"

"I hope so. My mother asked me to find him, see if he would come see her before she passes."

"I'm sorry. You were on your way to see him and I—"

"No, I was sitting in the hotel parking lot waiting for a friend to send me his address and then I saw—those guys had been hanging out there a while. I grew up around cops. I know the profile," he said, grabbing the sugar. He poured copious amounts—as if he didn't realize how much he was adding—and stirred it with a spoon.

Seeing the furrowing of Will's brows, how he stared into his mug as if life didn't seem worth living anymore, an impulse to comfort him shot through Claire. "I lost my dad when I was sixteen. Yesterday was the anniversary of his death."

Will tapped the spoon put it on a napkin. "Were you here because of the Caesar Palace Massacre?"

"No. A bachelorette party. We flew in yesterday for the weekend from Tybee Island, but a fake booking company scammed my best friend. I was somewhere else when my friends got kicked out of their room at the Luxor. I didn't know until I got back and found the door locked. My friends had already left. My phone was dead, so I couldn't call them."

"Doesn't seem like a very happy birthday."

Last night was amazing, but after . . .

Claire didn't let her thoughts continue. "If I hadn't got mugged, I'd be booking a flight back home. I would ask my friend Laura to call her pilot, but I don't want him making two trips."

"Your pilot fly a Cesna?"

"Um, yeah. How did you know?"

"Does your friend Laura have blonde hair? A bit hyper? I thought I saw her waving at me from your plane."

"You're the guy she kept telling me to look at. My—" Claire stopped herself. "My goodness that's uh, that's weird."

"What's weird?"

"That we, uh, both came here in a private plane." Claire wanted to crawl into a hole and hide.

Could I be any more awkward?

"I won't be able to call her until I can charge my phone," she informed him.

Will smiled and took his phone from his pocket, offering it to her. "You can borrow mine."

"I can't remember her number." Claire put her phone on the table. "I don't know why I thought the store would have a charger. According to some people my phone is ancient."

Aven came to Claire's mind. She wondered what he was doing, if he was thinking of her, but it didn't matter. She would go back home, work at the Bed and Breakfast, and never see or talk to him again. That's how one-night stands worked.

"You can use my charger in the car," Will offered. "I'll give you a ride when you find out where you're staying."

Claire looked at the phones. The only difference was the color. Claire's case was petal pink, and Will's was black.

Exhaling with relief, she put a hand to her forehead, thinking in the back of her mind how strange it was they had the same model.

Another coincidence?

"Again, thank you," Claire said, standing. "It won't take long. I'll just let her know where I am so she can pick me up." Before Claire could take two steps toward the door, Will called out her name.

Will knew it was too sudden, too quick to offer a ride, but he felt compelled to. He couldn't let her out of his sight, not after the flashes he saw, not after feeling like she was the girl he had seen in his dreams. The urge to protect her was too strong to ignore.

"I can fly you home," he blurted out, coming to her side.

"I'm sorry?" Claire turned, scrunching her brows.

"I can make a stop in Tybee. It's on the way."

Claire stared at her phone and then glanced back up at him.

"I'm a good pilot. You'll be safe."

"No, it's just—"

"I'm a stranger?"

"No, I mean yes, but I don't—"

"Trust me?"

Claire laughed and shook her head. "You beat up two guys, Jack Reacher-style. For a minute I thought I was dreaming. But no, it's not that."

Will halfway smiled.

"I don't want to be a burden. You need to find your brother, and I'm just holding you back."

Will wished he could tell Claire how wrong she was. The burden of his sick mother, a search to find a long-lost brother before she passed, all seemed to be lifted off his shoulders the moment he had seen Claire's face.

"You're not," he assured, softly.

As Claire stared at Will for a long moment, he had a sudden urge to touch her shoulder, to assure her he meant her no harm. He still couldn't understand their connection, the dreams of her, the visions at the touch of her hand, the fact she had the same exact birthmark. Holding her hand in the car, something had snapped into place, an unexplained familiarity of her touch.

"Um, okay," Claire said. "Thank you. I'll uh, I'll just go call Laura and tell her I'm going home."

Claire walked out the door, glancing at Will through the diner windows. When he ran his fingers through his hair, she felt as if she had seen him do that before. The visions from their touch had gone by too fast. She couldn't piece them together. She wondered if she would wake up, if she would find herself in her hotel room. Maybe this was all a hallucination from the pill Brittney had given her.

A very vivid hallucination.

Chewing the inside of her cheek, Claire plugged in her phone and waited for Laura to answer while watching Will take a call from someone as he paid.

"Oh my God, Claire! What the hell?" Laura screeched in her ear. "You could have at least called or something!"

"Well, I would have, but you have my charger and my clothes," Claire shot back. "You know I don't like to say I told you so, but I told you so. Thanks for ditching me."

"I ditched you? You're the one who didn't come back down to LAX. I tried calling you, but I guess you were too busy banging sexy Suit Guy. So was it amazing? How big is his—"

"Did you guys get another hotel?"

"Yeah, we're staying at the Flamingo. Daddy's going to be pissed I put it on his card. But, whatever. It's not like I'm making him go broke. If you're done doing the deed with hot stuff, bring him with you. We're heading to Fremont Street."

"I'm uh, not with him anymore. I'm with someone else at a diner."

"Who?"

"Well, no, thanks to your bogus booking, I was walking to the gas station to get a charger when two thugs came up and mugged me."

"Oh, shit! Are you okay?"

"I'm fine. This guy I'm with, he just came out of nowhere, and it was insane. I think he's Special Forces or something. He took apart a gun like he had done it a million times."

"A gun? You're joking, right?" Laura scoffed. "Look honey, I know you're new to this whole playing around thing, but you sound like you're serious or something."

"When have I ever lied to you?"

"Like a lot. Size *does* matter, Claire. So is this guy hot?"

"What?"

"Is. He. Hot?"

Claire glanced through the window of the diner and loosed a breath. "He's fairly attractive."

"Visual."

"Laura—"

"Details or I'm hanging up."

"Seriously?"

"Five, four, three, two—"

"He's gorgeous, okay? He has blonde hair and beautiful blue eyes. He's tall and built, and he smells really, really nice. He literally took the shirt off his back when I—"

"Wait, wait, wait. He took off his shirt?"

"Well, his hoodie." Claire glanced down at the Navy Seal emblem. "I'm pretty sure he served in the war."

"Hold up. Blonde? And a white hoodie?"

"Yeah, why?"

"He's the guy from the airport I kept trying to get you to look at!"

Claire sat back in the passenger seat and chuckled. "He remembers you waving like a crazy person."

"He does?"

"Yeah, I think he's wondering if you're just sometimes spastic or always spastic."

"How serendious is this! It's like you're living in a movie! Guy saves girl, they fall in love, have amazing sex and—"

"And you're delusional."

"Well, I'm not the one who dreamed him up and had him magically appear, now am I? Can I have your superpower? Can we bottle destiny?"

"It's not destiny. It's just some weird coincidence." Claire watched Will exit the diner and head toward the car. "He's flying me home. Tell Jenna I'm sorry. Tell her I forgot my medication, that I spazzed out after that pill Brittney gave me."

Not a complete lie.

"If you weren't taking off with your dream guy, I'd be giving you hell right now."

"I have to go. I just didn't want you to worry. I'll call you when I get home, okay?"

"Out of one stranger's arms and into another's. I'm totally rubbing off on you."

"You guys be careful. Watch you're back."

"Bye, Mom," Laura mocked and hung up.

Claire leaned back on the headrest, letting out a breath as Will opened the door.

"I have my brother's address. Can I make a stop before we head out?" he asked.

"Of course. It's the reason you're here."

As Will started the car, Claire found it hard to keep her eyes open. Not fighting her heavy lids any longer, she leaned against the window and soon was fast asleep, dreaming of a cave that sparkled like the night sky.

NOT A DREAM

Saturday, 6:58 a.m., Las Vegas

"Go. Away!"

When another knock came from his front door, Aven groaned, rolling over in bed. He covered his head with a pillow, trying to muffle another knock, but it was no use.

"Relentless demon," he grumbled.

A moment of silence.

Aven peeked out from the pillow and exhaled with relief. More knocking.

"Just give up already," Aven mumbled against the pillow over his face. "That trick stopped working months ago."

When the security system rang out from his smart device, Aven threw the pillow across the room and glanced at his phone. "Oh, now we're playing the ol' someone's in the house trick again. Google turn off security and play 'Sympathy for the Devil,' volume twenty."

Aven folded his hands under his head and closed his eyes. He focused on the lyrics, lip syncing the words until he felt a presence. The demon had played this trick before, pretending someone was clomping up the steps. Usually he would ignore her, but the footsteps sounded real. Too real.

Snatching his gun from the hidden compartment of his bed, Aven swung around, pointing it at the figure in the doorway.

"Whoa! Hey!" The illusion held up his hands. He was male, about six foot three, late twenties, with a grown-out crew cut.

Aven narrowed his eyes to the illusion's blue eyes. Not black, nor hollow as he assumed they would be. Did the demon learn a new trick?

Curiosity stirred as Aven stood before the ghost. He had never met this man—at least, not that he could remember.

"Now, this is new." Aven tilted his head with a partial smile. "Who the hell are you?"

"What?" the illusion yelled over the noise.

"Music off."

The music ceased.

"I said," Aven repeated. "Who. The hell. Are you?"

"William Stryde."

An encounter's significant other?

Aven rubbed his stiff neck. Stress. That was the demon's favorite time to mess with him. He reached into the jeans he wore last night, realizing his phone was still on the dresser. He would text Kitten later about getting him an appointment with the masseuse. Until then, he would play his demon's game.

Will kept his hands raised and stared at the shirtless guy pointing a gun at him. Black rimmed his eyes with a wild stare. Either this guy was crazy or a drug addict. By the half-sadistic smile spreading across his brother's face, he could only assume crazy. The resemblance of his younger brother was almost identical. The dark hair, the slender nose, his build, but he quickly reminded himself it wasn't Aaron.

"And?" Aven inquired.

"And what?"

"Why are you in my room?"

"I have a letter for you."

"Oh, goody. A letter," Aven mocked.

Will reached for his gun in the back of his jeans next to the letter, but Aven shot off his past his ear. The sound of punctured glass rang out and Will stared wide-eyed at the shattered pane.

Crazy. Definitely, crazy.

"Damn," Aven said, scratching his head with the gun. "I must be drunker than I thought."

"Calm down," Will ordered with a hand out before him, the other reaching in his pocket. "Let me get the letter."

"Is this some kind of telegram? Are you going to sing?" Aven asked. He grabbed a bottle of whiskey from a dresser and smiled. "'Cause if you are, I'll need a few shots first."

Claire startled from a deep sleep and sat up. Rubbing her eyes, she shifted her blurry gaze to the driver's seat. She remembered Will and how he saved her, assumed this was his brother's house. She glanced out the window, finding a mailbox with a number on the stone casing.

808. Claire's brows furrowed.

I've seen that number before . . . but where?

Squinting, she focused on the sign at the end of the road. She mouthed the street name and fumbled for her phone beside her. Swiping through her pictures frantically, Claire stopped at the one she was looking for. Her mouth dropped open, seeing 808 in the address of Aven's license.

"You seem very real," Aven said, poking his illusion in the chest with his finger.

The illusion swatted his hand away, and Aven took several steps back, taking another swig from his bottle of liquor.

"It's a fantastic trick, but you must jog my memory of who it was. Jessica? Penelope?" Aven asked, spouting off names from the body count list. "I got it." He snapped his fingers. "It was Sharon, wasn't it? I can't lie. That was a fun night. Is that why you chose this form? The brooding husband, the broken-hearted boyfriend. Go ahead, tell me what a horrible person I am."

"I'm sorry?"

"Look, I'm exhausted, and I'm sure there's only, oh, I don't know, about thirty minutes left until daylight. So you talk, I'll drink. Who wrote the letter?"

"Your mother. She asked me to find you."

Aven clutched the gun as his stomach rolled. Nehia hadn't brought up his mother in years, and after last night, having a glimpse of light, a reminder of her from his angel, Aven wondered what it would be like to see her again. It would be easy, quick, and he could finally be with her again.

Squeezing his fingers against the hard metal, Aven gave a wry smile. "I know how to solve this little predicament," he said, putting the end of the barrel to his temple. "When I wake up, we can talk face to face, you spiteful wretch."

"No, wait!"

Aven tilted his head with narrow eyes, putting his finger on the trigger. "You do not control my dreams, I do."

"Read this before you do anything else."

With a heavy sigh, Aven lowered the gun and snatched the letter from the illusion's hand. "I still think you should sing it."

He gave the letter a quick read of the first few lines. The car accident wasn't any new information.

"As if I don't know she was dead." Aven glared. "Care to try again?"

"Our mother's not dead, but in a matter of days or hours she could be. She asked that I bring the letter to you. She's hoping you'll come see her before it's too late."

"Our mother?" Aven's lips curled. "So that makes you my brother."

"Half brother."

"Right."

"There's a picture of you with her."

Aven took out the picture and gazed at it for a long moment as emotions flooded him. He smiled at first, tears welling in his eyes, but the smile quickly melted.

It was the same picture he had always looked at as a child, the same photo he kept on him at all times, a digital copy hidden in his phone. He hadn't looked at it in years, not until now.

"So we're back to this, are we?" Aven took another swig from the whiskey bottle and slammed it on his dresser. "Using my dead mother to taunt me. Always the same old tricks."

Aven crumpled the picture into his fist, tossing it and the letter into the floor. He strode to the illusion's face, coming inches from his nose. "Jealous of the angel of music, are we?"

The illusion took a step back, looking at him as if he had lost his mind.

Mad as a hatter, Aven noted to himself and wasted no time proving it, lifting the gun to his temple again. "Abandon all hope, ye who enter here."

"Stop!" the illusion ordered.

Closing his eyes Aven pressed the gun hard and he took a deep breath. He was ready to wake up from this nightmare, ready to face the demon in her true form.

"Aven, don't!"

As Aven's eyes flew open to the familiar voice, his arm went limp and his gun thudded to the floor. He fixed his gaze on the girl braced against his bedroom door, thanking the heavens above she had come to save him from his madness.

"Claire, go back to the car." The illusion drew his gun and put her behind him.

Aven squinted, his breaths growing shallow. He ignored the gun aimed at his chest. His focus was only on his angel. No matter the number of wrinkles lining her forehead, she was still just as beautiful as she had been last night—more so without all the makeup.

My savior.

"Milady–" Aven reached out for her, but the illusion blocked the way.

"Go back into the car," his illusion ordered her again.

A sharp pain split through Aven's chest. The devil was still there, and that meant he was still asleep, that his subconscious had conjured a tether to the real world.

She's not here. She can't be. She wouldn't be.

"Bravo." Aven applauded as if insulting a badly written play. "You can both take a bow now."

"I'll be there in a minute," the illusion assured dream Claire.

"So not only are we bringing my mother into this, but my lucky charm. So what? Am I, Aven Crey, supposed to be jealous of some blonde-haired, bulging-bicep rent-a-cop?" Aven chuckled and took up the bottle from the dresser. He took several large gulps and burped. "This just can't get any better. I must have royally pissed you off, sweetie."

"Aven's your brother?" dream Claire asked, peering up at the illusion.

"You know him?" the illusion asked.

"Yeah, sort of," she answered.

"Oh, she knows me, brother, and I know her." Aven tilted his head smirking at Claire. Even if she were a ghost, he would let the demon know how much he enjoyed last night without any interruptions. "Every. Single. Inch." He gave a quick glance back to his illusion. "A wonderland."

"Thinking about last night, Princess?"

Claire averted her gaze to the ground as her cheeks burned with embarrassment.

"Obviously not long," Aven continued. "Because now," he said, wincing through a smile, "you're here with my brother."

"Come on, Claire. I'll take you home," Will said.

I can't leave him, not like this.

"My number is on the back of the envelope," Will informed his brother. "You can call me when you sober up."

"Leaving so soon?" Aven asked. "I thought you liked games. If you want to play, I'll play."

"You're not dreaming, Aven," Claire tried to assure him. "Will really is your brother. Your—your mom is dying."

"My mom died in a car accident when I was two," Aven snapped.

Claire tried to swallow the knot in her throat, remembering the conversation about his mother last night. She couldn't imagine how painful this was for him. For Will.

"Whoever told you that lied," Will argued.

"Remember what happened last time you brought up my Uncle Jimmy?"

Claire looked at Will and he gave a sideways glance, seemingly just as confused as she was.

"Fine." Aven shrugged, glancing at the shattered window. "Nearly daylight. Why don't I play you a little song, and then you go back to whatever pit in hell you reside." Aven picked up his guitar from the corner and strummed a few chords. "Any requests?" He surveyed the room as if he had an audience. "No? Alright. My choice."

Whatever deep-seated pain Aven was hiding, Claire wasn't sure. She didn't understand the need to use the mask, couldn't stand his arrogant ego, but she couldn't turn her back on him, not after what he did for her.

She took a step toward the bed, but Will grabbed her hand and pulled her back.

"Claire, don't," he cautioned.

"What are you, like her bodyguard or something?" Aven quipped.

"It's okay," Claire assured Will, slipping through his fingers. She appreciated his concern, but she had to make Aven see the truth. She was real, and she was here for him.

Taking controlled steps to the bed, she kept her gaze on his and sat. She listened to the lyrics of the song, watched him press his fingers tight against the neck of the guitar.

Music. It was the tether to their souls. It was in the way Aven plucked the strings, the way his voice rasped with each strained breath. Aven didn't have to tell her of his heartache; she felt it. Mind, body, and soul.

With one last strum, Aven opened his eyes and tucked Claire's hair behind her ear. When she leaned into his touch, he put his forehead to hers. "I wish you were real," he whispered.

Claire put her hand over his on her cheek. "I am real."

"You don't know how much I wish that was true. Because there's something I want to tell you, a secret I held back."

Aven inhaled sharply. "Last night—I had every intention of keeping my promise, but every time I looked at you, I felt myself falling. I was lost before you, Claire. Wandering in a desolate land. And then by some miracle I was found in the green field of your irises. For the first time, I felt like I could stop pretending, like I found someone that could save me from my demons. For once in my miserable existence, I don't want to wake up from a dream. If I could, I would stay here, with you, remembering that hope, bathing in the peace and warmth of your light."

He could feel her pulse racing in her neck as he pulled her closer. "If you were real, I'd make love to you all over again. Right here, right now."

Claire trembled at his soft touch.

"You're the only girl I've ever made love to. The only one that made me regret sleeping with all those women. I could sleep with hundreds more, and it would still never bandage the wound of my bleeding heart the way you did last night. I was free—I had a reason to believe in something good."

"Hundreds?" Claire drew back.

"You were honest, vulnerable." Aven wet his lips. "Now it's my turn. I'll tell you the truth, I'll tell you everything."

Aven leaned in for a kiss, but Claire slipped from his grasp. Her horror cut him deep, another wound, etched in his battered heart. The demon knew where to stick the knife. It twisted against his ribcage as Claire turned her back to him.

"There's the torture I've been waiting for."

"Come on, Claire. We're done here," the illusion said, and Aven realized he had never left.

With a swift jerk of his hand, Aven wrapped his arms around Claire and looked her dead in the eyes. "Life's a bitch and then you sleep with one." He kissed her, hard, until she shoved him back, pressing her fingers to her lips.

The illusion came to her side, putting a comforting hand on her arm. "I'll meet you at the car."

Claire looked over her shoulder and nodded while tears pooled in her eyes, and then she left the room.

Well done, devil. Almost believable.

"Now's the part where you tell me to be a good little boy and—"

"You're one sorry son of a bitch," the illusion growled in his face.

"Oh, dear, dear, brother. Is that any way to speak about our mother?"

Aven grunted as Will's knuckles cracked against his abdomen and he crumbled to the floor, gasping for a breath. The urge to vomit rose in this throat, but he held it back with a cough.

"Nice meeting you," his illusion muttered as he walked out the door. "Call me when you sober up, asshole."

Aven listened to the illusion's boots stomp down the steps as he struggled to get to his knees. Gripping onto the footboard, his gaze caught something white. Snatching the letter from the floor, he clenched his teeth and squinted at the cursive of the handwritten letter. Reading what he could make out of the font, his heart sank.

I love you, my little blackbird. May you fly home if it be the Creator's will.

The Creator. The demon would never have mentioned him.

Aven moaned, favoring his middle as he stood. He stumbled to the shattered window, finding the first light of dawn.

"Shit."

Pushing from the wall, he yanked on his black V-neck t-shirt from the floor and ran out the door. Crossing the threshold of his front door, he groaned at seeing a rental car at the end of the driveway.

"Shit!"

Aven tripped over the threshold and ran. He stumbled into his garage, huffing for breath. He caught his fall on his Porsche, scratching the cherry-red paint job with his keys. His head was swimming. Too much liquor, not enough sleep, and he had been too stupid to know reality from a dream. Revving up his bike, he snapped down a front-faced helmet and peeled out of his garage as if he was Evel Knievel.

IMPULSIVE

WILL glanced at Claire in the passenger side. She was picking her fingernails, watching the desert passing by. "Hey," he mumbled.

Sniffing, she wiped her eyes and forced a smile. "Hey."

"Are you okay?"

"Yeah." She shrugged. "I'm fine."

Anger. That wasn't the only word for how Will felt. It was a mix of emotions swirling inside of him, a storm. He sorted through them, knowing the reason for them all. All except for jealousy.

Claire wasn't his, yet he felt something stir when Aven had kissed her. He wondered if he had been overprotective, but he couldn't help himself. The compulsion to protect her, even emotionally, was unexplainable.

"Are you hungry? I figured we could grab breakfast before heading out."

"Thanks, that would be—" Claire did a double take past him.

Will looked out of his window, finding a blacked-out motorcycle beside him. "What the hell?"

Car horns blared as Aven waved his arms in the air, signaling for Will to pull over.

"Have you lost your damn mind?" Will shouted over the wind as he rolled down his window.

Aven flipped up his visor. "Pull over."

"Like hell, I will," Will shouted over the wind.

"Will—" Claire began, but a horn cut her off and Aven swerved.

"Pull. Over," Aven repeated, leaning his bike back beside the rental.

"Hang on," he said before stomping a foot on the accelerator.

"You're not going to stop?" Claire asked in a shaky voice.

"No. The guy's off his meds."

Aven dodged another car.

"Please! He's going to get himself killed!"

Will glared at Claire, but he didn't slow down. He raced against the motorcycle as it avoided more oncoming traffic, cutting in front of them. It disappeared into the distance and appeared again, its rider standing in front of it.

"Will!"

At Claire's cry, Will slammed on his brakes, jerking the steering wheel. Dust flew as they came to a whiplashing stop on the shoulder. Unbuckling, Will reached over Claire and grabbed his gun from the glove compartment. He cocked it and gave Claire a stern look while exiting the vehicle.

"Stay here," he ordered.

As Aven approached, Will drew his gun. "Stay where you are."

"I'm unarmed," Aven announced, holding up his helmet in one hand. He surrendered with the other. "I just want to talk to Claire."

"I think you've done enough talking," Will bit out. He shoved Aven back as he tried to go past him.

"Are you like her royal guard or something?" He shot a glance to Claire in the passenger seat and shouted, "So you are royalty! I knew it!" He met Will's gaze again. "Five minutes is all I ask."

Will clenched his teeth, thinking of knocking him out this time. But when he glanced over his shoulder to Claire, he found her gaze expecting.

"Two," Will said flatly.

The smug smile only fueled Will's anger as Aven brushed past him, handing off his helmet.

Claire's heart raced as Aven ran his fingers through his wild hair. She dropped her gaze, staring at the handle of the door. She couldn't face him, not after storming off the way she did.

"Hey there, Princess," Aven said, leaning through the window.

She kept her eyes on the sandy landscape, thinking of running. "You could have been killed."

"But I wasn't, was I?"

Claire's brows knitted together as she whipped around. "Are you always this impulsive?"

"Isn't that what you liked about me?"

"What do you want, Aven?"

"I apologize if I hurt you with the kiss."

She didn't say it out loud, but no, Aven hadn't hurt her. Not physically. She pressed her lips, still tasting the alcohol from his tongue. She wondered if his drunken state had caused his temporary madness.

"And when I called you that—I wasn't talking about you."

Claire looked at him.

"I would never, *ever* call you that," he said, his gaze fixed. "And If I ever hear someone do, I'll see to it they are properly dealt with."

Claire wondered who he had been talking about, but there was only one question she needed an answer to.

"Is it true? That you've slept with hundreds of women?"

"Yes."

Claire cringed and averted her gaze back out the window.

"You have nothing to worry about. I have a clean bill of health."

"These days, that's hardly believable."

"It's true. I get a checkup after every—encounter. It's like a rule for the elite club I'm in. You sign the dotted line, agree to the appointments, and take a pill. So I promise you—"

"Dotted line? Will's right. You are crazy."

"No. Just have some issues I'm dealing with."

"Does your girlfriend know about your issues?"

Aven tilted his head. "Girlfriend?"

"There was a girl looking for you this morning after you left."

Aven raised a brow. "So you met Kitten?"

Claire scoffed. "Kitten, Princess. Does every girl you sleep with have a nickname?"

"This feisty side is kinda turning me on right now."

Ugh. Hello, Alter Ego.

"I think you should go." Claire leaned against the window, hoping if she closed her eyes the conversation would end and Aven would leave.

"Claire—"

She clenched her teeth, feeling like a horrible person for wanting him to disappear. "Please?"

Aven let out a sigh as guilt weighed him down. There was no fixing this, not with Claire so far out of reach. He needed more time think, another angle. But for now, he would leave her be.

"As you wish, milady," he said with a bow.

Turning, Aven let out a throaty groan as Will shoved his helmet into his stomach.

"Are you like an MFC fighter or something?" Aven asked, favoring his middle.

"You're a real prick, you know that?" Will glared, crossing his arms.

"I concur. A total prick. My apologies, for my appalling behavior. I'm quite inebriated."

A partial lie.

Aven was intoxicated, but he didn't want to admit his high tolerance for alcohol. He could burn it faster than he could drink it. The lie would buy him some time. He had to know about his mother, had to fix things with Claire. Drunk was as good of an excuse as any to grab a cup of coffee. "Can we go down the street and grab something to eat? My treat."

"No thanks," Will said, brushing past him, heading toward the car.

"Earlier I thought I was dreaming because there's been at least six impossible things that have happened to me thus far."

Will stopped in his tracks.

"I promise you I'm not mad, I just don't always think."

Will glanced over his shoulder. "Then you shouldn't talk."

Aven grinned as Will replied with a quote from their mother's favorite book: *Alice's Adventures in Wonderland.* A classic with no religious undertones, no morals, or so the government thought.

To dream the impossible, you have to first believe it, even if it's just a little.

"What do you say, brother?"

Will glanced at his watch. "You've got one hour."

DEATH IS PATIENT

CLAIRE followed Will and Aven into the diner, her senses elated by the sound and smell of sizzling bacon. She scanned the row of bodies at the bar, glancing at their plates. The sight of biscuits and gravy, scrambled eggs, and hash browns made her stomach gurgle. She hadn't eaten anything since the chocolate raspberry cheesecake last night and was dying for sustenance.

Coming out of the kitchen, Claire's gaze darted to a middle-aged woman with dark brown skin, singing as if she had a choir behind her. She stopped, her eyes lighting up as she saw Aven.

"Hey sugah! When you said tomorrow, I thought you meant tomorrow, not today!"

"I'm full of surprises, aren't I?" Aven gleamed.

"Go sit down, baby. I'll be there shortly," she told him, wiping her flour-covered hands on her apron.

As Aven led Claire to a table and pulled out a chair for her, Will headed for the restroom sign.

Mumbling thank you, Claire sat and leaned over the table to look at the menu—a real menu made of paper.

She glanced up after a moment, feeling Aven's eyes boring through her. "I'm not in the mood for a staring contest right now."

"Are you two like a thing?" Aven asked.

"What?"

"You and my brother."

"Will?"

"Yes, Sir William. The knight that shielded you from the evil villain."

"I've only known him for a few hours."

"A lot can happen in a few hours."

Claire raised the menu in front of her face, avoiding his charming grin.

"Well then," Aven said, peeking over it. "if he's not courting you, that means I can."

Claire lowered the menu and leaned in. "You have a girlfriend."

"I would like to ask you to a ball. There will be dancing, champagne, caviar."

Claire leaned back and crossed her arms with an irritated sigh. "I don't like caviar."

"Fine. I'll tell them to bring animal crackers, whatever you want."

Claire shook her head. "Sorry, can't do. I'm heading home after breakfast."

A rumble came from Claire's stomach, and she remembered her and Will's conversation on the way to the diner. No matter how hungry she had been when Will had told her about Aven's offer for breakfast, Claire had requested he drop her off. Will refused, said it wasn't safe to be alone at the condemned gas station she pointed to. No matter how much Claire had tried to convince him Laura would be back in a few hours to pick her up, Will wouldn't budge and promised to fly her home as soon as they ate. He also assured her it wasn't "weird" that she came, although to Claire, the situation couldn't be anymore awkward.

"Please, Princess."

Stupid Ego.

Claire stood up and shoved her chair under the table, hitting Aven in the knee on purpose. "I'm not your Princess."

Will pulled out a chair across Aven, giving him a look after seeing the knee incident. "Did you bring up the hundreds of women you've slept with again?"

"No." Aven grunted. "But I can assume it's still bothering her. Explains the judgy little eyes. Oh, you have them too. How cute."

"Don't like to be called out on your bullshit, do you?"

"Do you kiss our mother with that mouth?"

"Do you need another reason to end up on the floor?"

"Oh, I get it. You're diabetic. I, on the other hand, am hypoglycemic." Aven lifted the menu to his face. "S.T.A.R.V.E.D."

It was the paper menus that caught Will off guard, not Aven's ability to shrug off a threat. No eating establishments used real menus anymore, not for centuries. He slid the menu away, deciding his stomach could only handle a cup of coffee.

Aven kept his menu up, peeking over the edge. "Why is a raven like a writing desk?"

"Is this how you communicate with everyone?"

"I'm sure you know the answer." Aven smiled, laying down the menu. "But did you know she named me Aven because it rhymes?"

"Did you know she hates drunks?"

"When we get there, are you going to tattle on me?"

"She's dealt with enough. She doesn't need a stumbling dumbass by her side as she takes her last breaths."

"Okay, yes. I may have a slight drinking problem, but I think I can manage to stay sober during my visit."

Out of the corner of his eye, Will spotted Claire coming back from the restroom with a flushed face and a damp hairline. He watched her exhale a controlled breath, trying to avoid Aven's gaze as she sat beside him.

Will opened his mouth to continue his and Aven's conversation but was quickly distracted by a woman singing. The tune and lyrics were from a hymn his mother used to sing to him at bedtime when he was a boy.

"Aven, honey, I'm not used to seeing you with new friends," the woman said, pouring water in the empty glasses on the table. She glanced at Will and then at Claire. "Why don't you introduce me?"

"Paula, it just so happens that friend right there is my brother."

"Half-brother," Will noted.

"Will?" the woman asked, placing a hand on her chest.

Will met Paula's worried expression, wondering why she looked at him as if he was a lost puppy that had just been found.

"My, my child. I haven't seen you since you were . . . I mean"—she held out her hand—"I'm Paula."

"Will Stryde," he said, shaking it, although the words "haven't seen you since" made him wonder if they had somehow met before.

"Nice to meet you, baby."

"And this is Claire." Aven gestured.

"You are such a beautiful young lady."

"Thank you." Claire shook Paula's hand bashfully.

"Bright smile. I like that. Oh! Aven!" Paula poked him. "Is this the same Claire you were talkin' about this mornin'?"

Aven cleared his throat and handed Paula the menu. "I'll have my usual. And the number six with orange juice."

Paula smiled and shook her head, taking a pen from her ear to jot down the order. "Pancakes *and* the number six? You know it comes with pancakes."

"My usual is for Claire. She has a thing for chocolate." Aven winked at Claire.

"And for you, honey?" Paula didn't look up as she scribbled on the pad.

"Coffee, black, please," Will said, politely.

Paula nodded and headed to the kitchen as Aven put his napkin in his lap, and Claire's in hers.

"Now," he said, lacing his fingers, "about Mom."

Paula came back, sitting their drinks on the table. As Aven slid his milk in front of Claire, Paula lingered, setting up their silverware as if stalling to listen to their conversation.

"She's dying," Will began. "I think she's staying alive to see you. She told me there was something important she had to tell you. I have room on my plane if you want to ride with us."

"Where and when exactly?" Aven asked.

"Johns Island, South Carolina," Will informed her. "After breakfast. I promised to take Claire home first."

As Paula rushed to help a customer, Will wondered why he had caught wiping her eyes as she sniffed and walked away.

"Georgia is on the way." Aven wiggled his brows at Claire.

Watching Aven smile the way he did at Claire, Will knew there had been more than casual sex between them, and Aven was making that clear—not only with his remarks but in how he touched her at every opportunity. Fire lit Will's neck, watching Aven stare at her. He didn't know why he was jealous. There was no history between him and Claire, none other than him saving her. Still, it bothered him Aven was coming across so possessive. "Are you coming with us or not?" he asked.

"I'd prefer to take my private jet. Claire, you can ride with me."

"Alright!" Paula said with a tray filled with steaming food. "The number six and my famous chocolate chip pancakes." She put a hand on her hip and raised her brows to Will. "You sure I can't get you anything to eat, sugar?"

"I'm fine, thank you." Will smiled politely. His attention was brought back to Claire, who stared at her plate of pancakes. He could tell she was hungry but couldn't figure out why she wouldn't eat. Aven took his knife and fork and leaned over to cut up her food.

"Don't be shy, Claire," Aven said. He stabbed a few pieces and held them up as if she was a helpless toddler.

Claire took the fork from his hand with a light jerk and ate the bite, not bothering to look up.

"So how'd you two meet?" Aven asked, resting his hand on the back of Claire's chair. He kept his gaze fixed on her, waiting for her to answer.

Claire gazed at Will thoughtfully. "He saved my life."

There it was again. The spark, the tug.

"She was being mugged," Will said, ignoring the skipping of his heart.

"Crime these days." Aven shook his head, stabbing his eggs and sausage. "Evil running rampant in the streets. Which hotel?"

"MGM."

"My cousin owns that one. I'll get him to send the footage to the police."

When the bell on the door rang out, a chill slithered down Will's spine. He glanced at Aven who seemed to tense and to Claire who paused from a bite of her food. Something was wrong, he could feel it, but he didn't know what. He had a sense about these things but told himself it was nothing until Aven spoke.

"And speaking of evil." Aven tossed his napkin over his plate and leaned back. "Make that seven impossible things."

Will watched the dark-haired beauty walk over to the table. She wore skin-tight leathers and black high heels. They clacked against the floor as she peeled her riding gloves from her fingers with a sly smile playing on her lips. Will then looked at her face.

She reminded him of a 1950's movie star with her thick, wavy, black hair. Her eyelids were traced in thick charcoal eyeliner. Her full lips had been painted bright red.

"Hello, Aven," she said, standing beside him. "What a lovely surprise."

Aven stood as if it was expected, slipping his hands in his pockets. "Hello Ms. Delaroche. What brings you to Vegas?"

"If you had come to the party last night, you would know I was the guest of honor." Her smile grew deviant as her gaze went over Aven's shoulder to Claire. "Who are your friends?"

Stepping to the side, Aven gestured to Will, who stood. "Bree Delaroche, this is Will Stryde. Will, Bree."

Will nodded and shook her hand. They were soft but fiery hot to the touch.

"A pleasure," she said in a silky voice.

"And this is Claire Grace."

Claire stood and politely put out her hand and shook, but as she tried to pull away, her brows furrowed as Bree held on to her hand.

"Such natural beauty. You look as graceful and clear as your name. Talent in your fingers and your toes. Dancer and musician?"

Claire's throat bobbed, and her gaze darted to Will.

"Vincent was wondering what had become of you, but I can see you were busy. I was going to ask if you would be my date for the gala tonight." Bree grinned, tracing her finger along Aven's shoulder.

"Oh, that's a shame. I already have a date. Right, Claire?"

Claire took one look at Aven, and then Bree. "Um, would you excuse me?" she said, putting her chair under the table. She headed to the bathroom swiftly without another word.

"Is it just me or does she go to the bathroom a lot?" Aven asked Will. "Do you have a bathroom on the plane?"

"Are you staying in town long?" Bree asked Will.

Paula approached, narrowing her eyes at Bree.

"No, I'll be heading back home here shortly."

"Don't be so sure," Bree said to him.

Will gave her a wary stare.

"But you still have time. Death is patient." She set her gaze to Aven. "And so am I."

"See you tonight." Bree kissed Aven on the cheek then leaned into his ear. "Tell tiny dancer I said goodbye."

As Bree left, the bell on the door chimed. Will watched Paula dab something oily from her fingers on the frame. He didn't know what she was doing but could see her mouth something with her eyes closed.

Was she praying?

He brought his gaze back to Aven, who shoved his hands in his pockets. "Your friend, Bree, is—"

"Intense?" Aven asked, tapping his phone. "Don't bother. She's not your type. Believe me."

"I wasn't—" Will began. He cut his words short, watching Claire as she came back from the bathroom. He took notice of her damp hair as she rubbed her forehead.

"Claire?" Aven pointed with his thumb behind him as she came to the table. "Chocolate pie for the road?"

Claire looked in the direction of the bar to the dish, covering the fluffy meringue. "No, thank you," she answered.

Aven put a toothpick in his mouth and went to Paula. She frowned, pointing out the door, then shook her finger at him. He seemed to say something that appeased her before kissing her on the cheek.

As Will followed Aven and Claire to the door, he paused to thank Paula for the food, but before he could mutter a word, she spoke.

"What's Kate sick with?"

Will batted his eyes, wondering how she knew his mother's name. "Cancer," he muttered.

"The disease of grief. It eats away at ya. All these years I worried about her, wondered how she was. I've been looking after Aven just like she asked. Did the best I could anyhow."

"You knew she was alive?"

"No. Not for years. I grieved with Aven at her funeral, held that baby's hand as he wept. When Kate came back to Vegas to see me, you were a little boy. Your mama was pregnant with your baby brother, Aaron. Is he with her while you're here?"

"No, he's—she has a hospice nurse," Will answered, trying to wrap his head around all this new information. There were so many secrets, so many questions he had. He didn't ask them. He only listened.

"Kate made me promise I would never tell Aven she was alive. Said it wasn't safe. She gave me the Wonderland book and a picture of her and Aven at the piano. She told me his uncle Jimmy would let Aven come visit me, said he asked for the formula as a trade. His terms were that she disappear and that your father close all the cases on the Creys. After she told me all of that I hugged her, gave you a lollipop, rubbed her belly, and gave my word to watch over Aven. As soon as I overheard ya'll talkin', I was praisin' the Creator above. It was on his timin', but finally, they'll be together again."

"Aven hasn't given me an answer."

"Well, you better convince him. That boy needs his mama. He's got himself in a mess."

"What do you mean?"

"He's not a bad person, Will. He is Kate's son. But he's also a Crey. There's a war inside that boy, always has been, ever since he was little. He needs the light to guide him home, to show him the path that leads to his redemption."

Will's heart stopped.

Redemption.

It was the same exact word his mother had used.

"We choose good or we choose evil," Paula said. "There is no standing on the sidelines. Understand?"

"Yes, ma'am."

Paula wiped her tears before reaching into her pocket. "Tell Katy bug that Paula sends her love." She handed Will a lollipop and smiled. "May Aramis be with you child. I'll be praying."

"Aramis?"

"Baby"—Paula grinned wide, placing a hand on her hip—"don't you know the Creator's true name?"

Claire was as grateful for the silence between her and Aven. She was still shaken up by what she had experienced when Bree had touched her. The words echoed in her mind, over and over with an eerily familiar, silky voice.

My, my, Truth Keeper. You sound more like an outcast than a saint.

"You never gave me an answer," Aven said, interrupting the vision.

Claire blinked from her daze. "About what?"

"The ball. I apologize. I didn't have time to send a formal letter."

"I don't have anything to wear."

"You will. I have a fairy godmother."

Claire rolled her shoulders and rubbed her neck. She blamed the pinching pain on how she had slept in the car, but deep down she knew it was from all the tension between her and Aven.

"Just ignore Bree. She likes to get under people's skin."

"She didn't get under mine."

Aven leaned down to whisper in her ear. "You're not a very good liar."

Claire crossed her arms and took a step back, ignoring how much his words felt like déjà vu. "Is she your girlfriend too?"

Aven let out a light laugh. "No."

"Did you and her ever—"

"I know you're not fond of black. How about red?"

"Red what?"

"Gown, of course. For tonight."

"I'm not going to be any part of your cheat—"

"We should go ahead and get an early start," Will said, coming out of the door.

Aven wrinkled his forehead. "I need more time."

"She doesn't have time," Will pointed out.

"As Bree said, I have a gala I have to attend tonight. Some very important people will be there. If I don't show they will be quite disappointed. And so will my cousin, who is also my boss. And I really want to make partner. Twenty-four hours is all I ask."

Will crossed his arms. "I need to get Claire home."

"I'll call Laura," Claire interjected. "She can come pick me up."

"Then who will be my date?" Aven cut in.

"I'm not leaving you anywhere alone in this town," Will told her.

"But—" Claire stuttered.

"What time do we need to be ready?" Will asked Aven.

"I'll have the limo pick you up at six," Aven said, tapping on his phone. "I'll book you a room at a hotel."

"I have a room." Will glanced at Claire. "With two beds."

Aven's lips drew into a cunning smile, and he headed toward his bike but swiveled on his toes. "Oh, if you need to reach me, Claire has my number."

"No." Claire tucked her hair behind her ear. "I um, deleted it."

"Ouch. You get over people quick don't you, Princess? Take that as a warning, brother."

As Aven revved his bike, Claire's heart raced. She turned to Will to try to convince him she would be fine waiting on Laura but flinched as her phone vibrated in her pocket. She glanced at the number and rolled her eyes as she answered it. "Hello, Aven."

"Hello, gorgeous."

HARBINGER

CLAIRE followed Will into his hotel room and glanced around. It felt so small compared to Aven's penthouse suite. She walked past the beds, and then looked out the window. Without the bright lights, Vegas appeared dull; at least, from this view.

"Do you want to get in the shower?"

Claire's eyes darted to Will. "I'm sorry?"

"A shower. I was going to have one, but I thought—"

"Oh! You mean you, not us." Claire laughed nervously until she thought of something. "Do I need one?" she asked, sniffing her hair. It still smelled like gasoline with a hint of Aven's cologne.

Will's lips drew up slightly. "No. I was being courteous."

"Oh. Um. You go ahead. I don't want to use up the hot water."

"I'm used to cold showers."

Claire's brows rose.

"My unit was stationed in the desert when I served. It's a habit."

Claire pressed her lips as Will unzipped his duffle bag. She watched him get out his neatly folded clothes and place them in a drawer. He also got out a small bag she assumed was for toiletries.

"Which desert?"

"One with sand."

Claire sat on the bed, thinking of how Will was always avoiding questions about himself. She scolded herself in her mind, thinking of how fortunate she was never having to be drafted for the war. Before the worldwide peace treaty was signed, hundreds had been drafted, including her older brother. She remembered watching the bloodbath on social media several years ago, looking for him, hoping he would survive.

Top techies from all over the world were recruited and offered thousands of dollars to film the front lines. The feed was always on, always live. They edited nothing, never cut the sound of gunfire, or the screams of injured soldiers as they burned while running away from the blazes of the bombs.

Everyone talked about World War E. The E was short for entertainment. It made Claire sick.

How could such a horrible thing be entertainment to people?

During her senior year, she remembered how Laura and her whole class watched the bloodshed as if it was some TV drama. Claire couldn't stomach it, knowing her brother was on the other side of the screen among the soldiers. He survived three months of the field before a landmine almost took his life.

If it hadn't been for InfiniCorp, he would have never been able walk again.

Claire glanced up at Will, but he was typing on his cell phone. "It must have been really rough over there."

When Will lifted his head, she thought she saw a hint of pain lingering in his eyes. He parted his mouth to speak, but he said nothing. He only turned and looked out the window. Claire gazed at his reflection in the glass. It seemed as if he was trying to hold back from tearing up, keeping his emotion of anger and resentment buried. She could tell the things he had experienced and still haunted him, so she refrained from asking any more questions.

Will didn't hear the lock of the bathroom door. He was too consumed by his thoughts, searching for a way to make the images stop. Willing himself to exit the horrors of the past, he sent his message to Olivia over the phone. She replied quickly, telling him that his mother was comfortable but sleeping more than usual.

Death is patient.

Lying on the bed, he concentrated on his breathing, but it was a hopeless attempt to slow his heart rate. He couldn't get past the guilt, couldn't vanquish the images of the lifeless body beside him. He again felt the slick blood between his fingers, heard the gunfire getting closer, but then it faded as he closed his eyes and drifted off to sleep.

Combing her fingers through her damp hair, Claire came out of the bathroom, tying a hotel robe around her waist. She parted her lips to tell Will the bathroom was free, but when she glanced up at the window, he wasn't there.

She thought to wake Will as she stood over him, watching the rise and fall of his hands on his chest, but she didn't. She assumed he hadn't slept a wink since he had been in Vegas looking for Aven.

Then, as if she was in a dream, Will's face seemed to glow. The brightness from him grew, and before she knew it, she was sitting on a chaise lounge. He was lying in her lap, sleeping soundly. She glanced around the room, seeing a desk, bookshelves, and huge round windows. They looked similar to the one Laura had taken pictures of from a cruise. But out of these windows, Claire didn't see the ocean.

There were no clouds, no land or sea that she could find, only a vast darkness and gleaming stars. Somehow, Claire knew she was on some kind of spaceship, drifting through an endless space. Pressing a hand to the glass, her eyes reflected the backdrop of nebulas and a vista of vivid colors in every shade.

Pain shot through the back of Claire's skull, waking to a bright light. Squinting through the lamplight, her gaze met a towel, and the defined tight lines of Will's abdomen.

"I'm sorry," Claire mumbled, sitting up startled.

"For?" Will asked.

Claire's cheeks burned as she remembered the time she had accidently walked into the boy's locker room her sophomore year of high school. "For not telling you I was out of the shower."

"Do you need to get back in there before I shave?" Will asked, grabbing his toiletry bag.

Shaving. Claire covered her legs, remembering how she grumbled to herself in the shower about not having a razor. "Nope. I'm good. I'll just wait for you here. I mean, I'll wait until you're done."

Will picked up a garment bag hanging in the open closet and put it over his shoulder. "Yours is in there too."

Claire gave Will a puzzled look but stood and went to the closet as he walked into the bathroom and shut the door. She gazed at the slick black bag for a long moment and a white paper rose pinned on it. Aven. He must have had their formal attire delivered.

With a sigh, Claire took a step back and chewed the inside of her cheek. She didn't want any more of Aven's apologies, or worse, egotistical lines. Not after finding out he had a girlfriend, maybe more than one. With a groan, Claire snatched the rose off the garment bag and carefully unfolded the origami note, reading the calligraphy.

Your Majesty,

It's no use in going back to yesterday because I was a different person then.

However, I hope this atones for my trespasses so I can keep my head and delight you with a dance.

Claire couldn't help but smile. Not only had he quoted Lewis Carroll, but also in his own way, he had apologized for how he had acted. She couldn't go back to yesterday either. Everything about Vegas had changed her. She had never been the type of person to do all the things she had last night, and here she was, with yet another stranger in a hotel room. Morals. If she ever had them, they were leaving her little by little.

Her phone rang, and Claire yelped as the pin from the rose pricked her finger. She sucked on the tender spot, finding Laura's name on the caller ID.

"I can't talk right now."

"Is your mom okay?"

Startling panic shot through Claire. "What do you mean? What happened?"

"Didn't you hear about that earthquake in New Jersey? Like, New York even got hit. It's all over the news."

Claire grabbed the remote on the nightstand and turned on the TV. Her heart raced as she flipped the channels until she found the local news.

"The earthquake hit a 4.0 on the Richter scale," the news announcer reported. "Seismologists assure the citizens of the northeast they have nothing to worry about. The tsunami warning for the coast is still in effect until noon."

Claire put Laura on speaker and messaged her mom. "Did you call her?"

"No dummy. She's your mom. That's why I called you. This is some freaky shit. An earthquake on the east coast. That's like weird."

"It's probably nothing," Claire tried to assure herself. "They had a minor one last year."

"What if that Nibo stuff is true? You remember learning about it in class? That red planet that pulls Earth's gravity and— hey you never sent me pictures of your hot-ass flyboy."

She swore Laura had ADD. She showed all the classic signs according to her therapist. "You actually paid attention in class?"

"Mr. Brent was a very good at teaching, and other things."

"Gross. It's not Nibo. It's Nibiru, and I'll give you all the details about Will later. I saw an eyeful of him a minute ago."

"You've already seen him naked?" Laura screeched. "How big is his—"

"Laura! You don't need to know the size of everyone's—"

"Yes, I do!"

"He was in a towel!"

Claire's phone vibrated in her hand. It was her mother, assuring her everyone was fine but a bit shaken up. Claire rolled her eyes at her mother's pun, sending a message that she loved her, and she was glad she was safe.

"Mom's fine," Claire informed her.

"I'm glad she's okay. I'm kinda irritated at you, though."

"Why? What did I do?"

"Hello? Details. You keep leavin' me hangin'!"

"I'll tell you all about the gala when I get back."

"Gala who?"

"A charity ball."

"A ball!"

As Laura screamed, Claire held the phone from her ear until Laura's voice was at a semi-normal pitch. "You're Cinderella!"

"Seems that way doesn't it?"

"Gah! I hate you right now! You're going to a ball with your Prince Charming!

"Actually, I'm going with Aven, which from this note, yeah, he's masquerading as a prince."

"Wait, both of them are going? I really did rub off on you!"

Claire stared at the garment bag, wondering what style of dress was inside. She then found another bag in the closet and unzipped it. Inside was a change of clothes, a cosmetic bag, and everything she would need to prepare for the event.

She sorted through the makeup, finding her favorite brand of coconut lotion and stared at it until the faucet from the bathroom went silent.

"I have to go. I'll talk to you soon." Claire hung up, not bothering to say goodbye. When Will stepped out of the bathroom, Claire's mouth parted slightly, in awe of his transformation. He was clean-shaven, hair combed back and in a tuxedo that fit his form perfectly.

Claire wet her suddenly dry lips and swallowed. "You look, um, nice. Really nice."

"Thanks." Will appeared almost shy in his response. "I'll be downstairs. The limo is supposed to pick us up in thirty minutes."

"I'll be down shortly," Claire assured him, taking her new things with her to the bathroom.

Will picked up the remote to turn off the TV before heading out of the room, but as his finger touched the power button, he paused. Listening to the news about the earthquake sparked something in his memory, something he thought had been from a dream. He remembered when he had woken in the middle of the night, how he thought he could still feel the tremors. There was no question in his mind as the pictures of the destruction scrolled across the screen. He had seen this all before.

FOR A GOOD
CAUSE

CLAIRE lifted her sparkling red sequin dress nervously as she walked into the ballroom mansion. Arm in arm with Aven, she tightened her grip, leaning on him for support. She had yet to adjust to the high heels and bit her lip, concentrating on each step.

Aven ushered her to the middle of the room as if eager to make small talk with the clamoring socialites. Claire recognized them all. Celebrities and rock stars passed by, so close that she could have reached out and touched them. She smiled politely as Aven introduced her to a well-known movie star, dressed in a trendy suit, wearing stylish sunglasses. In the back of her mind, she promised to get pictures for Laura when the socialites weren't looking.

As the men talked about the event and how much money was donated, Claire's attention was drawn to the sparkling chandelier, glinting brilliantly against the ceiling. She was comforted by it, and yet a nervous tinge crept up her neck.

Her mind strained as she tried to remember why it seemed so familiar. She had never seen a chandelier before, but it was as if her mind brought a memory to her. She saw a cozy room walled with bookshelves, a desk by the window, and a plush rug with a golden emblem. Claire took a step back trying to make out the image, but it faded, replaced by a glossy floor.

"Claire Grace," Aven said, interrupting her thoughts.

Still in a daze, she took the celebrity's hand, shaking it. The movie star nodded with a smile and told her it was a pleasure to make her acquaintance, adding that Aven was a very lucky man.

"I'm going to get us some drinks," Aven said, slipping his arm away from Claire's. "Don't talk to any strangers until I get back. The artists are safe but the rest, well, I wouldn't doubt they would try to steal you away from me."

"Don't worry," Claire assured him. "I learned about stranger danger when I was five."

Kitten pulled her gaze from Aven, finding a familiar face at the open bar. Nick.

Trying to catch her breath, she turned back to the table of hors d'oeuvres, putting macaroons on a napkin. She rolled her eyes at a bowl filled with animal crackers, knowing Aven had requested them for Claire.

"No matter what anyone says that stuff is disgusting," she told Will, making a face at the black fish eggs. She pointed to the cucumber sandwiches. "They look fancy, but they're not. Want some fruit?"

She walked around the table, putting a few strawberries on her napkin. When Will didn't answer, she glanced up and followed his gaze. He was watching Claire's every move, had hardly taken his eyes off her since she came down the staircase of their hotel. He had got up to walk to her, but Aven had beat him to it. It was clear to Kitten, Will had already fallen for her, just as Aven had.

"She looks beautiful, doesn't she?" Kitten asked.

Will didn't respond.

Kitten swallowed the chewed-up cake and crumpled the napkin in her hand. "I'm going to go get us something to drink. What do you like? Wine? Jack and Coke?

Will scrunched his brows and met her gaze. "Water."

"Water?"

"Yes, please."

Kitten dusted the sugary crumbs from her palms and tossed the napkin in the trash. "Okay. Water it is."

Will eyed the shady socialites until he found Claire again. She was looking at the artwork, talking to the children standing by their work. Following her, he casually went to the largest painting in the room. He read the cards, finding that all of artwork had been done by young children. All but one.

He studied the abstract painting, wondering what the artist was thinking when he had chosen the dark colors. It was brushed with blue-black, dripping with a hue of crimson, as if blood had spattered on the canvas in the struggle of a heinous crime. His eyes darted to the corner, finding the name Crey brushed in a deep red.

"Some say art is a reflection of one's soul," a deep voice said.

Will turned, finding a man with jet-black hair combed back, holding a glass of champagne.

"It's an interesting piece." Will held back from touching the dried paint as he narrowed his eyes on the frozen red tears. Flashes came to his mind of bloody bodies, mangled on the ground as the dust cleared. Dried blood was on their faces, caused by his hands. He swallowed and blinked from the memory as the man took a step forward, gesturing with his hand.

"Vincent Crey. Aven's cousin."

Will shook his hand. "Will Stryde."

"Stryde. A pleasure to meet your acquaintance. An artist is always grateful to hear someone admires their work."

"It's yours?"

"You assumed it was Aven's?" Vincent grinned. "My dear cousin spends his time with keys and strings, not brushes. Do you paint?"

"I did. I haven't been able to in some time."

"Because of your mother. I'm sorry to hear she is sick. I gave Aven leave for the trip, although I must ask he return before next week. We are scheduled for a trip to Asia."

"Katharine mentioned you will be providing free health care there."

Vincent smiled and took a drink. "After Asia, everyone in the world will have access to our medicine. Soon, greedy government crooks won't be able to rob anyone of their health."

There was silence between the men as Will gazed at the canvas again. Past the dried red paint, Will thought he saw numbers. They were very faint, as if they were meant to be hidden. He studied them and before his eyes, they moved across the canvas, forming the words, "The End Is Near."

"Is the young lady going with you as well?"

Will brought his attention back to Vincent quickly, trying to ignore what he saw. "Yes, I'll be flying her home first. She was stranded here in Vegas after—"

"After her night with Aven."

Will nodded.

"He's taken quite a liking to her. He seems different. Perhaps because the young woman is unlike the other girls he partakes in every night."

"Every night?"

"My dear cousin has a problem. An obsession if you will."

"I'm not sure I follow."

"He's a womanizer, Mr. Stryde."

Will's mouth went dry. He knew by Aven's confession he had slept with a lot of women, but he assumed hundreds was an exaggeration. Now, he wasn't so sure.

"I've been trying to get him help." Vincent sighed. "But he refuses. It's a shame. I would hate to see him sent to a counseling center against his will."

"Always a new girl?"

"Yes. A shiny new toy to play with when he gets bored with the last."

Clenching his teeth, Will looked over Vincent's shoulder at Claire. The urge to go to her overwhelmed him. He parted his mouth, ready to excuse himself until Vincent's next words struck a nerve.

"Do you know what it's like to have an addiction, Mr. Stryde?"

Claire politely smiled at people beside her but avoided making conversation with the strangers Aven had teased her to be aware of. These people had money and lots of it. She was a simple girl who didn't know what it was like to live such a lavish lifestyle. Staring at the women in the room, she became self-conscious. All of them were stunning, adorned with diamonds and jewels that glinted as they laughed and drank.

Following in line with the crowd of people, Claire paused at a painting that set her soul on fire. The scene's backdrop was filled with galaxies and stars. Waterfalls cascading off the edge of a floating land disappeared into clouds. In the distance of the green lush hills was a crystal castle. It seemed to gleam, twinkle as if calling to her, whispering her to remember she was once there.

"This is so beautiful," Claire said to a little girl. The child's sky-blue eyes were fixed on Claire, but she didn't say a word.

"Abigail?" the little girl's mother softly scolded, placing a hand gently on her daughter's shoulder.

"Thank you," the little girl said, blinking.

"You painted this all by yourself?" Claire asked, astonished that a child of her age could paint such a distinct landscape.

"Yes, I've seen this in my dreams," Abigail replied, looking over her shoulder to the canvas.

"I wish I could dream of something so beautiful."

The little girl took a step forward and gazed up at her with a sweet smile. "Maybe you have."

GIFTED

AVEN watched Claire make conversation with the child as he waited for his drink order. Thoughts of children had never crossed his mind until that moment. In fact, he had never thought of his future at all. He had always assumed he would be a bachelor, living his life alone—always entertaining, always haunted.

Looking at Claire, he imagined what it would be like to have a family of his own. His thoughts traveled from being alone to dancing with Claire, teaching their children piano or guitar, tucking them in, and kissing them goodnight before heading to bed to make love to her.

He blinked. That wasn't him. That would never be his life, not if he was cursed. Putting the thoughts in the back of his mind, Aven listened closely to the conversation of the colleagues next to him. Picking apart their Italian, he smiled.

"Want to make a bet on how many times she's going to fidget with that dress?" Nathan, a short young man with brown hair and brown eyes, asked.

"Fifty says at least two more times," Nick, Aven's cousin, remarked.

"Eighty. She'll do it all night," Aven cut in, speaking their language.

Nick's dark brown eyes darted to Aven and then to Claire again.

"Aven," Nick said in English. "I assume you know her."

"I do."

"If you haven't ruined her already, you'll have to introduce me," Nick teased, putting his hands in his pockets, trying to copy Aven. "She must have just been initiated. What Circle is she in?"

"No Circle," Aven informed him.

"Then she's a donor or—" Nick began.

"She's been paid," Nathan jeered, glancing around the room at some of the women who clearly had been.

"Too bad you can't afford a mere five minutes with her," Aven poked. He was toying with them and he enjoyed every minute of it.

"Jealous of my big cock?" Nick taunted in Italian.

"You act as if you have one," Aven shot back in the same tongue. "Have you ever *not* paid a woman to sleep with you?"

"Bastardo."

"And the wolf in sheep's clothing bares his teeth," Aven noted in English.

"Does she know about your little *problema*?"

Aven narrowed his eyes.

"I'll take that as a no." Nick grinned. "Poor girl. Just another innocent victim of Aven Crey's *ossessione.*"

"Enjoy your visit, Nick," Aven said, taking his drinks. "From what Vincent says, it will be *breve.*"

Turning his back to Nick, Aven made his way to Claire but stopped as Kitten passed him.

"Katharine," Aven reproached.

She looked over her shoulder, rolling her eyes. "What? I'm getting a drink for Will."

"Don't talk to Nick."

"Okay Dad," she grumbled and walked off toward the bar.

Claire was rendered speechless. The child's words rang like a bell in her mind, tugging at her thoughts.

Maybe you have.

Images of a crystal kingdom swirled in Claire's brain until the woman gestured for her hand.

"I'm Cynthia. This is my daughter, Abigail."

Claire blinked from her daze and shook the offered hand before her. "Claire Grace. Hello, Abigail. It's nice to meet you," Claire said, but the little girl's attention was on the crowd.

"Abby's not ignoring you." Cynthia glanced at her daughter with a half-hearted smile. "She's over-stimulated. A sensory issue due to her autism."

"I have a cousin a few years older than Abigail on the spectrum," Claire informed her.

"Oh, then you understand."

"I'm surprised she is doing so well. My little cousin would have had a full-blown meltdown from the lights and people talking by now."

"We plan to leave before the auction. Abigail can cope with all of this for a little while, but when she's had enough, she's had enough."

"Are most of these children savants?" Claire glanced at the children in the orchestra. They hadn't missed a beat of Tchaikovsky's *Sleeping Beauty*.

"No. Which doesn't seem to help with the stigma of autism. To be honest, many of the children here are disabled."

"Yes, I see some in wheelchairs. Are they sick?"

"Some, unfortunately, but they are getting better thanks to the Solace trials."

"Solace?"

"InfiniCorp's latest medicine. It not only cures diseases, but also prevents them. It's very expensive. That's why Vincent holds these charities. He wants everyone in the world to be healthy. But the FDA doesn't approve. That's why Vincent has been going to other countries while Solace is still in trials here in America."

"Mommy, you're making her light go away," Abby interrupted, tugging Cynthia's dress with a whine.

"My light?" Claire asked, looking herself over.

The shy little girl that could have been a clone of Shirley Temple stood in front of Claire and gazed up at her. "Are you an angel?"

Claire squatted down, eye level with her. "No," she answered sweetly. "I'm not an angel."

Abby looked disappointed. "Are you sure? Because your light is very bright," she said, pointing at Claire's shoulder.

Claire looked at her shoulder and then at her right arm, confused. "My light?"

The little girl's mother took a step forward and gave Abigail a warning look. "Abby, we talked about this."

"I wish you could see it, Mommy. Her glow is white."

"I'm sorry," her mother said.

Claire rose, her knees aching from bending down so long. "It's okay."

"Every time she looks at that man over there, she lights up like the star on a Christmas tree."

Claire looked to where Abigail pointed. Aven was talking to an associate but met Claire's eyes with his charming smile. Claire flushed with heat as he stared.

"There it is!" Abigail pointed to Claire face. "Is he your boyfriend?"

Claire put a hand to her cheek and laughed. She didn't know what to tell this little girl. Adult relationships were complicated. "Does he have a light?"

"Only when he looks at you. I think he's sad, but you make him happy."

"Oh . . ." Claire glanced at Aven again. "Why do you think he's sad?"

"I think it's that scary shadow lady beside him."

Claire's heart stopped, thinking of the fire, of her own scary demon. "Shadow lady?"

"Abigail. Remember what we talked about."

"Does she watch TV shows about this kind of thing? She's very—"

"Inquisitive?" Cynthia raised a brow.

Claire smiled with a nod and bent down again to be eye level with Abby. "Are there other people with light in the room?"

Abigail searched the faces over Claire's shoulder. "No. But they could be bright if they wanted to. If they were good."

"Abby," her mother chided.

"You and that man over there are very bright—brighter than Mommy, and my mommy is very bright," Abby said, looking to her mother. "Well, not now."

"What is it that makes people bright or dark?" Claire asked, tilting her head to the gifted child.

Abby put her hand to her chest and said something that Claire would have never imagined would come out of the mouth of a child.

"We are not a body with a soul." She put a hand on Claire's chest and leaned in. "We are a soul with a body."

"That's very profound. Did you learn that in a Worship Center?"

"No, the Creator told me," Abby said, glancing at her painting. "I saw him in my dream. He told me how he made everything, he talked about the stars, told me they are dark because they forgot about him."

"He who?"

Abby smiled and cupped her hands to Claire's ear, tickling it with a whisper. "Aramis."

DEMONS HIDE

"ARAMIS?" Claire asked, furrowing her brows.

Abby frowned. "You forgot too." She glanced over Claire's shoulder. "Does he remember?"

Claire pointed to Will. "That guy over there with the blonde hair?"

"Yes, I like his blue eyes. He's very bright, but I can feel how uncomfortable he is around these people like me," Abby said, looking down.

"I'm uncomfortable too," Claire confessed, forcing a smile.

"Do–do you think he will dance with me?"

"I'm sure he would love to dance with such a sweet and talented young lady like yourself."

"Of course I would," a deep voice said from behind them.

Claire straightened and twisted around to find a man looking very much like Aven.

"I'll let you stand on my feet so I don't step on your toes, Abigail."

Abby didn't answer. She was staring off into the crowd again.

"Allow me to introduce myself," the man said, offering his hand. "Vincent Crey."

"Claire Grace."

"Cynthia, I'm so glad you could make it. In just the past hour there was a bid for twenty-five."

"Hundred?" Claire asked.

"Thousand." Vincent lifted his chin proud, glancing at Abby's work as if the prodigy was his own child. "I'll add the money to your account, Cynthia, but as I've said before, you should consider selling her work. You would have more than enough money by the time we get the patent."

"Oh, I don't know," Abby's mother said, smiling at the painting. "I treasure her work so much that I would hate to part with anymore, but my husband and I do plan on taking the money from his 401K. Please keep me updated. I want to know as soon as it's available."

"When we cure her, you will never have to worry about another seizure again." Vincent smiled.

As if on cue, Abby fell gently to the floor, her eyes fluttering.

"Abigail!" Cynthia fell to her side, cradling her head.

"I'll call the paramedics," Vincent said.

Claire knelt on the ground. "Is there anything I can do?"

"This isn't like her other seizures," Cynthia informed her quietly. "Sometimes she fakes them instead of having a meltdown."

The little girl's fluttering eyelids slowed, and she squinted, rubbing them. "Mommy . . ."

Cynthia gave Claire a look as if to say, that was exactly what Abby had done. "Mommy's here."

Claire watched as Abby's mother picked her up and kissed her on her head. "It's okay, sweetie. I'll take you home."

She tapped Vincent on the shoulder, and he turned, taking his phone from his ear. "Vincent I'm sorry. I need to get Abby home. Thank you so much for this auction. You don't know how much it means to the autism community here in Vegas."

As Cynthia apologized to Vincent, Abby lifted her head from her shoulder and looked at Claire.

"Abby," Claire whispered, "are you feeling okay?"

"I'm okay," Abby whispered back. "I just don't want to dance with Mr. Crey."

"Why not?"

"He scares me."

"What did he do to scare you?"

Abby put her finger to her lips, as if asking Claire to promise not to tell.

Claire nodded and came closer.

"I see his darkness," Abby began, "and the shadows around him. Their red eyes . . . they keep staring at me. They're looking at you too. Do you see them?"

Claire's anxiety sparked at the child's words, but she didn't let it show. "I'm sorry, Abby. I wish I could, but I don't have your gift."

Abigail seemed worried, but then appeared to be comforted by a thought. "Stay with the angel. He will keep you safe."

"The man you wanted to dance with?"

"He's your Guardian." Abby pressed her cheek to her mother's shoulder and closed her eyes as Cynthia turned around.

"Claire, it was such a pleasure to meet you," Cynthia said, holding out a card. "My cell phone number is on the back. If your little cousin needs any services I would be happy to assist any way I can. Abby would you like to say goodbye to Mr. Crey?

"She's asleep," Claire said, unsure if Abby was or if she was pretending. She glanced over at Vincent, trying to see the shadows Abby had mentioned, but nothing was there.

"I'll go alert the valet," Vincent informed and walked out of the room.

When Vincent was out of sight, Cynthia smiled at Claire, squeezing her arm. "Abby's a great judge of character. She sees something special in you."

"I'm just a regular person, nothing special about me."

"I wouldn't be so sure. We all have gifts, Claire. If Abby was awake, she would tell you not to waste yours."

THE BET

"ADORABLE little girl," Aven said, handing Claire her drink.

"She's so talented." Claire admired the painting once more. "It has to be one of the most amazing paintings I've ever seen."

"Makes mine look like a finger painting."

"You painted something for the auction?"

Aven offered his arm and escorted Claire around the room past the children's paintings to a table of abstract artwork. He stopped at one with a black background and two yellow circles inside of another large one.

"This one is yours?" Claire asked making a face, trying not to laugh.

"That's the one. Very modern isn't it?"

"Um, it's very . . . interesting. How many bids have you received for it?"

Aven looked on his phone. "Zilch."

Claire laughed. "Nothing?"

Aven glanced back at his panting and tilted his head. "Ah. No wonder," he said, flipping it right side up.

Claire let out a laugh.

"There it is," Aven said, grinning wide.

"What?"

"I've been waiting for that smile all night."

Claire looked at him and then the painting again. "You painted this for me?"

"You haven't smiled since we played *Chopsticks*. I had hoped this would do the trick."

Claire glanced down at her bracelet and began going back over last night in her mind, what Aven had said at his mansion.

If this wasn't a dream, I'd make love to you all over again.

Bringing her gaze back to him, she found his bedroom stare. She loosed a breath as he took her by the waist and leaned in.

"There's a reserved room at the Paris hotel with a bed covered in rose petals."

Claire's heart skipped a beat as Aven cupped her face. She leaned toward his lips, ready for his kiss, but startled to a loud voice behind her.

"Crey! I think it's time you introduce me to this exquisite young woman."

While Aven composed himself, Claire watched the man shake his hand. He looked very much like Vincent, like Aven, only taller, with a short beard and goatee with clean lines.

"Claire, this is Nicholas Giovanni," Aven informed her. "Nick, Claire Grace."

Nick took Claire's hand and kissed it. "Buongiorno."

"Nick is my second cousin. He's visiting from Rome," Aven informed her.

Claire forced a smile, but her stomach rolled as she eyed Nick's associate looking her up and down.

"We love our food and our women," Nick said.

"I hear Rome is a beautiful city."

"If you are ever in Italy, I would be happy to show you around the city."

"Thank you, that's very kind, but I don't travel much."

"Your first time in Vegas then?" Nick raised a brow.

"Yes."

"I assume Aven has given you a tour, then?"

Claire looked at Aven, reading between the lines.

"So he has." Nick gave a sly grin. "No doubt showing you how talented he is with his instruments."

Claire cleared her throat but tried to appear un-phased by how uncomfortable Nick was making her. "He's very good at piano."

"Oh, he plays more than piano, I assure you."

Aven took her hand, glaring at Nick with a warning. "I promised Claire a dance. Will you excuse us?"

"Don't be greedy, Crey. We're having a conversation. Did you know Aven could play all of the instruments on this stage?" Nick pointed to the children who were preparing for their next set. "Except the violin. I, however, play the violin beautifully. If you like I could give a private performance later."

"Oh"–Aven gave an arrogant smile–"so you've learned to play more than *Twinkle, Twinkle, Little Star*?"

"I can play anything the children on stage can."

"Vivaldi's *Summer*?"

Nick shrugged. "Of course."

"Two thousand denarius says you can't," Aven dared.

"Five hundred American dollars says I can," Nick shot back.

Aven gave a devilish grin, lifting his chin to the stage. "Prove it."

Nick took off his jacket and shoved it at his associate next to him. "È una scommessa."

"What did he say?" Claire asked as Aven unbuttoned his jacket and handed it to her gently.

"It's a bet. I'll be right back, Princess." He winked, folding back his sleeves.

Claire watched Aven jog up the stairs and talk to the children on the stage. He accepted one of their violins and plucked the strings a few times as they tapped on their tablets.

The music began, and Nick joined in the melancholy melody. After a few minutes, the children paused as did Nick, allowing Aven the solo. Surprise replaced Nick's arrogant expression as Aven's fingers slid from string to string, making the violin weep.

Claire's heart raced as the tempo rose, her brows lifting up and down with each crescendo. She watched Aven's tense facial expressions. He was serious and focused. She flushed with heat, seeing the same facial expressions he had made in bed. His brows knitted together, eyes closed, a small smile on his lips as he glided his bow across the strings with sincerity.

Nick could hardly keep up and broke a string as Aven ended the music three and a half minutes in.

The room filled with applause.

Aven bowed, keeping his confident stare on Claire. Her body throbbed to the pace of her beating heart, and she averted her gaze as Vincent approached the stage.

"Let's give these children another hand, shall we?" Vincent smiled, but Aven knew he was only doing it for show. He leaned toward Aven and Nick, covering the microphone skin chip on his neck with a finger. "Take your bets to the tables, this is not the place."

"My apologies, cousin," Nick said, handing him the violin. He walked off the stage, mouthing an Italian insult before pressing a button on his phone.

Aven's grin widened, hearing the ding of the notification at the money transfer. He handed the child his violin, told him a job well done, and went to the steps.

"Aven."

Aven swiveled on his heels, slipping his hands in his pockets. "Cousin."

"When are you going to stop acting like a child?" Vincent scolded.

"Nick started it."

"I mean it. You're jeopardizing my meeting with the Pope."

Aven looked over his shoulder with a smirk at Nick but frowned seeing him flirt with Kitten. It took everything he had not to jump off the stage and wring his neck, but he held his composure. "I doubt Nick has any true connections."

"Did you do this for a rise out of Nick or for her?"

Aven glanced back at Claire as she tucked her hair behind her ear with a meek smile. There was no question in his mind why he had showed off. "For her."

Placing a hand on Vincent's shoulder, Aven leaned into his ear. "Don't worry, dear cousin, I'm sure your trip to Rome this weekend will go just as your harlot Seer has predicted."

With the heat of Vincent's eyes burning into his back, Aven left the stage and took his jacket from Claire's arms.

"That was—" she began.

"Surprising?" Aven asked, lifting a brow.

"I don't know if that's the right word."

Aven grinned, buttoning his jacket and leaned in. "You're blushing."

Claire avoided his gaze, putting a hand to her cheek. "Am I?"

"I know I said I couldn't go back to yesterday, but I lied. I can't stop thinking about it."

Claire's face turned a brighter shade of red, and Aven thought of slipping her away to the Paris hotel. He envisioned himself unzipping her dress, trailing light kisses down her neck, but as the children struck up a new tune, he put his fleshly desires to the side.

"Care to dance, milady?"

When Claire took his arm, Aven led her to the dance floor, signaling Kitten with a glare to leave Nick's side and make Will dance. Kitten rolled her eyes but did as requested as Aven bowed and Claire curtsied to do the waltz.

Claire held Aven's gaze as he glided her across the floor until his stare wandered over her shoulder. As he tensed under her hand, Claire made a point to look while he twirled them in a circle. Her chest tightened, finding the dark-haired beauty she had met at Paula's.

Bree.

"What number was she?" Claire asked point blank.

Aven tilted his head, appearing slightly amused. "Jealousy doesn't suit you, Princess."

Claire waited for him to answer.

"Three."

"Are you still friends?"

"Bree and I were never friends, mere acquaintances."

"Is that not what we are?"

Aven paused in mid step and frowned. "I assumed after our intimacy last night, we were more."

"A one-night stand isn't intimate."

Aven swept her across the floor and whispered in her ear. "No. But secrets are."

Secrets. Not only did Aven know her dark past, he had cured her of the symptoms following her trauma. She remembered how he had held her in the bakery, the concern in his eyes. He was right. What she had experienced with him was much deeper, more meaningful than any action they had done in bed. She had told him her secrets, but he had yet to tell her his. She thought back to his room, how he had almost revealed them.

"Did you mean what you said this morning–about me?" she asked.

"Yes."

Claire's body went loose, finding the truth in his unwavering gaze.

"The question is, however"–he drew her in close, resting his cheek to hers–"will you admit you feel the same?"

Claire opened her mouth to answer, but her gaze caught Bree's fixed stare from across the room. A dizzying headache throbbed Claire's head and she closed her eyes as the room blurred.

Opening her eyes again, Claire found herself standing in the ballroom alone. There were no dancers, no Aven. No one. Nothing but a silky voice.

Give me your hand.

Claire turned, coming face to face with Bree.

She looked the same but different. Her hair was shorter, her face somehow prettier than before, and a wave of light crimson expelled from her silhouette.

Bree gave a cunning smile, waving her hand.

The room fell dark.

As if shoved back by some unseen force, Claire fell into something hard. Flames lit in front of her, and she found her wrists tied to a wooden chair. Bree walked through the fire, seemingly pleased. She leaned down to Claire, placed her hands around her bound wrists, and squeezed. There were no words for the pain, no way to describe how every nerve ending screamed as did she. Bree didn't release her hold; instead, she gave a sadistic smile.

This is the future, Truth Keeper.

Will clenched his teeth as Aven pulled Claire close. With Vincent's words echoing in his mind a rush of heat spread across his neck.

"What happened to the last girl? Vincent mentioned something about the last out of towner Aven dated."

Katharine's smile fell, her gaze snapping from another man back to him. "What did Vincent say to you?"

"If you don't tell me, I'll look Alex Anderson up myself and get the truth."

"Whatever Vincent said, Aven's not going to hurt Claire."

Will stopped dancing. "Do you mean physically or emotionally?"

"Excuso." The man Katharine had been staring at all night tapped Will on the shoulder. "May I cut in?" he asked.

Will took a step back.

"Gratcie."

Will walked away from the dancers, his sights still on Aven as he swept Claire across the room. He thought to slip her away, to tell her what Vincent had told him, but he knew it wasn't his place. Not to mention, he couldn't accuse his brother of such a violent crime. It was purely based off hearsay and he didn't exactly trust Vincent. Something about him was off. Still. The urge to protect Claire ate at him.

When his gaze went to the bar, Will quickly reminded himself of a promise he made to his mother. He needed to call Olivia. It had been hours since he had received any updates.

Walking down the hall to find a quiet place to use his phone, Will glanced at the paintings along the walls. All of them had Vincent's signature, all of them had numbers hidden in the dark art. The numbers shifted, making words again, sentences. Painting to painting he read them as they turned into a coherent story.

At the last painting, Will found himself at the doorway of a study. He went inside, finding it full of artifacts under glass cases. He paced the room, until one in particular caught his eye.

With cautious steps, he came to the glass case and fixed his gaze on the glittering gold script. Letters appeared from the numbers making words, words he felt he had said before.

The Book of Aramis.

THE SEER

"CLAIRE?" Aven asked, cupping her face. He wondered if she was having an anxiety attack, if the event had been too much for her. He leaned down but she wouldn't look at him.

"Claire," he said again.

Claire's lashes fluttered as she put a palm to his chest and held him at a distance.

"What's wrong?"

"I need air," she mumbled, brushing past him.

As Claire shoved her way through the crowd, Aven glanced over his shoulder, finding what had unnerved her. Anger swarmed in his chest when he locked eyes with Bree. She held a mischievous smile, circling her martini glass with her finger.

Wondering what spell she had used to get into Claire's mind, Aven made a straight line toward her. He was halfway across the room of dancers when his attention snapped to Kitten and the man's arms she was in.

He shot a glance at Bree telling her to stay put, then he took quick strides to Kitten and Nick.

"Excuse me, Nick, I need to borrow Katharine for a moment."

Hooking her arm, Aven dragged Kitten away from the dance floor to the corner.

"Is there a reason you're trying to piss me off?" he gritted through his words.

"Nice language," Kitten countered. "So what? You can break the rules, but I can't?"

Aven took a step forward, daring her to test him. "You know better."

"I was only dancing."

"With Nick."

"Yes. With Nick."

Aven cocked his head to the side. "Because he said you're pretty?"

Kitten's eyes narrowed, and Aven knew he had struck a nerve. Good.

"I was mistaken, Katharine. You're not a butterfly. You're a moth, mesmerized by the flame, drawn to the heat, and you will only get burned again."

"You don't own me, Aven. I can dance with whoever I want."

"You're supposed to be keeping my brother company. Where is he?"

Kitten surveyed the room. "He was here a minute ago."

"Find him, then go home, and pack," Aven ordered, glancing at his watch. "We're leaving for South Carolina in an hour."

"I'm not going."

"I'm sorry?"

"You have Claire." Kitten crossed her arms. "You don't need me holding your hand as your mother dies."

Aven's chest ached as Kitten's words cut him deep. He shot a glance at Nick, the man who had discarded her like a broken toy, only to want it again when it was fixed.

"He doesn't care about you."

Kitten's voice softened, her lips quivering at her words. "He's changed. He told me he was sorry, that he's cleaned himself up. He wants to take me to Italy with him this weekend." Kitten closed the space between them. "And he said he would teach me a spell that can protect you from—"

"Did you tell him?"

"Of course not. I said it was me."

"No."

"What do you mean, no?"

"I mean," Aven said, taking Kitten by the shoulders. He squeezed them gently, making sure she kept eye contact, "I would rather live the rest of my life dealing with my demons before I ever let you destroy yours again. Please. Go home and get your things."

Aven left it at that and walked away.

"Aven." Kitten's voice broke as she grasped his arm. He faced her, seeing her eyes pool with tears. "We may play house for your encounters, but we're not kids anymore, and I am not your wife."

Aven wiped away the tear rolling down Kitten's cheek, dying to ask her where this was coming from. Yes. He had asked too much of her these past few months, but seeing her tearful gaze, he realized this wasn't about business. This was something different entirely, something he wasn't prepared to figure out. But he knew. In every snide remark, every smart-aleck reply, Kitten had been confessing her feelings for him.

"Katharine," Aven and Nick said in unison.

"Stai bene?" Nick asked.

"Nick." Kitten wiped her tears quickly and faked a smile over Aven's shoulder. "Everything is fine. I was just telling Aven goodbye."

Heat coursed through Aven's body as his insides raged with jealousy. She didn't belong to Nick, but she also didn't belong to him. No matter if he was unsure of how he felt, he wasn't ready to let her go, at least, not into the arms of his deceitful cousin.

"So you finally figured it out," a voice slithered from the shadows.

Aven pivoted, watching Bree walk into the light, slipping an olive in her mouth. She licked her fingers slow, taunting.

"Should I assume this was all your doing?" he asked.

"Whatever do you mean?" Bree asked, tracing a finger across his chest.

Aven snatched up her wrist. "Keep your voodoo off of Katharine and my date."

"Poor little servant girl. She has a chance at happiness and you're too selfish to let her go."

"And you're still skipping around in minds as if they're your own personal playground."

"It's quite fascinating, seeing her pine for you just like she did before, and yet here you are again, too blind to see it."

"Don't start with that past lives crap again," Aven said, flinging her arm away.

"And the sweet innocent angel you brought," Bree continued, "you're terrified you'll dirty her white dove feathers, and yet you cling *so* desperately. Just as you did before." Bree narrowed her eyes with a sly grin. "Would you like me to tell you how it all ends?"

"You know me, Bree. I like surprises. Can't have them ruined by some whoring Seer."

"I hate to spoil it for you, Serus. But it happens the same way. You lose."

"Just because she-devil calls me that, doesn't mean I'll answer to it."

Bree gave a throaty laugh. "If you would use Nehia properly, you could see your past and possibly change your future."

"That's the thing about the past. There's no going back, so there's no point in knowing what I left behind."

"And your future? I can still tell you when—but only if you ask nicely."

"You only see a possible outcome."

"Come to my bed. Let me show you the moment before your heart stops beating."

Aven gave a clever grin and leaned to her ear. "I'd rather die."

TRUE IDENTITY

ARAMIS.

The name tugged at Will's brain as if asking him to say it, to remember that he had before.

"Find something that interests you?"

Will jerked his head up, finding Vincent leaning on the doorframe.

"Sorry." Will held up his phone. "I was just trying to find somewhere quiet."

"You won't get service in here. Best to try in the garden." Vincent motioned over his shoulder, then he set his eyes on the glass case. "Seems you found my collection."

Will turned back to the book under the glass. "I haven't seen a real book since I was a child." He glanced around the room. "I haven't seen any of this stuff."

"My father's personal history museum," Vincent said, walking over to stand beside the glass case. "Fascinating, isn't it?"

Will studied the numbers as they blurred into words again.

"Do you see something?"

Will glanced up at Vincent. "Do you?"

"No. But I've been trying to ever since I was a boy. The legend of this book says a time will come when someone can decipher the code inside, know the secrets of the pages."

"Has anyone been able to before?"

"Long ago. My father told me stories about those who could. How thousands of years ago, there was a time they spread its message across the world. Legend says the Creator himself came down and spoke to a chosen few, the Truth Keepers, and told them the words to write in it. Some even say the secret to eternal life is hidden within these very pages."

Will concentrated on Vincent's voice, how he enunciated his words.

"It's a very precious thing, life," Vincent continued, opening a cabinet. He took out a bottle of fine liquor and Will focused on the label as it came into focus. It was the very same brand he had drank after his service in the military, the same whiskey he had guzzled down many nights trying to drown out his guilt.

"May I ask what her illness is?"

"Cancer."

"Stage?"

"Four."

Vincent poured the liquor in a glass. "Care for a drink?"

"Thank you, but no."

"I'm curious, Mr. Stryde." Vincent leaned back on his desk and took a sip. "Have you ever served in the military?"

Will's clenched his teeth, noting the mocking tone of Vincent's voice. "No," he answered flatly.

Vincent sat his glass on his desk and unbuttoned his jacket. He reached inside, taking the pistol Will had dismantled and laid it on the table. "The hotel surveillance footage was quite impressive."

Will couldn't speak, his mind raced. He focused on the pin on Vincent's jacket. It was the same symbol he had seen on the screens during the art auction. A flashback lit his brain. The same symbol, a stamp on the vial the nurse drew from in the infirmary. He again felt the prick of the needle, the fire that had lit his veins from the injection.

The room blurred in Will's vision, but he managed to speak. "My father was a police officer. He showed me a few things."

At the click of the mag in Vincent's pistol, Will drew his gun from his back and held it at arm's length.

Vincent mirrored him, smiled, and tilted the gun back with a throaty laugh. "My father showed me a few things as well."

Will lowered his gun as Vincent put his in his jacket. "One thing you should remember, Mr. Stryde."

"And what's that?"

"Hiding one's true identity can only be achieved if you stay in the shadows." Vincent buttoned his jacket, picked up his drink, and walked over to Will's side. "Don't worry. Your secret's safe with me. Employee confidentiality, as you know."

Will's phone was quiet at first but became louder in his ears on the third ring.

"You should answer that," Vincent said. "It would be a shame for your mother to pass before she could see her oldest son again—or know the truth about your younger brother's death for that matter."

When Vincent was out of sight, Will glanced at the caller ID and answered quickly.

"Olivia?"

"I lost her, Will."

No.

"I brought her back but—I don't think her heart can handle anymore."

"I'm on my way."

Walking through the hall, Will's vision blurred again as a flashback from years ago returned. The same calm tone, the same haunting command echoed in Vincent's voice.

Shoot to kill.

POSSIBLE

FAIRYTALE

FIREWORKS screamed into the sky as Aven walked down the cobblestone path. He found Claire standing under a black iron arbor covered in rose vines. She held one of the flowers in her hand, letting the wilted petals fall to the ground.

"He loves me, he loves me not," Aven teased.

Claire glanced up at Aven, then toward the sky as a bang echoed and glittering embers rained down.

Aven came toward her, burning this memory into his mind. Her dress shimmered against the light in the sky, her skin a milky glow with each flash. He glanced at the arbor. He had seen it many times before, but it never stuck out to him until now. Standing under it with Claire, his mind flashed, his soul whispering.

I have loved you with a passion beyond measure . . .

Claire blinked free of the vision of the dark angel in a room of gold and met Aven's gaze. The words still echoed in her mind, and she wondered if he would say them.

Say yes to my proposal. Say you'll stay.

"You rushed off as if the clock had struck midnight," he said, caressing her cheek. "Not having a good time?"

"No, I mean, yes. It's been like a dream." She sighed, glancing at the arbor. "Some fantasy people used to read about." She met his gaze with furrowed brows. "But this isn't a storybook, Aven. And I can't keep pretending it will have a happy ending."

A smile spread across Aven's lips. It was a mischievous smile, and Claire had to ignore the fact that it reminded her of the Cheshire cat.

"I'm being serious and here you are smiling."

"I'm smiling because that's the first time you've said my name tonight." Aven put his arms around Claire's waist, pressing his lips lightly to her ear to whisper. "Say it again."

"Aven." Claire exhaled in frustration.

His grin widened as he leaned down to kiss her.

"I'm too unstable," Claire mumbled, slipping away. She leaned against the arbor post with a hand to her forehead. "Emotionally, to let myself fall for someone right now. Someone's heart I don't know if I can have. I can't pretend I'm okay with, whatever it is we are."

"If I put my heart in a box and wrapped it up with a pretty bow, would you reconsider?"

Claire shook her head and scoffed. "I might as well be talking to the man in the mirror. Do I need to speak in riddles to get a straight answer?"

Aven clasped his hands behind his back and tilted his head with a clever grin.

Claire let out a sigh. "Out of all the maidens of the land, has not one met your fancy?"

"Perhaps," Aven said, taking a step forward. "I've just been waiting for the fair maiden who fits."

"Fits what?"

"The glass slipper, of course."

Claire took off toward the veranda doors, but Aven took her hand, and drew her toward him gently.

"Give me this weekend. I promise to be myself."

"How can one be themselves when they're wearing a mask of so many faces?"

Aven swallowed as if the words he was about to say were painful. He caressed her face, tracing her lips. "Being with you is helping me remember."

"What was the secret you wanted to tell me this morning?"

"Grimm tales are not meant for bedtime, Princess."

"It's still torturing you." Claire put a comforting hand to his cheek. "You can tell me."

When Aven pressed his lips to hers, a fire ignited in Claire's chest. He deepened his kiss, smoothing his hand down her waist, pressing his hips to hers, but Claire drew back.

"Too much?" he asked.

"No, it's just, um"—Claire caught her breath—"can we talk?"

Aven gave another quick kiss on her lips and laced his fingers with hers. "As you wish, milady."

Claire followed Aven to a towering fountain in the middle of the garden. She gazed upon the golden sculpture, fascinated by how the water came forth. It was as if the water were wings, lifting the angelic figure off her feet.

"She's beautiful," Claire said.

"Yes, she is."

Claire caught Aven's stare. He hadn't been talking about the statue.

"There's something you should know about me, something no one knows," she said, slipping from his arm. She faced him, glancing up at the statue. "I still see things. I quit taking my medication because it made the hallucinations worse."

She glanced back at Aven, but he didn't speak.

"And if you haven't noticed, I have terrible anxiety, panic attacks."

Aven still didn't respond.

"That's what I wanted to tell you before this went any further. In case you might change your mind."

A smile spread across Aven's lips.

"Aven?"

He raised his brows. "Yes, Claire?"

"Why aren't you saying anything?"

"I'm waiting for you to infer another reason to assume I wouldn't want you."

"I'm an inconvenience. I still wake up with nightmares."

"You didn't last night."

Claire furrowed her brows. "Well, no, but—"

"What I told you," Aven said, closing the space between them, "about my demons this morning. I didn't mean it as a metaphor."

Aven watched Claire's throat bob. It was too soon to tell her everything, but he would let her know she wasn't the only one that was haunted.

"I don't sleep, Claire. Not at night, and if I do, I wake up screaming. So, I stay awake, reading books, playing music, waiting for the light of dawn to peek through my window. Being with you was the first time I had slept soundly in years. We could make this a contest of how broken we both are if you like, Princess, but I assure you, I'll win."

"You're not ready to tell me, are you?"

"It's not that I don't want to."

"It's okay. You were patient with me and my secret. The least I can do is be patient for yours."

Aven smiled and took her hand, folding her fingers into her palm.

"I was going to wait until later," he said, gently tilting her wrist. "It's not my heart, but I think you'll like it."

"I thought we were done with the bucket list."

Aven only grinned, waiting for her to open the tiny box.

"When I used to read fairy tales, I fancied that kind of thing never happened, and now, here I am, in the middle of one," Aven quoted, taking the charm of the dancing couple from her fingers.

"The first chapter to our possible fairytale." He clasped the charm on her bracelet and kissed her hand tenderly. "And no matter the beastly dragons, Your Majesty, we'll face them together."

Will neared as Claire and Aven embraced. His chest hallowed, aching while he watched them kiss. But something else caught his attention and his gaze darted to the fountain. The sight of the water lifting from the basin into the air stole his breath. It was as if he had seen this before, as if he knew the tiny orbs would float, expand into intricate designs like snowflakes.

When Claire pulled away from Aven's lips and looked up at him with wide eyes, the water fell with a splash back into the fountain pool.

"Will," she said coming to his side, "what's wrong?"

"We have to go." Will pulled his gaze from the fountain to Aven. "Now."

HOME SWEET

HOME

Sunday, 7:05 a.m., South Carolina

WILDFLOWERS. They were everywhere. Buttercups, poppies of orange and red, and golden wheat swayed in the breeze. Claire strained her mind, holding back from opening the door of Will's rolling pickup truck. She wanted to get out and run through the fields, touch the stalks, but held her hands tightly clasped in her lap.

"This is all your land?" she asked Will, gazing at the pasture.

"Twenty acres for the horses to graze."

"Do you have other animals?" Claire asked, looking at the red barn ahead.

"A dog."

"Oh, I saw the barn and thought maybe you had a farm."

"No." Will gave a faint laugh. "Boarding stables. There's seven that belong to clients. The three that live here permanently are rescues."

Claire's heart warmed as she stared at Will before looking back out to the pastures.

"Do they have names?" she asked, pointing to a speckled brown and white horse.

"That one there is Nil, the black one is Steve."

"Steve?" Claire laughed.

Will flashed his white teeth. "The client's son was five when he named him."

As Will turned onto a paved driveway, Claire set her gaze on a brown wooden fence, leading the way to a cape cod home. It was olive green, two stories high with white trim, and had a wrap-around porch.

There was silence a few heartbeats after Will parked. He stared at the barn for a long moment, but then looked over his shoulder.

"We're here," he said to Aven.

Aven didn't budge. He was sound asleep in the back seat, curled up like a small child.

"Aven." Claire pushed on his knee, but he only rolled over on his back. "I'll get him up," she assured Will with an irritated sigh.

Will nodded and shut the door hard, but Aven didn't flinch.

As Will went inside the house, Claire got out and went to the back of the truck. Swinging open the door, she placed her feet on the step and shook Aven's leg hard. "Aven, wake up, we're here."

Aven's eyes flew open as he gripped her wrist and gave it a good tug. Before Claire knew it, she was on top of him, only inches from his smirking face.

"Ever done it in a backseat before?"

"Have you?"

"No, but I want to."

Claire huffed, pushing herself off Aven's chest and backing out of the truck.

Aven climbed out after her, stretching his neck before observing the scenery.

"Pit stop on a farm?"

"Boarding for horses. Come on. Will's waiting for you."

Aven wrinkled his nose. "I hope the house doesn't smell like this." He turned to Claire, but her back was to him. "Claire?"

Her gaze was fixed on the field of lavender swaying in the breeze. Catching the scent, Aven stood beside her and cast his gaze on the open pasture.

Both Aven and Claire felt the same familiarity; the same tug spread from their chest to their fingers, beckoning them to touch the fuzzy tips of wheat. When they set their gaze on the pink dogwood in the distance, a soft blanket under it appeared. For Aven, it was if he was watching himself from afar, holding the glowing angel in his arms. As he leaned down to kiss her, the vision left him just as quickly as it had come. He glanced at Claire who was still in a daze.

"Claire?"

"Sorry. I thought I saw something."

"Yeah, me too."

Claire found Will's home much bigger on the inside than she had assumed. It was also tidy to her surprise. The theme of the home was traditional. Dark hickory hardwood floors were throughout, matching wooden beams that lined the ceiling. At the entrance was a small kitchen with a round table and two chairs. Nearby were the steps leading to the second floor. To the left was the living room.

Drawn to the pictures on the mantel of the fireplace, Claire looked closely at Will in his Navy Seal uniform, and beside his photo was another face that looked eerily similar to Aven in the same attire.

When Claire's gaze moved to the triangle case displaying a United States flag, her stomach tightened as the memory of her father's funeral came with the tone of the bell that had sounded before he was lowered into the ground. The memory faded as the bell was replaced with the ding of piano keys.

"Care to join me?" Aven asked, standing by a grand piano in the center of the room. He trailed his fingers along the ivory and paused at the one that sagged.

"Hm. Guess I'll need to fix that first."

Aven lifted the top of the piano but lowered it again as the sound of Will's boots clomped down the steps.

"She wants to see you," he said, looking to Aven.

Aven laced his fingers in Claire's and squeezed. Claire squeezed back, then slipped her hand away, but he took it and tugged her to follow Will up the stairs.

As Will opened a door down the hall, Claire's heart ached, seeing a frail woman on her deathbed.

A white and spotted Australian Shepherd laying at her feet jerked its head up with growl.

"Blue," Will said soft but stern. The dog ignored him and jumped from the bed, taking a stance in front of Aven.

"Nice doggy." Aven grimaced.

Blue growled again, and Claire found it curious the dog wasn't looking at Aven, she was looking past him.

"I'll take Blue outside," Olivia assured Will. "I gave your mama a dose. She should be comfortable for a few hours."

Will nodded in thanks as Olivia took Blue by the collar and tugged her out the door.

"You two need time alone," Claire whispered, slipping through Aven's fingers again. Aven bit his lip, staring at his mother, but didn't reach for Claire again. She went to door and took one last heartbreaking look until Will gently pulled it shut.

Exhaling a long breath, Claire leaned against the wall, gazing at a painting across from her. The canvas's glossy sheen mirrored the light fixture until she took a step forward, studying the oil painting of the grazing horses and the initials in the corner.

W.C.C.

"Do you want to go see them?" Will asked, glancing at the painting.

"I'd like that."

WHITE AS SNOW

CLAIRE followed Will behind the house to a wooden fence and watched him bite his lower lip. At the sharp whistle through his teeth, the horses in the field trotted toward them from the pasture. He opened the gate, leading Claire to the fence.

"This is Barnaby," Will informed her as Claire pet the grey dapple. "Valamier, Petunia." Will went to a brown horse with a white stripe down his nose. "And this," he said patting the mustang, "is my horse, Equuleus."

"Like the constellation."

Will flashed his teeth, picking up a saddle.

A whinny in the distance lifted Claire's gaze. Her heart leapt seeing a white stallion galloping toward them. Something inside made her want to run to it, to comb her fingers through its flowing mane.

"What's that one's name?"

Will grimaced, placing the saddle on Equuleus. "That's Snow. He doesn't come to us."

"Ever?"

"No."

"Why not?"

"I'm not exactly sure. I found him last winter on the side of the road, half-frozen with a broken leg. I brought him here and nursed him back to health, but once he got well, he wouldn't let anyone come near him. No one but my mother, and only if she was singing."

"What did she sing?"

"Hymns about a king."

Claire watched as the horse came closer until it stopped and stood several feet away. It leaned its head, staring at her but didn't come any further.

"Hymns of Old," Claire whispered." My father used to sing them to me. I would wake up in the middle of the night from bad dreams. The songs made me feel safe."

Claire walked toward Snow, but he huffed and backed away. Cautious not to spook the horse again, she took controlled steps and hummed a tune.

When Snow perked his ears and lifted his head, Claire sang words to the song and offered her hand.

As Snow reached out and touched her palm with his black muzzle, something inside Claire clicked. A childhood dream came to her: one of a white horse, a sugar-white beach, and the wind in her hair. And then, to Claire's surprise, Snow knelt, bowing his head.

"What's he doing?"

Will came to Claire's side, appearing just as confused as she was. "I think he wants to take you for a ride."

"Blackbird singing in the dead of night . . ."

Aven's heart warmed as his mother sang. She had used this song to sing him to sleep as a boy. He joined her in the lyrics of the second line, holding back his tears.

"Hey there, my little blackbird."

"Hey," Aven replied, kissing his mother on the cheek.

"Still as soft as raven feathers." She combed through his hair as he took her hand and kissed it.

"And you're still as just as beautiful as I remember."

"You have your father's charm."

"Is that a bad thing?"

Aven watched her slightly wince. He couldn't tell if it was for her father, or the pain.

"You have questions."

"Only one."

"About your ability."

Aven furrowed his brows and glanced up at the door, hoping no one was listening.

"I've seen it before, when you were a baby," Kate said. "I came in your room one night, finding your mobile moving on its own. You cried when you couldn't get it to stop."

"I remember."

"I know. That's something special about you, about the Crey family. They can practically remember the moment they were born."

Aven looked at his mother but didn't know what to say. He had missed her so much, missed her tender voice. It was weak now, raspy.

"Will you show me?" she asked.

Aven bit his lip.

"Don't be afraid, little bird."

Aven lifted his gaze to the vase of flowers on the nightstand and floated a wildflower into the air. It drifted toward him as if on an invisible string, and he caught it with his fingertips. He narrowed his eyes on the blossom, transforming it into a white rose before their very eyes.

"What am I?" he asked after a long moment.

"You're special Aven, but having this kind of power—you must use your gifts for good."

"Were you in some kind of nuclear accident when you worked for my father? Is that what's wrong with me?"

Kate smiled. "When you go home, I want you to look in your Uncle Jimmy's safe. There's a chip, a file labeled, The Ancient Ones. You'll find the answers to your questions there."

There was a space of silence as Aven let his mother hold his hand. There were so many things he wanted to tell her, so many questions about why she never told him she was alive. But he knew she didn't have the strength, so he reached into his jeans, taking a vial with the InfiniCorp logo on it.

"I brought you a gift."

When his mother's gaze darted to the vial, she squeezed his hand. "No, Aven."

"It's okay. I'm going to make you better. You won't hurt anymore." Aven took a syringe from its package and drew the black liquid from the vial.

"I don't want the cure, Aven."

Aven lowered the syringe and the line and glanced over his shoulder. "How do you know this can cure you?"

"I'm the one that discovered it. But InfiniCorp, they've changed the formula."

"What do you mean?"

"It was never about helping people with your father, it was about controlling them. Controlling me. That serum, it's tainted with the blood of the Fallen, that same blood runs in your veins."

"The Fallen?"

"I can't explain everything about who you are, just know you must fight against the urge to control."

"Even if it's for good?" Aven came to his mother's side and stared at her for a long moment.
You don't want to die.

"Don't do that." Kate shook her head slowly.

"Do what?"

"Use your gift of persuasion as your father did."

"You don't have to leave again." Aven's voice cracked and tears welled in his eyes. "Let me help you."

"It's my time to go, little bird, and it's your time to fly on your own."

Aven wiped the tears from his cheek and scoffed. "I've *been* flying on my own. I had no choice. You left me. Told Paula to lie."

"I did it to keep you safe, to keep Will safe."

"Will." Aven's face twisted in pain. "You started another family. You never even tried to contact me, never once came to see me."

"Aven—"

"You sent a stranger to kidnap me." Aven dug his fingernails into his palm. "And I . . ."

"Did you kill him?"

Aven averted his gaze and clenched his teeth. The past came back to him. How his uncle Jimmy had yelled at him to pick up the gun. How the man with blue eyes, Will's father, kept telling him he was taking him to his mother, that he was a friend. Aven remembered lifting the gun with his mind, pointing it.

"Did you kill Adam?" Kate rasped, bringing him back to the present.

"You think I'm a murderer."

"No," Kate whispered, squeezing Aven's hand. "You're my son. And you're good."

"And if I killed someone—if their blood was on my hands"—he met her wary gaze—"would you love me still?"

"You may have the Crey's last name, but you are not one of them. No matter how they've manipulated you, trained you to think like them, there's light in you, there's good, hiding from the darkness in your mind."

Aven looked at his mother for a long moment, seeing the same hope in her eyes. It was the same he had seen in Claire's the night they had met.

"All of us have demons, Aven," Kate whispered, "but it's free will that gives us the choice to fight them or set them free."

Claire exhaled a wistful sigh. Gallivanting through the pastures had been surreal. Images had flashed in her mind of the scenery, tugging at her brain as if asking her to remember it. The blooms of the pink weeping trees, the rolling hills. All of it felt so familiar.

"Looks like a storm's rolling in," Will said, setting his gaze to the cloudy sky as they came to a stop. He dismounted Equuleus and slipped the bit from his and Snow's mouth.

Claire swung her leg back to place a foot on the ground but lost her footing and tumbled.

Will held back a chuckle as he offered his hand. "Are you okay?"

"Yeah." Claire laughed. "It was a little further to the ground than I thought."

Brushing off the dirt from her backside, Claire looked to the open field. Her heart whispered, calling her to remember this moment. It was all so clear now: the way the sunlight glinted on the pond, how the poppies swayed, the scent of the lavender breeze filling her lungs. It was exactly how she had seen it in her dreams.

Bringing her gaze back to Will, she found him walking toward a towering oak. It welcomed him with its wide leafy branches, beckoning for him to come stand beneath its shade.

Will braced a hand on the trunk as if it were an old friend and grazed at the bark with sentiment.

"My dad proposed to my mom here," he said, "planted those daisies, built that bench so she could sit and read."

Claire glanced at the rotting wooden bench and back at Will.

"She was five months pregnant with me when they bought the stables. I've never seen two people more in love—he died in the line of duty when I was a boy. For the past month, she's been talking about how she can't wait to join him in Paradise."

Paradise.

Claire had only heard stories about that place from her father. He had said it was all around them but couldn't be seen.

Beyond the Veil is only accessible at our departure.

"What do you think it's like there?" Claire asked, glancing up.

"The afterlife?"

Claire nodded.

Will put his hands on his hips and surveyed the field. "Peaceful."

With a small smile, Claire followed Will to the center of the meadow. They stood, looking upon the landscape, not a word uttered between them as they listened to the bristle of the wheat in the breeze.

Peaceful.

Claire hoped it was true. She hoped that wherever her father was, it was as tranquil as where she stood now.

The silence broke with a crack like a whip.

"Time to go," Will said.

NO GOODBYE

AS thunder shook the house with a rattling boom, Aven's gaze darted to the windows. He watched them quake, but when he looked back at his mother, he found her eyes closed.

"Mom?"

He lifted her limp hand and pressed his fingers against her wrist. Low peaks mirrored her blood pressure on the monitor. With blurry eyes, he fixed his stare back on the syringe lying on the nightstand. Smoothing Kate's damp hair to the side, he kissed her forehead. "I'm sorry, but I'm too selfish to lose you again."

Holding up the line, Aven ignored the muffled bark outside the door and took a deep breath. He pressed the tip of the needle to the plug but froze at the ear-piercing tone that rang out.

As the door swung open and the nurse rushed in, Aven hid the syringe behind his back. "She's not breathing," he informed her, his voice cracking as the alarm sounded.

The nurse put the stethoscope to his mother's chest. "Kate? You can't go yet, honey. You didn't say goodbye to Will."

The monitor beeped again, slow and unsteady as the dog barked from the hall.

"Stay with her. I'll get your brother," Olivia said, rushing out of the room.

Will dismounted Equuleus and took him into the stables, placing a blanket over him. He glanced over his shoulder, expecting Claire and Snow beside him, but they weren't.

"It's stuck!" Claire yelled over the pouring rain.

Will ran to her side, but Claire tugged free of the stirrup, and slipped.

Catching her fall, Will's gaze fixed on her eyes, then the rain rolling across her lips. At a flash of lightning, he was somewhere else, holding Claire in a cave of pulsing starlight.

For a moment he saw the angel, but the cave, and her, disappeared at the sound of his name.

"Will!" Olivia shouted from the front door. "Come quick!"

Will froze at the door, listening to the monitor, gazing at his unconscious mother on her bed. Glancing at Aven standing in the corner, his chest ached. He had brought him here, asked him to see her like this, knowing the last memory of their mother had been much different.

"It's time to say goodbye," Olivia informed tenderly and walked out the door.

Will went to his mother's bedside and glanced over his shoulder at Aven.

Aven's jaw feathered as he took one look at their mother and walked out the door.

"Aven," Claire mumbled. She met Will's tearful gaze. "I'll get him back."

Watching Claire run into the hall after Aven, Will took his mother's hand in his. He had been brave in the war. He'd found the courage to stare death in the face. But death had the advantage now, and it was time to confess.

"Mom."

Kate didn't open her eyes, but she flinched at his voice.

"I'm sorry." His voice cracked. "I'm sorry I didn't tell you before, but Aaron . . ."

"Aven!" Claire called down the steps. "Aven, wait!" She took hold of his arm, tugging him away from the door.

As Aven looked past her, she studied his bloodshot eyes and cupped his face.

"Hey," she whispered.

"What?" he snapped, finally meeting her gaze.

"Don't you want to say goodbye?"

"No. And don't give me that look like I'm some wounded little boy. I'm fine," he gritted out, jerking away.

"You don't look fine."

Aven whipped around with narrow eyes. "Then stop looking."

Claire cringed as the screen door slammed against the house. She watched the rain drench Aven as he trudged through the mud to Will's truck. He slammed his fists against the window after failing to open the door and looked at the Mustang parked by the barn. When the car door opened for him with one swift pull, Claire bolted from the porch.

"Aven, stop!" She slipped in the mud, catching her fall gripping the car door. "Your mother is taking her last breaths. Don't you want to be by her side?"

"I don't do goodbyes."

He didn't look at her, only glared at the dash as if it had insulted him.

"Please don't do this. You'll regret it for the rest of your life."

There was only the sound of the pouring rain and the putter of the engine. Rain, maybe tears, trickled down Aven's cheeks. Claire wasn't sure which, but when he sniffed she knew he was silently crying.

"Aven, please don't go."

"Get in."

"What?"

He met her gaze. "Come with me."

"We can't just leave."

"Get in or let go."

A storm like the one above swirled in Aven's grey eyes. Pain, anger, resentment. Claire knew these emotions all too well, and she knew she couldn't make him stay. The second her aching fingers slipped from the door, Aven slammed it and fishtailed the Mustang down the driveway.

SCARS

WILL stood at his front door, looking at Claire through the screen for a long moment. As her shoulders jerked at her soft whimpers, his gaze drifted to the bald spot by the barn where the Mustang had sat.

"I couldn't get him to stay," Claire said softly as he opened the screen door.

Will sat on the porch beside her, resting his arms on his knees. He listened to the patter of rain and thunder trailing in the distance for a few heavy heartbeats.

"I wish there was something I could say," Claire murmured, "but knowing the loss of a parent—sympathetic words are not enough."

Will gave her a sideways glance, watching her lips quiver. He didn't know if she was cold or trembling with anxiety from all that had happened.

"Come on," he said, standing. "I'll get you something to wear until we can wash your clothes."

Following Will into his room, Claire glanced around the tidy space. Not a single wrinkle marred the navy duvet on the bed. There was no TV, no pictures on the walls, only a dresser and a nightstand.

Clean. Simple.

Movement in the bathroom mirror caught Claire's gaze, and she flushed with heat, finding the tight lines in Will's bare back. She glimpsed at the long scar wrapping around his ribs, then a round one on his right shoulder.

Lifting her gaze back to the mirror, she found him staring at her. Embarrassment lit her face to flames as she sucked in a sharp breath, swiveling on her heels.

She glanced at the nightstand, finding a spiral sketchpad and a dull charcoal pencil on top. The black wavy lines formed a face, and Claire squinted, thinking how much it looked very similar to her own. Reaching to move the pencil to the side, she flinched at Will's voice.

"You may have to roll the sweatpants a few times," he said, offering the folded clothes.

"Thank you."

"You can stay in here." Will pointed to the door across the hall. Claire went into the room as he gathered some fresh sheets from the linen closet.

While Will made the bed, Claire surveyed the room. It was smaller than Will's and not as tidy. Dust caked the dresser and shelves where baseball trophies sat. A glove and bat rested against a corner, and an image of a young man seemed to smile at her from the picture frame on the nightstand.

She knew it couldn't be Aven but was still in awe of how much this young man looked like him. She could only assume it was Will's younger brother, the one from the photo downstairs. This was his room.

Holding back the urge to ask Will where he was, she brought her gaze to the neatly made bed.

"Is this okay?" Will asked, lying the pillow case against the headboard.

"It's great, thank you."

Will ran his fingers through his hair and walked around her. "I need to make some phone calls. I'll schedule a cab to pick you up tomorrow."

"Laura should be home tonight. She can come and get me."

"The washing machine is downstairs under the steps."

Claire stared at the photo again.

"Claire?"

Claire turned, finding Will in the doorway. He wet his lips, hesitated before he spoke. "You're welcome to stay as long as you need to."

Claire shook her head and scrunched her shoulders. "I don't want to be a burden."

Will gave a thoughtful smile. His eyes were soft and so was his voice. "You're not."

1919

SUNDAY, 10:58 P.M., SOUTH CAROLINA

Claire stood on a balcony, peering down at jagged rocks below. She had to escape. She had to get away. Glancing at the red curtains behind her, she took hold, but they went up in flames at her touch. She turned back toward the balcony to jump, but a window appeared, blocking her way. She struggled to open it, but it wouldn't budge. Behind her, in the bedroom, the closet door swung open. Black smoke billowed out, ash spewed on the floor. A monster formed from smoke, glaring with red eyes. It floated to her, reaching out to choke her with its sharp claws. It disappeared and reappeared behind her. As it let out a deafening shrill and lunged, Claire cried out to the Creator.

Gasping for a breath, Claire woke, gripping the sheets. Her hands were stiff, her body frozen. She blinked, looking around the room, waiting for her body to catch up, for it to realize she was no longer asleep.

Sleep paralysis.

The weight of a cinder block pressed down on her chest. She struggled to breathe and begged her muscles to move. She had to think of something other than the fear, had to force her mind to focus. When her eyes allowed her to blink, Claire wiggled her fingers and her toes. She sat up slowly, wiping the sweat off her brow and groaned, grabbing her phone.

Eleven p.m.

Claire groaned, letting her phone fall to the side. She did a double take at the end of the bed, finding her clothes neatly folded. Heat warmed her cheeks as she picked up her underwear from beneath her romper. She hoped the nurse had found her clothes in the washing machine and not Will, but seeing how meticulously they had been folded, she wasn't so sure.

Mumbling to herself, she changed quickly before stepping out into the dark hallway. Two steps from the door, she collided with something hard.

"Aven," she hissed, but as the lights turned on, she realized it wasn't Aven she had bumped into.

"Sorry," she said all too quickly to Will. "I didn't mean to wake you."

"You didn't. Do you need anything?"

"Uh, bathroom?"

"It's this one." Will walked past Claire, tapping on the door to his left. He hustled down the steps and grabbed his jacket off the hook on the wall.

"Where are you going?" Claire asked, gripping the bannister. No matter if she had been cured of heights, it was still a habit. Before Aven's Mind Walk, this short distance from the ground would have made her woozy.

"To find the selfish prick who stole my brother's—" Will paused and zipped up his rain jacket. "I'm going to look for Aven."

"Do you know where he is?"

Will pulled his hood over his head and opened the door. Thunder clapped. Rain pounded the porch.

"No, but I believe he's at one of three local pubs in town. Dinner is in the fridge. I saved you a plate."

He was being short with her again. She didn't blame him. Losing his mother, Aven storming off. He had every right to be brief. "Will?"

Will waited at the threshold but didn't turn around until Claire stood behind him. She fidgeted with the end of her braid, thinking of what to say. "Maybe I should come with you."

Will didn't respond. He only looked at her for a long moment.

"To drive one of the cars back," she offered.

"Can you drive a stick?"

"No, but—"

"That's okay. You can drive my truck home."

After the fifteen-minute drive from the stables, Claire looked up at a neon sign as Will pulled into a full parking lot.

"1919?" she asked as he parked the truck next to the Mustang.

"Prohibition. Everyone in town meets here."

Claire wondered if Will came to this bar often, but she didn't ask. She waited for him to get out of the truck, but he didn't. He stared at the entrance as the muscles in his jaw slid back and forth. Something about this place made him uncomfortable. She wasn't sure what it was, but she could tell he wasn't thrilled about going in.

"I'll go look for him," Claire offered.

Will kept staring at the sign with no acknowledgement.

Claire unbuckled, reaching for the door, and braced herself for the downpour.

"Claire," he said, taking off his jacket. "If he's too drunk to stand, come get me."

"I'll be right back," Claire assured him. She took the rain jacket and pulled the hood over her head. It smelled just like the hooded sweatshirt he had offered her the night he had saved her. She breathed deep, comforted by the scent of him, and ran, dodging puddles on her way to the entrance.

The inside of the bar was foggy with smoke. It reeked of cigarettes and stale beer. Claire squeezed through the crowd of 1919's customers. They were about her age, at least from what she could see from the back. They jumped up and down with their hands in the air, singing along to the music.

Claire scanned their faces as she slipped her way through a mash pit, but her gaze was quickly drawn to the stage and a familiar face.

Aven held the microphone with both hands, a cigarette between his fingers. He took a step back and picked the strings of the electric guitar, too fast for Claire's eyes to keep up. She scoffed as he sang "It's the End of the World."

According to the lyrics, he 'felt fine', but Claire knew otherwise. This was just another mask of Aven Crey, and it was her least favorite thus far.

When Aven strummed the last chord dramatically, the crowd shouted in praise and raised their glasses.

"Thank you. I'll be here all night." Aven bowed slightly, flinging air kisses from his fingers to his roaring fans. Claire glared, watching him grab a full shot glass offered by a girl. He stooped down, tilting the shot glass back before he wiped a dribble of the liquid from his chin and stood.

When the crowd chanted encore, Aven took another shot and came to the edge of the stage. He flicked the remaining drops from his glass over them as if he was a priest, christening them at a worship service.

Claire burned with anger watching Aven blow kisses to women at his feet. He waved to the crowd, grinning wide, but the moment he brought his gaze back to the filled dance floor, he froze.

Hello, Alter Ego.

Claire motioned with her hands for Aven to come to her, but he only smiled. It was a mischievous grin Claire had seen so many times before.

"This one's for you, Princess," Aven said into the microphone.

At a three-count tap from the drummer, the band struck up the tune to "Creep."

Listening to the lyrics, Claire kept Aven's fixed stare. In his raspy voice, she could hear his confessions, knew he was admitting his flaws. It reminded her of being in his room, the morning he thought he was dreaming. He was being vulnerable. In his own way, he was pouring out his heart.

At the bridge, Aven tapped a device around his ear and replaced the microphone on the stand. He continued to play, standing in front of her as he changed the lyrics to the song.

"I've got a perfect body, but I want a perfect soul."

There was so much passion in his voice, so much grief. Her heart broke watching his face twist as he swept the guitar behind him. He reached out to her slowly, grazing his knuckles against her cheekbone.

Claire's lips quivered as he traced them. There was a storm in his eyes, and she almost thought she saw them glisten. Singing the last of the lyrics, Aven cupped Claire's face. He leaned down to kiss her, but the crowd erupted in applause as their lips brushed.

"Aven," Claire said, leaning back

"Claire." The trickster stirred in him as a playful smile replaced a grimace.

"VEGAS! VEGAS! VEGAS!" the crowd chanted.

Claire crossed her arms and raised her brows. "Vegas?"

"Nickname the good people of South Carolina gave me. You know how I like nicknames, Claire Bear."

"Don't call me that," Claire snapped.

She could deal with princess, deal with any nickname other than that one. That had been her father's nickname for her. She didn't want to think of her father. Not now.

"Someone's touchy," Aven teased.

"Will's waiting for you in the car," Claire shouted over the uproar. "We came to pick you up."

"As you can see, Your Majesty," Aven said, glancing around the room, "the peasants insist that I entertain them."

"Are you drunk?"

"Not yet."

"I think you've been the court jester long enough," Claire shouted. "It's time to go home."

"Home." Aven chuckled. "First of all, that farm is not my home and second—" Aven held up three fingers then looked at them with one eye.

As Elvis's "Viva Las Vegas" played over the speakers, Aven turned his back to Claire and jumped back on stage. "Drinks on me!"

The crowd grew louder, following him to the bar, shoving Claire out of the way. She gritted her teeth and shoved her way back through.

"One for you, and one for you . . ." Aven said, passing out shot glasses over her head.

"Aven!" Claire shouted, but he ignored her.

"To Vegas!" he said, holding up his glass.

"TO VEGAS!" the crowd said in unison.

"Claire?" Aven offered her a shot, but she shook her head.

"This isn't the time to be drinking."

"Fine, more for me." He tilted back the brown liquid, slamming the glass on the bar. "Keep 'em coming, Bobby!" he ordered, circling a finger in the air.

"Give me the keys, you can't drive."

"Back to being boring, are we?"

Claire reached for Aven's arm, ready to jerk him off his stool but was shoved back as three girls stood in front of her. The tall blonde in a red miniskirt and a strappy black top looked over her shoulder. She wrinkled her nose as if Claire's face was hard to look at. "You're not his girlfriend, are you?"

"No, I'm—"

The blonde swung her hair in Claire's face as she swiveled back around. Putting her hand on Aven's shoulder, she wedged her way between his legs. Claire's face lit with flames, but she held her tongue.

"So, as I was saying earlier," the girl said, "I'm coming to Vegas in a few months. Tell me more about this tour."

Claire's nose crinkled, disgusted as Aven's wandering gaze went to the girl's full rack.

"Roxy, right?" Aven asked with interest.

Roxy nodded, arching her back. "That's my name, don't wear it out."

Ugh. Really? A dumb bimbo?

"Well, Roxy." Aven grinned, shooting Claire a playful glance. "I'll have you know, I'm a great tour guide. Right, Claire?"

A brunette with fishnet tights and thick purple eyeliner came forward. "I'd like a tour too."

"I'm sure you would." Aven's smile widened.

Claire let out a frustrated breath. Aven's alter ego had taken over, and there was no talking to it. She hated that side of him but understood why he wore the mask. He was pretending to hide the pain, his grief. Playing the act at the bar had been his distraction.

"Let me know when you're in town," Aven said to the girls. "I can set you ladies up with a penthouse suite."

At the word "penthouse," any sympathy for Aven vanished. In that instant, she didn't care if he was grieving. There was no excuse for his actions. If he wanted to flirt with sleazy women, she wasn't going to stick around to watch. She turned toward the exit, ready to leave, but stilled, seeing a girl wrapped around Will's neck at the door.

46

HANNAH

WILL'S body went rigid as Hannah hugged him tight. This was why he had avoided coming to the city. This was why he ordered everything online, delivered by drone to the door of his house.

I should have never come here.

"I knew you weren't dead." Hannah said. "I've been praying for some kind of sign to know I wasn't crazy."

It felt unnatural not to return his ex-fiancé's embrace, but Will couldn't. It was for her own good, her own safety. His throat bobbed as he took a step back.

"I'm sorry, you must have me confused with someone else."

Hannah batted her lashes. Confusion wrinkled her forehead. "I just thought—you look like my fiancé, um ex-fiancé. I lost him in the war seven years ago."

"That must have been hard for you."

Hannah tilted her head as if asking if he would admit the truth. Will had never been a liar. He wasn't brought up that way, but he couldn't tell her the truth. He couldn't admit that he could have come home after his first tour; that instead, he went on a secret mission, lost his team, and his own life.

"I didn't know how to deal with it at first," Hannah said. "I missed him so much. There were days I felt like dying too."

"And now?"

"Now, I'm married and have two kids. A little boy and a baby girl."

Will recalled how they had talked about having children, about the songs they would play on their wedding day. It was a life he could never have now. No marriage, no children. He would always be alone.

"And your husband—he's good to you?"

"Gracen's a good man. He was a good friend of Will's."

Gracie.

That's what Will had called him when they had played football in high school together. He was a good man, and Will was glad it was him she ended up with and not some rebound jerk.

"Hannah! The taxi is here!"

Hannah acknowledged her friend that had poked her head through the door. She turned back to Will, hugging her jacket.

"Um, I have to go."

Will grimaced. He knew he shouldn't say it, but he had to. "I'm sorry."

"For what?"

"For your loss."

"Oh, um. Thanks. I'm sorry I hugged you. I've had a lot to drink."

"Don't worry about it."

Hannah put her hand on the door but looked over her shoulder. "It was the eyes."

Will raised a brow.

"That's why I thought you were him. You even smell like him."

Will held back a smile.

"Way too much to drink." Hannah laughed.

Relief spread through Will.

It's over. She's leaving. She's going home to her family.

He raked his fingers through his hair but when Hannah's eyes lit up, he tried to play off the nervous tick. She had always teased him about it, said she could always tell when something was wrong. The way she looked at him now, was the same way she had the day he told her he was going into the military. He wondered if that moment still haunted her too.

"Or maybe you're his spirit," she said," maybe the Creator heard my prayers." She came to him and placed her hand on his arm. "I don't resent you for choosing Aaron over me, Will. When your brother was drafted, I understood why you signed up to go to war. You were always protective of him. The only thing I regret is the argument we had the day you left. I should have told you that I was proud of your choice. I should have told you how much I loved you. But now you know, and I can let you go."

Will's rigid body went loose as emotions consumed him.

"Hannah!" her friend called through the door again.

Hannah wrapped her arms around Will's waist and gave him a hug. "Thank you for letting me say goodbye," she whispered and walked out the door.

DADDY ISSUES

GUILT ate at Will. Seeing Hannah had brought back too many happy memories. But they were memories of someone else's life, not his, not anymore.

Looking toward the bar, he found Claire. She was staring at him but averted her gaze over her shoulder to Aven and the two women in his lap.

Anger fueled Will's steps as he made a straight line toward his brother.

"I couldn't get the keys," Claire informed him.

He brushed past her, moving people left and right until he stood in front of Aven. "You stole something that doesn't belong to you."

"Little brother," Aven teased before tilting back a shot. "Can I ignore you some other time? A little busy here." His eyes darted to the women in his lap.

"She should have known what a selfish prick you've turned out to be."

"I'm a prick? You walked over here and didn't even acknowledge these beautiful women. It's kind of rude."

"Like the way you acknowledge Claire?"

Aven looked around the girls to Claire, and then he filled his shot glass. "There. Happy?"

"Give me the keys. You can catch a cab."

"Is that car special to you or something? Was it your father's? Was dear ol' dad as boring as you?"

"At least he wasn't a dick like yours."

Aven shoved the girls off him and took a step forward.

"Oh, I see," Aven said, tilting his head. "So, you read the letter too. Think you know about my father, do you?"

Will glared. "Enough to know he was a manipulating sociopath."

"Better a sociopath than a cold-blooded killer."

Will grabbed a fistful of Aven's shirt and jerked him forward. "You don't know what happened. Everyone that saw it is dead."

"You're right. But I do know your father shot mine and took my mother away from me because of you."

Will shoved Aven back. "I'm going home. I have a funeral to arrange."

"You should have a drink, Will—oh, wait. That's right. The oath."

Will clenched his teeth, holding his stance.

"AA's gaudy magnet on the fridge. Mom must have been so proud. Too bad you can't hold your liquor."

Will's crossed his arm. "I could drink you under the table."

"Wanna make a bet?" Aven taunted, dangling the keys to the Mustang.

Will reached for them, but Aven pulled them back. "Ah, ah, ah. I'll only give you the keys if you win a little wager."

"I can wager I'll be dragging your ass out of here on a stretcher."

"What say you and I play a game of darts?"

Will smiled. He was good at darts. Real good. That's what his unit did to pass time in the military when they weren't on duty. "And if you win?"

"Claire drives me home, you catch a cab."

Will and Aven looked at Claire, who looked back at them with worry.

"Deal," Will said, shaking Aven's hand.

"You keep score, Princess," Aven said, snatching up his bottle of bourbon.

"But I—" Claire sputtered

"But ta, ta." Aven waggled a finger, walking away. "The king has spoken."

PLAYING DIRTY

CLAIRE flopped down at a table near the dartboard as Will and Aven gathered their darts. She glanced at the girls hovering nearby. They eyed Will and Aven like vultures waiting for the traffic to clear so they could fight over the scraps of day-old roadkill.

"Rules?" Will asked, planting a foot at the red line on the floor.

"First to hit the little red dot ten times wins," Aven informed them. "Every miss, a shot of 1919's best bourbon."

"Better start saying your goodbyes."

"You seem awfully confident, dear brother."

"That's because"—Will turned his back to the board and flung the dart behind him without looking. At the sound of the thunk, he grinned—"I never miss."

Claire's mouth fell open, but when Will held up his finger at her, she shut it and tallied a point on her phone.

"Practice shot," Aven shouted to the crowd with a hand in the air to silence them. He shot a glance at Claire. "Let's see if you do that again . . . while looking."

Will aimed this time and flicked his wrist. The dart zipped straight for the bull's-eye, but as if by some force, it moved an inch, tapping the steel ring and bounced onto the floor.

Aven tossed his dart, and it sunk in the little red dot.

"See?" The first throw is always dumb luck."

Stabbing at the ice in her glass with a straw, Claire debated on ordering another Coke. Instead, she shoved the glass away. For the past hour, Will and Aven had been missing the board miserably. Claire was over their little bet, having sat in the same chair far too long keeping score.

Aven's dart missed the bull's-eye and the crowd moaned.

Claire let out a lengthy sigh. She watched Will head to the bathroom until Aven stumbled to their table and poured another shot. Rolling her eyes as Aven overflowed the glass, Claire sent Laura a video of the dart game and the three empty bottles of whiskey on the table.

Just walk out, Claire. Leave. Let the idiots play their games.

"What's the score, Princess?" Aven asked. He tilted back the shot and slammed the glass on the table with a throaty growl.

"The same since you asked me five minutes ago."

"Ha! I'm still winning." Aven poured Will's shot but squinted an eye when only a few drops kissed the top. "Bobby boy!" He called out, holding up the empty bottle. "Another!"

"Aven," Claire moaned, rubbing her forehead.

"Claire," he teased and kissed her cheek.

"Can't you guys call it a tie so we can go home?"

"That farm is not my home, and I'm pretty sure it's not yours either."

"You know what I mean."

"Let's play a game, shall we? Our own little bet. If I get this next bull's-eye, you have to sleep with me tonight."

"You're drunk. I'm not sleeping with you."

"If *you* get one, you don't have to."

Claire leaned back in her seat and crossed her arms, closing her eyes. It felt good to shut them. The jet lag had yet to wear off. "No, I suck at darts."

"If the dart touches the board?"

Claire met his hopeful stare. "No."

"No, what?" Will asked, coming up behind Aven. He took his shot as if it was water and flipped the glass over on a napkin next to the others.

"Okay, I got one." Aven snapped his fingers. "The past, the present, and the future walk into a bar." He paused. "It was *tense.*"

Claire groaned. Not only had Aven and Will been playing darts for the keys, but they added a contest to see who had the best bar joke.

As Will chuckled, Claire stood and grabbed her phone and the keys to Will's truck. "I'll wait outside."

"Whoa, whoa, whoa, Princess," Aven said, blocking her way.

"Aven, I am this close to giving you the Claire special."

"Oh, that sounds nice."

"I'm sorry, I meant a knee in the groin."

Aven twirled a dart in his fingers, grinned, and flung it at the board. As it punctured the bull's-eye, Claire glared at it.

"Yes!" He held up his clenched fists as if he was the champion of a boxing match.

Another thunk came, followed by steel clattering to the floor. Claire looked around Aven to the wall, finding Will had knocked Aven's dart clean off the board.

"Come on, Claire. Let's go home," Will said, heading toward the exit.

"That's not her home!"

Claire looked over her shoulder, watching as the crowd surrounded Aven with no way to follow.

"Do we need to call a tow truck for the Mustang?" she asked.

Will answered with a grunt and Claire swiveled on her heels, finding Aven's grip on his t-shirt collar.

"Back. Off," Will ordered, shoving Aven off.

"I called dibs before you even met her."

"Yeah, and we all know how that turned out."

"Are you jealous you get sloppy seconds or that you were never the favored son."

Before Claire could take a step to break them apart, Will swung his fist.

Aven dodged the blow, and Claire watched in horror as his fist pounded the back of a bald head.

The bald-headed man with an auburn beard turned around slowly. To Claire, he looked like a biker from a TV show with his black leather vest and chaps. His eyes went wide and he growled.

"Shit," Will said before taking a punch.

"Hey! Red Beard!" Aven shoved the bald man back, but he didn't budge. "If anyone's punching my brother in the face, it's gonna be me."

Aven swung and missed, punching Red Beard's friend beside him in the chin.

The guy punched Aven back, but Will caught Aven as he fell.

"Leave Vegas alone!" Roxy shouted as she stood on the bar.

The crowd charged Red Beard and his friends, and before Claire could blink, everyone in the room joined in on the bar fight.

Claire recoiled as chairs flew and beer bottles shattered on the floor. She attempted to push her way through the angry faces, but there was no escaping the brawl. Then, before she could react, she was knocked to the ground. A hiss escaped her lips at the sharp pain in her palm.

The broken glass from the window on her sixteenth birthday flashed in Claire's mind. Holding back a soft whimper, she plucked the shard from her bloody hand. She came to her feet, taking one last glance at Will and Aven in the midst of the fight.

Lifting her chin to the sky, Claire welcomed the shower of pouring rain. She didn't care if she would have to dry her clothes or sleep in Will's again. She just needed to sleep, and sleep was only fifteen minutes away.

Reaching for the handle of Will's truck, she froze, and swung around to her name.

"Claire, wait!"

The sound of Will's boots thudding across wet pavement didn't stop her from getting in the driver seat. She strapped on the seat belt and proceeded to put in the key.

"Claire!"

She stared at Will through the drops of rain on the windshield. The thin fabric of his shirt clung to his hard body. Rain trickled down his wrinkled forehead to the corner of his pleading eyes.

Claire cracked the window, told him to get in, but he didn't go to the passenger side like she assumed he would.

"Take the Mustang."

When he offered the keys, she glanced behind him to the sports car, not understanding why the Mustang was so important to him.

Maybe he was afraid someone would steal it and sell the parts? But who would buy them? It was illegal to run anything on gas.

"I can't drive a stick," she reminded him. "My dad tried to teach me but–"

"I can drive."

"No, you can't."

"Please."

Claire's heart leapt into her throat as police sirens screamed in the distance. She snatched up the keys, slammed the truck door, and got in the Mustang. When the car came to life with a growl, she gripped the steering wheel tight, and repeated a phrase over and over in her mind.

Left foot, gear, right foot, steer.

She could do this. She could drive a stick shift, just like her father had taught her.

A bang on the passenger side door made her jump.

"This is your fault." Aven's muffled shouted.

Claire put the car back in park and climbed out, finding Will shoving Aven off of him.

"My fault?" Will snapped "I'm not the one who hightailed it after she passed away."

When Aven pushed back, Will wrestled him down to the pavement as everyone running from the bar stopped and stared.

Claire ran around the Mustang and whistled to through her fingers.

Will and Aven both glanced up, holding their fists in the air.

"Both of you get in and shut up!" she shouted over the siren's calls.

"Shotgun!" Will said, punching Aven in the gut.

Aven groaned, curling into a ball.

"Who's got dibs now," Will taunted.

As Will fell into the passenger seat, Aven crawled in the back behind Claire.

"If I puke back here, you're cleaning it up." Aven groaned, favoring his middle.

"Get your seatbelt on," Claire ordered, pulling out of the parking lot.

Aven leaned forward. "Love it when you're feisty."

"Do you ever shut up?" Will asked over his shoulder.

"Just remember, Princess, your head, my bed."

"Are all the men in your family horn dogs or just you?" Will asked.

"At least I admit I want to see her naked."

Claire gripped the steering wheel, gritting her teeth. "Both of you, enough!" she said as if she was the mother of two toddlers having a tantrum. "I don't know what I'm doing, and I need to concentrate."

Will crossed his arms, watching Aven smirk in the rear-view mirror. He had said nothing the past ten minutes other than giving Claire directions left and right at the stoplights. As she turned onto his gravel driveway, he glanced over at her. She leaned forward, glaring at the windshield fogging up.

"Claire," he said softly, "let me drive."

"We're almost there. I see the fence."

"Let the lady be in control, brother."

Will glanced over his shoulder at Aven who was laid back, feet up, and his eyes closed. "Get your feet off the seat," he ordered.

As Claire shifted again, the car jumped and sped up the paved drive. Will leaned back as Claire seemed to relax until an ear-shattering crack came from outside.

A bolt of lightning lit the sky red, then zigzagged as if in slow motion several feet in front of the hood. As the car slid, Will narrowed his gaze to the figure standing in the middle of the road. It rose from its knees, sliding back a hood from a red robe, unfurling black wings. The Mustang snapped back as it fishtailed, and everything went black in Will's vision.

The blare of a horn grew loud in Will's ears as he woke. His cheek burned, and he blinked, finding the airbag in front of him.

The throbbing in his face was sobering. It reminded him of when his mother had slapped him across the cheek. A year ago, she had told him to choose.

Sober up or leave and never speak to me again.

He had seen the grief in her eyes, seen the fear of losing another son. That was the night he poured out the bottle, the night he vowed to never drink again.

Shoving the airbag away, he glanced over at Claire. She was leaned over the steering wheel, eyes closed. Panic gripped his chest seeing the bloody trail from her forehead down her cheek.

"Claire?" Will fumbled to unbuckle her as Aven groaned.

"I'm gonna vomit."

"Help me get her out."

Aven crawled out behind Will and came around to the driver's side, stumbling.

Claire coughed and moaned as he laid her on the wet pavement of the shoulder.

Aven bent down and scanned her with his phone.

A chime rang out at the completion of the x-ray.

"What's it say?" Will asked.

"It says she'll bruise in a few places, but it's nothing an ice pack won't fix," Aven answered. "Huh. This app has a better sense of humor than you do."

Will lifted Claire in his arms and headed up his driveway. "Claire, can you hear me?"

Claire muttered something, but Will couldn't make out her words; only a name.

"Where are you going?" Aven shouted. "I just ordered a cab to take her to the hospital."

No. No hospitals. No cops. They would ask for prints.

Will pressed Claire against his chest as she wrapped her arms around him. "I don't feel like getting arrested. Do you?'

"We won't get arrested. I know people."

"She's responsive, and I have a first aid kit at the house."

"You can't carry her all the way back, Dr. Stryde."

"It's only half a mile. I've picked up a man twice your size, put him over my shoulder, and carried him into the barracks running a fourth. I think I can handle it."

Aven let out a laugh. "Yeah right."

Will paused and looked at Aven with a pointed stare. "Wanna bet?"

"No more betting tonight."

"Agreed."

With the house in sight, Aven insisted on carrying Claire the rest of the way, as if he couldn't bear the thought of Will getting all the glory. He situated Claire with a light toss and glanced at Will beside him, passing the red barn.

"Look at us, getting along," Aven said.

"I'm only tolerating you because I'm too drunk to hit both of you in the face at the same time."

"Ah, so you *are* tipsy." Aven grinned. "How many were you from calling it quits?"

"About as many as you were."

"Did you see that huge birdman before we crashed?"

"Birdman?"

"Don't act like you didn't," Aven said, knowing he didn't imagine the figure. "You think we hit him?"

"I think you're drunker than you think." Will sighed, walking up the steps of his porch. "We landed in a tree. Thanks to you, the car is totaled." He opened the door, took Claire from Aven.

"My bed, remember?" Aven reminded him as Will headed for the stairs. "You really want to tote her up there?"

Will clenched his jaw but took Claire to Aven's room. As soon as he laid her on the bed, Aven unbuttoned her pants, wasting no time peeling off her wet clothes.

Will stood in the way, putting him at arm's length as if to protect Claire's honor. "What are you doing?"

"Like I haven't seen it all before." Aven shoved past him and pulled down the zipper. Will averted his gaze as Aven slipped a finger across her underwear. "Soaking wet and wearing a *thong*. No girl likes picking out a wedgie in the morning."

Will crossed his arm and hovered with a glare.

Aven smirked, peeling off her jeans. "You can wait outside if you're uncomfortable," Aven said. He cradled her neck and reached behind her back.

"Undergarments stay," Will ordered, covering her with the comforter.

Aven gave a sideways glance. "You really don't trust me, do you? Look, I may be drunk, but I'm not going to take advantage of her. It's a rule, not only in my book but—"

"My house, my rules. And the first one is assholes sleep on the couch." Will brushed past him, taking some sheets from the closet.

When he returned, he found Aven on the right side of the bed, propping up his feet.

"What the hell do you think you're doing?"

"Making sure you don't try to steal my girl."

Will tossed the sheets on the end of the bed and put his hands on his hips. "Didn't take you for a relationship kind of guy."

"I'm not."

"Then why mark your territory?" Will lifted his chin, setting his eyes on Claire.

Aven glanced at her and then back at Will with a shrug. "What can I say, I'm greedy."

"Someone needs to be with her that knows the signs of a concussion."

"I knew it."

"What?"

"You *like* her. This whole distant but protective thing, I have to say nice move. I wish I'd thought of it."

Will rolled his eyes and fell into the bed on the other side of Claire.

"Really?"

"You don't expect me to get up those stairs, do you?"

"Then sleep on the couch," Aven said, grabbing a pillow off the sheets at his feet. "Three's a crowd—literally." He threw it at Will's face but missed.

Claire stirred and moaned. "Alexander . . ."

There it was. That name again.

Somehow it felt familiar to Will. An image flashed in his mind of a training yard.

Gloves of electricity. Swords of light.

"Alexander's not here," Aven said a little too loud. He glanced over at Will and whispered, "Who's Alexander?"

"Hopefully not a dick like you."

"You're just jealous. I'm fun. You're not."

"It's four in the morning and I have to feed the horses at six. Could you at least attempt to shut your mouth for, oh, I don't know, five whole minutes?"

"Mm—no."

Will sighed and closed his eyes again. To his surprise, there was a long moment of silence, but it didn't last.

"Will?"

"I knew it."

"I'm sorry—about taking your brother's car."

Will wondered how Aven knew it was Aaron's car, but he didn't ask. He only let a smile tug at his lips. "Did you just apologize?"

"Don't expect it to happen again."

"Don't worry, I won't."

BOYFRIEND

Monday, 9:12 a.m., South Carolina

THE throbbing pain in her head wasn't what woke Claire; it was the ding of pots and pans. A groan escaped her lips. She touched her tender forehead, finding a bandage. Drawing back her hand, she found it too had been patched up.

The bar fight. The lightning. Squealing tires. The figure with black wings. An Angel of Death.

She remembered the concern in Aven's voice; Will's strong arms holding her. The arm around her now wasn't Will's. She knew by the way it drew her in, the way Aven sighed against her shoulder. Kissed it.

When Claire scooted away, she replaced her body with her pillow. Aven cuddled it and smiled as she tiptoed to the neatly folded clothes on the end of the bed. Now she knew for sure it had been Will who had brought her clothes yesterday and not the nurse.

Closing the door quietly, Claire walked into the kitchen, finding Will at the sink. He was washing dishes. She watched him for a moment, standing by the table covered in a wonderful array of breakfast foods.

"Good morning," she said finally.

Will threw the drying towel over his shoulder and leaned against the sink. "How's your head?"

"Pounding." She glanced at her hand. "Did you . . .?"

Will smiled before he reached into a cabinet. He took out a bottle of aspirin. "Anything else hurt?" he asked, making her a glass of water.

Claire shook her head. "Thank you." She graciously took the aspirin and gulped it down. "So I guess Aven got his way."

"He was just making sure you were okay. He was worried about you."

"So were you."

Will averted his gaze. "I made some homemade biscuits. The preserves are from my neighbors down the street and they," he said, pointing to the eggs, "really do own a farm."

As Will sat down, Claire pulled out the chair across from him. "You didn't have to go to the trouble."

"I didn't. Ms. Bleakly also gave me the breakfast casserole, the eggs. I already had the fruit and hash browns. I didn't want it to go bad since I'll be leaving next week."

"Leaving?"

"Is Aven getting up?" Will asked. He reached for the bowel of eggs and held them out to Claire.

Claire took the bowel and scooped the eggs onto her plate. "I didn't wake him." Claire glanced up. "You're not hung over?"

"No."

"Thank you for carrying me back."

Will's eyes were soft, but he said nothing as he chewed his food.

They sat quietly for a long moment, eating and shooting small glances at one another now and then. When Will was finished, he got up and washed his plate. Claire poked around her eggs with her fork, thinking about the fact that she was in South Carolina, that if she hadn't met Aven, she would be walking on the beach.

Had it all been a coincidence?

The date that had been changed for the bachelorette party, the hotel that was booked. It seemed as if it had all been planned out somehow.

"Do you think things happen for a reason?" Claire asked, not looking up from her plate.

"What do you mean?"

"Do you think we have a choice in life? Or do you think no matter what we do, we're set on a certain path, to be somewhere we're supposed to be?"

Will put his clean plate and fork in the drying rack and leaned against the sink with his arms crossed. "Like destiny?"

Claire glanced up, seeing the stern look on his face. She couldn't tell if he was interested or irritated. "Sorry. I'm getting all philosophical."

"It's okay." Will turned back to the sink. "Aaron always talked about those kinds of things. I'm used to it."

"Aaron?"

Will seemed to brace himself on the sink. He looked out the window, then over his shoulder. "My little brother."

"He's the one in the pictures?"

"Yeah."

"He looks just like Aven. Is he coming to the funeral?"

"I don't know."

"He lives too far away?"

"Pretty far."

Claire furrowed her brows. She could tell the subject was uncomfortable for Will, but she couldn't let it go. "Did he come to see your mom while she was sick?"

"Most likely while I was in Vegas."

"So he's not in the military anymore?"

Will shook his head.

"Where is he?"

Will turned, keeping his gaze on the floor. "I imagine on a sailboat fishing or maybe in a cabin in the mountains, reading."

Getting up slowly as if afraid Will would walk out of the room, Claire went to the sink to wash her plate.

Will took it and did it for her.

"I've got to get things ready for tomorrow, think you can keep Aven out of trouble until your friend comes to pick you up?"

"I'll try." Claire laughed.

"Make yourself at home. I'll try to be back by eleven to make lunch, but if I'm not—if you're gone before I get back—"

"Thank you for everything, Will."

"You're welcome to visit anytime."

Claire's brows rose with hope, thinking of the moment they shared in the rain.

"To visit Snow."

"Oh, of course. I would like that."

Will put a plate of leftovers in the microwave and then put up the rest of the food. "Guess I should get going."

As Will went up the steps, Claire glanced down at the empty dog dishes on the floor.

"Do I need to feed your dog while you're gone?"

Will rested a hand on the bannister and shook his head. "No. If I know Blue she won't leave Mom's bed. She doesn't do well with death."

Claire watched Will disappear before she grabbed her phone from the kitchen counter. She opened her messages, texting Laura about her accident, how Will had carried her, how heroic and humble he was, and about Aven's drunk flirting.

"Texting Alexander?"

Claire's heart skipped. The name. Somehow she felt she knew it, knew it meant something, but she didn't know what.

"Will made breakfast." She said walking to the microwave. She got out the food for Aven and sat it on the table before head toward the stairs. "You should eat."

"You said his name in your sleep," Aven informed.

"I don't know anyone named Alexander. I'm going to get a shower. Laura's going to pick me up in a few hours."

"I'm sorry for how I acted last night."

Claire paused from on the steps. He had lost his mother; he had been trying to hide the pain, but he had also acted like a complete jerk.

"It's okay. You were hurt. You weren't thinking straight."

"You've changed your mind about us."

Claire came back down the steps and stood in front in him.

"I didn't. I just—I don't know where I stand. Where we stand."

"Message Laura back, and tell her your boyfriend was a complete idiot, but you forgive him and don't need a ride because he's taking you shopping."

Claire's breath left her.

Boyfriend.

"Shopping for what?"

"A change of clothes—and a dress for the funeral."

"No. Aven—"

"Please? I don't want to hold Will's hand. They're calloused, and it would be weird."

"I honestly don't think I could handle it. The last time I stood in a cemetery was when my dad died."

Aven took a step forward and slipped his pinky into Claire's and gave a gentle squeeze. He smiled and glanced back up at her. "If you agree to stand by my side, I'll agree to tell you my secrets tonight. All of them."

After hours of shopping and several hundred dollars spent, Claire piled the bags from the boutiques into the cab.

"You said two outfits, not ten," she said to Aven.

"You didn't have fun trying everything on? I enjoyed watching."

Claire let out a sigh. "You can't keep doing this if we're going to be together."

"Do what?"

"Dote on me."

"You don't want to be wooed and courted?"

"Nope."

"Oh no." Aven's face scrunched. "You're going to break up with me."

"Why?"

"I already have something set up to arrive at your house."

"I don't need gifts, Aven. I just want you to be yourself."

"I'm compulsive, remember? Give me a spending limit."

"Twenty dollars."

"Ha. That's a penny to me."

"Aven."

"Alright, Princess. You win." He glanced at the sign above them. "One last stop?"

Claire lifted her gaze to the faded sign that read "Antiques."

"You want to go in here?"

"You look surprised?" Aven stepped up on the sidewalk and gestured for Claire to go ahead of him as he opened the door.

"I never took you for someone that liked this sort of place."

"*This* sort of place has what I like most."

The antique shop looked exactly like Claire expected it to. She and Mother had always gone in thrift stores, places that had anything used. Her mother was good at re-purposing, turning anything, even a toilet, into something beautiful. That's how she decorated the Bed and Breakfast. Claire didn't have that kind of creativity, but she wished she did.

Aven went straight for the counter where an old man with a thinning hairline welcomed them to his shop.

"Good afternoon, sir," Aven said, leaning on the counter. "You wouldn't to have any sort of special paper, would you?"

"What kind of paper?" The old man gave him a look.

"The kind that is *sparse*," Aven said with his charming smile.

The old man looked over his shoulder at the camera in the upper left corner of his shop, and then, back to Aven. "I may have something in the back," he said, rubbing his fingers together.

"I'll be right back, Princess. If you see something you like, make sure it's under twenty." Aven winked and followed the old man through a door.

Claire poked around the store, finding all the things her mother would have been thrilled to buy. To Claire, these items were useless, and nothing caught her attention until a dark wooden box stood out. She dusted off the smooth surface and opened it, but the music box didn't make any sound. It was expected. Just about everything in shops like this needed repair.

"Gorgeous."

Claire flinched slightly, but then she sighed as she glanced over her shoulder.

Gorgeous. He hadn't been talking about the box.

"It is," Claire stated, tracing her fingers along the intricate carvings. "Someone put a lot of work into it."

She put down the music box and looked at the cloth in Aven's hands. "Did you find what you were looking for?"

"I did," Aven said, fixing his gaze. Again. Not talking about anything in the shop.

"Is it delicate?"

Aven slid back the cloth, long enough for Claire to get a peek. Panic shot through her, seeing the faded title of the worn cover.

"Are those . . ." Claire didn't finish her sentence. She glanced at the camera behind the shop clerk and brought her gaze back to the illegal contraband.

Books. Real books made with paper and ink.

"They are."

Claire's heart thudded against her chest. "Aven, you can't," she whispered, but the horn from the cab sounded outside, cutting her off

"Tell him I'm checking out." Aven gave a quick kiss to Claire's cheek and went to the counter.

Letting out a long breath through pursed lips, Claire gave another quick glance to the camera as she walked out the door. Aven may have gotten away with things in Vegas, but they weren't in Vegas anymore, and what he had just done could get them both arrested on the spot.

There was no talking to Aven on the way back to Will's. He had been on the phone with his cousin, Vincent, talking about a trip to Asia. It sounded like a very important trip. Just from twenty minutes of overhearing the conversation, Claire realized how dangerous Aven's job was when he said words like "torture" or "machete."

When they got to the house, she went upstairs and changed into one of the outfits Aven had bought for her. She checked herself in the mirror, situating the black mini skirt and red top before she came back down to the living room and glanced at the grandfather clock as it chimed.

Six p.m.

"Will's not back yet?"

"Nope," Aven said, thumbing through his phone in the living room.

"Did he message you?"

"How's pizza and a movie sound?" Aven held up his phone, showing Claire a picture of the movie he wanted to stream.

"Phantom of the Opera?"

"Ever seen it?"

"No. What's it about?"

"A dark and mysterious man who seduces an angel." Aven wiggled his brows and pressed his phone, but the TV didn't respond.

"Hm. Looks like I need to buy my brother an upgrade. When I fly you back to Vegas, I'll take you to see it. It's better in the theatre anyway. Dinner won't arrive for another thirty minutes. Want to go in my room and fool around?"

"You promised," Claire said, trying to remind Aven that he had told her he would reveal his secrets. She, in a way, hoped he wouldn't. She couldn't stand the thought of going to a cemetery. Her pulse sped up just thinking about a yard of tombstones.

"Can't get anything past you, can I?" Aven disappeared into his room for a moment and came back, holding a pack of cards. He laid them on the table and pulled out a chair for Claire. "Milady."

Claire looked at the deck. She had seen these before at a carnival. Laura had insisted they go in and get their fortune read, but Claire didn't want to. She only watched Laura get hers. She remembered how the woman laid out the cards, what the pictures looked like. She rubbed her arms, uncomfortable. Her dad had been very much against messing with anything related to such Occult practices. No matter if people practiced it in the Worship Centers, her father had warned her to stay away.

Claire never understood how all beliefs could be worshiped at one time. How could devils and angels be called upon in the same room? Any and all deities were called during the services. All were welcome. No one was judged. No one looked down upon.

There is only one Creator, one being to be worshiped, Claire. No matter what the world says, truth is truth, her father had told her.

"The club you're in—you said you signed in blood. You didn't mean that metaphorically, did you?"

"What I'm about to tell you must be kept a secret. Can you promise not to tell?" Aven gestured for her to sit.

Claire gave her word with a nod and sat in the chair.

"The club I'm in, the Circle," Aven said as he sat across from her, "is a secret society. Only the elite can be a part of it. Millionaires, celebrities, people with respectable titles."

"Why is it a secret?"

"Because everyone that is a part of it has a plan to rule the world—some for good, some for evil. Sometimes you can't tell which because the law doesn't apply to any of the members. Money is power."

"Is that why you can buy things that are illegal?"

Aven's lips turned up. "Would you like to look at them?"

Claire wanted to look. She didn't want to admit it, but to see, to touch a real book was something she always wanted to do. As Aven unwrapped them, her heart raced again, this time not in fear but excitement. She took in the book's musty smell, the touch of the tattered tip of the spine.

"*Dante's Inferno*?" she asked, tracing the etched title. "What's it about?"

"Hell." Aven's answer was nonchalant, as if the contents of the book were no big deal.

Hell. Demons. What are you getting yourself into, Claire?

At the ring of the doorbell, Claire flinched. The book fell from her grasp and met the table with a loud smack. Aven picked it up and wrapped the books, putting them to the side.

When Aven greeted the pizza boy, the aroma of baked pepperoni and tomato sauce calmed Claire's nerves, but she couldn't take her eyes off the contraband sitting on the floor—not until she heard he front door shut.

"It's not what you had in Vegas, but close," Aven said as he brought in the pizza box with another small carton on top of it.

Claire watched Aven open the carton, revealing a chocolate cheesecake with raspberries on top. "They had that at the pizza place?"

"I paid the guy to go by a place in town," Aven admitted. "I'm stress eating. I've never been big on funerals and stressed spelt backwards is desserts, so I thought, why not."

"And that?" Claire asked, glancing at the six-pack of malt liquor by the door.

"After we eat, I thought we should play a little game."

"What kind of game?"

"Truth for a truth." Aven grinned wide, putting the drinks in the fridge.

"Truth or Dare without the dare," Claire said. She grabbed a piece of pizza and sat back in her chair. "Laura and I used to play it."

"Then you know," Aven said, tilting his head with a mischievous smile, "that, no matter the inquisition, the players must be indubitably forthright."

TRUTH FOR A

TRUTH

"NOT nearly as good as the one at the bakery," Aven said, taking the empty carton from their dessert to the trash. He put the rest of the pizza in the fridge and got out two malt sodas. "Ready to play?"

"Not really," Claire answered with a sigh, taking the drink from Aven.

"Do an easy one first," Aven said, shuffling the tarot cards. He kept his gaze on her, flapping the cards against one another in the air. They glided, one hand to the other and back again until Aven slapped his hands together. With a flourish of his fingers, he revealed nothing in his hands. He drew up his sleeves, silently saying that nothing was up them.

Flirt.

Aven winked—as if reading Claire's mind—before he slid a hand across the table. The cards appeared once more, spread in a neat line.

"Where did you learn magic?" Claire asked, glancing up from the trick.

"After my dad was murdered"—Aven frowned at the cards as he scooped them up and began flipping them over—"I went to live with my Uncle Jimmy."

Claire swallowed the knot in her throat, remembering the argument Aven and Will had at the bar.

"At the age of thirteen, my uncle asked me if I wanted to one day take over the family business, but I was a kid and obsessed with becoming a Las Vegas magician. So, we made a deal. If I went to the college of his choice, became his prodigy, he would show me sleight of hand."

"Your Uncle Jimmy, he's Vincent's father," Claire said, wording it like a statement and not a question. According to the rules of this game, only one question per player could be asked at a time. But if the player asked more than the first question during their turn, two questions could be asked of the opposite player as well.

"He was a great guy. I think I take after him more than my father; I'm pretty sure Vincent is still sore about me getting half of the estate, not to mention I was always called the favorite."

"He taught you the trick you used on me at the bar." Again, Claire made sure it didn't sound like a question. At Aven's grin, she could tell he had caught on.

"I came up with that one myself. But—"Aven flipped a card over and then tapped it. For a split second it appeared as a queen of hearts, but when Claire blinked, her heart stopped at the haunting image.

Death.

The skeleton wore a crimson robe. In one bony hand he held a white rose , in the other, a scythe. The image of the robe and the black wings of the figure before the car crash came to her.

Had it been Death that appeared?

"You're the only young maiden I've ever pulled out the queen of hearts for," Aven answered. "I could teach you."

"How to pick up women. No thanks."

"Sleight of hand. Let's start with something easy." He shuffled the cards.

"I'm a fast learner. Show me how you did that trick at LAX."

"Alright, milady." Aven held up a card that looked like a queen. "Let's pretend this is your card."

Claire took a good look at it and put it in the middle of the deck.

"The trick"—Aven folded his hands and leaned in—"is to keep the other person's attention on something other than the cards, even if it's only for a split second. You can pick the invisible lint off your clothes, glance at something on the floor like your shoes, or"—Aven shuffled the cards—"you look in their eyes, and *never* break your stare." He did the trick, much slower this time, revealing the card.

Claire's mouth parted, finding it had been in plain sight all along.

"The closer they look, the less they see." Aven wiggled his brows with a clever grin. "My turn."

Claire took a large gulp of hers, hoping he wouldn't ask about her past.

"What were the other things you saw when you took the medication?"

Of course he would ask that.

"Mostly things from dreams." She dared to glance up, to reveal another truth she had hidden. "Of places . . . people I've never met."

"Did you dream about me before you met me?"

Claire watched Aven's unwavering gaze. He tilted his head, waiting for her answer. But his turn was over. She could ask two questions to his one.

"Why do you carry around these cards?"

"I like to see what the future holds for me from time to time."

"You tell your own fortune?"

"Each card means something. A long time ago, I was shown which of these cards I was." Aven leaned back and tilted up his bottle. "Take a guess."

Claire took a good look at each card, avoiding the one of Death, and then tapped her finger the magician. "This one."

Aven grinned, shaking his head slowly.

Claire put her finger on the king.

Aven gave a throaty laugh and swept the cards into a stack. He stared at the deck for a moment and then lifted a brow.

Claire flinched as the top card slid off the deck and across the table into her hand. Her gaze flicked to Aven. He wiggled his brows with a grin, casually taking a sip of his malt liquor as if waiting for her to look at the card.

Peeking, Claire found a man adorned in frills, a jester hat upon his head. He appeared delighted, warmed by the sun, sniffing a white rose. He was a vagabond, holding a stick with a kerchief on the end in his other hand. He stood on the edge of a cliff, paying no mind to the danger as the earth crumbled beneath him.

The fool.

"In modern-day cards," Aven began, "the fool, is known as the joker or the jester. As for the tarot, the fool stands for each of us as we begin our journey of life. He is a simple soul with innocent faith to undertake such a journey with all its hazards and pain.

"The terms positive and negative do not imply good or evil in the tarot. All players are necessary for balance. In the Circle, we view the negative as our shadow, our weaknesses, our downfalls. Without these shadows, we cannot comprehend light, appreciate its warmth."

Claire asked him to explain further with eager eyes.

"At the beginning of this journey, the foolish child is trained in all the practices of his society, becomes part of a particular culture, gains status. He learns to identify with his group's worldviews and discovers a sense of belonging. He enjoys learning the customs of his society and shows his leaders how well he can conform to them.

"And then," Aven said, laying down another card, "the fool's world is turned upside down."

Claire looked at the card of a couple embraced, an angel behind them, its wings spread wide as if approving the union. "The fool was mainly self-centered, self-indulging," Aven continued. "Now he feels a balance, is led to reach out and become half of a loving partnership, yearning for a meaningful relationship. But . . . the fool must decide upon his beliefs, not his counterpart's. It is good enough to conform while he learns and grows, but at some point, he must determine his own values if he is to be true to himself. The lover makes him question everything he's ever known, ever encountered on his journey."

Claire glanced up slowly, finding Aven's fixed gaze. "Why do I feel like you're talking about me?" she asked softly.

"Because," Aven said, leaning forward, "I am."

Claire swallowed as Aven narrowed his eyes, tilting his head. "Did you dream about me before you met me, Claire?"

At a flicker the lights, Claire's blood ran cold and her heart raced with urgency.

Something was wrong. Very wrong.

The dream Claire had on the plane flashed in her mind again, then the vision she'd had in the hotel room. She closed her eyes, pressing a hand to her chest as it caved in on her lungs.

Not now.

"Claire . . ."

When Claire lifted her gaze, she found Aven's full of concern. She could see him, the real him behind the storm of grey. There was no trickster, no playful joker lingering as he reached for her hand. Her shoulders fell in relief at his warmth, but when something skittered behind his shoulder at the piano, she pulled away.

Sucking in a sharp breath, Claire stood up, knocking her chair back and jumped as it smacked against the floor.

"We should get some sleep," she mumbled all too quickly. "We can talk more tomorrow." She rushed to pick up the chair and then darted to the steps.

"Claire, wait." Aven's voice was almost pleading.

She didn't want to see the shadow again, didn't want to believe what Aven had said about his demons. If they were real, if they were what kept him up at night, they were now after her too. She forced herself to turn around, eyes closed.

"It was a little more than twenty-five dollars. But I knew you liked it."

Claire opened her eyes, finding Aven holding something from the antique shop.

The music box.

She steadied her wobbly legs and ran her fingers over the smooth carved wood until Aven turned the key and opened the top.

The tune was sad but beautiful, and Claire's eyes welled as the ting of metal plinked to the tune of *The Lonely Ballerina*. She had played this song on the day after her father had died, the last song before she closed her piano top and never played again. Not until the night with Aven, when he had asked her to bare her soul.

As she clutched to the box, Aven slid his thumb across her cheek and wiped the tear. "I told you we would face those beasties together."

Claire shook her head, pressing her lips hard. The memory of the fire and the casket of her father pounded the haunting guilt against her chest. Her body quivered with waves of emotion. She was drowning, gasping for breath, sinking deeper as the anxiety flooded her.

"I wish there was a way I could walk into your mind and take it away," Aven whispered, cupping her face. "Erase the memory of the fire reaching for you, how you tried so hard to hold on to that gutter, the sickening sound of your body as it hit the ground—"

Claire's gaze snapped to Aven's. "You saw it?"

Aven's throat bobbed as if he hadn't realized what he had said at first. "Yes."

"But you told me you weren't there, that—"

"You're the first person I've ever Mind Walked with that I could see what was happening."

"How is that possible?"

"I don't know," he answered, sweeping the hair from her face. "But I do know there's something between us we can't explain. Something buried so deep, that our souls are calling us to remember."

Our souls. A connection. The tug.

"What did you see, Claire?"

Claire stared at Aven blankly. She wanted to run away, wanted to escape his sympathetic stare. But as she drew back, the tug, the knowing of their connection, drew her toward him again.

"What's troubling you?" Aven whispered, caressing her cheek.

An image of the dark haired angel came with same words from his lips

"You'll think I'm crazy."

Aven's lifted her chin. "We're all mad here."

Claire exhaled at his words, teetering on the edge of telling him, of confessing everything.

"Did you see me in your dreams before we met?" Aven's gaze was pleading again. "Did it feel like a memory?"

Like a memory. How do you know? Are you him?

"Yes," she managed to say.

There was no hesitation, no other words spoken as Aven pressed her against the banister. His kiss was urgent, passionate, and Claire found pleasure in every tendril of her body, replacing the fear she had once had.

"Come to my bed." He breathed against her lips. "I'll tell you everything. No more secrets, no more games."

Claire answered yes with a kiss but jerked away, startled at the opening of the front door. She covered her burning lips in shame and met Will's defeated gaze as he stood at the threshold.

SIBLING RIVALRY

WILL didn't understand why it had surprised him, almost broke his heart, seeing Aven kissing Claire again. Part of him filled with relief. She had stayed. He had wanted her to, but not for Aven.

As Claire thanked Aven for the box in her arms and rushed upstairs, Will let out the breath he had been holding and tossed his keys on the counter.

"Perfect timing, brother." Aven crossed his arms and leaned on the bannister.

"Don't mind me."

"I do mind you," Aven shot back. "That's twice you have ruined my wooing."

"Wooing?" Will snorted as he opened the fridge. "Looks more like smothering." He gave an absent look at the shelves, the pizza box, then shut the door. He wasn't hungry. Not anymore.

"There's that darn jealousy again." Aven shook his head, clicking his tongue. "Pesky little thing, isn't it?"

"What's there to jealous of? I hardly know Claire. Come to think of it," he said, narrowing his gaze, "you hardly know her.

"Oh, I know her, brother. In ways you could only dream of."

"Are you trying to make this some kind of pissing contest?" Will crossed his arms and leaned back on the sink.

Aven shrugged as he picked up his bottle of malt liquor. He chugged it down and let out a satisfying sigh. "More like sibling rivalry, but yeah. And if you can't tell, I'm winning. Again." Aven wiggled his brows with a smirk. "Oh, by the way, she's coming to the funeral tomorrow. Just thought you should know."

"Claire's a good person, Aven."

"That's why I like her."

"Too good to make you feel better about yourself and then get tossed to the side when something new and shiny comes along."

Aven tilted his head. "You had a conversation with my cousin, didn't you?"

"I only believe half of what I hear. Actions speak louder than words."

"Last night I was drunk. We all know we do stupid things when we're drunk."

"Woke up a new man, did you?"

"Yep," Aven said, picking up a curious deck of cards. He put them in his back pocket and went to a cabinet in the kitchen.

"I didn't know you could trade a pitch fork for wings so easily."

"As you know, people can change." He took out a bottle of liquor from a brown bag and unscrewed the top.

Will glared at it. "Have you?"

"Work in progress." Aven poured himself a glass. "Nightcap?" he offered, holding up the bottle.

"The funeral is at eight." Will walked out of the kitchen to the steps and paused. "I'm going up there at seven to get everything set up."

"We should arrive separate, avoid the illegitimate child awkwardness. Makes Mom look bad. And out of respect, Claire and I will stand in the back."

Will didn't know if Aven was being thoughtful or if he couldn't stand to be that close to the casket. "No one else is coming except a few of my friends that knew her."

"No other family?"

"She didn't know her family. Her foster parents died in a car accident when she was eighteen."

"Seems we all have tragic little backstories, don't we?" Aven took a sip of his bourbon. "I'm curious to hear more about the one with your younger brother."

Sorry. Not in the mood for that conversation.

Will turned his back on Aven and ascended the stairs. "Eight a.m. Sober."

SUCCUBUS

AVEN glanced at the clock, walking into the kitchen to pour another drink. He ignored the cold draft lingering from the demon's presence and guzzled down the liquor, full of despair.

The demon had been playing with Claire, testing her, looking for a weakness, a way in. Part of him wished he had taken her to his room, swept her up into his arms like he had in Vegas.

His fingers twitched against the cold glass and he shook his head, making his way back to the piano to play. The longer he thought of him and Claire together, the harder it was becoming to avoid staring at the steps. He envisioned himself going up them, slipping through the crack of her door as she slept, waking her with a soft graze of his fingers beneath the silky nightgown he had bought. He could already hear his name on her lips, the creak of the bed, the panting of them both after a euphoric release . . . the irritating pounding of the door from Will's fist.

Nice timing, brother.

In a way, Aven had been glad of Will's entrance but wouldn't admit to himself he was right. He had been trying much too hard, breaking his own rules.

Aven had never been the clingy type. It had always been the other way around, and now, he felt guilty for shrugging off all the women who had been so interested in him. No closure, no knowledge of what might have been.

Only rejection.

Placing the glass of bourbon on the piano, Aven laid his fingers on the keys, playing the somber chords of *Moonlight Sonata*.

The grandfather clock struck midnight and Aven paused as the cool draft turned icy. Grimacing as the low chime came like a sledgehammer against his chest, he managed a deep breath and continued to play with stiff fingers.

"Can you feel the torture of the lover, written in the notes I composed?"

When Aven scoffed, his breath clouded in front of him. "Taking credit for Beethoven's brilliance. Charming."

Nehia nipped his ear with chilling lips. "Who do you think told him the notes to play?"

"The man was deaf. I doubt he was lured by your whispers of grandeur."

"Do you not hear me in your head?"

Aven gave her a sideways glare, catching a glimpse of the black wing lining her almond-shaped eyes. He averted his gaze from hers, watching her slender legs—revealed beneath her sheer black Egyptian goddess-like garb.

"Let's go back to the bar and play." Nehia sighed, tracing her slender fingers along the piano. "It's dull here."

"I'm not in the mood to entertain you."

She skittered like smoke and appeared, lounging on top of the piano. "If you won't play with me, then you should play with her."

"You would like that, wouldn't you?"

"You know what I desire." Nehia's red eyes lit with a fiery glow.

"I do. Every night it's the same."

"She likes that song. I hear her listening to it upstairs. Play it for her."

Aven ignored Nehia and changed the tune to a more upbeat tempo. Saint-Saens, *The Swan*.

"Come my dark darlings," she said, smiling as the demon dogs appeared out of thin air, "have a bite."

Aven slammed his fingers hard against the low keys and glanced up with a smile. "Perhaps the legion would enjoy a good hymn. Hm?"

Nehia let out a taunting laugh as the dogs gnashed their jagged teeth. "It only works if you mean the words." She slithered away in smoke again and sat beside him on the stool, giving an exaggerated pout. "But you don't believe. You're too bitter from losing your mother. Twice now."

"I may give him another shot. He has to be better than the master of the soulless bitch who delights in my torment."

"I'd like to see you say that after you die."

"I'm starting to think you and Bree only say that to control me."

"You've seen it." Nehia traced his neck with icy fingernails. "You know it to be true."

Aven's neck whipped back when Nehia grabbed a clump of his hair. She whispered an unknown tongue in his ear. Images of a possible future came forth as Aven's ears filled with the sound of licking flames, a girl's cries. A sharp stab came from his back. He looked down at his stomach, finding blood seeping through his shirt into his lap.

"Get out of my head."

"Play the song to the music box."

Aven gargled and cough up the blood.

"Or shall I go play with her again?"

Aven gasped, snapping back to reality. The illusion ceased, the pain with it too. "She saw you," he managed to say. "That's why she—"

"Take her to your bed, or neither of you will sleep tonight."

"Go to hell."

"Have it your way." Nehia skittered in smoke and was gone, only to reappear on the steps, a finger to her lips ascending the staircase.

"Wait," Aven gritted through his teeth. "If I do—will you leave?"

Nehia vanished and reappeared behind him, whispering in his ear, "Depends on what happens."

"When I get home, I'll have a threesome. Satisfied?"

"Never," Nehia said. She appeared in his lap, her legs straddling him. She leaned against him, licking his neck, combing her fingers through his hair. "You don't know how much I enjoyed watching you please her, how delicate you had been. I want to know what that feels like, I want to know what it's like to be loved."

"I think I'll tell her about you."

Nehia shook her head slow as if she felt sorry for him. "No, you won't."

Aven bit his lip and stared at the piano keys as she rocked forward and nipped his earlobe. No matter how much he loathed her, his body reacted accordingly.

"You're afraid she won't accept you, or worse, she'll leave you just like your little kitten did."

Aven's chest ached. He couldn't bear to think about what Katharine was doing with Nick right now.

"If you play the tune and take her to bed, you have my word, I'll only haunt you in your dreams."

"As if your word matters."

"No more than your pinky promise."

"Why didn't you interfere?"

Nehia's grin widened. "Because you were doing exactly what I wanted."

"You were watching the whole time."

"The sweetest taste of sin is when an angel and a devil collide."

Aven ground his teeth, but Nehia only giggled as she vanished. She appeared behind him, placing her hands over his, moving them to the piano keys. "Play, and I'll let you be with her, alone."

"Why would you give such a luxury?"

"Because when the time comes, you'll let me have her."

LONELY

BALLERINA

IN every step she took, Claire held her breath as she tiptoed past Will's door. She folded her arms over the silky nightgown Aven had bought her, going toward the sound of the piano. She had been listening to the music box on her bed, about to fall asleep, but her eyes fluttered open as the porcelain dancer had clicked to a stop and the tune continued.

Coming to the bottom of the steps, she peeked around the corner. A cold draft sent goosebumps down her arms, and she rubbed them, afraid of seeing the shadow again. She questioned if the music was in her head, if the dark imagination was playing the tune, luring her in.

"Go," Aven growled.

Claire froze at the doorway and pressed her back against the wall.

"I said leave!"

Claire quivered at the harsh tone of Avens voice as the floor creaked beneath her feet in her leaving.

"Claire?" His tone was soft now, meek.

"I'm sorry," Claire said, returning to the entry.

"For what?"

"You told me to go, and—"

"I wasn't talking to you I was—" his throat bobbed, his face twisting as if he was in pain. "Will you come sit with me?"

Claire fidgeted with the end of her fishtail braid, hesitating, but went to Aven's side and sat. He smiled sweetly at her, trailing his fingers gracefully along the ivory keys, then he glanced up at her as if asking her to join him, but she didn't.

"You can't sleep, can you?" she asked.

Aven stopped playing and stared at the piano keys for a long moment.

"You said you would tell me."

Aven frowned and braced his hands on the stool but didn't meet her wary gaze.

"What you saw Claire, the demon from your past, from the fire, do you think it was real?"

She shook her head. "Like you said. The meds. They cause hallucinations."

"I want to tell you, to bare my soul, but . . ." Aven bit his bottom lip and glanced over her shoulder before he averted his gaze back to the piano.

"But what?"

He met her gaze and after a long pause, he smiled through a wince. "I'm afraid to."

"Don't be," Claire said, taking his hands in hers.

"Tell me what you saw. What made you want to run up the steps?"

Claire stared into his soft blue eyes and built up the courage, remembering what he had told her.

We're all mad here.

"A shadow, I think," she admitted. "A young woman with long black hair, red eyes."

"If I tell you the truth, will you run again?"

Claire exhaled and watched as her breath clouded in the suddenly frigid air around her with her answer. "No."

"Most people don't know demons exist, and those that do either ignore them or live life unaware. But I've always been aware, Claire. Eu alimentei meus demônios."

"What's that mean?"

"It means—I chose to feed mine."

Claire rubbed her arms again as something icy slithered over them. Fingers. It felt like real human hands were tracing the goosebumps along her flesh.

"I did something, years ago. Something I regret. You remember Bree?"

Claire nodded.

"She is the Seer for the Circle. An oracle. When I was initiated after I graduated college, she offered to come to my bed, tell me my future. She was beautiful. I was young. Stupid. She offered what she called a gift, a present for my joining. At the time, I didn't understand the power of words, that intention holds meaning. So I said them and conjured a spirit by the name of Nehia."

"She's the demon that haunts you?"

"Not just any demon—a succubus."

Claire knew the stories of incubi and succubi from history, from studying medieval folklore. According to the legends, a succubus only visits someone at night, usually in their sleep, having their way with them if the person allows.

And listening to Aven's story, she knew he not only allowed it but also had asked for the demon with Bree's help. Claire didn't want to think about what had happened after the spirit had been conjured, assuming Bree had been involved in the union. Her stomach rolled, wishing the images of them together would leave her mind.

"My previous promiscuity wasn't by choice, Claire," Aven said. "Nehia required it. If I didn't partake in my fleshly desires, she would come to me in my dreams, but it wasn't as the stories say. There was no pleasure in her visits. Only tormenting nightmares. Some of them came true."

"Can you be free of her?"

"No more than the demon that haunted you."

Claire shivered, not from fear, but from the hope in his eyes as he gently squeezed her hands.

"She knows you're changing me, Claire, making me see that there's more to life than all that I have. I'm a better person with you. I'm a fool, blindly taking a step over the edge, and you're the voice of reason, pulling me back from sudden death."

"I know you think I'm strong but I'm not. I—"

"When you looked out to the field, you saw something, didn't you? Something that wasn't there."

"Did you?"

"I saw a picnic: you, an angel in my arms, pink blossoms drifting down on us like snow," Aven said, brushing the hair from her face. "I know it sounds like we're both two crazy loons, but what if we're not?"

Claire loosed a breath knowing Aven had seen exactly what she had. Somehow, they had a connection. Somehow, they had seen a vision of the two of them from a dream.

"When we're together. It feels like a memory, does it not?" he asked, leaning forward. "And when you kiss me, it's as if you've always known the taste of my lips."

When Aven kissed her again, familiarity washed over her like a wave as the taste of tart raspberries tingled her tongue.

"Why do I feel like I know you?" Claire exhaled against his lips.

"Perhaps from another life."

Leaning in to kiss Aven again, Claire froze, catching something flit across the room behind him, but when she blinked it was gone.

"Claire?"

Claire met his worried gaze. "Is she waiting for you to feed her?"

"Yes. She'll wait all night until dawn, or until I give her what she wants."

"What does she want?"

Aven slid his thumb across her lips. "For me to ravish you. Do things I know you're not ready to do."

A trickle of icy cold traced Claire's cheekbone, then her shoulder, and she flinched away. "Will that make her leave us alone?"

"You should go to bed," Aven said in a husky voice, "before she convinces me to take you to mine."

"We can talk. I'll stay up with you until sunrise."

"I won't be able to control myself. It's taking everything I have not to make love to you on this piano."

Before Claire could say another word, Aven lifted her trembling hand and kissed her knuckles.

"Goodnight, Princess. Sleep well."

POSSESSION

AVEN let out a ragged sigh, watching Claire walk away, listening to every creak beneath her feet. He guzzled his drink, but it wouldn't quench his desire. He only thirsted for her lips. His hands itched to be wrapped around her hips, to rock them in slow, even strokes. A low growl escaped his throat as he shook his head.

Now this . . . this was true torture.

He poured himself another drink and sat back at the piano. He could distract himself. He could drink himself to sleep. Reaching to place his hands on the keys, Aven jerked them away again as the piano top slammed shut, echoing a haunting noise.

"Such a tantrum," Aven taunted.

"I want her," Nehia hissed, revealing herself to him from a wisp of smoke.

The hellhounds appeared beside her from a pluming haze. They growled, baring their razor-sharp teeth as drool dripped to the floor.

"We all want what we can't have," Aven quipped. "Now you know how it feels."

"I know how it feels to have my fingers wrapped around a delicate neck."

Aven glared at the brown liquid in his glass on the piano top, remembering a morning he could never forget.

He had woken, seeing double with a splitting headache. Rolling over, he had reached for the girl he had slept with the night before. He wasn't greeted with good morning, only a hollow stare. There had been smudges of crimson fingertips on her bare shoulder. It had been blood. Her blood. His stomach twisted again as the image of his bloody hands came in clear.

He recalled the phone conversation with Vincent, how Kitten had held him, telling him it wasn't his fault. His crime— the murder—had been covered up. The girl's cause of death had been labeled a suicide in the morning news feeds.

How could it not when her throat had been cut?

"You're all about control," he said with realization. "When I lose it, you gain it."

Nehia's smoke drew in, a hint that he was on to something.

"You always find a way in through a weakness, a vice," he said, going into the kitchen. He snatched the bottle from the counter and poured the liquor into the sink. Holding it up after every last drop had dripped from the mouth, he smiled at the demon. "Now you have no way in."

Nehia gave a light throaty laugh. "I always have a way in." She disappeared only to reappear in front of him as a waving vapor of her silhouette. "And according to your deal," Nehia said with satisfaction, taking hold of his wrist, "I can do as I please."

The pain was tolerable at first, but as the heat of Nehia's grasp increased, Aven cried out as fire like a hot branding iron singed his skin. He fought to be free, looking down at nothing, nothing but black smoke wrapped around his arm, binding him.

Groaning, Aven watched to his horror as his blue veins turned black. The searing heat dug beneath his skin, clawing at his bones.

"You may not remember, but your soul will never forget. Serus."

At the release of Nehia's grip, Aven fell on his back, his head thumping against the floor. His skull throbbed like a beating drum, the room spun and blurred, taking the form of a place he had never been, but felt he knew.

Waves roared in Aven's ears and a scream like fireworks came from above him. He jerked his head up to the sky, watching the fireballs fall into the raging red sea.

I'm sure I can manage.

More red filled his vision. A uniform and a face he knew. His face. He rolled on his side and stood to his feet, observing his clone.

"There is one thing I must make very clear," a deep voice said.

Aven circled his double and the tall man with large raven like wings.

"And what's that?" his double asked.

"Your innocence will be completely void. Your soul will be damned by association, by the corruption of your genetics."

The two figures glitched as if they were holograms and the vision skipped forward like a damaged recording.

Serus. His name was Serus.

The name rang like a bell in Aven's mind. He now knew why Nehia called him by it. It was his from long ago, and he was sure now, that this was not a hallucination but his past.

He watched his past self in horror as Serus cut his wrist with the point of the feather, letting the clear fluid drip down his arm. He then took the angel's offered hand and gripped his forearm tight.

Fire blazed through Aven's limbs. He remembered the pact, the agreement that damned him to hell.

A deal to live lifetimes, a promise of immortality with the one you love.

As their combined fluids seeped into one another's cuts, Aven watched as his arm, his blood, turned as black as midnight.

Coming back into Will's house, Aven hissed, squeezing his arm only to find he wasn't the one clutching it. Nehia came into view, a smug smile plastered on her face. Crossing his arms over his chest as if to bind him like a straitjacket, she whispered something like a spell . . . words with meaning.

"Thy soul is damned
From a pact of blood
I have my way in
I'll fit like a glove
But you won't remember
All that I did
While I was doing
Unthinkable sins."

At the icy touch of Nehia's lips on his neck, Aven went limp, losing the battle to be free. Black seeped into his eyes as if splattered in drops of ink until nothing was left but hollow pits.

Aven bobbed as if he were a puppet on a string, then he snapped forward and straightened like the strings had been cut. A sly smile spread across Aven's face, but it wasn't him who found pleasure in this moment, it was the one who possessed him, the one who had control of his body until dawn.

The hellhounds barked, gnashing their teeth at one another, but as Aven put a finger to his lips, they whined and cowered.

"Shh. We don't want to wake the little angel now, do we?"

Occupying Aven's body with glee, Nehia climbed the steps but stopped as something buzzed in his jeans.

"Hello, Roxy," Nehia cooed in Aven's voice, answering the call. "Want to play?"

THE MASK

CLAIRE braced herself on the dresser, trying to steady her shaky breaths.

"You can do this," she coached herself in the mirror. "He needs you."

Smoothing down the black open-back dress Aven had bought her, she nodded in the mirror to her reflection and came down the stairs. She glanced at the kitchen table, finding breakfast covered.

Will.

She thought of how considerate he had always been as she passed the kitchen table and went to Aven's door.

Shaking out her hands, she exhaled through pursed lips, ready to get the funeral over with.

A few hours and this would all be in the past.

The door swung open. Claire smiled at first, but when she found a pair of brown eyes staring back at her, she frowned.

"Shit." Roxy laughed with a hand on her chest. "I thought you were his brother."

Claire averted her gaze from Roxy's full breasts peeking through her sheer top.

"No," Claire answered, her voice quivering. "He already left. I was just going to let Aven know breakfast is ready."

"Such a sweet sister," Roxy said as if Claire was child. She stuffed her hot pink panties and bra in her purse. "Sorry, I never got your name."

Claire swallowed the knot in her throat.

Please be a hallucination.

"It's uh, Claire," she said, meeting Roxy's gaze.

"That's kinda pretty. Sorry to hear about your mom."

Roxy pouted her lips, sounding somewhat sympathetic, but Claire could tell she didn't mean her words by the way she put a comforting hand on Claire's shoulder.

Not a hallucination.

"Your brother's in the shower," Roxy informed her, getting out her keys. "Sorry I kept him up so late."

As Roxy walked out the door, Claire cringed at the sound of the screen door slamming against the frame. She wanted to scream, to run away, all the way back to Tybee Island, but she didn't have the strength.

Every part of her was weak, shaking. She stared at her trembling fingers before curling them into fists and forcing her legs to take her into Aven's room.

Approaching the nightstand, Claire wrinkled her nose, finding an ashtray filled with butts. At her feet lay Aven's t-shirt, his jeans, and his boxers.

Adrenaline flushed her body as Claire sucked in a sharp breath, but she exhaled it as footsteps sounded behind her.

Aven clenched his teeth, seeing Claire by the bed. He quickly conjured a mask to appear, to look as if she had come in uninvited, betrayed his trust. It took everything he had to keep his hard stare as she turned with misty eyes.

He had hoped to make a clean break, had jumped out of his bed faster than Roxy could say "what the hell." Now, he would have to do something so despicable, so soulless, he would hate himself for the rest of his miserable life.

A bullet to the head would be better than this hell.

He gripped the handle of his rolling suitcase tight and waited for Claire to speak first. Her tearful gaze went to his luggage and back up at him with sudden confusion.

"Are you leaving right after the funeral?" The crack in her voice let him know she had run into Roxy. The shower hadn't washed him of the shame over what he had done, what Nehia had made his body do. He glanced at the trashcan full of empty bottles, holding back the bile in his throat.

"I can't go," he said flatly. "Vincent called. He needs me to go to Singapore tonight."

"You can't spare a few hours?"

"It's a billion-dollar deal," he said, brushing past Claire. He went to the mirror, fixing his tie, loosening it.

"Will's expecting you to be there."

"Well, I don't care what Will expects," Aven said, making sure to lace his words with venom. He sat on the bed, retying his black dress shoes.

Stall.

He wished the cab would hurry. The sooner it beeped from outside of the house, the sooner he could walk away, escape the flames licking his cheeks.

"What happened to you last night, after I went to bed?"

Aven glared at his shoe a long moment, making sure the mask was on tight. He stood in front of Claire, slipping his hands into his pockets. "Is it not obvious?"

"But why? What did I do wrong? I thought we . . . that you . . ."

Creator kill me now. Strike me dead right where I stand.

"It was a fun game." Aven shrugged. "And now it's over."

"A game. So now you're bragging, mocking me, after I've fallen in love with you?"

Aven's heart skipped, not once, but twice at her words. He hadn't been sure if she had fallen for him and now that he knew, it was harder to keep up the act. He called on another ego: the Jester.

"Look who wins a prize." He gave a dramatic wave of his hands and attempted again to walk past her. He would wait outside. He couldn't keep up the act, couldn't keep his cold stare.

"Aven, stop!"

He wished the small hands on his chest would reach inside his body, wished Claire would rip out his heart, slam it on the ground, and stomp on it.

Put me out of my misery.

But she didn't. She closed in the distance as a tear trickled down her cheek.

"I know you're hurting. We all make stupid decisions when we're in pain, but please. Don't push me away."

Stop being so perfect. Please.

Aven clenched his teeth, holding back the urge to wrap Claire in his arms and tell her the truth, to fall to his knees and beg her forgiveness.

"Because," she whispered, "I'm doing something that's hard for me too. I woke up this morning, thinking of coming down here to tell you I couldn't go, that I couldn't put myself through another funeral again. I couldn't bear the thought of standing in a cemetery, looking at a casket, remembering how I felt watching as they put my father's body in his grave...but then I thought about how selfish that would be. So I sucked it up, because I wanted to be there for you, because I care about you, and I know how hard it is to lose someone you love."

You don't deserve her.

"The first night we were together, you asked me to bare my soul, and I did. I bared it all Aven, and all I'm asking is that you bare yours too. Tell me the truth, tell me why you did this so we can move past it."

Do it now or you'll see blood on your hands, again.

"You want the truth?"

"Yes."

Aven swallowed, holding back the tears that threatened to wet his eyes.

The truth is I love you. That's why I'm letting you go.

"The truth is," he bit out, "you were a challenge."

A partial truth.

By the way Claire looked at him, he could tell she was beginning to believe the lie, some of it anyway. But it wasn't enough. He had to make it hurt, had to make it personal.

Aven leaned down, making sure his tone was lethal. Because what he was about to say next, there was no coming back from.

"I like who I am, Claire, and I don't want to change for anyone, especially not some self-righteous goody-goody who's fucked up in the head."

Don't you dare admit that's a lie, Crey. Don't you dare tell her it's you. You're fucked up in the head.

"But the demon, you saw it, you said—" she mumbled.

"I acted like I saw your hallucinations to get you in my bed. As fun as the game was, it was exhausting. So I called up Roxy."

Claire's gaze fell to the ground as she closed her eyes and clutched her chest. Aven feared she would collapse, watching her body sway back and forth.

Convince her you don't want her. Make her hate you.

"I'm surprised you didn't hear her screaming my name."

Claire's gaze snapped to his, her face curling up in anguish and disgust.

There it is. Slap me. Tell me you hate me. Run as far away as you can.

He braced himself for a lash, but Claire didn't raise her hand. Instead, she took a step back, shaking her head.

"You win."

The sound of Claire's charm bracelet jingling made Aven sick as she unclasped it and offered it.

"Take it as a parting gift," he said, pushing it back.

"Keep it." She took his hand, never breaking his gaze and laid it in his palm. It was torture how slow she folded his fingers, just like he had always hers before his magic tricks. "As a reminder."

As if I could forget.

"Of?"

"Your choice."

BIRTH PAINS

COOL water dripped down Claire's chin as she held onto bathroom sink. She glanced at her burning red eyes, and then her dry cracked lips in the mirror. She had sobbed too long after the cab drove away.

How will I explain it's my fault that Aven left?

Getting her phone from the dresser in the guest bedroom, she looked up Will's number. With a shaky finger, she thumbed past it and tapped on Laura's instead.

"If you tell me one more time to come get you I'll–" Laura answered.

"Laura," Claire croaked.

"Claire? Are you okay?"

"I need you to come get me."

"What the hell? Did you flip out at the funeral?"

"I'll tell you about it later. Please hurry."

Without saying goodbye, Claire hung up the phone and glanced at Will's number again. She couldn't message him, not now. The funeral was five minutes from starting. She would have to leave a note the old-fashioned way.

Flipping back the pages of sketches in Will's room, Claire looked for a blank sheet but paused at a drawing half finished. It was of a girl, gazing up at a waterfall as her dress waved in the wind.

This was the place Claire had gone to in her mind. The most beautiful place she could ever imagine during Aven's Mind Walk. Closing her eyes, she thought of that place again and remembered the glowing young man that jumped from the cliff.

See you at the bottom.

Slamming the sketchbook shut, Claire braced herself on the nightstand. She vowed to seek help, any kind of help, even if she would be prescribed the drugs again. She couldn't live like this: seeing thing that weren't there.

Aven was right. She was messed up in the head. She was crazy.

A raspy bark made her jump, and Claire turned on her heels, finding Blue in the doorway.

The Australian shepherd whined and trotted out of sight.

The empty dog bowls came to Claire's mind. She went to follow Blue but didn't find her downstairs waiting.

"What is it, girl?" she asked, coming to her.

Blue barked at a door, gazing up at her with sky-blue eyes.

"This isn't my house. I can't just let you in there."

Blue stood on her hind legs and scratched the door, scraping off the wood.

"Okay, okay."

When Claire turned the knob, Blue burst through and ran up a set of steps. Claire cautiously followed, but as she topped the staircase to the finished attic, she gasped at the colors that filled her vision.

Gazing around the art studio, Claire found canvases of oils, chalks, and watercolors. They were hung on the walls and stacked on the floor. She looked at each one, tracing her fingers along the initials in the corner.

W.C.C. The same initials on the canvas in the hall.

At a bark from Blue, Claire turned to find the dog scratching at a drop cloth draped over something tall. The six-foot ladder propped against it rattled as Blue tugged on the stiff fabric.

"Wait!" She caught the ladder before it fell and placed it to the side.

Blue tugged the splattered sheet away, revealing a colorful canvas.

With wide eyes, Claire traced her fingers along the dried paint, glancing at each depiction of the soft brushstrokes. There was a girl playing a white piano in a beautiful gown, a gold leaf adornment in her hair. Another scene of the same girl, picking flowers in a meadow of lilacs. Another of her riding a white horse on a beach with water so blue it reminded her of Will's eyes.

These were the same images, the same scenes that had flashed in her mind all her life, that she'd dreamed of, and somehow, staring at the mural, Claire felt as if she could remember doing all them all before.

She set her gaze to the bright light in the middle of the depictions, to a figure with a gold crown. He smiled, holding a glimmering star in his palm. Angels surrounded him, holding out their hands and singing a hymn as if they were a choir.

Claire smoothed her hand over the king's bright painted face and parted her mouth as if she could almost whisper his name.

"Jules?" Will asked, stepping away from his mother's casket as Julie stifled a whimper.

"Cariño, that is *not* Braxton Hicks," Jeremiah admonished, placing a hand to the small of Julie's back.

"Estoy bien." Julie winced, holding her pregnant belly.

"You're not fine." Jeremiah gave a pleading look to Will. "Tell her she needs to go to the hospital. She won't listen to me."

"I still have a few days left."

"You should go home and rest," Will urged, giving a thoughtful nod to her big belly. "Get off your feet."

"We'll wait until your brother gets here, and Claire. I want to meet her. Besides you shouldn't be here alone."

"I'm alright," Will tried to assure her. "Go home and take care of J Jr. I'll bring Aven and Claire over later."

"I hope they like Italian. It's all I've been craving lately," Julie said, hugging his neck. She winced again and met Jeremy's gaze. "I'll wait in the car."

"I'll be there in a minute, bebé."

When Julie was out of earshot, Jeremiah crossed his arms, staring at the tombstones in Will's family plot.

"Does it feel weird seeing your name on a gravestone?" he asked.

"I've seen it so many times; it's just a stone now." Will glanced at Aaron's tombstone beside his, beside his father's. "Did you find the rabbit hole?"

Jeremiah rubbed his five o'clock shadow. "It's much deeper than we thought."

"How deep?"

"Deep enough to get us both killed. You've already died once. I think it's time to leave it alone."

Will brought his gaze back to his gravestone, remembering how he died. He could never forget the hollow pit in his stomach at the fall from the helicopter, or the salt in his mouth as waves washed over his face in the shark-infested waters, how their fins had grazed his hands and his feet as he bled out. His chest burned again, remembering how water had filled lungs. He'd been weightless, sinking beneath the black, and then everything was silent.

He had opened his eyes to a bright light, standing in the place he had only heard stories of, the place Beyond the Veil. It was quiet, peaceful. A place he never wanted to leave, a place he could never describe with words.

Will had found himself standing on a lakeshore. He had surveyed the land, taking in the vivid colors of a breathtaking mountain view. Then in the distance, someone waved. It was someone who had died, someone he had held as they took their last breaths. Aaron. He had signaled to Will from a white boat with blue sails. The gold emblem stitched in the fabric shimmered, welcoming Will to Paradise. Aaron had motioned for Will to jump in the crystal lake, to swim to him. Will had taken a step to do so, but a light flashed in his vision and a warm glowing hand pressed against his chest.

"When I took that first breath on the beach in Mexico, after I came back to life," Will said to Jeremiah. "All I could think about was why. Why Aaron was so susceptible to the voice. Why he couldn't ignore it like I did. And then I thought about what InfiniCorps serum did to us. How it changed what we are. It made you think faster, Duke stronger, Blake—more of an asshole than he already was."

Jeremiah laughed. "But that asshole could make one hell of a shot."

"He never missed. He was the only one to ever beat me in darts."

"You remember the night he put a rubber snake in Aaron's bed. Kid jumped like three feet in the air. We picked on him way too much. I kind of regret it now."

"Have you ever wondered why the serum didn't work on Aaron?"

Jeremiah shrugged. "Maybe he was their control subject."

"No. I watched them inject him. It doesn't make sense."

"Well, you I both know he couldn't keep up with us in training. You were always watching his ass, making sure he survived those first couple of months on the front lines."

"Yeah, and it was all for nothing."

"Saving my ass from getting blown up is nothing?"

"You know what I mean."

"So what are you going to do now that you know the voice behind the COM? Sue InfiniCorp? There's no way you have any proof. Even if I could hack into Vincent Crey's computer and get the files on what they did to us, it won't hold up in court."

"You saw the feed, Jer. You were sitting right there at the computer as it happened in real time. You heard Aaron screaming for the voices in his head to stop."

"It haunts my dreams too, man. Aaron was like a little brother to me. I would have done anything for kid, for you, but I can't risk Julie's life, or our son's."

"I know, and I won't ask you to bear witness," Will said, taking a cracked vial from his pocket. He glared at the InfiniCorp's logo, knowing Aven could have been the only one to discard it in the yard. "All I need to know is if Aven was involved."

"And if he is?"

"You messaged me while I was flying back from Vegas, said you knew his whereabouts while all of it went down during that hour."

"He was at a club, had just graduated with honors from some prestige college in Britain." Jeremiah said, pulling up images on his phone.

"So he wasn't even in the United States."

"Oh, he was. Vegas, to be exact. But there's no way he could have been with Vincent during the op."

"And why is that?"

"Because I have footage of him at a strip club, at around zero hundred, carrying a girl, stage name, Kitten, aka, Katharine Reece, to a self-driving cab. He followed shortly after, but that's all the footage I have. A few months later the club was bulldozed down."

"I met Katharine." Will handed the phone back to Jeremiah. "I was going to ask her some things, but this Nick guy asked her to dance." Will ran his fingers through his hair.

"This the guy?"

Will glanced at the phone. "Yeah, that's him."

"The Elite club is full of hijo de putas. That Giovanni guy is really somethin'. You should see his search history. Some pretty gruesome mierda, man. Everyone in this club has a shady past. And I think all of them are somehow connected to the Genesis Project, working with the government."

"Do you think Aven knows about it?"

"Do you?"

"He's in the Circle, close with his cousin." Will handed the vial to Jeremiah. "If he doesn't, I'd be surprised."

"And if he does, what are you going to do then?"

Will put his hands on his hips and gave a pointed stare to Aaron's grave. "Get the answers to the questions I've had these past seven years."

"Jeremy!"

Will and Jeremiah's gaze darted to Julie waving out the car window.

"Our bebé! He's coming!"

REVELATIONS

AVEN watched Jeremiah's car speed through the cemetery and out of sight before he approached his mother's plot.

"He took you back," he said to his mother's casket, lying the roses on top of it. "Guess he needed his angel more than I did."

Aven idled a moment, sniffing back his tears.

"I wanted Claire to be the one, Mom . . . but I can't be free, and knowing what I know now, what I did from before, I never can be. I can't give her what she wants, what I want, but I can give my word. And I swear to you, no harm will come to her . . . I promise."

As the gravediggers came and lowered Kate's casket, Aven watched. Even as they shoveled the dirt on top, he didn't leave, not until they were finished. He laid the bouquet of roses, and one of daisies, on the piled-up dirt.

Wiping his tears, he glanced at the headstones by his mother's grave, tilting his head to the names.

William Carpenter
Aaron Carpenter
Adam Carpenter

Aven had seen these names before in a file on Vincent's computer labeled:

PROJECT GENESIS: CONFIDENTIAL

Walking back to the cab, he made a mental note to search InfiniCorp's files.

Seems I'm not the only one with secrets.

"Where to now, buddy?" the cab driver asked as Aven approached.

"The airport."

"You got it, bub."

As the cab driver tapped on the navigation app on his screen system, Aven froze as the car jolted slightly.

"What the hell?" the cab driver asked no one.

Aven pressed his palm against the window as it vibrated. "Earthquake."

"Earthquake?" the cabby sneered. "We don't get earthquakes on the east coast."

The car shook side to side slightly, then bobbed, as if the asphalt beneath it was a roaring sea. The plastic skirt of the Hawaiian bobble doll clacked furiously on the dash. Thunder came from all around, and Aven watched as the stop sign on the street wiggled back and forth.

"You do now."

Claire came out of her daze to the sound of artwork slapping the floor. She glanced behind her at the easel that jittered and the window as it trembled and cracked.

"Earthquake," Claire said under her breath, gazing at the ground as it vibrated beneath her shoes.

Blue barked, beckoning her to the door to escape as the ceiling cracked above her, but it was too late.

The ladder fell from the wall and met her face with painful smack on her cheek.

A throbbing ache pounded in Claire's skull as she rolled over. Then everything around her closed in, faded into darkness, and Blue's urgent barking quieted into a distant echo until there was nothing but silence.

Aven stood outside the cab, surveying the damage of the broken earth, the tombstones tilted by the quake as the ground still quivered lightly beneath his feet.

He glanced at his panicking cab driver that paced back and forth with his phone to his ear. Studying the movement of his lips, Aven picked apart his words.

I'm on my way home, I love you too, the cab driver mouthed. He shoved his phone in his pocket and approached

Aven. "You'll have to find another ride. I need to check on my family."

"I'll give you a grand to take me to the airport."

"I have to get home to my kids."

"Two thousand."

"Three."

"Done," Aven agreed, pressing a finger to his phone.

The cab driver glanced at his phone at the ding of the transfer and set his gaze back to Aven. "If we get another one you're on your own."

"Understood."

Aven fell into the backseat and let out a long sigh as the cab driver put the car in gear. He wondered if Claire was okay, knowing Will wasn't at the house with her, but he quickly pushed the thought from his mind.

Forget about her. Let her go.

The echo of Claire's last words made his chest ache. He rubbed his breastbone, trying to ease the guilt, until something in his inner pocket grazed his fingertips. Taking the pack of cigarettes from his pocket, Aven glared at them. Nehia.

"No smoking in my cab buddy."

A ding rang out on the cab driver's phone as Aven met his furrowed brows in the rearview mirror.

"That should cover detailing," Aven assured him. He put a cigarette in his mouth and withdrew his silver butane lighter from his suit. He stared at the engraving for a long moment with resentment. This was the symbol of his Circle, the same signet of the king he had served in his past life, the mark of his damnation.

Levitating the lighter from his palm, Aven flicked the starter with his mind and lit his cigarette from the waving flame. He took a long drag and leaned his head back against the headrest, holding the breath.

Who are you, Aven Crey? What are you? Man-whore... *mutt.*

The vision from Nehia's possession came as his head dizzied from the lack of oxygen. Black wings. Inky veins. A pact.

Serus.

Names. Aven had many, but this one he would seek out. He would find the out the truth about his lineage, his bloodline, the Ancient Ones.

"You're not from around here, are you kid?" the cab driver asked with a wary stare in the rearview.

No," Aven answered, exhaling a toxic plume of smoke in satisfaction. "Nowhere near here."

THE STORY CONTINUES . . .

THE
AEON
CHRONICLES

BOOK III

Have you picked a team?
Join the fandom!

THE
AEON
CHRONICLES

Use these hashtags on
Instagram and Twitter!
Fight for your ship!
Who do you choose?

#TEAMWILLSTRYDE
#TEAMAVENCREY
#THEAEONCHRONICLES

DISCOVER MORE

VISIT

www.aprilmwoodard.com

WANT BONUS CONTENT?

http://www.aprilmwoodard.com/beyondthepages/

JOIN THE MONTHLY NEWSLETTER

GET UPDATES ON...

NEW RELEASES
GIVEAWAYS
FREE SWAG

GET TO KNOW THE AUTHOR

C O M E   S A Y   H I   T O   A P R I L
S H E   W O U L D   L O V E   T O
H E A R   F R O M   Y O U

 @April_M_Woodard

 @April_M_Woodard

#THEAEONCHRONCILES

 authoraprilmwoodard

 april-m-woodard

ABOUT THE

AUTHOR

April M Woodard was born and raised in a small town in Virginia. She now lives in Georgia, near the big city of Atlanta, with her husband and three kids. She spends her days writing young adult fiction with three kitties at her feet. Scratch that. Two kitties and a mogwai. When she isn't typing away on her laptop, she is sitting on her back porch, sipping sweet tea, and reading a good book.

Photo taken by SHANNONTHOMPSON ART

CPSIA information can be obtained
at www.ICGtesting.com
Printed in the USA
LVHW091038180119
604348LV00001B/31/P